LEGENDS AND DREAMS

MAPLE HILL CHRONICLES BOOK FOUR

ELIZABETH R. ALIX

Legends and Dreams
Maple Hill Chronicles
Book 4

Elizabeth R. Alix

Printing History. First Edition, January 2025

Paperback: ISBN 978-0-9985243-9-9

E-book: ISBN 978-0-9985243-8-2

Cover illustration and layout by 100 Covers https://100covers.com

Supported by Palouse Digital Press, Pullman, WA USA: https//palousedigitalpress.com

Distributed by IngramSpark

❀ Created with Vellum

To Thaddeus J. Gesek, Bill Miller, Bill Rothwell,
Everett Sprinchorn, Holly Hummel
and Genevieve Kenny
who worked at the other Avery Theater

CHAPTER 1

Tommy Verplank made the rounds through the tired hush of the Avery theater, checking that all the doors were locked and the house lights were off. He doubled back to peek into the auditorium to be sure that the single bare bulb in the middle of the stage was on. The rest of the cast and crew had gone home an hour ago.

Sleepy Hollow had demanded another late rehearsal. They had four weeks before opening, and the play was a mess. More than usual. The leads were missing their blocking, people still struggled with their lines, and the sets and costumes were a long way from being done. It didn't matter. Casting could be a complete crapshoot sometimes. But this time it felt different. Even though the three leads had very little theater experience, it was almost as if they were made for the roles. He'd written the script himself in a fit of inspiration. It was a great script, based on a classic, well-loved story. *The Legend of Sleepy Hollow* was the personification of the Hudson Valley. With a few modifications of his own, he was confident it would save his grandfather's theater. It had to. *He* had to. Where would he go if he lost the Avery? Nowhere. The Avery was his home in every sense of the word.

The aroma of popcorn disguised the hint of dust that

emanated from the worn red velvet seats and old carpeting. Could he afford a professional cleaning before opening night? A good impression was critical. Maybe he could move a few things around in the budget. Take something out of his savings. The Wednesday and Saturday movie showings were hell on the upholstery but helped fill the bottom line. When this show was a sold out hit, the investors would come back, the bank would back off, and Old Miss Avery would get a face lift. All the upholstery would be new again. Maybe royal blue this time.

Tommy paced through the lobby in his worn loafers over the threadbare carpet to check the front doors. They were locked. He continued to the door of the box office, cocked his head as he always did, and heard the faint rattle of the front doors behind him. He nodded. That was just Miss Avery's way of saying good-night. The money was safely locked up, and the lights were out. He touched the framed photo of his grandfather standing with his family outside the old theater and straightened it slightly.

"I won't let you down," he said softly.

His old navy blue fedora settled over his bushy gray-brown hair, and he zipped up his jacket before stepping out into the chilly November air. The push-bar doors locked themselves securely behind him. He descended the three broad steps into the chilly night and walked the couple of blocks home.

Marianne dreamed she was wandering through the Maple Hill Cemetery at night. The tombstones stretched out in rows on all sides, and she was searching for something or someone. She peered at each stone, but the letters were too worn to be read. Something tickled her foot. A small round globe like a soap bubble was attached, and she shook it off in disgust. Another bubble drifted down from the sky and bounced gently on her head. She flung up an arm to brush it away, but it tangled in her hair and stuck to her arm. In a panic, she lifted her other arm to push it off, but little black blobs clung to her skin. They gently swarmed her, feeding like butterflies on sugar water. She felt herself grow cold as they sucked the life out of her.

Gasping, she snapped her eyes open and felt her heart beat fast and heavy in her chest. She was lying in bed in her own room. Ruari snored softly next to her. She pulled her arm free of the covers and groped for Oscar where he lay next to her hip. His soft fur met her fingers, and she felt the cat startle then curl tighter as he fell asleep again.

It had been ten days since the fight at the cemetery. She'd had nightmares off and on since then. One had been about Byron Mandel, the others had been about *draugers* chasing her. This was the first night they'd caught her.

We killed them or pushed them back into the Shadowlands that night. There are no more. Stop worrying about this. Byron is gone. We closed the portals to the Shadowlands. We finished the spell.

A treacherous thought added, *But did we? Sarah said she couldn't tell if we'd finished it in time.*

There's no reason to think we didn't.

She'd had this conversation with herself many times since Halloween. Somehow her brain hadn't gotten the message that she was safe.

It was just a dream. It wasn't a true dream. It was just me processing a scary event.

She took a deep breath and let it out and tried to get comfortable again. She turned this way and that. Oscar went down the hall to the litter box and returned, and she was still awake.

I've got to get some sleep.

With a flash of inspiration, she flipped her pillow. Maybe all the bad dreams would stick to the underside and disappear. Her cheek nestled against the cool side of the pillowcase, Oscar resettled himself, and she snuggled closer to Ruari.

Morning came and Marianne roused, feeling heavy with sleep. Oscar was a warm weight tucked behind her knees. She vaguely remembered having a nightmare but pushed it away. Ruari rolled over and put his arms around her.

" 'Morning," he said.

"Mmm. What time is it?" She murmured.

"Probably time to get up and go to work."

"Wish you could stay here." She burrowed closer to his chest.

He sighed. "SueAnn Talmadge waits for no man."

She grunted. His boss was awful, but Ruari had worked that job for ten years. He had his coping skills firmly in place. "I'll get the coffee going," she offered, "and make us some breakfast."

"Deal."

Oscar stretched, his crooked tipped tail shaking with the effort, and jumped off the bed. He put his paw under the door to the hallway and pulled, opening it wide enough to slip through. Marianne slid out of bed and shivered while she found slippers and a fluffy blue robe. Fall and winter were not her favorite seasons. She was a spring and summer girl. Ruari stretched, his back and shoulders moving under his sleeping shirt. She admired the view. A life of physical work both in his job as a handyman and in his hobby as a woodworker had given him plenty of wiry muscle.

Following Oscar, she went down the hall into the kitchen

"Alright, Mister, let's take care of you." She fed Oscar, refreshed his water, and scooped the litter box while the electric pot boiled water for tea. She set the coffee pot for six cups to cover Ruari and Erin's caffeine preference and started sausage and eggs.

It was nice to have a semblance of a routine again, and she relished the peace and quiet. When the orange and white tabby was done with his food, he meowed to be let out, and she obliged. By then, Ruari had showered and come into the kitchen, his ginger blond hair still damp. He wore a Kelly green polo shirt with the Gloria's Valley Homes and Properties logo on the right breast.

"I love waking up to coffee and breakfast with you," he said, kissing the back of her head.

"I love having you stay over." She handed him a plate of hot sausage patties which he took to the table.

She delivered a couple of scrambled eggs to the table for Ruari and a couple of eggs over easy on toast for herself. He poured coffee, milk no sugar, for himself and a cup of Earl Grey with milk and honey for her. She appreciated that he'd learned to make her favorite drink. It was more than her ex had ever done.

They ate in companionable silence while the morning beverages slowly percolated through their systems. She tensed at the sound of footsteps overhead. Those footsteps used to mean her ghostly roommates were up and about, but Anne and George had been evicted.

"Mmmm. Coffee." Erin, Ruari's younger sister, padded into the kitchen in stocking feet, black leggings and an oversized sweatshirt, her red hair sticking out in all directions. She clattered about making a mug of hot, sweet, French Vanilla flavored coffee for herself before joining them at the table. Her eyes glazed over staring at nothing while she sipped, waiting for the coffee and sugar to jumpstart her brain.

In a fit of generosity and camaraderie after they'd all survived Halloween in the cemetery, Marianne had invited Erin to live with her. The redhead had jumped at the offer. She had refused to return to her own apartment over the flower shop on Main Street which she claimed was haunted. Living at her parents' house was also a non-starter, and Marianne couldn't fault her for not wanting to camp out at Ruari's studio apartment. It wasn't awful, but it was definitely a minimalist bachelor pad prone to piles of papers and sawdust in odd places. Now, ten days later, Marianne was having regrets. But, she told herself, it was only temporary while Erin job hunted.

Ruari finished his breakfast and cleared his place, tucking the dishes into the dishwasher and cleaning the pan. Marianne smiled and sipped her tea. No regrets there. He returned to the dining room and hugged her as she sat.

"I'm going to try and do some work in the studio later."

"Okay. Let me know if you want me to save you some dinner. Have a good day. Don't kill Casey or SueAnn."

"I'll try not to."

He went out the front door, letting Oscar back in at the same time.

Marianne tried to bully her brain cells into coming up with a plan for the day. After Halloween, she'd been exhausted and needed time to do nothing. But she was getting restless and feeling guilty. She'd finished the cozy mystery she'd been reading last night and had the next in the series. But she really should buckle down to actual work.

As a researcher with a PhD in history, she was qualified to dig into the past. Since moving to Maple Hill in August, she'd become familiar with the local library, local history, and Mrs. Caldwell, the grumpy librarian. After dealing with the ghosts in her own house, and Ruari's family ghosts, she felt somewhat qualified to cope with spirits in general. All that had led her to the conclusion that if no one would hire her to teach history, she could start her own business as a researcher for hire and a sometime ghost investigator.

During her trip around Canopus County, she'd met several spirits who were unable to move on, and she'd offered to help them. She'd begun looking into the fate of a little boy who'd gone missing in the 1950s. His mother, Astrid Delaney, haunted a church in Centerburg. But Marianne had run into a dead end and hadn't yet had the motivation to push through it.

Then there was Peter O'Meara and his men, the intimidating ghosts of miners who'd died in the 1880s, who'd helped them at the cemetery on Halloween. In exchange, she'd promised to get a memorial plaque put up at the place they'd died. He'd sworn to haunt her if she didn't. That was an incentive to get going. But she hadn't done it yet.

"Erin, what are you up to today?" She asked.

Erin had finished her sweet coffee and was looking marginally more awake. She'd moved back to Maple Hill after she'd lost her job as an accountant at an Arizona firm during the economic recession. She'd applied to over a hundred new jobs so far with no prospects in spite of her excellent qualifications. Like Marianne, she'd fallen into a slump after Halloween.

Erin shrugged. "I got halfway through my new video game last night. I'll keep going on it."

Marianne finished the last swallow of tea and made up her mind. She would do something concrete about starting her business if it was the last thing she did today. She put her dishes in the dishwasher and went to shower. Oscar followed her into the bathroom and sat on the counter grooming himself while she cleaned up. *Pretend I'm going to the office and someone expects me.* Clean hair, fresh clothes, turtleneck, jeans, and her favorite gold sweater with the twisting cables down the front helped her feel more decisive.

Erin had disappeared upstairs, leaving her mug on the counter. Marianne shook her head and went into her office to get organized. Oscar hopped up on her desk and settled down among her papers.

Her first task was to call Sarah. Before their road trip, Sarah's cell number had been like a hot line. Marianne could call it day or night, and Sarah would answer and help her with whatever ghost question she had. Since Halloween, however, she had been missing in action. Marianne had left three messages and gotten no replies. Granted, Sarah had been exhausted in mind and body for many reasons and needed rest, but it was hurtful that she wouldn't text or email a reply at least.

Her call went to voice mail again.

"Hey, Sarah, it's me Marianne. I haven't heard from you in a while and hope you and Kelly are doing okay. Give me a call if you have time. Thanks. Bye."

If Sarah didn't get back to her this time, she'd call Kelly at her salon, Hair Magic, and find out what was going on. Firmly putting her mentor out of her mind, she turned to research.

Ruari was still steaming as he drove back to the office at the end of the day. Casey had abandoned him in a tantrum halfway through the job this afternoon after Ruari had yelled at him and pulled him physically away from exposed wiring. The dumb shit was going to get himself killed one of these days. His assistant had been more distracted than usual of late, forgetting to finish things and ignoring basic safety precautions. Casey's flash of fear had turned into anger, and he'd stormed off. Ruari had secured the loose wires and finished the job, all the while muttering furiously under his breath.

He piloted his old, white, Ford pickup truck into the lot behind Gloria's Valley Homes and Properties. The flashy red truck wasn't there. Maybe Casey had taken his wounded vanity and gone home for the day. Good thing. Ruari was still mad enough to yell at him again. He grabbed his paperwork and went inside.

Alyssa, the receptionist, gave him a pained look and tilted her head toward the boss's closed door. She said in a low voice, "She's on the phone, but I think she wants to see you."

Ruari grunted and nodded. No surprises there. He managed to complete the day's paperwork and give it to Alyssa before the door opened.

SueAnn Talmadge stuck her head out and nodded curtly, "Allen, get in here."

Resigned, Ruari followed her in.

"Close the door," she said curtly.

Who was going to overhear them? Alyssa was the only one out there at this time of day.

Talmadge returned to her desk and sat down. She was short and plump and wore her curly dark hair in a high fluff, and always reminded Ruari of an angry poodle. If poodles wore red suits and glowed with a livid red corona. His newfound ability to see auras gave him clues as to the emotional state or personality of the individual. He didn't always know what it meant. Today was easy: Talmadge was furious with a tinge of fear and embarrassment. Her lips were the thinnest of lines.

"Sit," she said curtly.

"No thank you." He remained standing, and she gave him an annoyed glare.

Over the years they'd developed a relationship where she depended on him for his expertise in repairs and maintenance. Instead of being reasonable and grateful, she insulted him and demanded his 24/7 availability. He'd come to care about the elderly tenants of Gloria's Valley Homes and Properties and been reluctant to bail on them.

"I just got off the phone with Gloria Hopper. The owner. Casey's *mother*, in case you forgot. She is very unhappy about your treatment of her son. You were supposed to teach him the maintenance aspect of the business, but according to him you only criticized him, and all he learned were menial jobs."

"What—?" That was not what he'd expected. "What else does she think a handyman does all day?"

"I'm not finished." She leaned forward and folded her pudgy hands on her desk. Her voice dropped to a deadly calm. "She told me to find another repair man. I put my neck on the line for you, Allen, and told Gloria you were the best maintenance guy I have, and I couldn't afford to lose you. What have you got to say for yourself?"

Her words this time were accompanied by a bloom of dark smoke as if she breathed out a swarm of gnats. She was lying. What had she told Gloria for real? Had they commiserated on his shortcomings? He worked his jaw, clenching and unclenching his fists. With an effort he put a leash on his anger.

He tried to match her calm. "Casey nearly grabbed live wires and electrocuted himself today. I gave him a verbal warning and then pushed him out of the way. He could have been badly hurt or killed."

Talmadge gaped, then rallied. "That's not the story he told his mother."

"I'm sure it isn't."

"Are you sure that's what happened?" She narrowed her eyes.

His anger snarled silently at her insinuation. He clenched his jaw. "You've known me for ten years. I don't lie."

She compressed her lips again and shook her head. "Gloria is livid over the treatment of her son." *And what are you going to do about it?* She silently challenged him.

"I have done my best to train him, but Casey ignores what I tell him if he doesn't want to hear it. He is not suitable for this line of work. For his own safety, I strongly suggest you let him go."

That was not the answer she'd been looking for. Her face flushed. "If what you're telling me is true, Gloria nearly lost her precious son today. All because you failed to communicate the dangers."

He made up his mind in a flash. "You know what? As of today, I resign. I quit. I refuse to be part of that kid's dumpster fire life." He hadn't planned on saying that, but something came over him. He was done. A touch of the Allen Scots brogue emerged as he added, "And I am sick of working for a *crabbit* old *feartie*." Without waiting for a response, he turned and exited the office.

"How dare you!" She shrieked. "Get back here, Allen!"

He closed the door behind him with a deliberate click. Alyssa gave him wide eyes.

In a perfectly normal voice he said, "I've resigned. Please send my last paycheck to my address on file. Thank you." He walked out to his truck. On autopilot he cleared out anything that belonged to Gloria's and brought it inside. He didn't want to give her any reason to call him back here.

Talmadge's door was still closed, and she was on the phone again. Probably telling Gloria that their terrible handyman was finally gone. Ten years of damn good service keeping all thirty properties going. Out the window like heat on a winter day.

He drove to his converted garage/studio apartment but couldn't bring himself to go into his workshop. He was much too keyed up to work on anything. Not so long ago, he would have gone to The Dutch, a favorite watering hole for the locals, and had beer or three. But that no longer appealed to him. Instead, he gunned the engine and headed for Marianne's house.

He hesitated at the front door. She'd generously given him a key a couple of days ago, but he still knocked every time.

She opened the door and said, "Hi, I thought you were going to the studio?" Then she frowned and added, "Are you okay?"

"I quit my job today." He still felt shell shocked.

Her mouth made a little "o," but all she said was, "What happened?"

Over a cup of tea, they sat on the couch, and she listened to everything.

When he was done, she giggled. "Calling her a grumpy old cow was the kindest thing you could have said." Seeing his glum expression, she added, "She doesn't deserve to have you." She took the mug from him and added, "More tea?"

He nodded. The chamomile was bland and flowery, a little like drinking hand lotion, but surprisingly soothing. He felt better.

At dinner that night, Erin heard the news.

"Woohoo, you finally quit that bitch!" She crowed and called Talmadge something far nastier in Scots she'd learned from cousin Seamus. "She's been horrible to you since you started."

"Yeah, I did." Ruari's dazed feelings had morphed into relief.

Marianne said with a warm smile, "Guess what? You don't have to go to work tomorrow."

"I think it's going to take a while to get used to that."

"No more being on call 24/7 for floods, furnaces, or lock outs," she added.

Erin added with a grin, "Now when Casey nails his hand to the wall or offs himself with a screwdriver, you're not responsible. We should celebrate! Do we have any champagne?"

Marianne shook her head. "I do have ice cream and apple pie, though."

They cleared the table and served themselves in the kitchen. They returned to the table to enjoy their pie à la mode.

Erin grinned. "Welcome to the ranks of the unemployed, big brother! I can help you with job hunting if you want, since I'm such an expert now."

"Maybe this will give you a chance to start your woodworking business," Marianne suggested.

Ruari said, "I've been thinking about that. What do you think of Sylvan Woodworks?"

"I like it."

"If you're going that route," Erin said around a mouthful of pie, "I could set up a website for you. I started to work on some pricing a couple of weeks ago when you were talking about doing a business. I can just fold that in."

"Only if you don't charge me," Ruari said with a wry smile, knowing his sister all too well. "Remember, I don't have a paycheck, and I'm poor now."

She screwed up her face in mock concentration. "Well, I guess I could do it pro bono, now that I don't have to pay the rent anymore either."

Just then, Oscar strolled through the dining room licking his whiskers ostentatiously.

"Did anyone put the ice cream away?" Marianne asked. Head shakes around the table. She leaned down and picked him up. "What's with you and the counter top grazing all of a sudden?"

He sat in her lap and began washing his white front ruff. She cuddled him indulgently. "Okay, we're going to have to be sure the food gets put away. I don't know what's gotten into him lately. He's not usually like this. Though he does have a thing for vanilla ice cream, don't you, Mister?"

"And pepperoni," Erin added.

"Anyone want to watch a movie?" Ruari asked as they cleaned up.

Marianne had increased the size of her meager DVD collection through the discount DVD section at the local pawn shop, and they settled on *My Big Fat Greek Wedding.*

Erin rolled her eyes and went back to her video game upstairs.

"Good call," Ruari whispered as they settled on the sofa, snuggled under her favorite tropical patterned plush blanket.

CHAPTER 2

"Katie, where are my shoes?" Tayloe asked. She'd gotten off work at the Golden Years Retirement Home, eaten a hasty dinner, and hurried to the theater. Her role as Katrina VanTassel had been a fun last fling before nursing school, but there had been some odd moments. Two nights ago, her wig was missing. It had turned up along with all the others lined up along the backs of the chairs in the house, looking like a bizarre audience. Mr. Verplank had started rehearsal by lecturing the cast for not taking the play seriously, but no harm had been done. Even though she'd had nothing to do with it, she'd felt vaguely guilty.

Tonight, her shoes were missing. She'd put them right on the shelf above her costumes. She knew she had. She didn't want to hear another lecture.

"I don't know," Katie replied, her hand feeling all the way to the back of the shelf. "Mine are gone too. Maybe Brendan took them for some reason."

They ducked out of the women's dressing room and headed down the hall. A tall-ceilinged, narrow hallway ran behind the stage, opening onto dressing rooms, props storage, costumes, green room, and the scene shop as well as the odd closet. Their footsteps echoed.

"It's kind of creepy back here," Katie said in a hushed voice.

"It really is." Tayloe remembered getting lost the first couple of times.

They heard voices up ahead and entered the costume shop.

"I don't have them," Brendan was saying.

"They have to be somewhere," a rich tenor responded.

Brendan ran his hands through his curly brown hair. "I don't know who's doing this, but it isn't funny."

"None of the guys have joked about it, so I don't think the prankster is in the cast," the other man replied.

"I don't think it's the women either," Tayloe said.

The two men turned. Tristan, who played the narrator, was clearly on the same mission as they were.

Brendan shut his eyes and pinched the bridge of his nose. "Tell me your shoes aren't missing, too."

"Sorry, they are," Katie said apologetically.

The costumer swore. "We have to find them before rehearsal. Check the house, the bathrooms, the box office, everywhere. With any luck we'll find them. So far, everything else has turned up."

Tristan nodded. "I'll check the house. Would you ladies check the bathrooms and foyer? Maybe we can locate them before Mr. Verplank finds out."

Katie and Tayloe nodded fervently and headed back, glad of the company.

After a ten minute search, Tristan called out that he'd found them. Tayloe and Katie ran into the auditorium to see where. Tristan was standing behind the very back row. Twenty pairs of shoes were carefully lined up behind the last row of seats as if people were standing there facing the stage.

Tristan was tucking his phone back in his pocket. "Looks like they're all here. Would you ladies take the shoes for your dressing room, and I'll get the ones for ours?"

"That was so weird," Tayloe said, her arms full of footwear, as she and Katie headed back.

"No kidding."

"Who do you think it is? Do you think it's Tristan?" Tayloe asked.

"Nah, my money is on one of the other guys, maybe Casey or his friend Jake."

"They seem like the type."

"Hey, I think Casey is sweet on you," Katie said slyly.

Tayloe gave a half laugh, "Maybe."

Katie gave her a sideways glance. "But you like Randall better don't you?"

Tayloe blushed all the way to the roots of her brown hair.

Katie giggled. "Still fending them off with a stick, just like in high school."

"Shut up."

They returned to the ladies dressing room which was now full of other cast mates getting out of street clothes and into their costumes.

"Oh thank goodness, you found the shoes!" Someone exclaimed.

Tommy Verplank had been in bed for a couple of hours after another late night at the theater. He awoke from a sound sleep to someone shaking his shoulder. A powerful feeling of calamity gripped him. He had to get to the theater *now*. He fumbled his way into pants, shirt, socks, and shoes from where they lay discarded on the floor next to the bed.

The feeling of *hurry, hurry* gripped him, and he grabbed his jacket, phone, and keys as he headed out the door. He'd had these moments of prescience several times in the past, always to do with the theater, and he'd learned to trust them. Once it had been a frozen pipe that would have burst and damaged the costume shop. Another time it had been a door left open after a movie showing. A couple of kids had gotten inside and were roaming around. They could have damaged the theater or gotten hurt. Theaters were full of dangerous things like machine shop tools, open traps, flies, and counter weights for the stage. The theater could kill you if you weren't careful.

Oh God, I hope no one's hurt.

The front doors were still locked, that was good. He let himself in and locked them again. No sense in leaving the door open for more trouble. He paused for a moment in the lobby to listen. Perhaps his intuition would draw him to the source of the trouble. He'd been lucky before.

"Where are you this time?" He murmured. A faint tugging on his sleeve drew him toward the auditorium. The silent rows of seats in the darkness showed nothing amiss. Darkness? He could have sworn he'd left the ghost light lit on stage. He was religiously careful about it. Maybe the bulb had burned out. He made his way down toward the stage, aiming for the house light switches at the foot of the stairs.

A soft whimpering moan raised the hairs on the back of his neck. He stopped.

"Hello?" He called.

The moan came again. Definitely on the stage.

"Hello?" He called again, louder.

"Tommy?" came a faint voice.

"Teddy?" Tommy hastened to the light switches and flipped all of them. "Teddy, where are you?"

"Down here."

Holy crap. The central trap was wide open. He hurried to the edge and bent over. The crumpled form of Teddy Miller, his set designer, lay ten feet down. "Oh my God! What happened?"

"I broke my leg, and I think a couple of ribs. It hurts a lot," he panted.

Tommy stepped back from the edge, hauled out his phone, and dialed 911.

"911, what is the nature of your emergency?"

"I'm at the Avery Theater." He gave the street address. "Someone's been hurt. He fell. He's got broken bones. Please hurry. I'll let you in the front door." He leaned back over the edge of the trap. "Teddy, the ambulance is on the way. I have to go unlock the front doors for them. I'll be right back." He stood up. "Yes, ma'am, I'll stay on the line. I have to unlock the doors."

He switched on the lights in the foyer and propped the doors open to the house. In the distance he heard the wail of the siren. Thank goodness Maple Hill was relatively peaceful and had its own fire house. It meant emergency services were quick to respond.

They were going to need a ladder. He went back stage and fetched an extending ladder and brought it to the stage.

"Teddy, I'm here. My God, man, what were you doing here?"

"I had an idea to fix the set we've been having trouble with and came back. The stage light was out, but I didn't remember the traps being left open. Stupid. I know better. God, it hurts."

"You didn't have to come back. It could've waited till tomorrow." Tommy ran his hand through his sleep disheveled hair.

"But we're behind schedule. It wasn't going to take long."

"Hello? Where's the emergency?" A loud voice called from the front.

"On stage. Down here."

Two paramedics came down the center aisle, rolling a gurney between them. They went down the ladder, assessed the situation quickly, and got Teddy strapped to a back board. Together they lifted him out.

Tommy caught a glimpse of his set designer's ashen face as they rolled him back toward the ambulance. The theater was silent again. His heart still pounded. Slowly, he worked the lever to close the trap and latch it. How had it fallen open? Dave Binkler, his stage manager, was supposed to be in charge of making sure everything was reset for the next rehearsal and everything was safe before he left. He'd call Dave in the morning.

What were they going to do with the sets, now that Teddy was down and out?

He needed this show to be a success, to bring in lots of people, and improve the cash flow. He needed to prove that the Avery had what it took to be a vibrant community theater. Without that the much-needed renovation wouldn't happen. He would lose the theater to his creditors. It would be sold and then torn down. He couldn't let that happen.

Now that Teddy was in the hospital, they were going to be even further behind. His own set building days were over, and Binkler and Scotty didn't have the chops to build a picnic table much less half a dozen sets. How were they going to get the show up in time?

It had been a couple of days since he'd quit Gloria's, and Ruari still couldn't get over the reflex of waking up early before reminding himself that he didn't have to go to work. SueAnn Talmadge had called the morning after to ask where he was when he didn't show up at eight-thirty like usual. He'd told her in no uncertain terms he wasn't coming back. She'd huffed and blustered and demanded he return everything that belonged to Gloria's. Then she'd hung up.

Good luck getting someone willing to put up with you. I'm sorry, Mr. Carter and Mrs. Rosalind. I hope someone comes on board by the time your furnaces need service.

It had been a decade since he'd been unemployed, and not having a job made him restless. He puttered in his wood shop studio, an old converted carriage house and auto garage, but couldn't settle on anything. Marianne had been wonderfully supportive and encouraged him to start the woodworking business he'd been dreaming of. Erin had made noises about setting up his books. But working full time and suddenly having no work felt like driving in a convertible at eighty miles an hour and then stopping suddenly. He was flying over the windshield without direction. He'd been splitting his time between his studio apartment above the workshop and Marianne's house with a definite preference for Marianne's place, but Erin was living in the upstairs bedroom now. Having his little sister living in the same house again was not great. He loved Marianne's generous nature, but who knew how long it would take Erin to find a job? Erin was high in energy and low on boundaries.

He needed to jump start himself. He breathed in the comforting smells of wood, Tung oil, and the fainter smells of shellac and varnish as he tidied up the already clean shop. He sat on one of the tables closest to the big sliding door to the alley. It was the best vantage point to see the whole place. With a sketch pad in his lap, he tried designing the best space for him and jotting down ideas for simple, crowd-pleaser projects that he could sell while making larger commissioned furniture. Lazy Susans and cutting boards were obvious. He'd done some inlaid wood and had recently seen some intriguing designs involving poured epoxy resin set into wood. That would be fun to learn to do. He'd have to figure out how expensive the materials were and how time consuming it was. If it wasn't too bad, he could see doing some really cool table tops. He put a star by that idea and stared off into space.

Not for the first time, he wondered if Vivienne would awaken in the spring or not. His artistic muse was a tree spirit who was over a thousand years old and had been a secret partner of his for several years. She'd taught him quite a few woodworking techniques after Granda had died, and she'd helped him carve the intricate tree stump with animals, insects, and foliage that took pride of place on a nearby table. The level of design and detail still took his breath away. He wasn't sure if he could do it again without her guiding his hands. He also hadn't realized how much she'd urged him to create and work on the next project. How much of his love of wood had been her not him?

He would have to figure that out whether she returned or not.

His phone rang. The number was not Gloria's Valley Homes and Properties.

"Ruari Allen," he answered.

"Hey Roar, this is Scotty."

"Hey, haven't heard from you in a while." His friend Scotty worked IT at the Maple Hill Food Co-op, but he hadn't seen him lately.

"Yeah, I've been busy. Listen, would you have some time? I've been working at the Avery on lights and sound for the new play, and they need a set builder."

"I don't know the first thing about building sets."

"But you know your way around a saw and hammer and nails. Our set designer and builder is out, and we really need someone to finish the sets."

"I don't know a lot about theater, but I'd be willing to take a look. Are there plans?"

"Yeah, don't worry, Miller left lots of plans and sketches. Can you come down to the Avery after work today?"

"I can do you one better and come now."

"That would be fantastic! Verplank is about to have a nervous breakdown."

"What happened to Miller?"

"I'll fill you in when you get here."

"Okay. Be there soon."

Glad for the interruption, Ruari put on his jacket against the cold November breeze and put a few basic tools in the steel box attached to the bed of the truck, enough to do some simple things if he had to.

The Avery Theater was an old brick building at one end of Maple Hill. It had two slim towers and an arched roofline with a marquee over the sidewalk. A second run movie and a classic movie were listed for the weekly showings. The glass-fronted cases on either side of the entrance showed a silhouette of a Headless Horseman rearing up with a grinning jack-o-lantern in one hand and the words "*The Legend of Sleepy Hollow* Anniversary Production: 100 years."

He tugged on each glass door until one opened. The foyer was a deep burgundy red in both carpet and wallpaper. The carpet was rumpled along the edges, and one of the light fixtures was askew. Voices came from an office to the right, and he followed them.

Three men sat in a cluttered office. He recognized his friend Scotty and vaguely recalled the older man with bushy gray-brown hair, heavy features, and a slightly desperate air as the theater owner. The third man had a youthful face, but his hair had gone prematurely white. He wore it styled in a pompadour that had a little twist to it that resembled a soft serve ice cream cone. This man looked over at Ruari's arrival.

"The theater is closed today. You'll have to come back on Saturday for the movie." His tone was polite but dismissive.

Scotty turned. "Hey, Ruari, thanks for coming so fast! This is the guy I was telling you about. Ruari Allen, this is Tommy Verplank, the owner and artistic director of the Avery. And this is Dave Binkler, the stage manager."

Hands were shaken all around. Tommy Verplank looked like Ruari might be the answer to all his prayers. Binkler looked skeptical. Scotty's wide smile told him he hoped Ruari would say yes. To what, Ruari wasn't sure yet. He was tempted to open his auric vision and see what lay beneath their expressions, but there would be time for that later. So far, no one was lying at least.

"I'm not sure how I can help you," Ruari said.

Scotty pulled up a chair. "Have a seat, and we'll show you."

"What we need, frankly, is a magician who can turn these drawings and plans into a reality," Tommy Verplank said.

They showed him a dozen sketches. They were much better than the back-of-the-napkin variety he'd feared. They had measurements and suggestions for painting and finishing as well. But there was a lot of building involved.

"Has any of this been done?" Ruari asked.

"Yes, about half has been started but not finished," Tommy answered.

"When's your deadline?"

"Opening night is in three weeks."

If half of it was done, he could probably finish the rest in good time. He wasn't much of a painter, though, so the sets with forest and old fashioned interiors were beyond him.

"That's okay," Scotty assured him, "we're using a projection for most of them, and I can help you with the ones that need a little more than that."

"Do you have all the materials to build them? Do you have tools or a shop?"

"Of course we do," Binkler said, like it was a ridiculous question.

"Dave, why don't you give Mr. Allen a tour and show him what we have before he gets started," Tommy suggested.

"Wait a moment," Ruari said. He wasn't willing to give away his time quite so fast. "What are you offering in terms of pay?"

Binkler and Verplank looked at each other, and Ruari had the feeling that some telepathy was happening.

"My going rate is $35 an hour," he interjected before they could finish.

Tommy looked at him. "The theater runs on volunteers from the community for the most part." A slight trickle of dark smoke emerged with his words. Likely Binkler got paid and probably the former set designer had. Ruari had a sinking feeling that this gig wasn't going to be a walk in the park.

"I really can't do it for free." He had to treat this like an extension of his new business. Like Erin said, "Don't do nothin' for free, big brother, or you'll never get paid."

"Let's start you at eighteen dollars an hour and see how it goes."

"Thirty."

"Twenty-five."

"You're killing me." Tommy shook his head. "All right. Deal."

Not great but better than free. He had enough money as a cushion from all the overtime he'd done for Gloria's, but he couldn't coast on it forever. "Okay, for now," he agreed. "I'll look over a paper contract when you've drawn one up."

Tommy pressed his lips together, then said, "Dave, show Mr. Allen around."

The stage manager rose from his chair, his white, soft-serve hair bobbing gently, and tucked his clipboard under one arm. He motioned to Ruari.

"Follow me."

Marianne sat in her home office, notes and papers in organized piles on her desk. Oscar lay like a big fluffy paper weight, snoozing in the middle of them all. She had gotten a text from Ruari earlier saying he was headed for the Avery theater for a possible job opportunity. She'd texted back an enthusiastic, *Good luck!*

When he'd quit his job, she'd been worried. Her divorce settlement had been limited. Her ex and his lawyer had successfully hidden a majority of his assets and convinced the judge that he didn't have to split his considerable fortune with Marianne even after ten years of marriage. Instead, she'd been given a modest five-figure settlement and had been eking it out ever since. An apartment in New York City followed by a move to Maple Hill had depleted her savings, and she had to find paying work. Soon.

After some reluctance on her part, she'd allowed Ruari to help with the rent while she job hunted. So far, she'd had no luck finding a job in her chosen profession of history in spite of leaving resumés across Canopus County. If neither of them had jobs for a prolonged period, they were both going to be in trouble. But a job at the theater, even a temporary one, would be good. In the meantime, she needed to fulfill her promises to the people she'd met during the drive around Canopus, even if they were very unlikely to pay her. She'd have to make it quick and find a way to drum up business from paying clients.

She dug out her notes on Peter's and Astrid's cases and reviewed them. Telling the story of the mining accident was simpler than searching for a missing child from more than fifty years ago. She made a manilla folder for Astrid and the notes she'd taken so far and set it aside in a drawer. Then she dove into research about mining in the 1800s, Turner's Hope Mine in particular, the immigrants who worked there, and the terrible working conditions. She barely noticed when Oscar abandoned her for his food bowl.

She was in the thick of things and making progress when she heard a scrabble of paws on the floor upstairs and soft thuds as Oscar came racing down the stairs, down the hall, and flashed under her desk.

"What the—?" She pushed her chair back and looked under the desk. Oscar's orange and white fur was fluffed to twice his size. His crooked-tipped tail twitched madly. His ears were laid back, eyes wide.

"Good heavens, what happened to you?" Maybe some boxes had fallen over while he was exploring upstairs? Erin's possessions had been tossed hastily into boxes, and most of them were still stacked in the hallway landing upstairs. It took a few minutes, but she coaxed him out and into her lap where she petted and soothed him until his fur settled down.

"You want to go outside for a bit?" She took him to the front door and set him down where he stood on the front step and surveyed the neighborhood.

She realized she was hungry and called up the stairs, "Hey, Erin, you want some lunch?"

No answer. Marianne climbed the stairs and went to the younger woman's room, noting the undisturbed pile of boxes on the large landing.

Erin sat with headphones on, hands glued to the keyboard, staring fixedly at her monitor. Her eyes narrowed and lips compressed as she did something on screen. Marianne knocked on the door frame. Erin paused her game, slid one earphone off, and looked up. "Hey."

"You want some lunch?"

"Sure. I just got my ass handed to me for the tenth time. Time for a break."

"Oscar just came tearing downstairs scared out of his mind about something. What happened up here?"

Erin shrugged. "I don't know. He was up here for a while contemplating which of my shoes to leave cat litter in and then took off."

Marianne smiled. Erin and Oscar seemed to have a rivalry going. Each one blatantly snubbed or offended the other. She wasn't worried about either one's safety, since they seemed to keep their antics to a reasonable level. "He doesn't do that on purpose you know. I get litter in my shoes too sometimes."

Erin rolled her eyes. "He's a little angel, right? Well, he also eats the pepperoni off the pizzas I get."

Marianne looked over the room. "A mess" was putting it politely. She winced. She'd spent several hours making the place a pleasant guest room before Erin had moved in, and now it looked like a tornado had come through after looting a mall and a food court first.

"Erin, I hate to ask this, but would you mind not eating food in your room. Please? I don't want mice and roaches to feel at home." Years of living in apartments in New York had given her an acute appreciation of cleanliness.

Erin seemed to look at the room for the first time. Her fair cheeks reddened. "Oh, sure. Sorry. You've been really nice to me letting me stay here. I'll clean it up."

"Thanks. I'll go get lunch started." Back downstairs in the kitchen she realized that Erin's messiness and sharing of all the meals without paying her back had started to feel like freeloading, and Marianne was beginning to feel resentful. Maybe her hint would turn Erin back into a polite guest.

Erin came downstairs with a full trash bag and several plates and cups. She was fully dressed, had lightly gelled her hair into a spiky crest off the back of her head, and done her makeup with dark eye-liner and elegant eyeshadow in shades of maroon and dusty tan. Marianne was always slightly envious of the woman's apparently effortless ability to look gorgeous.

"Thank you," Marianne said as Erin stepped out the side door to the trash cans along the side of the house and deposited the bag.

"What's for lunch?" Erin asked when she came back in.

"We're running out of things, but there's enough for a couple of sandwiches, and then I have to go to the Co-op on a grocery run."

"Cool." Erin made herself a ham sandwich and poured a glass of milk before leaning against the counter to eat.

Marianne sighed. Taking a page out of Sarah's notebook of blunt talk, she addressed Erin. "I know you don't know how long you'll be here, but I'd appreciate your contributing financially to groceries while you are."

"But I don't have a job." Erin stiffened, looking hunted.

"Neither do I, and yet I still have to pay for rent, utilities, and food." Marianne gave her a pointed look. In the bad old days, when she was married, she would have to bring up delicate subjects like money from roundabout angles in order to get what she needed. It was time to try Sarah's directness even if it made her squirm.

Erin looked abashed. "You're right." She dug in the pocket of her black jeans and pulled out a couple of twenties and set them on the counter. "There's a start." She ate a few more bites pensively while Marianne made her own sandwich and ate it.

Coming to some conclusion, Erin sighed. "I have a bunch of apps out to employers in Boston and elsewhere, and I spiced up my professional profile. I have no idea when people will finally feel like hiring again. So, I'll check around in town and see if anyone needs a financial specialist. Or a receptionist."

Marianne nodded sympathetically. "I haven't had much luck getting work as a history teacher. Starting my own business might at least make me feel like I'm doing something. 'Shades of the Past' will have a history side and a ghost side. I'm still figuring it out, though."

"Ooh, you mean paranormal investigation?" Erin looked intrigued.

"Yeah, I figured I could mostly do history research, genealogies, things like that, and, once in a while, if someone had unexplained phenomena happening, I could check it out."

"Can I do that part with you?" She looked eager.

"What part?"

"The paranormal investigation thing. We could get all kinds of cool instruments and gear and go set up in people's houses at night and record EVP's, and orbs, and stuff. It would be way cool!"

"Um, I hadn't thought that far." What about just sensing for spirits the way she normally did? "Do you think we need all that?"

Erin set her sandwich down on the counter and brushed her hands off. "Okay, say, I'm Jane Doe and I think my house is haunted, what would you do?"

"I would ask you what makes you think it's haunted. Tell me your experiences."

"I tell you I've seen apparitions, and I hear footsteps on the stairs when no one's there."

"I guess I would have to come to your place and check it out."

"Right! And I would come with you."

Erin had spent most of her life denying that ghosts and the paranormal existed but had recently changed her mind. Marianne still marveled at how far she'd come.

"I was hoping that Ruari would be able to come," Marianne said. "Because what if the house isn't haunted, but they have wind in the eaves or the pipes knock? That's something he could figure out."

"True, but I still think you need a fellow spooky person to help you."

Marianne smiled. "I'll think about it."

"And," she pressed, "it would look so much more professional if we had a bunch of equipment like a ghost box, EVP recorder, and a camera that we can set up and record video on."

"That sounds really expensive. Why can't I just go and sense ghosts the way I usually do? It's what I would do anyway."

"People want a show. You might look less professional and more like a fraud."

"Really? That seems unlikely."

"Trust me. People think having the equipment makes you look more real."

"I'll take it under advisement for now," Marianne replied.

"Cool. Could I borrow The Flea this afternoon? I wanted to run a few errands outside of town. I promise I'll bring it back in one piece."

Marianne had been gifted her mother's little tan Ford Escort and dubbed it The Flea. She was careful with it in case her mom wanted it back someday, but Erin had driven it responsibly the last time she borrowed it. "Sure. I'll walk to the Co-op and try not to get more groceries than I can carry."

"Perfect. Thank you."

Erin finished, put her dishes in the sink and started to move back upstairs when Marianne said, "All the way in the dish-washer, please." Ugh, she was channeling her mother. Well, if that's what it took.

Erin returned and put them and her dishes from upstairs into the dishwasher before she ran to her room. She came back in a short black leather jacket and grabbed the keys from the bowl next to the front door.

"Ciao! See ya later!" She called on the way out.

Erin's role playing had gotten Marianne thinking. She was

going to need a more concrete plan. Having both Ruari and Erin on a house call could be very useful. And much safer. Not that she was worried about being overwhelmed by ghosts, but living people could be dangerous. That reminded her: she needed to cleanse and recharge her personal charm.

She pulled the little gauze bag out of her nightstand drawer and emptied the semi-precious stones and dried herbs and flowers into a bowl. Then she buried them in sea salt. According to the pamphlet she'd gotten from DreamTime, the New Age store in town, it would take twenty-four hours to remove any accumulated negative energies. Then she could lay them on a window sill for reenergizing in sunlight and moonlight.

As she left via the front door, Oscar darted out from the copse of trees at the end of the cul-de-sac and ran up the steps meowing.

"You want to be inside again? Okay, Mister. I'm going out to get food for all of us, and I'll be back." She stroked his back as he twined around her ankles before heading inside.

Dave Binkler was shorter than Ruari by several inches but walked with the air of a man who knows his stuff and owns the place. They went through an unmarked door in the lobby into a pale green painted hallway. Ruari estimated they were walking parallel to the auditorium headed for the rear of the building.

"What do you know about the theater, Mr. Allen?"

"Not a lot. I've seen a few plays but never did theater myself."

"Well, you'll see that a lot goes into creating the grand illusion the audience sees on stage." He sounded smug.

They walked down a long hallway with twelve foot ceilings and came to a short staircase leading to a door. Binkler led him down into a space with a huge vaulted ceiling that was easily three times the size of his own workshop.

"This is the scene shop where we build sets and store old set pieces."

Ruari followed Binkler down to the shop floor. Several things were partially built from two-by-fours, and Ruari thought he recognized pieces of the school room from the drawings. Binkler led him to the machine shop, and Ruari was glad to see they had all the basic saws, drills, and even a sander.

Binkler gave him a dubious look. "Do you think you can handle these?"

Most of the equipment looked like it had come from the 1950s and 60s. There wasn't a computer chip among them, and a lot of men his age wouldn't have a clue how to use them. But Granda had taught him how to use very similar equipment, and his own shop was a motley collection of vintage machines. It was nice to be able to tell Mr. Softserve, yes.

"Yeah, sure. Could you show me what set pieces have already been built?" Ruari asked.

Binkler gave him a wintry smile and motioned for him to follow. They went through another door, and Ruari found himself in a dimly lit narrow space defined by black curtains and ropes.

"This is backstage. You can move finished or partially finished pieces through the special doors and onto the stage this way."

They emerged from the curtains onto the open stage. A couple of two-by-four pieces were out there. That was it? The drawings had looked much more complicated than that. That wasn't even half of the projected sketches. Tommy either was overly optimistic or was terrible at evaluating things. Ruari revised his own estimate. He'd be lucky to finish everything in three weeks.

Binkler looked like he expected Ruari to make his excuses and abandon ship.

Ruari rubbed the back of his neck. He needed a project to focus on. He just hadn't expected it to be quite so...crisis driven. He made up his mind.

"Alright, I'll do my best."

Binkler looked faintly surprised. "Mr. Verplank will be very pleased." He led him back to the front office area where Scotty and the director were still conferring.

Ruari cleared his throat, smiled, and said, "Mr. Verplank, I think I can build your sets as long as I have some help with the painting."

Scotty grinned and clapped him on the shoulder. "That's my man, Roar. Painting I can do."

The director stood and offered his hand. He looked like a huge weight had been lifted from his shoulders. Ruari suspected he knew where that weight was going to settle. "Please, call me Tommy. Glad to have you on board. If you have any questions, Dave or Scotty will be able to help you." He handed Ruari a messy stack of papers and drawings.

"Is there a contract for me to look over? I'd like things in writing, please."

Tommy hesitated for a moment. "Sure, sure. I'll have Dave draw something up for you before the end of the day." A trickle of black smoke accompanied his words. Ruari was going to have to stay on top of it or they would conveniently forget. He'd be lucky to get paid.

Dave's confident demeanor dimmed slightly with the look of a busy man who's just been handed one more thing to do. His brow creased, then he nodded.

Scotty stood. "Well, that about covers everything, right? I'll show Ruari around a little more."

Tommy nodded, sat down, and picked up the phone.

Scotty ushered Ruari out the door and headed toward the auditorium. "This is great! You really saved us."

"I haven't done anything yet." Ruari paused at the concession stand and used the countertop to tidy the small stack of drawings.

"You will. You're a wizard in the shop."

Scotty gave him a much more thorough tour of the building

before ending up in the glassed-in booth at the back of the auditorium. Ruari's head spun with all the theater terms and places he'd been. He hoped he could remember it all.

"Don't worry. You mostly only need to know about the shop, backstage, and the stage area. You'll be fine. This is my inner sanctum. I control all the lights and sound effects from here," Scotty said proudly.

The small room was filled with electronic boards, gadgets, buttons, and dials arranged around a huge window that gave a perfect view of the stage. Ruari was no techno-wizard and was glad he didn't have to fill in for Scotty.

"I think I need to sit down with these drawings and figure out what needs to be done first. Do you mind if I lay things out here? In case I have questions."

"Sure. I have a shift coming up at the Co-op in about thirty minutes, but I can get you started. I'll be back after six tonight for rehearsal."

Ruari laid out all the sketches and went over them with a fine-toothed comb. Scotty filled in some of the gaps Teddy had left. By the time Scotty had to go, Ruari had a handle on what was required and headed back to the stage to walk through each set.

"By the way, what happened to Teddy Miller?"

"He fell down an open trap in the dark last night."

Ruari had gone below the stage on his second tour and gave a low whistle. That was a good ten foot drop onto a concrete floor.

"Is he okay?"

"Busted leg, broken ribs, and a punctured lung. They said he'd recover, but it would be a good eight or ten weeks."

"Wow, poor guy."

"Yeah, the ghost light had burned out."

Ruari's neck prickled. "The what?"

"Ghost light. It's a regular light that stays lit on stage whenever the house lights are off. It's supposed to keep people from falling into any open traps or tripping over set pieces."

"Why is it called that?" Ruari felt a little spooked himself.

Scotty laughed. "Supposedly the theater is haunted. According to legend, the light either keeps the bad spirits from causing mischief or it allows the ghosts of dead performers to relive their heyday. It's really just for safety. I gotta go. See you tonight if you're still here."

Scotty might not believe in ghosts, but Ruari had plenty of reason to believe in them.

CHAPTER 4

arianne returned laden with shopping bags and was glad to put everything down. She should have asked Erin for a ride back from the Co-op, and she'd grumbled more and more as the bags got heavier on the way home. She shook out her sore hands and put things away. Clearly she was going to have to be more direct with Erin, or she was going to lose her temper and toss her out. Then she'd feel guilty about it. She resolved to find a way to say something before it came to that.

It was late afternoon and time to start dinner. Marianne did all the cooking. Ruari and his sister were more of microwaved meal or take out kinds of people, and she didn't understand why. Their mother was a great cook from the couple of meals she'd eaten with the Allen family. Anyway, it was nice to make food for more than one person again, and they were appreciative. She rubbed sage and other herbs over a roasting chicken and put it in the oven to slow bake. The rice and squash wouldn't take that long to prepare.

Ruari had texted mid-afternoon that he'd gotten a temporary job at the theater for the duration of the show, and she was eager to hear more about it. Erin was still out, and Oscar was snoozing on the sofa in the living room. She made herself go back into the office and continue writing up the history of the Turner's Hope Mine disaster. The trick was telling the story in as few words as possible and getting people to care about what had happened.

She hit save on a decent draft and looked up. It had gotten dark out, and Ruari and Erin should be back any time now. The aroma of roast chicken permeated the house, making her mouth water.

Erin was the first to walk in the door. She dropped the keys in the bowl in the front hall.

"Wow, it smells like my mom's house! When's dinner?"

Feeling gratified, Marianne replied, "In the next half hour or so. It'll hold till Ruari gets back."

"Cool, I'm starved!" She ran upstairs.

Ruari arrived not too long after. He let himself in and came into the kitchen where he gave her a hug and lingering kiss.

"Dinner smells wonderful, but your kisses are better," he said when they broke apart.

"We can eat anytime." She smiled.

"Great, I'm starved."

"That's what Erin said. I was hoping we could have an evening together."

He sighed. "I have to go back to the theater after dinner."

"Oh, okay." She was a little disappointed. A new job took precedence, though. She and Ruari had all the time in the world to explore their relationship. "Rain check then. Would you set the table and call Erin down while I get things out of the oven?"

"Will do."

They gathered around the table in the dining room. Erin was wearing a black bolero jacket Marianne hadn't seen before. Under it was a red lacy shirt with a high neckline. She was humming and smiling slightly to herself.

"You look exceptionally Goth tonight," Ruari commented.

"I'm going dancing at that new club on Route 9 in Fishkill. A friend is coming to pick me up." She looked at Marianne, her darkened lips curving in a smile. "You want to come?"

It sounded awful. "Thanks, but no. I'm not into loud music really."

Erin looked a little disappointed. "Aw, it's fun. You should try it sometime!"

"Maybe I will but not tonight. I'm kind of tired. I think I'll read a book."

"Wish I could stay," Ruari said. "But they asked me to come in during rehearsal so I could see what set pieces they need first and how they're using them."

"That's right, how did you end up in the Avery anyway?" Marianne asked.

He told them about the phone call and getting the job as an interim set builder while the original designer was in the hospital.

"What happened to him?" Marianne asked.

"He fell down the trap in the middle of the stage last night."

"Who sets pit traps in a theater?" Erin said, looking startled.

"They're holes in the stage where set pieces can come through or a way for people to appear or disappear during a scene. I had a crash course in theater-speak today."

"Is he okay?" Marianne asked.

"Broken bones and a punctured lung, Scotty said."

"Yikes. What is it they want you to do?" Marianne asked.

"The set designer left detailed plans for what he wanted built. I think I can get them made."

Marianne smiled. "I'm so glad you got work that's right up your alley."

"Yeah, I was kind of spinning my wheels, trying to get motivated, and it fell out of the sky into my lap. What did you guys do today?"

"I worked on the text for the plaque at Turner's Hope Mine and did some shopping."

"I did a little job hunting in town and got sucked into the thrift store off Main Street," Erin volunteered.

Marianne looked at Erin's new jacket and shirt. "It looks cute on you."

"You should come thrifting with me sometime. It's fun!"

"I've never thrifted. I've antiqued, though. Is it the same?"

"Pretty much, just at a much lower price and quality. Sometimes you find treasures, though."

Everyone helped clear the table, then Ruari looked at his watch. "Gotta run. I'm so sorry to stick you with all the dishes. I promise I'll make it up to you."

Marianne kissed him and said, "I'll hold you to that. Have a good time. Don't fall down any holes."

The doorbell rang a Big Ben chime.

"That's my ride." Erin shrugged into her leather jacket. "Are you sure you don't want to come with us? You're totally welcome."

"Maybe another time," she answered. "Have fun, be safe. When will you be back?"

"As late as one, depending on the music."

"Okay, bye." The door slammed behind her.

Ruari kissed her. "I really am sorry about not being here tonight. I'll figure out what the schedule is and when I'm supposed to be there, and then we can make plans."

"It's okay. It's a new job. When do you think you'll be back?"

"Maybe ten?"

"I love you." It was still new to say, and she liked it.

He grinned and kissed her again. "I love you too. Dangit, I wish I could stay."

"I'll hold the fort."

The house was quiet after the front door closed. As she did the dishes and cleaned up in the kitchen and dining room, Marianne surprised herself by feeling lonely. Oscar strolled through as she wiped the last counter.

"Oscar, I can't believe I'm saying this, but the house is too empty. We used to be able to spend a quiet night together without thinking twice. What's happening to us?" She scooped the orange and white tabby into her arms and carried him to the sofa in the living room. She spent several minutes cuddling with the big cat. He purred and rubbed his face on her cheek. Eventually, he settled on the sofa next to her and began grooming himself.

She remembered she hadn't told Mrs. Thomas, her landlady, about Erin living with her yet. She should be honest about the addition and now was as good a time as any. It was still early in the evening. She could call Grandma Selene afterwards.

She dialed Mrs. Thomas and waited. The phone rang for a while, and Marianne imagined the elderly lady slowly making her way with her walker to the landline. Finally, she picked up.

"Hello?" She sounded as shaky as she always did.

"Hello, Mrs. Thomas, this is Marianne, your renter."

"Renter?"

"Yes, at 25 Violet Lane."

"Oh, yes, of course. How are you, dear?"

"I'm fine. I wanted to tell you I finished painting the inside of the house."

"That's lovely, thank you. I'm sure it needed it."

"It did. You've been kind enough to give me a break on the rent because of it."

"Have I? Well, good for me."

"I wanted to tell you also, that a friend has moved in with me."

"A friend? Who is it?"

"Erin Allen. She needed a place to stay after her apartment situation changed, and I offered to let her stay here. I hope that's okay."

"Is that Douglas and Margaret's little girl?"

"Yes." Mrs. Thomas had lived all her life in Maple Hill, and there were times when she seemed to know everyone.

"She's a bit rowdy isn't she?" Mrs. Thomas said dubiously.

"She's a character but has been a good roommate so far."

Marianne crossed her fingers. "Do you want us to pay extra rent as long as she stays? She's planning to get a job elsewhere, but the market has been tough."

"Well, if you want to put in an extra hundred dollars a month that wouldn't hurt."

Marianne suppressed a sigh. Being an honest person was not great sometimes. Aloud she said, "Absolutely." Hopefully, Erin would chip in.

"How is your young man?"

"Ruari is fine. He just got a job helping with the play at the Avery."

"Oh, that's wonderful! I miss the theater. Selwyn and I were in many productions in our day."

"I didn't know that."

"Oh yes. *Hello Dolly, Mame, Annie Get Your Gun, Anything Goes*." She warbled a verse of the signature song from *Anything Goes*.

"Are you planning to go to the show when it opens?"

"Of course. It's not a musical, but I do like supporting the theater."

"Ruari will be building the sets."

"I'm sure they'll be fine. Well, if there's anything else, dear?"

"That's all. Have a good night, Mrs. Thomas."

"Good night, dear."

It was a relief to know that Mrs. Thomas didn't mind Erin staying here, though the extra rent would be tricky. Damn her stingy ex. Time to call Grandma Selene. Maybe they could plan to have tea together soon.

Something landed with a thud overhead. Oscar paused in his washing, his tongue sticking out between his teeth, and his ears swiveling this way and that, listening. She tensed, listening for telltale footsteps, but none came, and she relaxed.

"What do you suppose that was, Mister? Sounds like something fell over in Erin's room. We should go check it out. Are you coming with me?"

Oscar licked his nose and thrust a hind leg in the air, clearly planning a long session.

"Guess that's a no." The house had been very peaceful since her ghostly roommates had vacated. It was probably nothing, but she'd better check just in case.

She mounted the stairs off the front hall to the little landing on the second floor. The stack of boxes looked undisturbed. Peeking into Erin's room, she saw with relief that the room was much tidier, and all the food boxes were gone. Thank goodness. The desk chair was lying on the floor. That might have made the noise. Or Erin might just have been in a hurry on her way out. Marianne stood it upright and glanced into the bathroom. Her sweet little bath under the eaves was a disaster zone. Makeup and hair products were everywhere. Squashing the urge to tidy up, she made a note to ask Erin to deep clean in here as well. As far as she could see, there was nothing to create a loud bang.

Her eyes fell on the little four-foot-tall access door to the attic space. One of the times she'd been in there, a ghostly presence had made itself known. With some trepidation, she pulled the door open and flipped the light switch. The wan bulb illuminated the rafters and the little boardwalk down the center.

The space always made her feel anxious, and this was no exception. Something was a little off, but she didn't know what. She looked around for a moment trying to identify what might be making her uneasy. The roof looked okay from here, and the window at the far end was intact. Maybe a branch had hit the roof. She shook her head and closed the door.

Back in the living room, she returned to the couch, pulled her tropical-printed blanket over her lap, and dialed up Grandma Selene.

She picked up on the third ring. "Hello, lovey!"

Marianne grinned. Her grandmother had grown up in England, and her voice still held traces of her British accent, something Marianne adored about her. "Grandma! How are you?"

"I'm doing well. To what do I owe the pleasure? Are you well?"

"I'm good. I just wanted to call and catch up with you." She'd already told her grandmother about the events at the cemetery on Halloween and trusted her implicitly with things supernatural. Grandma Selene also had clairvoyant dreams on occasion and was Marianne's favorite relative in her small family.

"How are things at your house?" Grandma asked.

Marianne told her about Erin and Ruari and then about her research for Peter O'Meara.

"I think you're doing good work to help those men find peace."

"I've researched how to get a historic plaque for Turner's Pond, but I have to go through the State Parks history review board for approval. It might not be done until spring. I hope the miners can wait that long."

"You told me that time passes differently for ghosts sometimes. I think knowing that you are trying will help them wait. Have you started the review process yet?"

"No, I'm close to being done, though. I have a couple more things to chase down."

"I'm sure it will be well-researched and well written."

"Thanks, Grandma. Would you be available for tea in the next week or so?"

"That would be marvelous." They discussed a few dates and decided on Tuesday. Marianne promised to make pumpkin bread.

"See you then, lovey."

"Love you, Grandma."

Marianne always felt better after talking to Grandma. She debated briefly about calling her mother up in Hyde Park and guiltily decided not to. Her mom had called about a week ago asking about Thanksgiving. They had been close when Marianne was growing up, but her marriage to Geoffrey had distanced them. Her mother had been all in favor of her marriage to the well-connected Chubb family, but the Chubbs hadn't thought much of the widowed, single mother from a simple, middle-class upbringing and kept themselves distant. After Marianne's divorce, she'd started reconnecting with her mom, but her newfound ability to see and speak to ghosts made her mother very uncomfortable. Mom had consulted her pastor and been told it was a slippery slope to unChristian behavior. Marianne kept their conversations cordial and polite but didn't tell her much about her life. No, she didn't need to call again so soon.

Instead, she put in a movie. Oscar curled up in her lap, and she tucked the plush blanket around them.

Ruari arrived at the Avery a little after six. He felt bad leaving Marianne alone for the evening, but she'd been so encouraging that he couldn't dwell on it. None of the front doors were open, and he couldn't see anyone in the foyer. Where else could he get in? Maybe the shop door was open. He went around the side of the building, but it was locked too. Was he too early? He pulled out his phone and texted Scotty.

I'm here. How do I get in??

I'll let you in the stage entrance around back, he replied.

Scotty arrived shortly. "Sorry about that, man. I forgot to tell you. We keep the shop locked for obvious reasons unless someone's in there. And we keep the front doors locked unless there's a public event. Just trying to keep the riff raff out," he chuckled.

Ruari could see his point. The house lights were on, and the general stage lights were on. Scotty led him back to his booth.

"Where should I be for this rehearsal?" Ruari asked.

"They're going to run through Act I tonight. You should have Teddy's sketches with you and sit somewhere in the first couple of rows so you can see the stage well. Just get oriented. Then when you come back tomorrow, you'll have a better idea of where to start and what is needed. Oh, and you should probably check in with Binkler and Verplank."

"Okay, where are they?"

"They're around. Fran and Brendan are around, too. You might introduce yourself."

Ruari looked blank. He didn't recall those names from this afternoon.

"Fran Turk's the prop mistress, and Brendan Nailer does costumes. They should be in their shop spaces in the back hall."

"Got it." He'd left the set design sketches in the scene shop this afternoon and headed backstage. Climbing the steps to the stage, he ducked behind the curtains into the wings where the oversized door to the scene shop was. An older lady with short iron gray hair, wearing jeans and a button up cowboy shirt was coming from the opposite direction.

"Excuse me," she said brusquely, "Can I help you?"

"Hi, I'm Ruari Allen. I'm filling in for Teddy Miller."

Her expression relaxed, and she stuck out her hand. "Fran, props." She shook her head. "I've known Teddy for years. He's lucky to be alive. Well, let me know if you need anything."

"Thanks, I will."

He reminded himself that props were all the items used by the actors in a scene from furniture to handheld items like dishes or umbrellas. Sets were larger and created the ambiance of a scene. He continued to the scene shop and made his way to the power tool area. He'd spent some time earlier in the day cleaning up and making sure everything was in working order. He'd cleared a table to one side for desk space and left the drawings there. They were gone now.

He spent several minutes searching for them but couldn't find them anywhere. Tommy and Dave Binkler must have them. He grabbed a pencil and a couple pieces of paper and a clipboard for notes and headed back toward the auditorium. He retraced his steps down the hall the stage manager had shown him that afternoon. Voices drifted out of the men's dressing room as he passed. The costume shop was next.

A dense forest of costumes hanging from two tiers of racks

suspended from the ceiling made a narrow corridor to the back of the room. A large work table littered with bits of cloth, scissors, a huge multicolored thread caddy, a pair of shoes, a sewing machine, and other things foreign to Ruari occupied the back of the shop. Half a dozen mannikins stood in various stages of dress or undress, but there was no costumer. Ruari left and continued down the hall.

Women's voices signaled the ladies' dressing room. A male voice was part of the mix. Unwilling to intrude, Ruari loitered for a couple of minutes hoping the other person was Brendan, but no one emerged. He continued down the hall up to the front of the theater and out the door into the lobby.

Tommy was conferring with Binkler in the director's office, the stage manager's white pompadour nodding gently in response to something Tommy had said. Ruari knocked on the door frame. They looked up.

"Hi, I'm here to observe the rehearsal tonight. I left the set drawings in the scene shop earlier today and hope you have them."

Tommy nodded. He gathered up the pages from the top layer on his desk and handed them to Ruari. "I've made some changes since we added a few things to the script. You should sit up near the front. We'll get started soon. Act I."

"Do you have a contract for me?"

Binkler hesitated for a moment then flipped through the stack of papers he kept inside the cover of his spiral bound script. He pulled out a two-page document. Ruari read through it. It was bare bones but seemed to be in order. He promised to build sets for the production <Legend of Sleepy Hollow> before the opening night <December 3> and to be present for the duration of the run of the show in order to address any last minute changes or repairs. They promised to pay him twenty-five dollars an hour. He would have to keep track of his hours and submit them once a week. He had no idea if this was an enforceable contract. Erin would likely have pithy things to say about it. But he wasn't union. He was just filling in for the one show.

"I need to look this over tonight. I'll bring it back tomorrow."

Binkler said, "It's no big deal. Just sign it, and we'll pay you for your first week's work at the end of next week." He smiled as a thin stream of smoke accompanied his words.

Damn. Vivienne's gift of seeing people as they truly were was coming in handy. He smiled back. "Sounds great. I'll bring it back tomorrow. I'd better hurry. It's nearly time to start." He tucked the contract under his papers and walked out of the office.

He chose a seat along the central aisle about six rows up from the stage. The slanted floor afforded each row a reasonable view over the heads of the people in front of them. He'd read a synopsis of the play this afternoon and had a general idea of what was going to happen. Act I introduced Ichabod Crane, the itinerant teacher, Katrina VanTassel the beautiful daughter of a local landowner, and Abraham Van Brunt also known as Brom Bones, the local bully. There was a drawing for a road, a schoolhouse, and a local alehouse. There was a new sketch with a lot fewer details showing a cemetery. That must be the addition Tommy mentioned. The painted scenery behind everything was out of his wheelhouse. He truly hoped Scotty would take care of that.

Tommy slid into a seat in front of Ruari a couple of rows closer to the stage with a large notebook. The stage manager, clipboard and script in hand, went up the stairs and behind the curtains. Ruari could hear him clapping his hands and urging everyone to come out on the stage for a quick meeting. People began filtering out into view. The women wore long dresses with square necklines and had blond or brown wigs and white caps or bonnets. The men wore dark brown or black trousers with light colored button up shirts and open coats. There were about twenty people in all, including several children. One of the men had brown hair pulled back in a small ponytail. He seemed vaguely familiar, but Ruari couldn't get a clear look at him.

"Okay, people, settle down," Tommy said. "Does everyone

have their wigs and shoes tonight? Is anything else missing? No? Thank goodness. I just wanted to take the opportunity to tell everyone how well this is going. We have three weeks till opening night. Plenty of time to iron out the details and make this the star production I know it can be.

"You are all part of the proud tradition of musicals and plays performed on this historic stage, the Avery, for the last one-hundred years. I know we've had a few hard times, but this anniversary show will revitalize the Old Girl and make Maple Hill a Mecca for the cultural arts once more."

Ruari looked at the cast. Tommy was giving them a pep talk, but they didn't look very uplifted by it. Tayloe and her friend looked dubious. The director rambled on a little longer before concluding.

"I have the utmost faith in our cast, particularly our leading men and lady, for an extraordinary performance and a solid run for this show. All right. Okay."

He cleared his throat. "Tonight, we're going to do a run through of Act I. Let's try to be off book as much as possible. If you forget something, say 'line,' and Dave will prompt you. Fran has your props, and Brendan will be on hand for any costume issues. Okay, people, places."

The stage cleared and the house lights dimmed and stage lights came on. A wooded hillside with a quaint colonial village appeared on the background, and Ruari remembered that Scotty said they were using projections for some of the sets. A youngish man in a deep blue open coat with tails and shiny gold buttons stepped out from the left side of the curtains. He wore a tricorn hat and carried a black cane. He bowed and smiled at the audience.

"In the bosom of one of those spacious coves which indent the eastern shore of the Hudson, at that broad expansion of the river denominated by the ancient Dutch navigators the Tappan Zee," he began, gesturing with his cane in a welcoming and expansive fashion. He got through his monologue flawlessly as far as Ruari could tell. When he finished, the scene changed to a country lane.

Ruari looked at the next drawing and saw there needed to be a bridge and a fence and possibly some fake greenery. A younger man entered the stage and began walking slowly across as if he was traveling. The narrator continued, introducing Ichabod Crane as "a worthy wight." The scene continued as more people entered the stage and populated the village. Several of them glanced at discreetly carried papers as they walked. Ruari realized they must be scripts. Scotty had said not everyone was "off book" yet.

Tommy yelled, "Stop!" after several people looked like they didn't know where they were going. Binkler reminded them where they were supposed to be, and Tommy started the scene again.

Ichabod taught classes in a one-room schoolhouse made of logs. His young charges were unruly, and prone more to spitballs and snickering than learning until Ichabod applied a birch switch. He was telling them class was done for the day when a pretty young woman with golden curls appeared at the door. Another woman sat on a chair with a book in her lap on the other side of the stage. Ruari glanced at his set drawings and realized that the chair was supposed to be a tree stump.

Ichabod dropped the book he was holding, and several boys laughed as they pushed past the woman in the doorway.

"Mr. Crane, I'm here for my lesson," she said. Her hands were behind her back, and she leaned forward slightly, showing her cleavage under her bodice.

"Mistress Van Tassel, you're early," he stammered.

"Of course, I am. I could hardly wait."

"Stop!" Tommy yelled. "The line is, 'I keep forgetting the line in that hymn you were teaching me.' "

Katrina looked at the director and pouted a little. "Oh fine." She cleared her throat and focused on Ichabod again. "Mr. Crane, I'm here for my lesson."

Ichabod's eyes had not left Katrina throughout the director's correction. "Mistress Van Tassel, you're early."

Ruari was impressed. It was as though there had been no interruption.

"I keep forgetting the line in that hymn you were teaching me."

"Of course. Please come in."

He gave her an impromptu voice lesson. Ruari became aware of two men carrying a ladder and a pillow. They were sneaking in an exaggerated fashion, completely obvious to the audience but out of sight of the two people in the schoolhouse. The girl reading the book ignored them. One held the ladder while the other climbed up and laid the pillow over the chimney. Then the two grabbed the ladder and jumped into the bushes, laughing silently.

"There will be a puff of smoke from the wood stove," Tommy called.

Ichabod and Katrina pretended to cough, waved their arms about, and fled the school room.

The two pranksters stifled their laughter and emerged from the bushes as if they had just arrived.

"Why Katrina, what are you doing here?" The man with the dark hair tied in a ponytail spoke first.

Ruari got a jolt. He knew that brash, slightly nasal voice. Brom was being played by none other than the terrible Casey. He groaned inwardly. He thought he'd gotten away from the little twerp, but against all odds, here he was. Ruari hoped the gloom of the theater was enough to cover his presence at least for now. There was no way to avoid meeting Casey at some point; the theater wasn't that large. Ruari hoped he could keep his temper.

Katrina's coughing ended, and she smiled. "Why Brom, I'm here for my singing lesson. Mr. Crane is teaching me a hymn for the Sunday service."

Brom scowled at Ichabod before saying, "Schoolmaster Crane, I thought lessons were over for the day."

"They are now. Something seems to be stuck in the chimney."

Brom's friend snickered as Brom said, "Katrina, I have a message from your mother, she wants you at home."

She turned back to Ichabod and gave a little curtsey. "Thank you, Mr. Crane. I'll see you on Sunday." She gathered up her friend with the book, and they exited arm in arm.

The scene continued with Brom and his friend trying to goad Ichabod into a friendly wrestling match, but he refused and went back into the school house to fiddle with the stove. Brom and his friend exited. Ichabod came out, found the ladder, and climbed to the roof where he found the pillow. He looked after the two men and scowled.

The next scene had more people and more forgotten lines. Tommy stopped each time and made them say the line correctly. Ruari had the brilliant idea to photograph each new scene so he could compare Teddy Miller's drawings with what was actually on stage. After they finally made it through most of Act I, Ruari began to think the whole story reminded him of *Beauty and the Beast* with the out-of-place person being Ichabod instead of Belle, and the bully being Brom instead of Gaston.

With all the stops and starts, it was a very long night. Ruari had a new appreciation for a finished play where everything ran smoothly from start to finish.

CHAPTER 5

Ruari slid gratefully into bed with Marianne when he returned to her house. She put her arm around him, and he relaxed into sleep. It seemed like only minutes had passed when an insistent ring roused them both from sleep. Ruari was instantly awake. Years of being on call for Gloria's had left their mark.

She mumbled, "Oof, yours or mine?"

"Mine, I think." He reached down to the floor and fumbled his cellphone out of his pants pocket and answered without thinking, "Ruari Allen."

The faint sound of music pounded in the background. "Hey, it's me. Could you come pick me up? I'm down at Pulsar Club in Fishkill."

"What happened to your ride?"

"She bailed on me."

He sighed. He didn't really want to get out of his nice warm bed and go get his sister, but he said, "Sure. Give me directions."

She grumbled something about, "Google it," but gave him verbal directions.

"Be there in about half an hour. Are you safe till then?"

"Yeah, I'm fine." She hung up.

"Who is it?" Marianne asked sleepily.

"Erin's ride left without her, and she wants a lift home."

"Can't she call a cab?"

He sat up and started putting his clothes back on. "I suppose she could, but I promised her when we were teens and I could drive before she could that I'd come get her if she needed it. Mom and Dad would give her hell first before they'd get her—"

"And now she just calls you," Marianne finished.

"Yup."

"You're a good man. She'd better not call you if she moves to Boston or New York." Marianne patted Oscar apologetically before getting out of bed. "I'll come with you." She tugged on her pants.

Ruari stopped. "No, stay here and keep the bed warm. I'll be back in an hour."

She hauled her sweater over her head. "Somebody's got to keep you awake on the way down."

They finished dressing, and he gave her a hug. "You really don't have to, but I'm glad of the company."

They took The Flea, and Ruari drove, since Marianne was still yawning. He was used to after hours calls from tenants and woke up fast. Marianne navigated, having pulled up directions on her phone.

As they sped down the dark switchback road that led from Maple Hill to Route 9, she asked, "Did you have to rescue Erin a lot when you were kids?"

"A few times. Parties that didn't work out, too much drinking. And once, a date that had gotten too personal too fast."

"Have I told you today what a good man you are?"

He grinned. "It's always nice to hear."

"How was rehearsal?"

"You're not going to believe this. Guess who's in the cast?"

"I don't know. Kelly? Sarah?"

"Casey Hopper."

"You're kidding?!"

"Not only that, he's Brom Bones."

She snorted. "Type casting. Did he see you?"

"Not sure. I was in the auditorium in the dark the whole time, but maybe."

"Ugh. Well, maybe you won't have to deal with him much."

"I'm hoping."

They pulled up in front of Pulsar, a club in one of the big strip malls. Colored running lights outlined the door and the name, and muffled music throbbed from within. A large guy stood vigilantly beside the door. A handful of other people in punk clothing and spiky, colored mohawks smoking cigarettes, vaping, and who knew what else loitered on the sidewalk. When they pulled up, a lone figure detached herself from the wall and sauntered over. She climbed into the back seat and slammed the door.

"Thanks for coming," she said, and slouched, leaning her head on the back of the seat.

"You okay?" Marianne asked her as Ruari pulled away from the curb and headed back out to Route 9.

"Just pissed that my ride stranded me here."

"Why did she do that? If you bring someone to a place, why wouldn't you take them back?"

"Exactly! She just decided she didn't want to be there anymore."

"Then why didn't you go home with her when she did?"

"She was being weird."

And she wouldn't say anything else, no matter how gently Marianne inquired.

When they got home, Erin mumbled another thanks and went upstairs to her room.

"Is she always like that?" Marianne asked.

Ruari shrugged. "When she doesn't want to talk about something, she doesn't."

"She acts like she's still a teenager."

"I know. I don't know how she survived business school and her first job so far away from home."

"She's going to have to grow up one of these days."

"Yup."

"And we're going to have to stop picking up after her."

He paused in pulling his socks and shoes off. "Did she do something else to make you mad today?"

Marianne sighed. "Yes and no. I asked her to chip in for groceries and she did. Then she took the car and didn't offer to help me shop."

"I'll talk to her."

"No, I need to sort this out for myself. My ex used to run me over a lot, and I have to learn to stick up for myself. She's good practice. By the way, I called my landlady tonight and told her Erin had moved in. She asked for an extra hundred a month to cover." She felt bad mentioning it. She really needed to be able to pay her own bills. But Erin and Ruari were straining her resources so it was fair. Right? She was too tired to sort out her feelings.

"Erin and I will help out," Ruari promised.

"Thanks."

They undressed and climbed back into bed. Oscar rearranged himself, putting his back against her thigh where she could reach him.

Ruari put his arm over her waist, loving how she fit against him. "If you need to kick her out, let me know. I wouldn't mind having you all to myself again."

"Thanks. I'll let you know."

He drifted off as the long day hit him all over again.

Marianne dreamed she was walking through a building with many rooms. It was important to get somewhere but it was taking forever. She finally passed into a large lecture hall and realized she must be late for a class, but she'd forgotten her books. They were in her dorm room, so she stepped into the nearest stairwell and started climbing. On the third floor, she pushed through the fire door and headed down the hallway. The carpet muffled her footsteps. The sounds of a loud conversation drifted down the hall, and she stopped at an open doorway. Two men and a woman were arguing vigorously about something, but she couldn't make out the words. A boy sat in one corner, idly playing with a piece of string. Noticing her in the doorway, the three students stopped, and the girl said, "Hey, you can settle this for us!"

Marianne said, "I'm sorry, I'm late. I can't stop right now. I'll come back later." She continued down the hall passing through section after section, up and down more stairs. She was missing class all this time. Maybe she should just go back and listen to the lecture without her notebooks. The longer she walked, the farther away her room seemed.

She surfaced from sleep feeling annoyed. It had been a long time since she'd had an endless walking dream where she never reached her goal.

Well, at least it wasn't about draugers this time.

She rolled over and sank back into sleep.

Marianne woke Saturday morning from an uneasy dream about John Irving, the caretaker at the cemetery. It had been something about him digging a grave by hand while Jason and Jesse helped. Digging graves was something John did for others for a living, so that wasn't too strange. But getting help from the two resident ghosts made her feel uneasy.

She shook her head and got up, leaving Ruari to sleep a little longer. Oscar was already gone, and she heard the sound of paws in the litter box down the hall. She put on her fluffy bathrobe and slippers and headed to the kitchen. Oscar met her there, complaining vociferously about his empty food bowl.

"You've been extra hungry lately." She refilled the kibble and put out some wet food, then cleared the litter box, and refreshed his water. Oscar scarfed the wet food with alacrity, licked his lips, and meowed to go outside.

"So demanding first thing in the day," she said affectionately, opening the front door for him to exit. He stood on the front step, twitching his crooked tipped tail as he surveyed his neighborhood. Marianne nudged him out so she could close the door.

She started the coffee maker and was pleased to note that it had been rinsed out. Perhaps Erin had taken her hints to heart. Humming, she put the electric kettle on for her own tea and got some bacon going.

Ruari joined her with a hug and a kiss as she stood at the stove turning over slices.

" 'Morning, Mahri," he murmured into her hair.

She leaned into him and smiled. " 'Morning. You sleep okay?"

"Mmhmm. Want to turn that off and come back to bed with me?"

"Give me two seconds." She scooped eight slices of bacon onto paper towel and turned the stove off. He swept her off her feet and carried her into the bedroom. She nudged the door shut with her foot as they passed by.

Sometime later, they heard clattering in the kitchen. Erin was up.

"Guess we have to get up soon," she sighed.

"Coffee and bacon will hold her for a little while. She'll figure it out."

They dozed a little longer before Marianne roused again. "You want French toast?"

He murmured agreement.

She dressed for a second time and went back to the kitchen, her stomach growling. Erin stood in her oversized hoodie and sweats, sipping coffee full of cream and French vanilla flavoring, eating the last piece of bacon.

Marianne's annoyance from yesterday resurfaced. "Hey, I was hoping to have some of the bacon." So much for reestablishing boundaries.

"There were only two pieces left by the time I got here."

"Oh really? I made eight."

She shrugged. "Then your cat ate the other ones."

"He's been outside all this time."

"Huh." Erin washed the last bite down with coffee. "I grabbed the last two slices figuring you guys had the rest."

Marianne took a deep breath. "I said you could live here temporarily, and I still mean that. But it's starting to feel like you're taking advantage of me. I need you to chip in for groceries and help with chores. I'm not your mother, and I don't want to be."

Erin looked stricken. "I'm sorry. You're right. You've been so nice to let me live here. I lived by myself in Arizona and didn't have to care about a roommate. Coming back here and having to live with my parents made me feel like I was twelve again."

Still feeling rankled, Marianne added, "Well, you're not twelve. I need you to help out here. Didn't you have roommates in college?"

"I did. I was the neatest one of the group." She drained her coffee and said, "I promise to do more to help out." Then she rinsed her cup and stuck it in the dishwasher.

Relief swept through Marianne. "My landlady asked me to put in another hundred dollars a month while you're here. Can we start there?"

"Would making a website and setting up your business be a good enough payment?"

"Yes, but I need some cash as well. You must have been paying the rent with something at the other place."

"Yeah. Savings. I was hoping to keep that for a downpayment on an apartment when I get a job in Boston. Rent there is as crazy as New York rent is."

"I get that, but I need help with the rent and utilities *now*."

"Your new business will bring in some money, right?"

"Ghosts don't pay. And I don't have any living clients yet."

"Are you asking Ruari to pay in?"

"He already is."

"Okay." She sounded resigned.

"Thank you."

"I'll get started on making a website and business plan for you today."

Marianne relented. "I'm making some French toast. Would you like some?"

Erin perked up. "Sure, I love your cooking!" With that she headed upstairs.

Ruari came in showered and dressed for a day in the shop. "I caught the tail end of that. Did she agree to pitch in?"

Marianne nodded. "She agreed to give me the hundred bucks Mrs. Thomas asked for and help with groceries."

"Do you need more from me?"

"No, you've been more than generous."

"Tell me if you need any more."

He poured himself a cup of coffee with a bounce of half and half and watched over a fresh batch of bacon while she made French toast.

When everything was cooked, Ruari called up the stairs to let Erin know.

He and Marianne sat at the dining room table and applied butter and syrup. "Where are you headed today?" Marianne asked.

"I'll be at the theater, building sets. I have a good idea of what they need, and I'll get started on that."

"Will you be home for dinner or are you at rehearsal again?"

"No rehearsals on weekends, so I'll be back around five I think."

"Movie tonight?"

"Yes!"

Erin returned wearing black leggings, Doc Martens, and a plaid knee length skirt with a wide belt. She had a black turtleneck with a green vest up top. No makeup yet.

"Erin, where are you off to today?" Marianne inquired.

"I'll keep looking for a short term job in town," she said unenthusiastically. She sat at the table and added a liberal amount of syrup to her two slices of toast.

Marianne said, "I thought I'd visit John Irving today." Her

dream had reminded her that John had helped them on Halloween night, and she hadn't heard from him since then.

Erin brightened. "Can I come with? You could drop me in town on the way back."

"I guess. I'll give him a call first and make sure he's available."

They cleared the table, and Marianne heard Ruari ask Erin to help him clean up. She smiled as she went into her office to make a call.

❦

Tayloe's cheeks hurt from smiling all Saturday morning. She assembled the umpteenth snack special, a cardboard tray with popcorn, a small package of candy, and a small soda, for another parent and child while Katie rang them up. Today's movie was *The Little Mermaid,* and the attendance had been especially good. She was glad for Mr. Verplank. His theater needed the income. But she was so ready for a break. After the show, she and Katie would have to go through the theater and clean up all that popcorn and mop up the sticky floors. Ugh.

The last parent-child combo hurried into the theater, and Tayloe breathed out a sigh of relief. There were always a few late-comers and a handful of people always came for seconds on the popcorn and drinks, but she and Katie could sit on the bar stools they'd sneaked behind the counter.

"Jeez Louise!" Katie said. "I thought they'd never be done!" She theatrically blew a stray lock of hair out of her face, making Tayloe laugh.

"We have about ninety minutes to ourselves," Tayloe said.

Together, they tidied up behind the concession counter and put another small batch of popcorn on to pop in case someone wanted more.

"How are you liking being in the play?" Katie asked her.

"It's a lot harder than I thought it would be in some ways."

"Really? You learned your lines really fast. I was impressed."

Tayloe shrugged. "The script feels like a conversation, I guess." She frowned. "If Mr. Verplank didn't keep changing the lines, I'd do a lot better."

Katie nodded vigorously. "No kidding. Just when I think I have it, he changes something. I sure hope he settles on the final version soon. Everyone else is tired of the changes, too."

"Here here." Tayloe was embarrassed that the acting was coming so easily to her. She hadn't expected that, but maybe she was just a natural.

"If the lines aren't the problem, what is?"

She shook her head. "I don't remember all the blocking. I keep ending up in the wrong place for some scenes."

"Well, Mr. Verplank must like you an awful lot 'cause he changed his blocking to accommodate you in the school house scene."

At her nursing home job she was a CNA with very ordinary duties: bathing and feeding residents, making sure they had their meds on time, and dealing with the childish and sometimes dangerous temper tantrums of the residents in the memory care wing. She always had a bruise or scratches healing.

But when she was on stage, she could be someone else completely. Putting on the Katrina wig and clothing made her feel very much the flirt: pouting and sassy. She enjoyed batting her eyelashes at Ichabod and mooning over Brom. She felt like a starlet. She'd be sorry when the play was over. Maybe she could take up community theater in whatever place she ended up doing nursing?

"Earth to Tayloe," Katie teased.

"What?"

"I said, what are you going to do about Casey and Randall? They both like you and sometimes I wonder if they're going to get into a fistfight over you. Though I think Casey would win that one."

Tayloe frowned. "Casey's so mean. I can't stand him."

Katie gave her a look. "Really? All that flirting you do on stage with Brom looks awfully real to me."

"I'm acting!"

"Huh. Not sure he sees it that way."

"Never mind. At least we haven't had any new pranks for a couple of days. That thing with the wigs and shoes was really weird. Did you ever hear who did it?"

Katie shook her head. "No one 'fessed up as far as I know. Mr. Verplank didn't seem too upset about it, though. I guess as long as no costumes or props were harmed or lost, it doesn't matter."

Tayloe paused, then lowered her voice. "Do you ever get a weird vibe when you're here? Like, if you come early before the rest of the cast gets here? It feels like someone is watching you or maybe just went around the corner out of sight."

Katie shivered. "Yes. That's why I wait until you get here before I go in. And poor Mr. Miller. He's still in the hospital."

"I heard he has broken bones and internal damage. He'll be recovering for a while before he can go home."

"Maybe he'll end up at Golden Years, and you can ask him what happened," Katie suggested.

"Hey ladies! Got any extra popcorn for us?"

They looked up. Tristan and the new guy were crossing through the lobby.

"Hi Tristan!" Tayloe said. Tristan was really sweet, and his plummy tenor made him a great narrator.

Katie was already getting a paper bag of buttered popcorn ready.

Tristan leaned on the counter and gave them each a warm smile. "I want you to meet Ruari Allen. He's filling in for Teddy Miller."

Ruari was taller than Tristan and broader in the shoulder. He was fair and freckled and had short, sandy, red hair. *Good looking for an older person*, Tayloe thought.

"Nice to meet you," Ruari said. "You're playing Katrina, right?

I almost didn't recognize you without the wig. And you're in the ensemble?" He nodded at Katie.

They nodded.

"Well, we gotta go make some sets, ladies," Tristan said, picking up the bag of buttery corn and giving them a wink. "See you later."

They giggled. " 'Bye!"

When the guys were out of earshot, Katie said, "Tristan's such a sweetie, isn't he?"

"Yeah, I always feel safe around trans guys. What do you think of the new guy?"

"He looks okay. Hopefully, he can get the sets made. I'm tired of pretending to walk around things and look at things that aren't there."

"Same."

❦

John Irving was available until eleven that morning when he had to close up a gravesite after a funeral. He sounded tired and old for the first time since Marianne had met him in August and that worried her. John was in his seventies but did all the maintenance at the cemetery with the energy of a younger man. Maybe he was sick and would be glad of the non-work related company.

The day was chilly and overcast, and Marianne bundled up. Erin had changed her attire after learning where they were going. The leggings and shoes were the same but the tartan skirt was considerably shorter. Her eye makeup was shaded and perfect as always. Marianne felt very Plain Jane in her jeans, olive turtleneck, and a dark brown sweater under her jacket. Her hair was pulled back in a ponytail under her black knit hat with a white pompom.

"Who are you dressing up for, John or interviewing?" Marianne teased.

Erin reddened a little. "I just wanted to look nice for potential jobs."

They drove through downtown Maple Hill and over the little bridge that crossed the Schuykill Creek at the end of town. The road wound its way up and around with the Hudson sparkling in the distance on the left and the imposing mass of the Hudson Highlands on the right. The trees were bare, and the car stirred up leaves on the road in its wake.

"What kinds of jobs are you thinking of?" Marianne asked.

"Maybe someone needs an outside person to straighten up their books or answer phones. Anything but waiting tables. One summer was too many."

"I hear you. Erratic tips and too many hands," Marianne agreed fervently.

"You waited tables?" Erin turned to her. "I thought you were ivory tower all the way."

"Right after my divorce I needed to earn money and that was the quickest way. The first way, I should say. I think I lasted two months? It gave me a lot of incentive to find something better."

They pulled through the fieldstone gates under the wrought iron arch. The parking lot was crammed full, and Marianne squeeze-parked the little Ford Escort off to the side between a Subaru and the low cemetery wall.

"It must be a big funeral," she commented. They both had to eel out of their doors in the tight spot.

Together they went to John Irving's old stone cottage. The machine shed was behind and off to the right. Marianne told herself she needed to stop by there to say hello to Jason and Jesse before she left.

John Irving opened the door, and Marianne received a shock. He had always been a wiry, spry seventy-something and sported the best Mark Twain mustache Marianne had ever seen. When he smiled, the crow's feet crinkled around his lively blue eyes.

Today, he looked like he'd aged a decade. His shoulders hunched, and he moved slowly. His mustache drooped. Marianne felt like someone had punched her in the gut. He ushered them inside.

"John, I'm so sorry I haven't been to see you before this," Marianne said. "I didn't realize you weren't feeling well."

The mustache twitched as he ghosted a smile. "I'm all right. Do you want some tea or coffee?"

"Sure. Can we help?" Marianne slipped her jacket off and hung it on the coat rack by the door.

Erin hadn't removed her jacket yet. She fidgeted and said, "Um, I need to step outside for a minute. I'll be back." And she left, closing the door behind her.

"Where is she going?" Marianne wondered.

"Probably visiting," John said, unruffled. He led her into the small kitchen at the back of the cottage.

Jason or Jesse, no doubt. "I'll be sure to say hello before I leave. Here, let me do that." Marianne filled the kettle with water while John pulled out a chair for her at the small kitchen table. Marianne recalled coming by when she felt overwhelmed with her newfound ghost abilities. John had been a calm, steadying presence.

They settled at the table with steaming cups.

"Are you doing okay?" Marianne asked, looking at John's lined face.

"Getting by. I don't seem to have as much energy as I used to. Good thing it's going into winter. I don't have as much to do."

"Erin told me you'd been attacked by *draugers* on Halloween night," Marianne said. *How could I have forgotten? Sarah was in her thirties, and she'd been knocked flat for days when she'd been attacked. I should have come by sooner, made sure he was okay before this.*

He gave a one shouldered shrug of agreement.

"Is there anything I can do? Want me to get groceries for you? Are you in pain?"

He shook his head. "I just don't have the energy. It's time to retire. I notified the higher ups at City Hall that they needed to find a replacement. The old place deserves someone younger than me."

"Where will you go?" *Who could possibly take John's place? Who would she ask for advice about spirits, if Sarah and now John were gone?*

"Not sure. Something will come up." He paused and looked at her earnestly. "Have you ever seen the Grand Canyon?"

"No, never. I've heard it's amazing, though." Her ex had not been into visiting natural wonders grander than himself. Doubtless, if people were allowed to ski the Grand Canyon, he would have thought it was more interesting. "Why?"

"I'd kind of like to see it."

"That sounds like a great idea." Silence fell between them while they sipped tea and ate a cookie each.

She asked, "Do you have family in the area?"

"I have a niece and nephew in Poughkeepsie."

"Do you get along?"

"We don't see each other very often."

"If you need anything, call me, please?" If Erin wasn't currently occupying her spare room, she would have asked him to come stay with her.

He smiled and patted her hand.

"Have you seen Sarah?" Marianne asked. "She hasn't returned any of my calls since Halloween."

"Kelly stopped by the day after and went up to the bonfire area. Said they'd lost something. I didn't ask."

Sarah and Kelly, now John. Erin acting mysterious. Ruari quitting his job. Everyone had been changed by the events at Halloween.

"How are Jason and Jesse?" She was half afraid to find out.

"They're well. They help me out when they can. How are you doing?"

Marianne told him about considering starting a paranormal investigation business and about her research for her first two clients. He got them each a second cup of tea and listened.

When she finished, he said, "You're doing good work. The dead need someone to help them out sometimes just the way the living do."

"Sarah told me that if you help out everyone who comes to you, you could run yourself dry. She said the number one killers of psychics were cancer and autoimmune diseases like MS. Is that true?"

He thought for a while before answering. "Everyone dies of something. You have to decide for yourself if helping people is something you feel strongly about. Once you start, it may be hard to stop. You won't always be thanked, and some folks won't appreciate it at all. But those you do help will be worth it. If you decide to spend your life helping people, always save something for yourself and don't feel bad about asking for help."

Marianne let his words sink in. *Don't feel bad about asking for help. Well, I know where that advice comes from. Sarah is terrible at asking for help.* Having Ruari's help, maybe Erin's, would be good. She nodded.

John glanced at the white clock on the wall. "I need to go and close up the graveside."

"Of course." She helped him wash up the mugs and wiped the counter with the sponge. If John was retiring, she was going to miss the spartan neatness of this little cottage. Who knew what his replacement would be like. She'd have to find out where John ended up, so she could visit him regularly.

She stepped back outside, tugging her black knit hat over her ears against the cold breeze. Where had Erin gotten to? Marianne headed for the machine shed and ducked inside.

"Erin? Are you in here?" She called into the dimness. No flash of a red beret. "Jason? Jesse?"

No one answered her, and the shed felt empty. She closed her eyes and turned her head from side to side but saw nothing new. Marianne returned to The Flea. She slid into the driver's seat and waited, feeling the chill seep into her jacket. She texted Erin that she was ready to go but got no answer. After a few more minutes, she called Erin's number. No answer. She left a brief message when prompted. "Hey, I'm done. Come back to the car."

Finally, Erin emerged from a path beyond John's cottage and sauntered up to the car. She was smiling.

"Where did you go?" Marianne asked.

"I just went for a walk." She looked at Marianne and really saw her. She blanched. "Oh no! I'm sorry. Did you wait for very long?"

"Well, kind of. I texted and called you."

Erin pulled her phone out of her pocket. "Shit, I'm sorry. I must've been out of signal range. Hey, I owe you tea or something, okay?"

"I'll hold you to that." Marianne started the car. She dropped Erin at the end of Main Street where it started after the Schuykill Creek Bridge.

"I promise I'll treat you next time. Be home for dinner around six." Erin shut the passenger door and gave her a cheerful wave.

Marianne waved back and continued down Main Street. Erin might've been out of sight, but Marianne had been all over that cemetery and never lost signal.

When she got home, she decided to refresh the magical wards around the house. She'd hung a horseshoe over the front door after Halloween, but more vigorous protection would be better. She didn't want *draugers* or full grown Shadow People showing up on her doorstep. Or worse, Byron Mandell.

She shivered as she got a box of tea lights out of the pantry, a long handled lighter, and a bundle of smudging sage. Byron had been Sarah's mentor and had gone as bad as a person can go. They'd stopped him, but he'd escaped into the Shadow Lands, taking the spirit of his sister with him. But not before he'd made it very clear that he loathed Marianne and would take revenge on her if he could.

"You've got to get through my wards and the locks on the doors and windows first, buddy," she said. Oscar looked up from snacking at his food dish, licked his lips, and came to rub against her ankles.

"Would you help me protect our house, Mister? Sarah said you're an essential part of my family and add to the power of the wards."

He said, "mrow-row" in agreement and followed her to the front door. She stood with her back to the door and closed her eyes, settling her mind into the right frame. When she felt focused and calm, she lit the end of the sage smudge and blew the flame out leaving it smoking.

"By Earth and Sky, and Fire and Water, I call on the spirits to protect this house from negative energies and evil entities. Surround us with light. May peace be in this house." Slowly she walked from room to room wafting the pungent sage smoke in all corners. She paused at the windows to light new tea lights and dust off the polished semi precious stones in their saucers. At each doorway, she inspected the little dried bundles of herbs and flowers. Those that no longer gave off a scent when she crushed them, she made a note to replace.

As she walked, she began to feel a humming in her ears. Before her wild ride around Canopus County with Sarah, she'd been unable to feel magic and had to take it on faith that it even existed. Now, she could feel the humming tension building like a faint chorus. She felt her own throat humming along on the same notes. Oscar followed her from room to room purring.

She descended the stairs to the basement. Once a source of anxiety and fear when the ghost of Anne Rutherford was there, it now felt neutral, just another level of her house. She wafted sage smoke into every corner, behind the huge old furnace, into the old coal bin where she kept a few boxes of things. At each of the small windows, she lit the tea lights in their clean, empty cat food tins filled with a few ounces of water to extinguish any flames that got unruly. Oscar leapt up into the big window which had been the old coal chute. She put a floating tea light on the deep sill.

"By Earth and Sky, and Fire and Water, protect this basement from things that dwell in darkness. Keep all who live here safe." Her prayers were free form. Sarah had emphasized the power of the intent behind the words more than using specific phrases. Marianne sent her positive intentions into the universe fervently. Keep us safe from *draugers*, Shadow People, and Byron Mandel. Tell me if they try to get in.

They proceeded up the stairs to the second floor. Marianne continued to wave the purifying, protective smoke into all the corners and lit the tea light on the window sill overlooking the front of the house. When she'd first arrived, she'd seen a face in the window here. She still wasn't entirely sure if it had been Anne or George, but since those spirits had moved on, she hadn't seen the face or heard the footsteps.

She chanted again on the landing.

They entered Erin's room and lit the light on the windowsill and dusted off the stones nearby. Erin had taken them out of their dish and made a little spiral pattern with them on the sill. Marianne smiled and swirled smoke around them. Dutifully she included the little bathroom under the eaves and then paused in front of the little attic door. It looked as though it led into another world. The bundle of sage was burning down, getting warm near her fingers. She'd better hurry.

She opened the door. The attic always felt a little menacing with its low ceiling and sharp nails from the roofing shingles poking through. She appreciated being on the short side as she stepped onto the beams and carefully walked to the far end of the house to the little vent and dirty window at the far end. There was no sill, so she'd pinned up a little bundle of herbs and dried flowers instead. She waved smoke everywhere and hastened out, closing the door behind her just as the sage singed her finger tips. She dashed into the bathroom and dropped it into the sink. Cold water cooled her hand and extinguished the last of the smudge with a tiny fizzle. The faint hum of magic closed with a pop, and she felt the protection settle over the house like a warm blanket. It was nice to know when it worked.

Oscar yawned and shook his head before loping down the stairs. She tossed the crumbly sage ash into the trash. She felt damp and flushed with exertion, though all she'd done was walk around the house. She splashed some cold water on her face and patted it dry with the hand towel. That should keep her from feeling uneasy about the attic and help keep out bad dreams.

CHAPTER 7

"I know it's a little last minute, but do you want to go thrift shopping with me?" Erin asked Marianne over breakfast.

It was Sunday and Ruari had said he had to build sets at the theater all day. His deadline was looming, and Binkler was breathing down his neck to get things finished. Marianne sympathized. The white-haired stage manager's passive aggressive behavior reminded Ruari of Talmadge's and part of him was tempted to dig in and go slow. But the cast had been doing the best they could under trying circumstances, and he didn't want to disappoint them. So, he got his keys, kissed her goodbye, and headed out in his truck.

With her day free, Marianne had planned to do some work. Erin's invitation felt like an abrupt non sequitur. "Now?"

Erin looked hopeful. "Yeah, just a girl's day out. I promised to take you, and Renata's Closet is open from ten to four today."

"I guess I could. For how long? I was going to do some reading and research this afternoon."

Erin looked thoughtful. "We could start at Renata's and then see where the spirit takes us. There would probably be coffee or tea in there somewhere."

That could be fun. Marianne had never spent much time with Erin socially. It might be nice to get to know her a little better. Thrift shopping would be so much better than going to a club with loud music and awkward dancing and drinking. "Okay, sure!"

Erin grinned. "Perfect! Meet you back here at ten." She put her dishes in the sink and headed out.

Marianne said, "Erin, would you mind putting those all the way into the dishwasher?"

Erin paused halfway through the pantry on the way to the front stairs. "Oh, sure."

Once the kitchen was tidied up and the dishwasher was going, Marianne retreated to the bedroom to dress. Ruari had made the bed, and she loved him all over again. Smiling, she showered and dressed in jeans, a turtleneck, and a loose fitting sweater that would be easy to get in and out of if she found clothes she liked. She hadn't been shopping with a girl friend in ages and was beginning to feel excited about the prospect.

Erin was waiting by the front door in black leggings, an olive green canvas kilt, doc martins, and a black turtleneck sweater. Her make up was perfect, as always. She grinned through dark red lipstick. "Are you ready to take Maple Hill by storm?"

Marianne quirked an eyebrow. "Well, I'm certainly willing to go shopping with you. Want to walk?"

"Let's."

Marianne locked up, leaving Oscar on the doorstep contemplating the neighborhood, and they headed up Violet Lane. Erin was voluble and chatted about this and that at a great rate. Marianne didn't need to say much. She just let it wash over her.

Main Street was moderately busy at this time of year. Stores were putting out their holiday displays, and the town was beginning to look festive. Marianne had lived in Maple Hill for only a few months, but she knew they depended on sightseers and weekend tourists from the city and elsewhere. There was a flyer for a holiday-themed shopping weekend after Thanksgiving in many stores, and she made a mental note to check it out.

Renata's Closet was open with racks of summer clothing at deep discount out on the sidewalk. Inside, the decor was themed with travel and concert posters from the 1950s through 1980s. Having been born in the late 1970s, Marianne was amused and slightly horrified that the era she'd grown up in was now considered retro. She hadn't been old enough for bell bottoms, peasant blouses, and maxi dresses. Her idea of cool had been velour and big hair.

Renata's had divided clothing by type and by color. Erin drew her to a rack.

"Okay, there are a couple of methods. You can be ultra methodical and just look at everything, or you can go by colors, or be random, but you might miss things if you go totally random. Don't forget to go through the bargain bins. You can find some really good stuff in there sometimes. Good luck. If you see something you like, holler!"

They were different sizes. Marianne was short and curvy. Erin was a little taller and sturdily built. They also were attracted to very different things. Marianne started to look through a rack by size and was quickly overwhelmed by the sheer variety of styles and started skipping to things with colors that caught her eye. She tended to prefer warm gold, caramel brown, and emerald green but sometimes brighter magenta, orange, red or purple worked. She looked at the next rack over. Erin was clearly the methodical type, giving each new item a quick scan.

Marianne drifted between racks and found a dress that looked promising as well as a couple of sweaters. After ten minutes, Erin found her. She had a huge armload of things and was beaming.

"I found a couple of things you'd look really cute in!"

They went to a couple of empty changing rooms. Erin hung up all of her finds outside the door on one side. Marianne took her four finds into the room with her. She tried on the dress first. It was deep blue and green with threads of the Allen family tartan colors in it. She liked it and decided if Ruari wanted to wear his kilt sometime, she now had a dress to match. The sweaters were less exciting, but there was a dark brown cable knit that looked warm. She glanced at the prices and raised her eyebrows. They were both under twenty bucks. So much easier on the wallet than antiquing or shopping in the city.

"Hey, Marianne, I found this for you!" Erin thrust two hangers into the dressing room.

One was a pair of dark brown leather pants, and the other was a bustier style velvet top in dark green and purple with blousy sleeves. It was very low cut.

"Are you sure these aren't for you?"

"Just try them on! And you have to show me!" Erin laughed.

Marianne shucked off her jeans and put on the pants. It was like wearing a pair of driving gloves over her legs: as snug as a second skin. She looked at herself in the mirror. They were absolutely the last thing she would have chosen for herself. She put on the top and winced at the amount of exposed cleavage. She wasn't in danger of falling out, thank goodness, but, wow. Again not her first or even her tenth choice. The two items together made her feel like a renegade from a '60s folk rock band. It just needed a paisley headband to complete the look.

"C'mon, show me!" Erin called from the other side of the curtain.

"Is anyone else we know out there?"

She laughed. "Nope, it's safe!"

Marianne pulled the curtain aside and stepped out.

"Holy shit, you look gorgeous! Like a badass babe!" Erin admired her. "Ruari's gonna flip!"

"Oh no, I'm not getting them. I'm just showing you!" Then she looked at Erin's outfit. "Oh! You look amazing in that." It was a deep red, rib knit, sleeveless dress that hugged her figure. The neckline was high around her throat, exposing her pale shoulders. It came to her mid thigh. "You should definitely get that!"

Erin grinned. "Stay there, I'll be right back." She dashed off into the store and came back a couple of minutes later. "Here, put this on."

It was a velvet choker with a single pearl in the middle. Erin helped her fasten it around her throat. It felt weird. She looked at herself and conceded that it certainly went with the outfit. Now she looked more like a gypsy witch than a hippie. She would never wear this. Ever.

"You *need* to get this." Erin was adamant. "I'm getting mine. You're getting that."

"But I'll never wear it!"

"That is certainly true if you don't own it. I bet you there'll come a time when that will be the perfect thing to wear. Mark my words."

Marianne disappeared back into the dressing room to take the outfit off but only after she looked at herself in the mirror again. Her mother would be appalled, and she certainly would never have worn anything remotely like this while she was married to Geoffrey unless she wanted to be called a slut. She narrowed her eyes and turned one way and then the other. If Erin showed her how to do make up like hers, then maybe she could wear this outfit. Let that part of her out to see the world for a little bit. She shook her head and took it off. The pants needed extra work. Getting back into her jeans, turtleneck and sweater felt safe. But a tiny part of her sighed.

When she emerged from the dressing room. The huge pile of clothes outside Erin's curtained stall had partly shifted from one side to the other. Marianne folded the items she'd chosen over one arm and left the unselected items on the hook outside.

She paid and put them in a paper bag with a Renata's Closet logo stamped on it and drifted around the store looking at things. Eventually, Erin came up behind her with her own bag of purchases.

"Want to get some coffee?" Erin asked.

"Let's." They walked to Hudson Valley Trading Company and ordered drinks. Marianne got a tropical green tea, and Erin ordered a mocha, and they sat in the window overlooking the street.

"So you grew up in Maple Hill, right?" Marianne asked.

"Preschool to high school. Same bunch of kids." She did not look enthusiastic.

"That sounds kind of nice. My mom and I moved around a couple of times. She went wherever she got a job."

"That sounds nice to me." Erin sounded a little envious.

"Being the new kid all the time wasn't great. Everyone else already had their friends, and there wasn't a lot of room for me. And when I finally made a friend, I had to leave them behind."

"But you had the chance to start over. And you could leave all the jerks behind."

"I suppose. But there were always new jerks. Do you still have friends who live here?"

Erin sipped her mocha. "I thought I did. But they turned out to not be my friends anymore."

"What happened?"

Erin sipped her mocha and didn't answer. When Marianne was about to let it go and try another topic, Erin spoke softly.

"I knew everyone at school. The people I didn't know, weren't worth knowing. Or so I thought. I hung out with mostly the same girls from ninth grade to senior year. I guess you'd call us the popular girls. We went to parties together, did homework together, got in trouble together. But I was good at math, and they weren't. I played it down." She took another sip, staring at something in the past.

"When I left for college, we kept up with each other, but it wasn't the same. I went to B-School in Chicago right after I graduated and got my first job in Arizona. I was really stoked. My high school friends had gone to college, but a lot of them came back, got married, and had kids.

"When I moved back, I tried to reconnect, but they made it clear they'd stayed tight with each other, and I was not part of that group anymore." She sipped her drink.

"That sounds really painful."

She grimaced. "Almost as painful as my stupid haunted apartment. But, hey, at least that helped you out."

Marianne had to make a few quick mental connections. Ruari was right; his sister did jump topics. "I'm sorry I wasn't here to help you with that."

Erin's smile was wry. "That's okay. I probably wouldn't have believed you. I had to live through it to believe it. Anyway, thanks again for letting me stay at your place. I promise I'll be out of your hair as soon as I get a decent job. If you need me gone sooner, just tell me. I'll figure something out."

Marianne considered the offer. Erin seemed to be genuine about it rather than playing the martyr. Marianne smiled. "You can stay as long as you pitch in."

Erin's shoulders relaxed a trifle. "Thanks."

They sipped in silence for a while. Erin stared into the middle distance, clearly in a world of her own. Marianne let her thoughts drift a little. The rest was nice.

"Um," Erin said quietly, bringing Marianne back to the present. "Have you ever been with someone but know you can't really be with them? And they know you can't be together too, but you both pretend because it's nice to pretend?"

Taken aback, Marianne had to process Erin's words. For a moment, Erin looked small and unsure.

Seeing her hesitation, Erin's expression snapped closed. "Never mind. Just being stupid." She stood up with a wry expression. "Better get these clothes back home so we can try them on again."

They headed back to Violet Lane, talking about nothing of consequence. Marianne replayed Erin's words but couldn't make much sense of them. Erin surprised her one last time by giving her a quick hug before heading up to her room. Thoughtfully,

Marianne put her purchases away at the back of her closet and plunged into research for the rest of the afternoon.

CHAPTER 8

Tommy spent every daylight hour and more getting things for the play lined up: tickets printed, material for the Playbill, and lots of publicity, including a radio interview, and ads in the Canopus, Dutchess, and Putnam county newspapers. He also called old friends from New York theaters to schmooze and tell them about his upcoming production. He always invited them to come see it with comped tickets at the door. On Monday, he called one of his oldest friends.

"Charlie, this is Tommy Verplank, how are you?"

"Tommy, haven't heard from you in a long time. What are you up to? You must be retired, drinking a mai tai on a beach somewhere."

"Not ready to retire yet, Charlie. I saw you were doing *Guys and Dolls*. I've got tickets to see it next week."

"That's terrific! You're lucky you got them, we're nearly sold out for the next six weeks."

"Congratulations. Listen, I'm doing a production of *Sleepy Hollow* up here at the Avery, and I wanted to invite you and your wife to come opening night. Tickets are on me."

"Oh, yeah? That's real swell of you, Tommy. When's it opening?"

"December third."

"I'll tell the missus. *Sleepy Hollow*, huh? Which adaptation? Burton? Bloedel? More horror or more comedy?"

"Actually, I've adapted it myself from the original. I'm pretty pleased with it."

"Your own, huh?"

"Picture this: Ichabod is an educated outsider to the town of Sleepy Hollow. Katrina is beautiful and talented and torn between staying in the village or marrying him and becoming successful in the larger world. Brom represents the town, protecting its ignorance. Ichabod is all things modern, and Katrina represents the village. The style is in the realm of magical realism with a Dutch Colonial look. I added a ghost of a Van Tassel who never left home and regrets it. She tries to convince Katrina to make better choices than she did. I think you'll really like it."

Charlie gave a low whistle. "Say Tommy, that's...that's something."

"I think it illustrates many of the same things we're facing today: ignorance and worldliness, small town and the wider world. It's very relevant."

"You've always been very *aw current*. But do you think it will entertain people and make them happy?"

"It'll make them think."

"But will it sell tickets?"

"If we market it right, I know it will. I was hoping you could get us a spot in your Playbill. Maybe a half a page?"

"Tommy, I'll talk to our marketing person this afternoon and have them call you back. And I'll tell Susie about the invitation tonight. We'll be in touch. Thanks again for your call."

Tommy hung up. That had gone better than his two previous calls which had ended much sooner. At least Charlie had heard the whole spiel. Of course *Sleepy Hollow* would sell tickets. It was perfect for the season. Maybe he needed to add in another ghost or two and beef up the *Christmas Carol* feel to it. This adaptation might become the new holiday play. There could be royalties.

He had to focus. Get this production on the stage. Get people in the seats. If he could fill the auditorium, he could renovate. Get a new roof. Fix the old boiler. Hell, replace the whole HVAC system. New seats, new curtain, new lights, new sound booth. New marquee.

If only the ghosts of the old theater didn't get in the way, there would be room for a new Avery theater.

Monday night, Ruari sat through the first few scenes of Act II while Binkler and Tommy reminded the cast how and where they were supposed to move and stand. This was the first time through for these scenes in two weeks, and most people still walked around with scripts in one hand and a pencil in the other. At least Tommy seemed to have stopped changing lines.

Ruari referred to Teddy's sketches with a more experienced eye. He was getting the hang of set building after the first couple of epic fails. He'd built flats that were sturdy but heavy, and no one would be able move them easily. Binkler's scathing looks had reminded Ruari of his Granda's glare: "ye-daft-idiot" mixed with a dash of contempt. He'd wondered if he'd gotten in over his head. Would Vivienne have known better? Probably not. Scotty had stepped in quietly and given him some hints and pointers.

Ruari made notes on what was needed for the next few scenes including a complete interior of an old Dutch Colonial great room with a fireplace, furniture, and a huge table for the feast scene. He planned to borrow a huge old spinning wheel from the antique store in town. Maybe Marianne would be willing to help him research the time period and make his sets more accurate. Scotty had been true to his word and started painting the existing flats and sets. More importantly, he'd shown Ruari the basics of painting in perspective, creating the illusion of three dimensional objects on a flat surface. Scotty was good at it. It was going to take Ruari a long time to master. Tommy's irritated voice made Ruari look up.

"No, Casey, I need you to stand *up* stage from Randall and *then* cross to the other side. Do it again. And Randall, what's going on with your costume?"

Casey grimaced in annoyance, caught himself, and nodded before backing up to his original position.

Ruari and Casey had finally crossed paths for the first time that evening. Ruari had been passing from the scene shop to the bathroom along the back hall, and Casey and Jake had stepped out of the men's dressing room. His former assistant had done a visible double take swiftly replaced by a sneer.

"What are you doing here?" Casey said.

Ruari bit back his first reply, *unemployed thanks to you, asshole,* and said, "Filling in for Mr. Miller while he's out. Congratulations on getting a lead role," he added, proud of himself for handing out a complement under the circumstances.

"Who's this?" Jake nudged Casey.

"We used to work together. He was the handyman at my mom's real estate business, but he got fired." Casey smirked.

Ruari tightened his jaw. "Actually I left because I couldn't stand to watch you get killed on the job." Erin would've been proud of him for standing up for himself.

Casey's self satisfied expression vanished, and his pale face flushed. "Well, you suck as a teacher. I didn't learn a thing." His words were accompanied by a roil of black smoke that quickly dissipated.

Little liar. Ruari felt the slow burn of anger but shook his head. He lobbed a parting shot. "Don't grab any live wires, idiot." He felt like he had a target on his back as he walked all the way to the men's room at the end of the hall. Part of him wished Casey would take a swing. The smarter half said, *that would be the end of this gig which would be a shame after all the work I did to get a contract.*

He finished his business and splashed cold water on his face until he'd calmed down. *I'm here to build sets. I don't have to spend any more time with him. Just do my job and be done.*

Sitting in the auditorium now, watching Casey aim his petty little smirk at someone else, Ruari was able to steer clear of his own anger. He'd heard from Tristan and some of the others that there was a rivalry between Casey and Randall, possibly of a romantic nature over Tayloe. It wouldn't surprise Ruari in the least, though he had thought Casey was fond of the girl at the pizza parlor. Either way, it wasn't his problem.

Now, during rehearsal, Ruari was curious. He opened his auric vision and scanned the stage. With the full stage lights on the two men, it was an ideal place to see auras. He unfocused his eyes and stared a little past each of them. Casey, as usual, had a dull green aura that Ruari associated with his former assistant's peevish, petty nature. Randall's aura had a flash of blue which Ruari had come to think of as being loyal and self-confident. A metallic edge to it meant predatory, but Randall's had a cleaner hue. The other actors in the scene had the usual mix of hues, nothing strange there. He blinked and focused on individuals again.

Randall was in Ichabod Crane's dull black suit he'd worn for rehearsals last week, but the sleeves seemed to be tearing off at the shoulders.

The young man looked acutely embarrassed and replied, "I'm sorry, sir. I got here late, and it was like this when I put it on. I don't know what happened. It was fine when I put it away on Friday."

Casey sniggered with his buddy Jake.

"For the love of Dane," Tommy said in exasperation. "Brendan, can't you do anything to keep Ichabod together for the rehearsal?"

Brendan, in a Hawaiian print, short-sleeved shirt, was already out of his third row, aisle seat and mounting the steps to the stage two at a time. A dressmaker's tape was draped around his neck, and a kit of emergency supplies in a pouch was at his waist. He examined Randall's jacket, whipped out several safety pins and secured the seams in short order. He descended the stairs and took a seat in the first row.

"Thank you." Tommy rubbed his brow. "Okay, let's go back to the top of the scene and run it again."

Tristan walked out as the narrator again with his black cane and set the scene for the viewers. "It was, as I have said, a fine autumnal day," he proclaimed. "The sky was clear and serene, and nature wore that rich and golden livery which we always associate with the idea of abundance. It was toward evening that Ichabod arrived at the castle of the Heer Van Tassel, which he found thronged with the pride and flower of the adjacent country."

Tristan had also been extremely helpful while Ruari was building sets this weekend and had shown Ruari several useful tricks. Tristan said he'd spent a good deal of time in theater growing up and that he was a singer, though he did straight plays too. All in all, Ruari liked the man, but something was a little odd about Tristan. He wasn't exactly sure *what* it was, though. In the light of the stage, Ruari could see a double yellow and red aura around his body signaling a happy, passionate, creative person. At least his aura was clean.

Ruari continued to mull over what it was about Tristan that felt "off." The actor looked sharp in his tailored suit, but Ruari realized his figure was more rounded in the hips and backside than most men he had met. Suddenly, it dawned on him. Tristan was a trans man; his body had been masculinized, and his voice had deepened throughout his transition. Ruari had met several trans people in college and found them to be creative, interesting people; more thoughtful than those who didn't have the same life experiences. Now that he'd put two and two together, Ruari's confusion dissipated and he relaxed.

The rehearsal moved on, and Ruari grudgingly acknowledged

that Casey sounded confident and professional. Nearly everyone had asked for a line prompt except the three main actors.

They must take their responsibility as leads very seriously and spend a lot of time memorizing their lines. Maybe that was one of the reasons Casey had been so scatterbrained at work: he'd been thinking about his lines instead of paying attention to drywall and plumbing repairs. He wasn't perfect, though. Tommy had to correct his blocking several more times.

The play followed Washington Irving's storyline fairly closely, elaborating on particular moments for the sake of the audience. When the feast came, Ruari was jolted out of his thoughts as Tommy interrupted the rehearsal.

"And, everyone freeze. Katrina, you don't freeze. You're the only one aware of the ghostly figure coming toward you out of the fireplace. Maud Van Tassel," he called, "come on out. This is where your part starts."

An older woman stepped out of the fireplace. She wore a pale gown, her hair was white, and her face, neck, and arms were pale. Earlier in the day, Ruari had been tasked to cut a hole in the back of the fireplace and drape a black curtain over it to mask it. Binkler hadn't told him why at the time.

"Katrina!" Maud called.

Katrina turned around, looking confused then placed a hand on her chest and leaned back melodramatically. "Who are you?" She gasped.

"I am the spirit of your great-grandmother. I never left Sleepy Hollow even though I had a choice. I married a pig farmer and lived a tiresome life of farming, babies, and making food. I've been watching over you. You are beautiful and smart and have a good man offering to take you away from Sleepy Hollow. Don't throw the chance away to leave and have a better life than I did."

"Great-grandmother Maud! But everyone said you were happy here."

"I did the best I could. I was never happy, though. Ichabod

Crane is an educated, kind man who would show you the world, if you let him."

"But great-grandmother, Brom loves me too."

"Brom will never be more than a country farmer."

Katrina put her hands on her head as if she had a headache. "Great-grandmother, what shall I do?"

"Be brave, my child. You will choose the right thing when the time comes." And she backed up into the fireplace and disappeared through the curtain.

Katrina straightened up and looked around her. The rest of the cast was staring at her.

"Well, that's new," someone said.

Tommy said, "Remember I said that this play was allegorical. I added a scene to emphasize the choices Katrina has."

Maud came out from the wing nearest the fireplace and waited with her hands folded.

"Um, what are we supposed to do now?" A father of one of the school urchins who was playing a prosperous farmer spoke up. Ruari admired him. He tended to be the one to ask questions everyone else was thinking and didn't seem to mind if Tommy was a little brusque.

"All I want the ensemble to do is freeze in place when the music stops. This signals that we are in Katrina's head. When Maud disappears and Katrina looks up, you can start moving again as if no time has passed. Okay? Let's run the scene again. Maud, go back to where you were. That was good. Katrina, that looked good."

Tommy and Binkler ran the scene again two more times. Each time, people got a little better incorporating the new part. At the end of the night, Ruari had more notes on what he had to build, and he was thoroughly tired of watching everyone go through the same moves and lines over and over. He didn't think theater would ever become his new passion. He walked backstage to the shop doors to leave his notes on the desk by the machine shop. As he walked into the cavernous open space and strode between the stored flats of other shows, he felt a prickling sensation along his neck.

He scanned the area, alert for any signs of trouble.

Surely Casey wouldn't be so vengeful as to hang around in the set shop to give him a scare or to start a fight? Their whole conversation earlier had been stupid but not inflammatory. As he walked toward the saws and drill press, he thought he saw movement in the back corner. He didn't usually get spooked by big empty spaces, but he'd overheard some of the cast members talking about how creepy the old theater was, and he felt a momentary shiver.

"Hello?" He called.

No answer. Placing his notes on the desk, he then walked a quick lap around the shop. He ensured everything was turned off and secured, and the master switch was firmly in the off position. He checked the outer door: locked. Confident there was nothing amiss, he climbed the stairs to the hallway that led back to the front door. Maybe he could avoid Casey if he cut through the front and left through those doors instead of the stage door. The front doors locked themselves when they closed.

Marianne snuggled on the sofa under her blue green plush blanket while she waited for Ruari to come back. She'd begun the second book in a cozy mystery series, and she could totally relate to to the haunted house problems of the main character. The sound of scrabbling claws on the landing upstairs broke into her story, and she looked up in time to see Oscar streak down the stairs, his fur and tail bushed out to twice his size.

"Again? Oscar, what's the matter?" She put her book down and leaned over to peer under the sofa. Two green eyes glinted from the darkness in the back accompanied by a hiss of displeasure. She got up and called from the bottom of the stairs, "Hey, Erin?"

She had to call two more times before her guest answered. "What?"

"Did you and Oscar get into a fight? He just came down here like his tail was on fire."

"No, I'm playing a video game."

"Okay. Huh." It took a few minutes to coax the cat out from under the couch. "I don't know what's going on, but you're okay now, Mister." She brought him into her lap and snuggled the blanket around them both. After a moment he began purring and settled down to groom his fur into order.

She picked up her book and went back to San Francisco with the plucky home renovator.

Ruari arrived around ten-thirty. Marianne suppressed a yawn and greeted him with a hug and a kiss.

"How was the theater tonight?" She asked.

"Eventful."

"Uh oh, that doesn't sound good."

While they brushed teeth and got ready for bed, he told her about meeting Casey, the rehearsal, and the slightly spooky shop. They climbed into bed where Oscar lay, already settled for the night.

"Casey sounds like the perfect awful Brom Bones," she said.

"He certainly fits the role of an entitled bully rather well."

"Hopefully, you won't have to interact with him much."

"That's what I'm relying on."

She snuggled closer and lay her head on his shoulder. "You said you felt something in the shop on your way out. Do you want me to see if I feel anything?"

"Would you? I'd like to have your take on it."

Pleased to be asked, she said, "I'd be happy to."

"Oh, hey, I wondered if you would also be able to do some research on Dutch Colonial styles for the play?"

"Sure. You can be my first living client to use both the history and the supernatural side of my business! Erin offered to make a website for me today to tell prospective clients what I offer."

"What are you thinking about?"

"There would be two services: researching history, doing genealogies, et cetera, and the other would be investigating paranormal events in people's houses or businesses."

"How would that work?"

"I guess I'd go to their houses and get a feel for the place."

"The idea of you going alone to look for ghosts makes me worry."

She looked at his profile in the dim light coming through the window. "I was sort of hoping you would come with me on house calls."

He squeezed her. "I would absolutely come with you."

"That would be great. I wasn't sure how you'd feel about it. If I can't find a ghostly explanation, then maybe there's a practical, physical explanation which you might pick up on."

"When are you planning to start this venture?"

"Not for a while yet. I have to iron out the details."

"The play won't be done till the second week of December, and then there's the holiday season. Would you consider holding off till January?"

She nodded. "If you aren't available for a house call, I thought maybe Erin could be my back up. She seems more comfortable around ghosts these days."

He snorted. "Yeah, she changed her mind pretty thoroughly."

"By the way, something scared Oscar tonight. He came racing downstairs like a demon was after him."

"Did you figure out what it was?"

"Nope. Erin swore it wasn't her. This isn't the first time."

"He doesn't seem like a high strung cat, easily spooked."

"He hasn't been before. Except when Anne and George were haunting the house. But they're definitely gone, and I refreshed the wards earlier, so nothing bad should be able to get in."

"Erin keeps talking about losing her pepperoni. And there was the infamous bacon incident."

Marianne giggled. "I know. She and Oscar have a rivalry

thing. He's probably been mooching off her pizza. I only just got her to clean out all the food things from her room."

"If it's not Oscar, maybe it's a pepperoni eating demon?" He teased.

"I doubt it. The wards are supposed to keep anything like that out of the house."

He yawned. "Tomorrow's problem."

"That's right." For once, she fell asleep without tossing and turning first.

Marianne dreamed she and Oscar were at the Co-op together drinking at one of the little wire tables on the patio. It was sunny and warm, and they enjoyed the shade of the big umbrella. Marianne had an Arnold Palmer with a sprig of mint, and Oscar was lapping at his favorite hazelnut latte.

"What's with you and eating off the counter lately?" She asked.

He sat up and licked the foam off his whiskers. "I can't help it. I eat when I'm stressed. You know I can't resist vanilla ice cream and chicken." His voice was an orange and white purr.

"I'm sorry for not checking with you before inviting Erin to live with us," Marianne said. "I just couldn't say no after she'd risked her life on Halloween like that."

He snorted. "Would you have said no if you'd known what a gargoyle she is?"

"Well, *you* weren't there!"

He licked one paw with dignity. "Someone had to hold the fort while you were off gallivanting through the cemetery."

"She's not a gargoyle. She's just a bit of a handful."

"Oh fine, I take it back. She's not a gargoyle. She's a hellion, a hag, a red-headed troglodyte."

Marianne grinned. "So, you *do* put litter in her shoes!"

"Well, yes. To be fair she has a lot of interesting smells on her shoes, and the litter gets stuck in my paws. Besides, the one time she vacuumed her room, she dropped me in the middle of a circle of hose and cackled when I bounced straight up."

Marianne snorted into her tea.

"It's not funny! You try keeping your cool surrounded by the coils of your ancestral fear of snakes." He glared at her. "And then there was the time she laid a lovely, soft-looking blanket over her bed, and it turned out she'd put slippery things underneath, so I fell off when I tried to jump up on it."

She put her hand over her mouth to suppress her giggles.

Oscar sniffed and licked his paw to clean latte foam off his whiskers. "She's a treacherous hag, not to be trusted."

"I'm sorry, Mister." Marianne got her amusement under control.

Oscar pointedly ignored her, licking his tail with long strokes.

"So, you put litter in her shoes and eat the pepperoni off her pizza when she isn't looking. Sounds like fair payback to me."

Oscar stopped, tail in mid air, and looked at her with an intent gaze. "That's not me. I don't like pepperoni. Too spicy. Burns my tongue. That's the other one."

Marianne swallowed her mouthful of lemony tea. "Other one?"

Oscar was back to grooming his tail with long licks. "Scares me every time."

By Tuesday at noon, she'd gotten her wording for the Turner's Hope Mine plaque settled and written a cover letter. After fiddling with her word choices a little, she bit the bullet and sent it by email to the appropriate Canopus Parks department along with a copy of her CV in case they needed proof of her skills as a researcher. She felt like she'd just submitted a term paper to a critical prof.

"What's the worst they can do, say no?" She asked Oscar where he lay on the papers on her desk. His eyes were shut, and his crooked tipped tail tapped gently. She stroked his fur.

"Actually, that would be the worst thing. Then Peter O'Meara and his men would be furious, and I'd have to worry about them haunting me for the rest of my life."

"Meo-ahh," Oscar said, turning his comment into a yawn.

"You're not impressed. Fine, I'll try to not to stress about it."

Time for a break. She dug out the recipe for pumpkin bread and spent a happy hour or so making two delicious loaves. She left one on the counter under a tea towel to cool and wrapped up the other one in another tea towel to take with her to Grandma Selene's house.

She backed The Flea out of the driveway onto the cul-de-sac.

The faint hum of the charm bags pinned to the visors, the glove box, and the back seat made a pleasant background noise that faded quickly as she steered the car toward town. Once she'd learned to sense magic, it was possible to tune into it and, more importantly tune it out. But she'd protected The Flea magically as soon as she had the energy to do it after Halloween. She'd also put charm bags into Ruari's old truck. While not exactly excited about it, Ruari had at least not taken them out. The magical aspects of the battle in the cemetery had taken on an unreal, dreamlike feeling in the days afterwards. Sometimes she wondered if it had really happened.

The drive to Vandenberg was pleasant as The Flea wound along the road through the hills. The Hudson River flashed in the distance through the thinning tree cover. It was a chill, grey day and definitely felt like winter was coming.

Vandenberg was in the Hudson Highlands along with Maple Hill, and Grandma Selene had lived there for fifty years. Grandpa Claire had passed away more than ten years ago. Marianne hoped he'd been reunited with his son, Marianne's dad, who had died of pneumonia when she was five. She missed her dad. Her mother had raised her alone and now lived an hour north of Maple Hill. Since acquiring the ability to see and hear ghosts, Marianne had secretly hoped she'd catch a glimpse of her dad. But she hadn't yet. He must not have had any unfinished business, and she supposed that was a good thing. That didn't keep her from wishing, though.

Feeling melancholy, she pulled into Grandma's long, narrow driveway. It took her back through the trees to the huge old Victorian farmhouse with gingerbread trim along the eaves and a big wrap-around porch. She parked The Flea next to the garage. Today, the garage was closed, keeping the big old Lincoln Town Car safe from the weather. Grandpa Claire's pride and joy and now Grandma's. She kept it spotless and rumor had it, she'd made grown men weep with joy at seeing it. She'd refused offers to buy it and turned down one proposal of marriage.

The porch steps creaked as she climbed up and knocked on the door. It was a few moments before Grandma Selene unlocked and opened the door.

"Come in, come in out of the cold!"

Marianne entered and hugged her beloved grandmother. Her iron gray hair was in a tidy bun, and she wore a coordinated pair of wool trousers and soft sweater with a turtleneck under it. A gold brooch in the shape of a spray of maple leaves was pinned on the left side.

"I'm so glad you came today!" Grandma said. "I've been feeling a little blue, and this is just the thing to perk me up."

Marianne thought Grandma's voice was like a cup of Earl Grey tea, smooth and creamy. She took off her jacket and hung it on the coat tree in the front hall. "I was thinking about Dad on my way up."

Grandma Selene put one arm around Marianne's shoulders and squeezed gently. "He'd be so proud of you."

"Thanks."

Then she put her cane into operation and headed for the kitchen.

Marianne followed her as she moved slowly through the formal dining room to the kitchen at the back.

"I see you're using your cane today. Are you doing okay?" Marianne asked anxiously. She was used to her grandmother being strong and steady, and Marianne hadn't seen her use her cane since the one time she fell a few years back.

"The cold makes my bones hurt," Grandma confessed.

"Winter isn't my favorite season either. I'm already looking forward to Spring."

"Me too. Maybe I'll take a trip to Santa Fe this winter and soak up some sunshine."

The dining room always looked picture perfect, with a seasonal centerpiece. Today's decoration was an assortment of pinecones and large, fall colored leaves on a creamy white runner. Portraits of stuffy looking ancestors lined the walls. It looked like a perfect showcase room. The kitchen was much cozier with a wood stove going in the corner. The small wooden table was set for two.

"Just put the bread on a plate, and I'll get the water started," Grandma said.

They moved with practiced ease around each other, getting cups and saucers, matching sugar bowl and creamer with silver tongs and spoons. It was a dance they'd done since Marianne was four.

The tea kettle whistled, and Marianne put water in the pot with a generous helping of tea leaves. "This smells delicious. What kind is this?" She asked.

"I discovered a tea called cream Earl Grey. It's wonderful. I think you'll like it."

They sat at the table, and Marianne cut slices from the pumpkin loaf. It still held enough warmth to melt the butter, and they enjoyed their repast in appreciative silence. The new tea was indeed delicious, and Marianne vowed to get some for herself on the way home.

"How are you, my dear?" Grandma Selene asked after finishing the first slice of bread.

"I finally feel like I'm back to normal after the craziness around Halloween. Whatever normal is. I still don't have an income, but I've been working on projects for people I met when Sarah and I were driving around."

Marianne caught her up briefly about her research for Peter O'Meara and his men. Grandma Selene nodded and cut each of them another slice.

"I've been preparing to start my own business for history research and offering help to people who think they have ghost problems. But I haven't had the nerve to take the plunge yet."

"Maybe part of you isn't ready. It's a lot to offer to go into someone else's home, listen to their problems, and try to help them. You'll know when you're ready."

"Ruari said he would come with me on house calls."

"That's a very wise idea, though Erin seems to be coming along both in her comfort with spirits and as a boon companion."

Marianne gave a rueful laugh. "Still waiting on the boon companion part."

"How is Ruari's theater experience going?"

"He's spending a lot of time there, building sets and being a general handyman."

"Your landlady, Lily, and her husband Selwyn spent a huge amount of time at the Avery when they were active in community theater. Local productions will consume all the time you want to give them and then some."

"That reminds me, I wanted to ask you something. Last night, Ruari mentioned he got the willies being in the scene shop after everyone had gone home. Is the theater haunted?"

Grandma raised her eyebrows in mild surprise. "Of course it is."

Her candor surprised Marianne.

"I'm pretty sure every theater is haunted in one way or another," she continued. "All that creative energy and those melodramatic personalities. As for the Avery, there have always been rumors about ghosts."

"Why don't I know this? Tell me more!"

"I'm sure Lily will have more details, but there's a story about a little boy who plays pranks on people. He's not harmful, just mischievous. There's another one that says a ghost will warn people before a tragedy strikes."

"That's cool! I like the warning ghost better than the prankster. I've never been good with practical jokes."

"The outcome of being an only child of a somber mother."

"Probably. Geoffrey's idea of a joke was always at my expense."

"He was a maggot," her grandmother sniffed.

Marianne snickered. Grandma's Britishisms always made her smile, especially when they were so blunt.

Grandma continued blandly, "I had several cousins when I

was growing up who were quite clever with their jokes. They were always meant for a laugh, not to humiliate."

They talked for a while longer.

Marianne drained her second cup of tea. "Well, I should be getting home before it gets dark. I find myself a little nervous driving after dark now. Let me help you clean up."

Together they tidied up, and Marianne gave her grandmother a big hug before she put her jacket back on. "I love you, Grandma. Thank you for the tea and company. I really needed it."

"I needed it just as much. Take care of yourself, lovey. Drive safely."

"I will." Marianne got into The Flea and carefully backed up and turned around. Grandma Selene stood in the doorway with the porch light on and waved as she left.

Grandma lived alone in that huge old house. She'd never talked about being lonely or frightened. *She's got friends and committees. I wonder if she and John Irving would get along? Oh stop matchmaking,* she told herself sternly. Nevertheless, she resolved to call her grandmother when she got home and ask her.

"Mahri, thanks for coming with me this evening," Ruari said as he and Marianne walked up to the side entrance of the shop that evening. He'd been given keys earlier that day and was eager to show her what he'd been working on. As a carpenter and wood carver he was accustomed to working in isolation for days or weeks at a time, but it got lonely. One of the few things he liked about the theater job was that his work was in the open with regular feedback.

"Are you sure it's okay for me to be here?" She asked.

"I think so. I'll tell them you're helping me conceptualize the sets, which you are, and you just wanted to see the stage to get more ideas."

"I'll need someplace quiet to get a feel for the space. It's hard to sense ghosts if they don't want you to see them or if the area is too noisy."

He pulled the door open and ushered her inside.

"Wow, this is a huge space," she said.

"Pretty neat, huh? Scotty told me they sometimes build huge props. And, of course, there's lots of storage of old stuff. I looked through some of the old flats. Lots of fragments of old plays. It's pretty cool."

She smiled. "I'm glad you're enjoying yourself. I was a little worried you'd get depressed because you didn't have something to do all the time."

"I would never be depressed about leaving Gloria's, trust me. But I was spinning my wheels a little. I don't think I'll suddenly take up theater, but this is a good transition to something else." He waved her toward another door. "I'll show you the stage and the scary hallway."

She followed him out of the scene shop into a dark-curtained space. Voices up ahead told them others were busy at work. They emerged onto a brightly lit stage where a couple of people were conferring over a long wooden table. They looked up when Ruari and Marianne approached.

"Roar," Scotty said, "we were just talking about the feast set. We could totally use your input."

"Sure thing. I wanted to introduce you to Marianne. She did a little historical research for me into Dutch Colonial styles. Mahri, this is my friend, Scotty."

Scotty stuck out his hand and Marianne shook it. "Nice to meet you," he said.

"You as well. Do you also work at the Co-op?"

"I do their IT."

"Do you do the announcements sometimes?"

"Aye, I do," he said with his best Star Trek engineer's voice.

Ruari rolled his eyes. "That's a terrible accent."

"Only you would know." He winked at Marianne and she chuckled.

A throat cleared. "I'm Dave Binkler, the stage manager." He shook Marianne's hand. "Do you have set design experience?"

"No, I'm a historian. I specialize in the Victorian era, but research is research no matter what era it's in."

"Well, Teddy Miller left us with some good sketches," Binkler continued, "but they need more details."

"I brought some printouts. Maybe they could be useful." She pulled a handful of pages from her backpack and handed them to the stage manager.

He took them, his white, soft serve swirl of hair nodding along gently, as he reviewed the images. "I like these. Heavy wooden beams overhead, large china cabinet, big walk-in fireplace for cooking. Uh-huh, uh-huh." He looked at Scotty and Ruari. "We could use elements of these in the projected set. Ruari, do you think you could find or build a simple dish cabinet like this? It doesn't have to be a real piece of furniture, it just needs to look the part. And be light enough for people to move it on and off stage quickly."

Ruari thought about it and nodded. "I could come up with something."

"Good. Also this trestle table needs to be longer. Again, light enough to move quickly but big enough to take all the prop foods we have for the feast scene."

Ruari nodded again.

Marianne made a restless movement next to him, and Ruari came out of the sketches and plans. "I'm sorry, Mahri. Did you want to look around on your own?"

Binkler stepped in. "The stage area isn't very safe if you're not familiar with stages, but you can sit in the audience if you like."

"I'll stay off the stage. Is there a bathroom I could use?"

"Certainly. There's one in the lobby. It's out that way." He pointed toward to top of the auditorium.

"I can find it. Thanks. See you at home, Ruari?"

He nodded. "See you at dinner."

Marianne made her way to the back row. She hadn't been inside the Avery since she was a kid. Her grandparents and mom had brought her to see a kid's production of *Pinocchio* when she was about seven. Her memories lined up pretty well with what she saw now, except the upholstery on the chairs looked more worn and the carpet a bit more threadbare. It was the perfect atmosphere for haunting. She patted her jeans, feeling the lump of her charm bag. The salt and sunlight had recharged it fully. It hummed softly in her pocket. She wanted to be ready just in case she ran into any Shadow People.

She took a deep breath and let it out, trying to center and settle herself. She tried to ignore the conversation on stage and listen to the quiet of the auditorium. Closing her eyes, she slowly turned her head from one side to the other, scanning with her other senses. Nothing. The voices on stage were very distracting.

She moved out into the front lobby and walked slowly through, enjoying the old posters. The concession stand was closed and tidy, waiting for the next show. The aroma of popcorn and butter smelled like movies.

"Excuse me, miss, can I help you?"

An older man with bushy graying hair and a heavy face leaned out of an office.

"Hi, I'm Marianne, a friend of Ruari's. I did some research for him about Dutch Colonial styles to help with the sets. I hope you don't mind that I tagged along with him today. He showed me the stage and the scene shop."

He smiled and stuck out his hand. "Tommy Verplank, owner and artistic director of the Avery Theater. Call me Tommy. Ruari has been doing a great job. I hope you're coming to the show? We open in a few weeks."

"I'm planning on it. Can I buy tickets now?" She hadn't put much thought into it, but there was no time like the present.

"Absolutely. I'm between phone calls, and I could sell you a couple."

She followed him into his office. While he pulled out a receipt book and a pack of tickets, she looked around the cluttered office. Framed newspaper clippings as well as old posters crowded the walls. Her eye was drawn to a group of black and white photos. One showed an old theater. Another showed a man and woman with five children around them. They were smiling, and the man had his hand on the shoulder of one of the boys. The other photos showed a younger Tommy Verplank shaking hands with a couple of men who looked vaguely familiar. A scrawled signature slanted across the bottom of each picture.

"The tickets are twenty dollars each," Tommy said. "How many do you want?"

"I'll take two," she said, and he wrote out a receipt and handed her two cardstock rectangles. "I'll see if my friends and family will come to opening night."

He put the book into his top desk drawer. "That's great."

A thought struck her. "I could write a little piece for the Playbill. Maybe a short history of the Avery? Would you like that?"

"That would be a fine idea! It would add a little bit of sparkle and give people something to read."

He gave her a word count and a deadline. That would give her a solid reason for wandering through the building if she needed one.

"Would it be okay for me to walk around a little? I'll stay out of the way. Maybe I could see the costume shop? I saw pictures of the period clothing, and I would love to see the costumes for the show."

"Sure." He led her to a door on the far side of the lobby. "Just follow this hallway all the way to the end and make a left. The costume shop is on the right a couple of doors down. Brendan is our costume designer. He might or might not be in."

"Thank you, Tommy."

A phone began ringing.

"You're welcome." He hastened back to the office and shut the door behind him.

Marianne opened the door and stepped into the hallway beyond. When the door shut, a hush descended. She stood in a long hallway with a very high ceiling. Green paint reached up the first eight feet and an oatmeal white finished the trip up to the ceiling. Pipes for heating and cooling, and an outdated sprinkler system ran below the ceiling. Old fashioned, six-panel, wooden doors made dark patches in the green all the way to the end. Curious, she tested the nearest door handle. It opened into a closet with mops and buckets and cleaning products.

She moved down the hall to a set of stairs that descended three steps before continuing. She must be parallel to the sloped seating. Sitting on the top step, she closed her eyes again, listening with all her senses. There was a faint sound of music from a radio up ahead but not much else. After a few minutes of stillness, she opened her eyes and continued down the hall.

A couple of other wooden doors were locked. Finally, she got to one that said "Green Room" and peeked inside. The shabby sitting room had mismatched chairs, a long mirror with enough lights to illuminate a surgical suite, and shelves with an odd assortment of objects that looked like everything from dishes and pretend food, to a stick with a bundle, woven baskets with handles, and other items she couldn't distinguish. She was about to continue down the hall when something brushed her senses. She closed her eyes and looked around the room, hoping to catch sight of whatever it was.

She didn't see anything, but she heard a soft giggle from the other side of the room.

"Hello?" There was no answer, but she felt a faint sense of amusement. "All right, you don't want to show yourself. Are you the prankster?" There was a light quick step and a cold, featherlight touch as someone brushed past her into the hallway.

She withdrew and continued down the hall. Another set of bathrooms were at the corner where the hall turned left and went down the back of the building. The sound of the music grew louder, and she passed doors marked "Women's Dressing Room" and "Men's Dressing Room" before coming to an open door. The music emanated from there, a classical station, playing something sweeping and romantic.

She knocked on the door frame and heard a voice say, "I'm in the back." The rows of neatly organized clothing reminded her of Renata's Closet. A narrow corridor led to a lighted workspace.

A man in a bright Hawaiian print shirt looked up, a dressmaker's tape around his neck. "Can I help you?"

"Hi, are you Brendan? I'm Marianne, a friend of Ruari's."

Brendan smiled and leaned over the table offering his hand. "Nice to meet you, Marianne. What brings you to my domain?"

"I did some research on Dutch Colonial architecture for the sets and came across pictures of what people wore in those days. I wondered if I could see some of the costumes for the play?"

"Sure. I've finished most of the basic ones, and they're hanging in the dressing rooms already. But here's Katrina's dress for the last act at the feast, and Mr. Van Tassel's suit is over there." He pointed to two mannikins.

The first one was for a slender figure, taller than Marianne, with modest hips and bust. The fitted light blue bodice and floor length skirt had a brown floral design. A darker blue, plain underskirt peeked through the gap below the corsetry.

"It's beautiful!" She imagined herself wearing such a confection and smiled. She wouldn't want to be confined to a corset all day, but a lace up bodice that defined her waist and bust would be fun to wear on a special occasion. She touched the sleeve and sighed. "Look at all the lace!"

Brendan beamed. "Our Katrina will be the belle of the ball for sure."

"I'm sure she'll feel like a princess in it."

The second mannikin had been expanded for a portly figure and wore a cream colored waistcoat and breeches with a dark green open jacket accented with shiny brass buttons and big cuffs. A pair of knee high black leather boots stood nearby to complete the outfit. "Very handsome. That's not for Brom is it?"

"That's for Mr. Van Tassel at his big party."

Brendan ushered her to the other side of the costume shop.

"Here is a sneak preview at the *pièce de résistance.*" He gave a flourish with one hand at a black cape draped over a third mannikin. A large grinning jack-o-lantern rested on the neck of the figure. It had a sinister expression with one large and one small triangle eye and a cruel, toothy grin.

"It looks like Jack Skellington's mean older brother. I would absolutely run away if that was chasing me!"

Brendan took a small bow, looking pleased.

"I just bought tickets for opening night," Marianne said. "I can't wait to see the play! Thank you for showing me. I shouldn't take any more of your time."

Brendan looked at his watch. "Rehearsal begins in about forty minutes, and I have some things to finish."

Marianne headed for the hall and nearly collided with a man who was on his way into the costume shop.

"Oh, excuse me," she said.

"Pardon me," he said at the same time.

They both stood back. He was a little taller than she was, though not so tall or broad as Ruari. He sported a smallish beard and mustache on his rounded, boyish face, and his eyes were amused as they dodged each other in the doorway.

"You're a new face," he said. "Are you here to help our esteemed costumer?"

"No, I'm just helping a little with the sets."

"One of Ruari's friends, then."

"That's right. I'm Marianne."

"Ah, Ruari told me all about you." His eyes twinkled. "It's nice to meet you. I'm Tristan Kitteby. The Narrator and a couple of miscellaneous background characters." He stuck out his hand with a big smile.

Marianne's smile froze as she shook his hand automatically,

covering for her sudden cold rush of dread. Tristan Kitteby. *There can't be many people named that.* TK. The initials on the evil charm bags she and Sarah had found during their cross county trek. The supposed magical protector of Dutchess County.

"Nice to meet you too," she babbled. "I'm sorry. I have to get going. 'Bye."

He gave her a puzzled, slightly hurt look as she walked away.

She followed the hallway to the end and walked into the scene shop, grateful to be back where she'd started. Ruari was nowhere to be seen, so she let herself out and headed home on foot, thinking furiously.

Tristan Kitteby is in the play? Why is he here? She thought he lived in Dutchess County. *Don't be silly, he can go where he likes. Maybe he just likes theater.* Didn't Ruari say one of the people who'd helped him was a theater person? There's no reason to think he's here on magical business. Besides, Byron had all but told them he'd faked the involvement of the other Protectors to hide his own evil actions. So, Tristan Kitteby probably wasn't involved in the events leading up to Halloween at all. But Sarah had had a very low opinion of him and the other Protectors for a long time. *We don't talk to each other,* she'd said. She must have had a reason.

Her shock wore off and turned into embarrassment. Meeting him like that had given her quite a turn. She must've seemed very rude to him. She was going to have to apologize when next they met. In the meantime, maybe she could find out more about him and figure out who Tristan Kitteby really was and why he was here.

CHAPTER 10

$\mathcal{R}$uari sat in the fourth row from the front in the semi darkness of the auditorium while Tommy and Binkler ran the rehearsal. He'd had a scare earlier in the evening when the two benches for the schoolhouse collapsed under the weight of the kids sitting on them. No one was hurt, but he'd scrambled to screw them back together and get them back on stage. He still couldn't figure out why they'd suddenly fallen apart when they'd been fine the last time they'd been used.

The sets for this scene looked good from here. Marianne's research into Old Dutch Colonial styles had given him plenty of ideas, and he was sketching additions onto a couple of sheets of paper while the actors ran their lines. Tommy had added a scene where Ichabod takes a shortcut through a cemetery to get home, and Marianne had found some very cool looking tombstones with rounded tops. They had angel-winged figures with death's heads and blocky writing featuring old fashioned spelling like, "Heere Leys Cornelius Van Wyck" with birth and death dates. Scotty and Binkler had enthusiastically embraced them, promising to look for images to project onto a scrim and add to the spookiness of the background.

Lost in his thoughts about adding this detail or that, Ruari more or less ignored the goings on up on stage until shrieks pulled him out of his reverie.

The ladies in the cast had pulled into a group and were staring at Ichabod and Brom. The two men were glaring at each other. Randall looked furious enough to take a swing at Casey.

"That's it! I'm sick of your stupid pranks!" Randall said angrily. "This is the last straw." He held out two little fluffy things accusingly at Casey. From Ruari's vantage, he thought they looked like ear muffs.

Katrina's look of shock turned into giggles.

Ruari blurred his gaze and used the stage lights to focus on each of the leads in turn. Randall's aura had been a pretty consistent blue since Ruari had first seen it. Tonight, it was dull and murky to the point of being almost brownish. That was weird. Ruari associated dull, muddy colors with negative emotions and illness.

His former assistant always had a dull green aura of pettiness, but tonight it was a roiling dark green. Thank goodness it wasn't a black void. His one experience with a person possessed by Shadow People had not been good. At least Casey's aura didn't look like that. He shifted to Tayloe in her Katrina costume. She'd had a bright turquoise aura on previous nights. Tonight, her aura was also a roiling dark green of something ugly. What was going on?

"I didn't put them there!" Casey protested, but his innocence was undermined by his maliciously delighted expression.

"I know you were here before me tonight," Randall snarled, "and they weren't there yesterday."

Ruari snapped his focus back to the stage. For a moment he wondered if he'd have to break up a fight. Where was Tommy? Hell of a time to step out to the bathroom.

"Hey, hey, hey!" Binkler was up on stage, clutching his binder and script to his chest. "That's enough of that." Ruari gave him credit. Even though he was a head shorter than the two actors, the officious little man interposed himself between them. "Randall you can throw those in the trash. There's a can in the green room. And wash your hands."

Randall hesitated, looking like he wanted to push the stage manager aside to get at Casey. Instead, he stalked off stage, fury in every step.

Binkler turned to Casey. "These pranks have to stop."

"I didn't do it!" His amused bluster turned to anger.

"I didn't say you did. I want you to do your part to take care of your fellow actors. Remember, we're a team and everyone needs to work together." He turned to the rest of the cast. "That goes for everyone. These pranks might be funny to someone, but they're disruptive and slow down our precious rehearsal time. Okay, everyone, let's go back to the top of the scene."

Tommy chose that moment to return and sat down again. The folding seat's springs creaked in protest. The cast watched in nervous silence while Binkler walked down the steps, made his way through the row, and leaned over to whisper in the director's ear.

Everyone held their breath wondering if there would be an outburst. Instead Tommy nodded and said pragmatically, "Let's go again from the top of the scene. Is everyone in their places?"

Belatedly, everyone reset from the beginning.

The new cemetery scene started with the lights filtered through a mish-mash of bare branches, casting a spiderweb of shadows on the floor. Ruari had gathered a bunch of dead branches from the city compost pile at the dump (he knew a guy) and put them in front of the lights. He'd have to rig something else later, but this was a good test run. Abruptly, every light in the house went out.

There were some startled cries and suppressed curses from the stage.

"It's okay everybody, stay where you are," came Tommy's weary but calm voice. "We'll get that fixed in a couple of minutes. Just freeze in place. Don't let the children wander and get hurt. Scotty?" He shouted the last word.

"I'm on it," came Scotty's voice from the vicinity of the light booth. Ruari laid his sketch pad on the floor under the seat next to him, drew out his phone, and put the flashlight on.

"I'll help," he volunteered. "I know my way around electrical panels."

Tommy had both hands pressed to his temples. He waved one of them without looking and said, "Go."

Ruari scooted between the seats and hurried up the aisle where Scotty waited for him with a flashlight. Together, they left the auditorium and headed for the side hall.

The hall was still bathed in light. Scotty switched off the huge metal flashlight and made his way up the hall to a door that Ruari guessed was behind the light booth.

"What's going on?" Ruari asked.

"A fuse blew."

Ruari didn't like the sound of that. "A fuse, not a breaker? That's pretty ancient for a building like this."

"No kidding. Here we are." Scotty opened a closet door like all the others. Inside, was a small room with a huge metal box. Horizontal rows of metal tubes came off a central line with fat red and black wires. Each cable split off into one of the fuses.

"Holy shit," Ruari breathed. The sheer amount of power demanded by the modern lights, HVAC, and scene shop tools alone easily outweighed the power provided by this dangerously outdated system.

Scotty gave him a grim look. "Tommy swears this is the first thing to be refurbed when he gets the money." He looked down the line of metal tubes. Each line was labeled with a number painted in white, and a handwritten list on the inside of the door to the box indicated what area of the theater each line served.

Scotty peered at the lines until he came to one that was blackened on each end. The center was a twisted lump of glass and metal. "There you are. Hold this for me." He handed Ruari his flashlight and reached for the top of the box. He retrieved what looked like a pair of pliers with a bright orange insulated coating and reached toward the blown fuse.

Ruari caught his arm. "Hey, don't you have to turn the line off first?"

Scotty gave him a pained look. "I did the first two times this happened, but it's not necessary if you don't mind working hot. These are fiber glass and don't give you even a little zing." He tipped his head toward a box on the floor. "Grab me a new one, would you?"

A box on the floor had two BUSS cylinders left. He handed one to Scotty and stood off to the side. In electrician class, one old timer had told them that these old-style fuses occasionally exploded.

Fascinated and horrified, Ruari watched Scotty grasp the hot end and give an authoritative jerk. The old cylinder pulled free, and he handed it to Ruari. Then he fitted a new one into place. "And, voila. Bright lights again."

Ruari let out a little breath. "Crap, man. You're either really daring, or really crazy." He was going to say dumb, but Scotty was a friend.

Scotty gave him a lopsided grin. "Just crazy, Roar, just crazy." He ran his hand over the other fuses without touching them, feeling for excessive heat. Satisfied, he closed the metal door with a firm snap. "Well, now you know how to do it, if I'm not here."

Ruari looked at the twisted fuse in his hand. "Tommy knows about this?"

"Yeah. Like I said, he swears this is first on his list to replace. All the 'big money' from this show."

"Why do I think he's said that before?"

"This is the third show I've done for him."

Ruari shook his head. If he'd been an electrical inspector, he'd have shut the whole place down for safety reasons.

They closed and locked the hall door and headed back to the auditorium. Scotty said, "If it's any consolation, they used to have huge arc lights to light the stage. Those things set fires all the time. You should see the list of old timey theaters that burned down because of those things. This is safer than that, at least."

Ruari returned to his seat and watched the rest of the rehearsal. At least the angry mood on stage had been dispelled by the power outage. Tommy got the cast back on track, and they were able to finish out the scene and go through the next couple. Tommy seemed pleased with the outcome, oblivious to the interpersonal dynamics of the three leads, and unconcerned with the condition of the fuse box. The auras of the three principals cleared up and returned to their former states.

After rehearsal, Ruari approached Binkler and showed him the blown fuse.

"I don't know if you're aware of the electrical situation," Ruari began.

Binkler's white pompadour waved gently as he nodded. "This has happened before. It's perfectly normal."

Ruari was shocked by the dismissive attitude. "But it's not normal or safe. They blow because there's too much power going through them. You're lucky there hasn't been a fire before now."

The stage manager hugged his binder to his chest with both arms and looked at Ruari confidently. "Tommy assures me the theater has stood for a hundred years like this and will stand for another hundred. Just get us through this show. We have only two weeks to go before we open. It'll be fine."

A cloud of ephemeral smoke from Binkler's words filled the air around his head for a few seconds before dissipating. Wow. The man was very worried and refused to admit it.

Unwilling to press the issue, Ruari slipped the distorted tube into his pocket. "Okay, if you say so."

With visible relief, Binkler turned and walked away.

Thoughtfully, Ruari secured the shop and turned the lights out before heading back to Marianne's place. Maybe she would have some insight from her visit earlier.

❧

When Ruari got to Marianne's house, she was drowsy, and he was reluctant to wake her. So he climbed into bed and kissed her good night, letting his thoughts slip away.

The next morning, as he was putting on his jacket he felt something heavy in the pocket. He removed the burned out BUSS fuse.

"Mahri, were you at the theater when the lights went out?"

"No, when did that happen?"

"During rehearsal." He showed her the burned and twisted tube. "We were in the middle of rehearsal, and the lights just quit. Scotty and I changed this out."

She looked it over. "That looks really bad. Is that normal?"

"Well, the good news is that the fuse did its job of cutting the power off before the wires overheated. The bad news is that this isn't the first time, and the electrical panel is really out of date for the power draw."

"What does that mean?" She looked faintly alarmed.

"At the very least, the lights are likely to keep going out. At the worst, there's a risk of fire."

"Do Tommy and Mr. Binkler know?"

Ruari ran a hand through his hair. "Yeah. Scotty says Tommy has been promising to upgrade the box for quite a while. Binkler said he wasn't worried, but he was lying through his teeth."

"Is there anything you can do?"

He shook his head. "I'm a journeyman electrician, not a master, and an upgrade of the box would require a very expensive rewiring process and a lot of down time with no lights and no HVAC."

"So, the owner is just crossing his fingers that he makes it through each production?"

"Pretty much."

"Yikes. Well, I'll cross my fingers, too, if that's any help. When you're done with this project, maybe you shouldn't do any more until the box gets replaced."

"Until then, I'll stay alert."

She hugged him. "Please be careful."

"Absolutely. I have to head back to the theater again. There's still a ton left to do, and Tommy is breathing down my neck to finish." He kissed her and headed out the door. Only after he'd left did he realize he hadn't heard about what she thought of the theater's spookiness, and he hadn't told her about the altercation during rehearsal.

Tayloe glanced up and down the street surreptitiously in the early morning light. No one from her family was around, not that she expected them to be at this hour. A man was sitting in a blue Honda Civic a couple of doors down. She squinted and then wondered what Tristan was doing here so early. Maybe waiting for another business to open? She smiled and waved. He made a small wave back as if he hadn't expected her to see him.

The door to Hair Magic was unlocked, and she slipped inside and locked it behind her, leaving the Closed sign in place.

"Hey, hon, it's good to see you."

Aunt Kelly enveloped her in a strong embrace. Tayloe relaxed for the first time in days. She'd figured out by the time she was ten that Aunt Kelly and Aunt Sarah were not the social deviants her parents made them out to be. Instead, they became trusted, safe spaces for her. She had to sneak off to see them without telling her father, but she wouldn't have to do that for much longer. When she went to nursing school, she'd finally be out from under the watchful eye of her parents.

"I'm sorry to get you up so early," she apologized.

"Happy to do it for my favorite niece. Besides I was up for my run at six anyway. What's up?"

She sat on the faux leather sofa in the waiting area, and Kelly sat in the matching chair.

"I don't know if you know, but I'm in the play," Tayloe began.

"I heard. Your dad wasn't super excited at first, but he seems to be okay now."

"Yeah, he's telling the whole family to get tickets and come see me in 'my' show."

"Are you okay with that?"

She shrugged. "I guess."

"If it's not about your dad, then what's going on, hon? Something's on your mind."

Tayloe frowned and looked at her aunt. "I think… I'm losing my mind."

Kelly's dark brows rose. "How so?"

She looked down at her lap. "I liked doing theater in high school, and I thought it would be a fun to do before going to nursing school, you know? But this is different. It's like," she groped for words, "I'm living in the character."

"Is that a bad thing?"

"Or, no, it's like Katrina Van Tassel is living in me. Whenever I get on stage, in the costume and the wig, it's like I become her for the rehearsal."

"Isn't that what any actor wants?"

"I suppose, but this feels weird, like I'm not myself. Oh, I can't explain it! Do you think Aunt Sarah could, you know, do her woo-woo thing and make sure I'm okay?"

Kelly regarded her with sympathetic blue eyes. "Sarah is out of town at the moment."

Tayloe gave her an agonized look. This had been her last resort.

"But, I could send you to another friend. She's good with this kind of thing too."

"Is she like Aunt Sarah?"

"Yes. She's recently decided to help other people." Kelly rose and went to her reception counter and got something out of a drawer. She returned and handed Tayloe a Hair Magic business card with a phone number on the back. "This is Marianne's number."

"Okay. Do you think she can help? "

Kelly nodded. "Give her a try. If she can't help, come back, and Sarah and I will see what we can do."

Tayloe stood up and hugged her. "Thank you. This is really freaking me out."

"Marianne is a good egg. I think you'll like her."

Tayloe tucked the card into her purse and checked the clock on the wall. "Oh my gosh! I'm going to be late! Love you, Aunt Kelly. Say hi to Aunt Sarah for me."

"Will do, hon."

During her six-hour shift at Golden Years Retirement Home, Tayloe was so distracted by her worries that it took her twice as long to do her chores. She made several mistakes and had to backtrack to fix them. At last it was three-thirty and her shift was over, and she had a chance to call the number Aunt Kelly had given her. A woman's voice answered.

"Hello?"

"Hi, is this Marianne Singleton?"

"Yes, who's calling please?"

"Um, my name is Tayloe Walker. You don't know me, but Kelly at Hair Magic gave me your number."

"Hi Tayloe. What can I do for you?"

"Aunt Kelly told me you might understand about weird happenings..."

"I don't follow you. Weird happenings?"

"I'm not explaining this very well, sorry. I'm in the play at the Avery, and I think something weird is going on there."

"What kind of weird things?"

"There might be a ghost and...other stuff."

"Sounds like something that might be easier to explain in person. Would you like to meet somewhere over tea or coffee? Do you have time before rehearsal tonight?"

"Yes, please!" She knew she sounded desperate.

"Okay, can you meet me at the Hudson Valley Trading Company in about ten minutes?"

"Sure."

"Great, I'll see you then."

CHAPTER 11

*M*arianne hung up and looked at Oscar where he lay on the couch snoozing. "Hey, Mister, I think we might have our first client." He twitched his ears and curled into a tight orange and white, cinnamon roll shape, turning his little white chin up. She gave him an affectionate look. "Well, don't get too excited."

She threw a notebook and a couple of pens into her backpack. At the door, she put on her knitted hat with the big pompom and a warm jacket before walking into town.

The bell over the HVTC shop door jingled as she entered into the warm, cinnamon and coffee-scented shop. She scanned the handful of customers at the counter and at the tables, locating a younger woman with medium brown hair. Her pretty features and full lips were currently twisted with anxiety.

Marianne approached her. "Hi, are you Tayloe?"

"Yes, are you Marianne?"

"Yes. Have you ordered a drink yet?"

She shook her head and got up. Together they went to the counter. Marianne got Earl Grey with a shot of vanilla, and Tayloe ordered chamomile tea. They paid, got their drinks, and picked a table away from others to chat.

Marianne took her jacket and pack off and set them on the chair next to her. Tayloe occupied the chair opposite her.

"So, what's going on?" Marianne asked gently.

Tayloe let out a breath. "Thanks for meeting me here. I really appreciate it. I auditioned for the play for a bit of fun before I go off to nursing school in January. I did a little acting in high school and enjoyed it. My best friend Katie is in the play too. It started out as fun, but lately when I go, I feel almost like I'm too into it, you know?"

Marianne shook her head.

Tayloe laced and unlaced her fingers as she explained how weird things had gotten. Her big brown eyes were anxious.

Marianne said, "So, it's more than just acting. Who do you think you're becoming? Katrina?"

She frowned. "Maybe. She's not just flirty, she's a little mean, a little selfish. Last night we had to stop rehearsal because Randall found dead mice in his pocket. Randall is playing Ichabod. It was really gross, but part of me thought it was very funny, and I couldn't stop laughing." She looked at Marianne in anguish. "I felt so bad afterwards, 'cause I really like Randall, and he looked so hurt."

"Do you still feel like that—mean and selfish?"

"No! I'm really worried I might have made Randall feel bad."

"Did you talk to him about it afterwards?"

"No, I couldn't." She shook her head vehemently.

"Maybe you could talk to him before rehearsal tonight."

"That's the thing. When I get to the theater, I forget about things like that. It's like I put on the character when I get there and can't take it off till I leave."

"Do you know where Randall works? Could you speak to him outside the theater?"

"Maybe. He works for his dad at Merritt Motors."

"Maybe you could stop by on the way to the theater."

Tayloe looked hopeful for the first time. "Yeah. I can do that."

"Good. So, what other weird things are going on at the theater?"

"Well, there are rumors that the theater is haunted, and it feels creepy when I'm walking around backstage. But I haven't seen any ghosts, so maybe it's just an old building? Then, there have been a bunch of pranks, mostly harmless things. Like the wigs went missing one night, and we found them all lined up along the seat backs in the auditorium. Then the shoes went missing a couple of nights later. And there have been a couple of times when the sets have fallen over or didn't work right."

"That does sound odd. But maybe there's just a mischievous person playing tricks." Marianne remembered the soft giggle she'd heard in the Green Room the night before. *Or maybe not. I've got to eliminate the more obvious culprits first before I go blaming everything on ghosts.*

"No one's bragged about it or confessed, so no one knows. Mr. Verplank doesn't seem to be super upset about it at least. But Randall has been the target of some really mean pranks. Someone tore the seams in his costume, and Brendan had to fix it so he could keep rehearsing. Someone stole his street clothes and hid them in the balcony. It took forever to find them, 'cause the balcony is off limits. Then there were the dead mice last night."

"Those sound very different from the other pranks. Is there any idea who's behind those?"

"No, but Casey and Jake always look really smug. They swear it isn't them, but I think Casey has it in for Randall."

"Why? Do they know each other outside of the theater?"

Tayloe's fair cheeks turned pink. "It might be because of me. I think they both like me, and Katrina is supposed to flirt shamelessly with both of them. So she—I— kind of do when we're rehearsing. Katie thinks Casey takes it personally as if I'm flirting with him. He's asked me out a couple of times, but I said no. He's kind of a jerk."

"Hmmm. I've heard of him."

She looked surprised. "How?"

"My boyfriend Ruari worked with him for a while."

"Oh, is he the new guy working on the sets for Mr. Miller?"

Marianne nodded and counted off on her fingers. "Okay, so the weird things at the theater are the stories that it's haunted, pranks, both general and specific, and you feeling like maybe Katrina is taking you over while you're at rehearsal. Is that right?"

She nodded. "I'm not losing my mind am I? I'm not making this up, I swear!"

Marianne laid her hand over Tayloe's and said, "I believe you. Would it help you if I went to the theater tonight and checked things out? Maybe I could watch a little of the rehearsal and see what you've been talking about."

"Would you? That would be great. Aunt Kelly said you handled the kind of things Aunt Sarah does. Paranormal things."

"Kelly and Sarah are your aunts?" *What were the odds? Kelly trusted me enough to refer her niece to me, so she can't be too mad at me.*

"Yeah, my dad is Aunt Kelly's brother. He doesn't like her very much because of, you know, her relationship with Aunt Sarah. But I've always liked them. Now that I'm over eighteen, he can't stop me from seeing them if I want. But Aunt Kelly said Aunt Sarah was out of town, and you would be the next best person to help me."

Marianne hoped her trust wasn't misplaced. Not that she couldn't figure things out, but it might take more time than they had. She smiled. "Thank you for sharing your worries with me. I'll do my best to figure out what's going on. " She looked at her phone. "It's nearly four-thirty. Maybe Randall is close to getting off work? You could ask him out for a coffee," she added with a conspiratorial smile.

Tayloe grinned back. "Maybe I will." She put her jacket back on and tossed her empty cup in the trashcan, looking much happier than when she'd sat down. "Thank you so much!"

"See you at the theater tonight," Marianne said as the young woman left. She remained at the table for a little longer, thinking hard.

Hmm. Several things came to mind. Shadow People was one of them. *Sarah said she wasn't sure we'd closed the gate in time on Halloween.* Maybe this was a variation on being possessed by Shadow People? But in her limited experience, Shadow People didn't let go of their hosts when rehearsal was over and let them go back to their normal lives. Maybe this was a different kind of behavior?

Kelly had told Tayloe that Sarah was out of town. Maybe Marianne could get a message to her and she'd call back.

She dialed Kelly's number, and it rang a couple of times.

"Hair Magic, this is Kelly. How can I help you?"

"Hi Kelly, this is Marianne."

"Hey hon, how are you? Do you need a hair appointment?"

"Probably, but not right now. I just met your niece, and she told me she was worried about things going on at the theater."

"Oh good. I gave her your number."

"She mentioned feeling like she wasn't herself and feeling negative emotions. It made me think of Shadow People, honestly. But I don't have a lot of experience with them. Would you and Sarah be willing to confer with me?"

"Sarah's out of town for a couple of days."

"Is she at a law conference?"

"No, a personal matter."

"I've tried to call her cell a couple of times since Halloween to say hi and see how you guys were doing."

"We're doing okay. She recovered fine from the *draugers*, if that's what you mean. She had some stuff at work and then had to go take care of this personal thing. I'm sure she'll call you back as soon as she can."

"Well, if I have questions about Tayloe, can I call you? I'm going to the theater tonight to see if I see anything unusual."

"Perfect. I'll let Sarah know you're on the job."

"Kelly, thank you for trusting me with your niece. I'll do the best I can for her."

"I knew you would. Let us know if you need anything."

"Will do." She hung up and stared at her phone. Well, Kelly sounded friendly enough and not like she was avoiding Marianne. That was good. But she was clearly hiding something and protecting Sarah. Hopefully, Sarah would get back to town in the next few days and be around for back up in case things at the theater turned out to be beyond Marianne's abilities.

She got out her notebook and wrote 'Tayloe' at the top of a new page. She made notes on the things the young woman had told her while they were still fresh in her mind. Then she drained the last of her Earl Grey. Pulling on her hat and jacket against the cold, she slung her pack over one shoulder and started home.

When Ruari got home for a quick dinner, Marianne told him about her first client while she served hamburgers, chips, and salad. Erin had opted not to join them. She'd found a temporary job at her old dentist's office while they hunted for a more permanent receptionist. Today had been her first day, and she claimed exhaustion. She was upstairs, probably deep in a video game. Marianne made sure to leave her a plate of food under wraps in the fridge.

"Tayloe asked me to stop by the theater during rehearsal tonight," she told Ruari. "She's afraid something spooky is happening to her there."

"That reminds me. I forgot to tell you that something odd happened last night at rehearsal."

"Did it involve dead mice?"

"Yeah, Randall and Casey got into a huge argument on stage about it. Randall thought Casey had put them in his costume pockets. I thought he was going to punch Casey out."

"I'd be mad if someone put dead mice in my pockets, too. Have they been at odds before?"

"There have been a series of pranks at the Avery over the last couple of weeks."

"Tayloe also mentioned something about shoes and wigs."

"Yes, but someone seems to have it in for Randall in particular. Given Casey's childish nature, it wouldn't surprise me if it was him, but he keeps swearing it's not."

She nodded. "That squares with what Tayloe told me. So what happened?"

"The Bink stepped in and defused the situation."

"Who is that?"

Ruari grinned. "Jake and Casey have been calling Dave that when he's not around."

She snickered. "So, that was the weird thing that happened?"

"Not entirely. I watched their auras during their confrontation. They were subtly different from what they have been before. They all had darker, more disturbed auras."

"What do you think that means?"

"I'm still learning to read them, but generally, the brighter and purer the color, the healthier the person. Murky, dark colors often mean negative emotions of some kind."

"I suppose if they were angry at each other that might do it."

"Maybe." He sounded dubious. "Auras seem to reflect deeper, more consistent emotions rather than transient ones."

"Then what does it mean?"

"I don't know." He looked thoughtful.

"Tayloe told me she feels like she's not herself. She felt 'mean and selfish' and laughed at the two men last night."

He nodded and finished his dinner.

"I'd like the chance to observe, and do a little more poking around," she said. "Can I come with you tonight?"

"Of course."

"Do we have to come up with another reason for me being there?"

"More research for the sets?"

"That works." They were running late and left the dishes in the sink for later.

On the way to the Avery in Ruari's battered white pickup, Marianne said, "I met Tristan the other day when I was there. What do you know about him?" She hadn't had any time to research him yet.

"He's a nice guy: handy with a hammer and helped me with the sets a bunch. He said he does a lot of community theater, mostly musicals."

"What does he do besides theater?"

"No clue. He hasn't said. Why do you ask?"

"Well, Sarah told me a person named Tristan Kitteby was the magical Protector for Dutchess County. I don't suppose that's a common name."

"If it's the same person, he doesn't seem particularly magical. Then again, you and Sarah don't either, so I suppose that doesn't matter. If he is, that's okay, right?"

"I guess."

"What's bothering you?"

"Sarah avoids the neighboring Protectors completely. She says they 'don't get along.' Also, the letters 'TK' were written on the evil charm bags we found in the stone chambers."

"You think Tristan was working with Byron?" Ruari sounded alarmed.

"I think Byron wanted us to think that. Byron struck me as the kind of person who worked alone. I think Tristan is probably okay. I just don't know him at all." Marianne knew she was trying to convince herself that she didn't have to watch Mr. Kitteby for signs of evil.

They parked in the side lot near the scene shop door. Ruari took her hand.

"If he makes you uncomfortable, Mahri, you don't have to be around him. I'll run interference."

"Thanks. I'll ask around and see what I can figure out and let you know."

They got out and entered the theater through the scene shop. Ruari headed for the stage, and Marianne went up the stairs to the hallway that ran out to the lobby. She encountered Tommy Verplank.

"Marianne, what are you doing here?" He asked, puzzled. "The play doesn't open for another two weeks."

"Ruari asked me to sit in on the rehearsal and see if there were any more Old Dutch Colonial touches he could put on the sets. I hope that's okay?"

"Alright but don't give away all our secrets to other people. No spoilers." He waggled a finger admonishingly.

She laughed. "I promise. And I'll be quiet as a mouse."

"Okay, then." He continued on to his office.

Marianne chose a seat off to the side in the front half of the auditorium. She could still see the stage but wouldn't be near Ruari or the others who had staked out several chairs along the center aisle.

Eventually, the manager called everyone to the front of the stage. She suppressed a grin. Between his soft-serve pompadour and being called The Bink, it was hard to see how he got his job done.

People gathered on stage in full dresses and colonial suits, and Tommy gave them notes and instructions about rehearsing Act I. Marianne almost didn't recognize Tayloe in her blonde wig and rusty brown dress. Kelly's niece giggled and whispered to another young woman in a blue-gray dress and brown wig. That must be her friend Katie. Maybe Tayloe had cleared the air with Randall and that made her happy.

Marianne had no trouble identifying Casey. He was the thick set young man in the dapper costume. Brom was the village darling after all. Randall was taller and thinner than Casey, wearing a dull black suit that had been tailored with the sleeves and pants slightly short to indicate his relative awkwardness and emphasize his height. Tayloe had been right about one thing: both men cast surreptitious glances at her when they thought no one was looking.

When Tommy was done, everyone left the stage purposefully, and the lights dimmed. Mr. Binkler came off the stage and glanced at her briefly, a slight frown on his face. She smiled blandly. *Keep going, I'm no trouble at all.*

The cast ran through Act I, and Marianne was amazed. The shy, agonized young woman she'd met at the coffee shop was gone. In her place, a confident, teasing coquette welcomed Ichabod to the village. Her focus was entirely on Ichabod as the new schoolmaster. Ichabod's abashed looks, stammered lines, and stumbles over benches may have been staged, but they had a sincerity that added another level. The school children gave their lines around them, but the magic was happening between Katrina and Ichabod. It was not hard to believe that Ichabod had come to teach at a sleepy village expecting to be the only sophisticate among the bumpkins, but he was quickly falling in love with the beautiful farmer's daughter.

Brom Bones and his pal arrived in the middle of Act I. Ruari had described his former assistant as a lazy, self-important, entitled, whiny twerp. Casey's Brom, however, had turned those qualities into a confident, arrogant man. Marianne had only heard descriptions of Casey and seen him once or twice at a distance. Casey's Brom was nothing like the teenager playing him. She would have thought he was at least five years older. When he strode onto stage, all eyes went to him. Katrina broke off her conversation with Ichabod and immediately went to his side. She took his arm and introduced the new schoolmaster. Brom tried to put a possessive arm around Katrina's waist, but she slipped out of reach while still managing to linger a moment longer. The look of jealousy on Ichabod's face was plain. Brom laughed and welcomed the newcomer, but it was clear that trouble was brewing already.

Marianne was mesmerized by the interaction between the

three lead actors. The flow was broken when Mr. Verplank called them to stop. Someone had flubbed a line or been in the wrong place at the wrong time. Marianne shook her head, feeling like she'd been absorbed in a movie or play done by professionals not amateurs. The cast reset to the top of the scene. The energy between Tayloe, Randall, and Casey was less intense than it had been, but jealousy and envy still flowed as strong undercurrents. Marianne could well believe that each man thought Tayloe had eyes only for him.

Marianne didn't know any of the actors very well at all. But she would have sworn they were seasoned veterans and speculated that there was plenty of off-stage chemistry between the three of them. She got out her notebook and made notes by the light of her phone. At this point, she didn't know what she was looking for. It was like researching any new history project. She had to collect enough information and wait for the pieces to get big enough to begin connecting to each other. All she could do for now was observe. Ruari found her after rehearsal was over. He was done for the night. Marianne opted not to go back stage and bother Tayloe. The young woman most likely wanted to keep her worries to herself. If Marianne had any questions, she could call or text her later.

When they got home, all was quiet upstairs. Either Erin had gone to bed or was still immersed in her game. Oscar met them at the door with a meow. Marianne picked him up and snuggled him on her way to the kitchen where the dishes were still in the sink. The plate she'd made for Erin was piled on top of the others. Marianne was exhausted, and all she wanted to do was brush her teeth and fall into bed. But she was loath to leave the kitchen a mess. At least Erin had eaten dinner.

Ruari looked embarrassed. "I'm sorry. I'll talk to Erin in the morning. I can do these for you. I'll meet you in bed." He sounded equally tired.

"It's not your fault. We'll do them together."

Ruari put things into the dishwasher while Marianne

scrubbed the remaining hamburger grease from the pan.

Ruari grinned. "Did you know you lick your lips when you wash dishes? It's really cute."

She felt a flash of embarrassment. Geoffrey had rarely done dishes and the few times he had, he'd teased her about her unconscious habit. On top of all his other demeaning comments, it felt like one more elbow in the ribs. She had to take a moment now and check herself. This was Ruari and he was nothing like her ex. Instead of folding up and retreating, she stuck her tongue out and flicked a few suds at him. He grinned at her and splashed back. They ended up damp and laughing, her tension gone.

"Let's go to bed. I'm beat," she said.

CHAPTER 12

Marianne woke excited to get to the library. After observing the rehearsal, she agreed with Tayloe and Ruari that something odd was happening, and she needed to do some research. Once Erin and Ruari were off to their respective jobs, she loaded her backpack with pens, water bottle, and her growing notes about Tayloe and her problem. She let Oscar out for the morning and headed into town.

The old fieldstone building of the Maple Hill Library was located next to the Avery Theater. Built in 1781, it had been an early colonial home and now was on the National Register of Historic Places. A modern addition had been built on the side opposite the theater and connected to the stone building with a glassed-in walkway.

Marianne descended the steps into the basement of the old stone building where the Maple Hill Historic Society was housed. Whenever she had ghost-related research, she always started there.

Mrs. Caldwell was at her desk across from the stairs. Mrs. C was of indeterminate age from sixty to eighty, had sharp eyes under penciled eyebrows, and wore her bronze-colored hair in a low bun. She guarded the historic records as closely as a shepherd did her sheep. She looked up as Marianne entered. Marianne smiled and waved before choosing a table to settle into. She hoped after doing the map filing project that the librarian had softened a little. Mrs. C did not smile or wave back, but she did give Marianne a tiny nod of recognition before returning to her work, and Marianne considered that a win.

She got out her materials and prepared to dig through the microfiche files to look up anything related to the Avery theater over the last hundred years. However, she detoured to Mrs. C's desk first.

"Good morning, Mrs. Caldwell, how are you?"

The older woman looked up from her current project. As always, it seemed to involve lists and cross checking. Cataloging something no doubt. She always seemed a bit irritated to be interrupted. "What do you need today?"

"I'm not here for maps, though I see you found a place for the flat file cabinet. It looks good over there."

"Thank you for your help in organizing things. I put in a request to the library committee for lignin-free folders to protect the maps. Maybe they'll find the money to get some."

That was the friendliest Mrs. C had been. "I hope they do, too. Those are fascinating maps and deserve to be preserved."

"What are you researching today? More dead people?"

Marianne was speechless for a moment. She hadn't realized Mrs. C was looking over her shoulder. Did she also know about Marianne's ghost seeing abilities?

The older woman's pinched nostrils flared defensively. "I notice what people research. It allows me to direct their inquiries."

"Um, I don't know if dead people are involved. Possibly? Probably? I want to find out everything I can about the Avery Theater. Do you have any suggestions where I should look? I figured the newspaper archive would have something. Are there other resources I should look at?"

Mrs. C considered. "Try *Maple Hill Register* back issues, particularly in the early 1910s. There have been a few pieces written by the local Chamber of Commerce. Canopus County has a tourism board, and they may have done a writeup. That should get you more leads, anyway. Do you need me to write that down?" She looked like she would rather not.

"No, I've got it."

"You're welcome." She turned back to whatever she'd been working on.

Marianne headed for the microfiche reader.

"Did you ever get paid?" Mrs. Caldwell asked suddenly.

"Yes. I got a check a couple of weeks ago."

"Good." Her tone sounded like there would've been hell to pay by someone if it hadn't.

Marianne's opinion of Mrs. C rose another notch. "Thank you for asking." Mrs. C did not reply, absorbed in her task once again.

Marianne spent the next several hours combing through the old copies of the *Maple Hill Register*. She took Mrs. C's advice and started with the earliest issues of the *Register* rather than working her way back in time. As she recalled from her initial foray into Maple Hill history, it used to come out once a week, and there weren't a lot of local news articles at first. Instead, there were what she called "exotic culture pieces" and lots of advertisements for farm equipment, home accessories like canning jars, newfangled gadgets like clothes washers and vacuum cleaners, and clothing—$1.50 for a pair of men's canvas work pants. She passed the notices for the Anne Eddy's family tragedy in 1905 with a pang and quickly moved on.

Finally, there was an article in 1909 for an Averill Theater. Located in downtown Maple Hill, it was described as a "cultural magnet for theater and vaudeville." However, the reason for the article was that the theater had suffered a tragic fire during a show. The audience had escaped in spite of a near stampede for the fire exits. A number of people had suffered from smoke inhalation and minor injuries and had been taken to the hospital.

At least one person had died, an actor named Loren Demarko who had been "a rising star of stage with aspirations for the silver screen." He had been overcome by smoke and died at the scene. Maybe he was responsible for Ruari's feeling of being watched?

Well, that explained the ghost at the theater. She kept reading. Then her jaw dropped and her stomach plunged.

The performance had been the opening night of what theater owner, Anthony Verplanck, had hoped would be a long run. He was staging a production of the "Hudson Valley favorite, *The Legend of Sleepy Hollow,* adapted by Mr. Verplanck himself."

How crazy was it that *The Legend of Sleepy Hollow* had been on stage in Maple Hill a hundred years ago? And, that the theater had burned down opening night

Marianne re-read the article. It concluded that the fire was suspicious, and an investigation was ongoing. There was a grainy photo of the burned out remains of an old wood and brick building. She pressed the copy and print button on both pages of the article and collected them from the printer after paying.

Over the next several issues of the *Register,* there were reports of the investigation. The day after the fire, a second tragedy had been uncovered. Anthony Verplanck's son, Dane, age twelve, missing since the night before, had been found in the ruins. It appeared he had been trapped during the blaze, unable to escape. It was unclear whether it had been an accident or deliberate. Investigation ongoing.

Another possible ghost. She printed and kept reading.

It took six months for the inquiry to conclude that the fire had occurred as a result of sparks from an arc light igniting a muslin curtain backstage. The resulting flames had quickly gotten out of control. The only reason more people hadn't died was that innovations such as an asbestos fire curtain had been installed as a result of previous theater fires elsewhere in the U.S. It had shielded the audience for a precious few minutes allowing them to escape. The other innovation had been the installation of doors that opened outward allowing panicked people to escape rather than getting caught in a crush.

It was still unknown how Dane had become trapped in a closet and overcome by smoke and flames. Investigators concluded that he'd accidentally locked himself in, and no one had heard him in time. Marianne winced and tried without success to stop her imagination from picturing the scene. Poor Dane. His poor parents. She wondered how he had ended up in the theater in the first place. Nowhere in the articles did it say.

She jotted her questions down and kept reading.

Loren Demarko and Dane Verplanck had been buried in the Maple Hill Cemetery. Well, she could check that out. Maybe John Irving would know where their graves were. Another note.

The other major actors had been Wilhemina Trent playing Katrina Van Tassel, and Clifford LaSalle had played Ichabod Crane. More notes.

Then there were no more articles about the Averill Theater. She read through the next several months of *Register* issues until she came across an article roughly a year later entitled, "Theater Rises from the Ashes." The Verplanck family had built a new theater on the site of the old one and christened it the Avery Theater. It was considered fireproof, and they had added modern safety equipment such as sprinklers, electric lighting to the asbestos curtains and outward opening doors for the public. Their first production was *A Stubborn Cinderella*, a musical in three acts. It ran successfully for three months. A lighthearted farce about life at a modern college was about as far as one could get from the moody, dark *Legend of Sleepy Hollow*.

Mrs. Caldwell announced to the room in general, "The library will be closing in five minutes, please put your research materials away."

Marianne looked up in surprise. It had gotten quite late, and other researchers had arrived while she was absorbed in her reading. She made a few more printouts, put the microfiche away, and shut the reader off. She tucked them into her pack, pulled on her jacket, and tugged her hat on.

She was headed out the door when Mrs. Caldwell said, "Did you find what you were looking for?"

Marianne paused and stuck her head back around the corner, one foot on the stair. "Yes. I'll be back to keep going. Thanks for your help, Mrs. C. Have a good night!"

She was half way up the stairs before she heard a distant, "You as well."

❦

Marianne called John Irving the next morning. He answered after many rings.

"Maple Hill Cemetery, John Irving speaking." He sounded tired.

"John, it's Marianne. How are you?"

"I'm alright. What can I do for you?"

"I wondered if you knew where Loren Demarko or Dane Verplanck were laid to rest? They died in 1909, if that helps." John took care of the grounds, but he also had a great memory for where people were.

"Well, the older plots are generally closer to the road, but there are a few scattered up and around the hill. I'll see what the records say. Do you want to wait or I could call you back?"

"I forgot you have records at the cemetery. I thought they were only at the library."

"We have records of every burial here. I send a batch of the newest ones to be added to the ones at the library when I think of it."

"If it would save you time, I could look them up myself. I just wondered if you knew off hand."

"Not off hand, no. But you're welcome to come out and look for yourself."

"Thanks, I might come later today. Have you done anything further about moving?"

"The county knows I'm retiring, and they said they'd find an interim caretaker in the next few weeks."

"Do you have a place to go?"

"Not yet."

Marianne took a gamble. "Do you remember my grandmother, Selene Singleton? You met her at my housewarming party a couple of months ago."

"Sure. We know each other a little."

"She lives in a big, empty house in Vandenberg and told me she wouldn't mind hosting you while you find a more permanent place."

There was a silence before he replied. "That's nice of her, but I couldn't impose."

"It wouldn't be an imposition at all. She could use the company."

"Thank you for the thought, Marianne. But you know us old people, we're kind of set in our ways."

"Okay. Well, please know the offer is out there. She'd be glad to have you. I'd be glad for her to have some company rather than living alone off in the woods."

"Thank you."

"I'll see you later then."

"Very good."

When she hung up, she dialed Grandma Selene. After a short conversation, she breathed out a sigh. It was out of her hands, Grandma would handle it.

Yesterday's research had produced more leads. She wasn't sure how the story of the fire at the Averill Theater and the building of the Avery was connected to Tayloe's problem, but she felt like they were related. Internet research was in order, but that could wait for nighttime hours. The library was open till four-thirty, and there was more she could do there. First, a phone call.

When the phone picked up, she said, "Mrs. Thomas, this is Marianne, your renter."

"Marianne? Oh yes. Hello, dear. How are you? Is the house okay? How are George and Anne?"

"George and Anne left at the end of August."

"Oh, I hope they're alright. Anne was such a good pianist. A lovely woman too."

"Yes, she was. Mrs. Thomas, you told me you and your husband had been involved in community theater at the Avery."

"Oh yes! Selwyn and I were in lots of shows."

"Right, I was wondering if you would be willing to talk to me about the Avery, particularly the early Avery in the 1910s and 20s."

"Well, I'm not that old!" She chuckled. "But, of course, I'd love to talk to you about it. I have a couple of scrapbooks, if you'd be interested."

"I'd love that! Could I come tomorrow?"

"No. I have a big bingo tournament this weekend at the senior center. But maybe next week on Monday or Tuesday?"

Disappointed, Marianne said, "Sure. That sounds fine. Monday afternoon?"

"Yes, I'll put it on my calendar." She covered the phone. "Miss Gina? Come write this down for me, please? Marianne, Monday two o'clock, tea. Thank you, dear."

"Mrs. Thomas, I'll put it in my calendar too and look forward to seeing you then."

"Wonderful. Wish me luck. I have high hopes of beating Marge DeVries. She's been my nemesis for the last five years."

"May the numbers be with you, Mrs. Thomas."

"Thank you. Bye-bye."

"Bye."

She glanced at the time and made up her mind. She could make a trip out to the cemetery to find those graves and see if the spirits of Dane Verplanck or Loren Demarko were still around. That might be the fastest way to stop the haunting at the theater.

Then she could return to the library to continue her research if need be.

She ate a hasty early lunch. Oscar cruised into the kitchen shaking his crooked tipped tail and meowed for more food in his dish.

"Hungry again? I don't know how you manage to stay so trim, Mister, with all the extra cat food you've been eating lately." But she put an extra quarter of a can in his dish which he wolfed down. She cleaned up her dishes and let the tabby outside on her way to The Flea.

The drive out to the cemetery was easy. The weather was overcast and chill, but it hadn't snowed yet. Snow was the worst. She hadn't driven in snow in years, and the prospect made her nervous. She drove through the gates and parked near the caretaker's cottage. There was no answer when she knocked on the cottage door. She didn't know where he kept the cemetery records and hoped she wouldn't have to walk through every row to find the ones she was looking for. A short walk brought her to the machine shop, and she stuck her head in.

"John, are you in here? It's Marianne." She called a few more times but no one answered. Maybe he was out and about. She stepped back and heard a voice in her ear.

Boo!

She nearly jumped out of her skin as she spun around. Jason was laughing uproariously, his semi-transparent form doubled over and shaking.

She clutched her chest. "Oh my God, you nearly gave me a heart attack!" Her heart thudded under her jacket.

You have no idea how many people I've tried that on. You're the first real jumper.

"Very funny." If she could have punched him in the arm, she would have. Unfortunately, although she could see and hear ghosts, she couldn't touch them unless they wanted her to.

She scowled. "I'd punch you in the arm if I could."

He laughed. *But you're such a fun scare! Even if you could, it would still be worth it every time.*

She couldn't stay mad for long at his good humor. "Do you know where John is?"

I think he's up tending a fresh gravesite. Why?

"I need to look up two graves, and he's got a record book somewhere. Do you know where he keeps it?"

He's got an office in his house and keeps it on a shelf. Who are you looking for?

"I'm looking for Dane Verplanck and Loren Demarko from 1909. Any chance you know where they are?"

He thought for a moment. *I might. My man Jesse has been showing me around and getting me familiar with everyone here.*

They started walking toward the lower end of the cemetery where the oldest graves were. Jason glide-walked in his hoodie, oblivious to the cold, and Marianne walked with him, shivering in her jacket.

"Are Dane or Loren still here? I mean, can you see them, talk to them?"

No. I've met most of the people who are still here, and I don't know anybody named Dane or Loren.

Marianne's booted feet crunched over the hard ground and stiff grass. "Did you know John is retiring?"

He nodded. *Jesse and I have been doing what we can to help him out.*

"I'm glad."

Jason looked sad. *He's a good guy. Jesse wishes we could do more. He might be changing teams soon.*

She was momentarily puzzled, then her stomach plunged. "Oh no! Can you tell if someone's going to die?"

He shrugged. *Not really. He's just old, you know? The fight at the portal was really hard on him.*

"I'm trying to get him and my grandmother together. Just to keep each other company," she added hastily at his sly look. "He doesn't seem to have anyone he can move in with otherwise. And she lives alone. I worry about her. I guess the county will have to get someone else to be a groundskeeper and to dig and fill the graves."

I suppose if they have some fun while they're at it, more power to them, he added.

She tried to block out an image of her Grandmother in a slinky dress. *It's their business, not mine,* she told herself.

They arrived at a modest headstone with the engraved words: Loren Demarko 1884—1909. There was no other information. Jason led her down another row and stopped in front of a smaller marker with Dane Verplanck's name on it. A larger monument had other members of the Verplanck family listed. She looked around and realized it wasn't far from Samuel Eddy's tiny marker. There wasn't any more to see, so she headed back toward the parking lot. Jason continued to drift and walk along with her.

"Thanks for showing me around. Are you guys going to stick around?" She hoped so. She'd really miss Jason and Jesse, the previous caretaker before John.

He shrugged again. *Kinda depends on who the next dude is. If they're cool or not.*

"Where would you go if you weren't here?"

Guess I'll go wherever my man Jesse goes.

"Let me know, will you?"

He gave her a mischievous smile. *Would you miss me?*

"Who else would give me a heart attack when I visit the cemetery?"

He gave her a sly look. *Could I stay with you, like I did that one time?*

"I'd rather have some warning if you don't mind."

You mean I can't just hang out and watch you on a hot date?

"No!" The thought horrified her.

He laughed again. *Oh fine. I'll be really polite and knock first.*

"Thank you." She unlocked The Flea. "Take care of John as long as he's here, okay? And say hi to Jesse for me."

Will do. He faded away, leaving her alone in the empty parking lot.

❦

After dinner, Marianne took The Flea to the Avery and parked near Ruari's truck. Light spilled out of a crack around the scene shop door Ruari had left propped open for her. She slipped inside and shut it firmly. No one else should be able to sneak in behind her. She paused. The scene shop was currently empty. There were distant voices in the direction of the stage as the rehearsal got underway. Her plan was to prowl the back halls, listening for ghostly presences, and watch the rehearsal from an unobtrusive place at the back of the theater.

She climbed the stairs to the side hall that ran to the front of the building and hoped she didn't encounter anyone. She only had half-baked excuses for being here. This hall was very similar to the one on the other side of the auditorium. She checked the handles of the doors along the inside of the hallway as she went. A couple were locked, and others led to small storage rooms with a jumble of things that looked like they hadn't moved in fifty years ago. About half way down the hall there was a set of three steps like on the other side. She sat and closed her eyes, listening for whatever might come to her.

The sound of distant voices and footsteps echoed along the hall, then silence. No noises escaped the wall between her and the auditorium. The pipes clanked overhead as water moved along the ancient heating system. She was about to get up when she heard faint footsteps brushing along the passage and someone muttering like they were talking to themselves. She couldn't make out the words but felt a faint presence as it whisked down the hallway from behind her. She swiveled her head, eyes still closed, to see who it was but saw nothing. A chill breezed brushed by her and was gone.

Well, that was interesting. Someone was definitely here but didn't want to be seen. Hmm.

She stood and walked slowly up the hall toward the front. Lost in thought, she opened the door to the lobby and stepped out. The faded red wallpaper and carpet with their infused scent of popcorn reminded her she was on the job. Maybe she could stroll down the other hallway to see what she could see and then sit in the back of the theater for the rest of the rehearsal. Halfway across the lobby, she heard voices coming from the auditorium. Mr. Binkler and someone else. She hurried the rest of the way and went through the door just as their voices emerged into the lobby.

Not sure why she was worried about being spotted, she slowed her steps down. *Hurrying makes you look guilty of something,* she told herself.

"Excuse me!" A voice called out behind her.

She sighed and stopped. Busted. Turning, she put on a smile. "Yes?"

Mr. Binkler, vanilla swirl pompadour waving gently, trotted down the hall after her. She stayed still and waited for him to catch up. He was only an inch or so taller than her. Hardly intimidating. But he made up for it by looking officious with his clipboard and script under one arm. "Excuse me, Marianne was it?"

"Yes?" She smiled sweetly.

"What are you doing here?"

Nothing nefarious. I'm just looking for ghosts, trying to find out if people are getting possessed, and maybe nab your prankster in the act. "I'm helping Ruari out with something, and I'm writing a short history of the theater for the Playbill."

He gave her a pointed look. "Did Tommy put you up to this?"

"I suggested it, but he liked the idea."

Mr. Binkler rolled his eyes. "He's always doing this to me. As if I don't already have enough on my plate."

"Do you know anything about the history of the Avery? I'd be happy to include it."

He frowned. "No, not really. Please don't wander around alone. You heard what happened to our other set designer, right? I'd rather not have any more injuries." He stood aside and gestured her back up the hall to the front lobby.

"Of course." If she was restricted to the public areas, ghost hunting and protecting Tayloe were going to be more difficult.

She headed back to the scene shop through the front lobby where Tristan stood in the doorway to the auditorium watching. He made eye contact with her briefly, a slight crease between his brows. She felt a little zing of anxiety. He was keeping an eye on her, and he wasn't happy about it.

CHAPTER 13

$\mathcal{E}$rin pushed the front door closed with her elbow, so glad it was Friday night at last. The smell of the pepperoni pizza in the box made her mouth water. After answering phones and filing all day at the dentist's office she was starving. Desperate to take off her horrible office clothes, she wanted to put on something comfortable and eat the whole pizza without having to talk to anyone. She cast a guilty look down the hall. Marianne wasn't in the living room or kitchen. She was probably in her office doing some research thing. What she didn't know wouldn't hurt her. Erin wouldn't leave any crumbs in her room and would ditch the box as soon as she was done. Easy-peasy. She tiptoed upstairs and put the forbidden box of pizza on her desk.

She kicked off her shoes and sighed in relief. Curse the inventor of high heels and their stupid association with femininity. She pulled off the matching jacket and skirt combo and slipped into an oversized black sweatshirt with a sigh. The angled black skyline of 'Black Parade' on the front had faded a little, but it was still her favorite. A pair of ratty black sweats kept her warm. Marianne sure liked to save her pennies on heating. It was freezing up here. Better eat a couple of slices before the pizza developed icicles.

She slipped on her headphones and logged into the game of *Dragon Age* she was deep into. Two slices later, she grabbed a third piece while she explored a village and became aware that the growling noise she'd been hearing wasn't part of the game. Pausing, she slipped the phones off one ear and listened.

"Oscar?" She said.

Another growl.

"You little stinker, you'd better not be stalking me."

A louder, deeper sound came from a throat too big to be a cat's. The hairs on the back of her neck stiffened. Marianne didn't have a dog. Erin's suddenly pounding heart had nothing to do with the game. There were demons in *Dragon Age* that corrupted your psyche if they got ahold of you. Her avatar had just barely avoided that fate in the game. Wait, what if it was another form of Shadow Person? Yanking off the headphones, she bolted for the door and pelted down the stairs two at a time.

"Marianne!" She'd better be home. Finding out her roomie was out would not be a great discovery right now. "Marianne!"

"What's the matter?" Marianne appeared in the doorway of her office. Oscar sat on her desk washing his face.

Erin skidded to a halt in front of her, panting. "I think there's a demon in my room!"

"What? That's not possible. I just refreshed my magical wards for the whole house."

"Whatever it is, it's growling at me."

Marianne's eyebrows vaulted skyward. "Growling?"

Erin took a deep breath and forced herself to calm down. She wasn't alone. Marianne would be able to handle this. She was the professional, and it was her house. "Please, just come upstairs with me."

She frowned at the slice in Erin's hand. "Is that pizza?"

This was no time to mince fine details. Erin lowered the offending food and tried to hide it behind her. "I got it on the way home."

"I asked you not to eat in your room." Marianne's look of disappointment was piercing.

"If you set a pizza-eating demon on me, I repent! I won't do it again."

"Don't be ridiculous. I wouldn't do that even if I knew how to."

"Please just come up and take a look." There was no way she was going back upstairs alone.

"Give me a sec." Marianne located a little gauze bag of stones and herbs under a pile of papers and tucked it into her pocket.

"Oscar, are you in on this daring mission?" Marianne asked. The orange tabby paused in washing his paws and gave them both a look of, *are you kidding?* He pulled back one forearm and began licking his front ruff.

Worthless cat. Erin stuck her tongue out at the orange fur ball. He stopped and stared at her with a look that said, *who's a scaredy cat now?*, before he returned to washing himself.

"Lead the way," Marianne said.

After leaving the theater, Marianne had gone home and done a little online research. Searching for "Tristan Kitteby" had turned up a number of theater references to plays and musicals he'd been in. Other than that, he didn't own any businesses and didn't seem to be employed by local governments or medical facilities. And, as usual, there was no webpage for magical practitioners or county Protectors. If she wanted to know more, she'd have to ask him herself.

David Binkler didn't have anything particularly unusual other than theater credits. He'd worked with Tommy Verplank at the Avery for at least five years and about a dozen productions. He wasn't sinister, as far as she could tell, just very avid about protecting the theater.

She'd switched to searching for any leads on the Averill or

Avery Theater. Way down a rabbit hole, she found a reference to a periodical called *Theater Talk*. Printed between 1891 and 1921, the magazine contained photos of actors from stage and screen as well as interviews. Many of the articles seemed to be fluff pieces similar to those in modern teen and star magazines, but some of them were in-depth accounts of more specific events. It had been produced mainly in New England but included New York, New Jersey, and Pennsylvania sometimes, according to the description.

The chances of the Maple Hill Library carrying issues of *Theater Talk* were pretty low, but you never knew. Mrs. Caldwell had come through before. She went online and found an interlibrary loan form and made the request. She was about to call it a night and read a book when she heard feet pounding down the stairs and Erin calling her name as if the house was on fire.

Ruari's sister raced into the office looking wild-eyed, bearing some cockamamie tale about growling, pizza-eating demons. Marianne felt a small spike of fear at the word demon. Sarah hadn't expressly said they existed, nor had she said they didn't. Maybe a *drauger* or Shadow Person had infiltrated the house somehow? Marianne still didn't know entirely how they worked. She reached for the ward, and the warm-blanket feeling was still there. Presumably if the magic had been broken, she'd have felt it somehow. What was Erin up to?

Ruari's sister seemed genuinely panicked. So, Marianne found her protective charm and slipped it into her pocket. It would heat up at least and tell her if Shadow People were nearby.

"Lead the way," she said.

At the top of the stairs, Marianne paused and listened. Silence except for Erin's chewing. A throb of annoyance pulsed through her. If they had mice or roaches now...She pulled herself back to Erin's current problem.

If it really was a demon or a *drauger*, Marianne didn't have any holy water to banish it with. A major oversight. She'd have to get some more. She patted the charm in her front pocket. It was only just warming up to skin temperature. A good sign.

Marianne cautiously peered inside Erin's door. The box of pizza lay on the floor. All of the pepperoni had been eaten off the top.

"What on earth?" She muttered.

"I did not do that!" Erin said, wide-eyed. "I told you there was a pepperoni-eating demon in my room."

Marianne pondered for a moment. Something seemed familiar. "For the sake of solving this mystery, would you be willing to sacrifice your last slice?"

Erin looked pained.

She held out her hand. "We can always order another pizza."

Erin sighed and handed her the half-eaten slice. Marianne closed the lid of the box and laid the slice on top. Then she motioned Erin back a couple of steps. "This better work," she muttered. Clearing her throat, she addressed the empty room.

"Rita? Are you here?"

A faint doggy whine tickled their ears.

"Rita, is that you, girl? It's okay, you can have the last slice. Erin doesn't mind." Marianne closed her eyes and scanned the room, looking for an apparition.

A spectral Newfoundland, the size of a small pony, emerged from the space between the bed and the book case. She wagged her tail uncertainly.

"Holy shit!" Erin whispered. "Is that the dog from the cemetery?"

Marianne opened her eyes and saw Rita's pale, shaggy form standing in the room. "It's okay, girl. I didn't know you were here. You can have the last pepperoni, but no more stealing okay?"

The tail wagged more, and she bent over the slice and delicately nibbled the last of the pepperoni.

"How does she do that?" Erin whispered.

"No idea. She was abandoned in a motel room that Sarah and

I stayed in. We fed her pizza to appease her. I guess she didn't want to go back after helping us at the cemetery."

"She's been living here in my room all this time?! That is so not cool!"

"That might explain the missing pepperoni, bacon, and maybe the canned cat food. She must be why Oscar keeps getting spooked." It might also explain the dream she'd had the other night.

Erin stared at the ghostly dog and narrowed her eyes. "You're the one who's been eating my pizza."

Rita licked her lips, swished her tail in acknowledgement, and regarded Erin uncertainly.

"Huh, I guess I owe your cat an apology," Erin admitted reluctantly.

Marianne addressed the dog. "Rita, what do you want to do, girl?"

Rita sat, her ears perked up, and whined hopefully.

"You're not thinking of letting her stay, are you?" Erin sounded appalled.

"I can't send her back to that motel room. She hated it there."

"She cannot live in my room." Erin was adamant.

"She's really a big sweetheart. She's also really smart." Marianne told her the rest of the story about the motel room, and Erin's lips quirked up.

"If she did that, she can't be all bad. But she can't stay in here. I need a ghost-free space."

Rita watched their exchange, her ears twitching back and forth. Her tail wagged slowly.

"Okay, Rita," Marianne said sternly, "you can stay, but you have to behave yourself. I'll make sure you get your share of pepperoni, but you have to stay out of Erin's room, and you and Oscar have to make peace. Can you do that?"

Rita tilted her head and opened her jaws in a pant.

Erin said, "She's a dog! Why do you think she'll pay any attention to you?"

"Look at her face. She understands. Don't you, girl?"

Rita barked once and gave a happy grin.

Erin threw up her hands dramatically. "Fine." She glared at the ghostly dog. "No more stealing my pizza. And stay out of my room."

Marianne patted her leg. "Come on, Rita. Let's go downstairs. You and Oscar can work it out." Rita followed Marianne out of the room, half gliding, half walking. Erin closed the door firmly behind them.

"We'll have to find some way of explaining this to Ruari when he gets home," Marianne said to the big Newfie.

The meeting with Oscar did not go well. The big orange tabby arched his back and hissed, bristling ferociously, before he raced off and hid under the sofa, growling. Rita barked a couple of times before Marianne could shush her. "Rita, no! If you guys can't get along, I'll have to banish you to the garage."

Rita wagged her tail and panted happily.

"Maybe I should get you a bed. That would give you a place to call your own. I'll look for one tomorrow. In the meantime, Rita: go lie down." Marianne pointed to a place on the floor in the living room.

The dog turned and faded out. Oscar's hissing growl stopped, and she picked him up and cuddled him. "I know you're used to being an only cat, but she has no where else to stay. I'll send her to the garage, if we have to, I promise."

Oscar gave her an irritated look.

"Don't be too mad. You know what it's like to have no home." She rubbed the soft fur under his chin, and he closed his eyes and leaned into it.

Marianne curled up on the couch with a book for the rest of the evening, Oscar by her side. Ruari returned from rehearsal after ten o'clock, looking tired and frazzled. Marianne put down the Haunted Home cozy mystery and gave him a hug. "How did it go?"

He sat heavily on the sofa. "One of the set pieces I made collapsed on Randall and Casey."

"Oh no! Were they hurt?"

"No, they wanted to blame each other, but they couldn't." He sighed. "I think Binkler and Tommy are wondering if I'm shit with a hammer and screw gun though." He put his hands over his face and rubbed his eyes.

"You know you're not."

He threw up his hands and let them fall in his lap. "I could have sworn everything was fine when I put the flat out, but somehow it had come unscrewed from the base and fell over."

"Is it okay now?"

He nodded. "Nobody said anything to my face, but they all looked worried. Did you have a nice quiet night?"

"Not exactly. Erin came home with a pizza and tried to eat it in her room."

He gave a small smile. "Did you get on her case?"

"Not exactly. We have another guest."

His smile faded. "Guest?"

"Do you remember I told you about a ghostly dog Sarah and I encountered in a motel room about a month ago?"

"Yes, you said she helped us fight at the cemetery."

"She did. Apparently she didn't want to go back to the motel room. She's the one who has been eating the pizza and scaring Oscar."

"She's here?" He looked around a little wildly.

Marianne recounted the events of the evening.

He ran his hands through his hair in dismay. "So now we have an invisible dog living here? Do I have to worry about this? Is she going to be under foot and eating our food?"

"No, I think if we give her her own space and share pepperoni with her occasionally, she'll be okay. I couldn't send her away."

He sighed and rubbed his eyes. "I'm too tired to deal with this. It's your house. You can have whoever you please stay here. Except Casey."

She hugged him. "Absolutely no Casey. If Rita overstays her welcome, I'll ask her to leave."

He kissed the top of her head. "It's been a long day. Let's hit the hay."

"I can't wait to curl up with you."

Fifteen minutes later, they switched off the light and pulled the covers up. Oscar lay down in his usual place next to Marianne. There was a certain amount of thrashing by everyone to get comfortable, then Ruari sighed contentedly and put his arm around Marianne's waist.

"Good night," he whispered in her ear.

"Good night, I love you," she whispered back.

"Love you too."

They were just relaxing when end of the bed dipped as a heavy weight descended. Oscar stiffened and hissed.

Ruari jerked his head up. "What the hell is that?"

"Rita," Marianne said sternly, "no, girl, off the bed. Now."

There was a soft whine and the end of the bed bounced back.

"I'll get her her own bed tomorrow," Marianne promised.

Ruari lay back down and tightened his grip around her waist. "I don't know about this."

CHAPTER 14

arianne woke on Saturday and snuggled up next to Ruari who was peacefully asleep. Reflexively, he curled around her, and she drifted off. Sometime later, she woke again. Oscar was gone, and she smelled coffee. Ruari was still next to her, so Erin must have gotten up early and made coffee. That was a first.

" 'Morning," Ruari murmured.

"G'morning. You sleep okay?"

"I did. It's so nice not to be called for rental emergencies at all hours."

"Yup. Someone else's problem."

He inhaled deeply. "Is that coffee?"

"I think Erin made it."

"Wow. Maybe the dentist's office is having a good effect."

"That or Rita is."

He opened his eyes. "I dreamed you told me we had a ghost dog."

Marianne looked away feeling guilty. "Rita wanted to live with us. I told her yes."

He winced. "I was hoping you were kidding."

Her discomfited look was her answer.

He sighed. "What does Oscar think?"

Maybe he was relenting if he was asking about Oscar's opinion. "He's not thrilled. I'm hoping they'll make peace with each other."

"I thought you closed the house magically. Wouldn't that have kept her out?"

"I've been thinking about that. Maybe? They're meant to keep out negative spirits, and she's not particularly negative. I'm guessing she was already inside, and I just didn't notice."

Ruari rolled out of bed and headed for the shower. Marianne could tell he was unhappy but didn't know what to do about it. He might come around given time. On the other hand, having him be unhappy with her made her feel a little queasy.

She would think of something. Maybe Jason and Jesse would be happy to have Rita live with them? She dressed warmly, digging into her turtleneck and sweater collection and coming up with a toasty pink turtleneck under an olive colored cable knit. They convened in the kitchen and found the coffee half gone. Erin had disappeared back upstairs, probably to play her video game again. They made sausages and eggs and toast in remembrance of their Scottish breakfasts at the Allen family farmhouse. It was so quiet they could imagine they were alone.

"What do you want to do today?" She asked.

"I don't have to go to the theater till the afternoon."

"Let's do something fun together," she suggested. That might help mend things between them. "The weather is good and not too cold. Is that garden place you took me to open?"

"Innisfree in Millbrook? No, they close for the season. When you and Sarah were out, did you go to the Kent Gardens?"

"No. I vaguely remember driving by them."

"They have some nice paths, and there's a small café."

She shuddered. "As long as they don't have a stone chamber, I'm up for it."

"Not that I know of."

They took The Flea, and Marianne drove. Ruari pulled up

directions on his new phone. He'd fried the old flip phone some weeks back and been forced to get a new one. Marianne and Erin had been showing him how to use it, and he wondered how he'd gotten along without it for so long.

Kent Gardens turned out to be a popular destination that morning, but there were lots of paths, so it wasn't too crowded. Marianne enjoyed the beautifully kept grounds all put to bed for winter. Large wicker sculptures of animals dotted the lawns. People smiled and said hello when they walked by, and she was irresistibly reminded of Hyde Park during the Victorian era when people got out to see and be seen. They stopped at the little café and warmed their hands around cups of hot chocolate. Ruari was still acting distant with her, and she knew he was still bothered by something. She was reluctant to probe, unwilling to cloud the nice time they were having.

"Thanks for binging me here," she said.

"They have a pond for ice skating later if it gets cold enough," Ruari said, making the effort to be sociable.

"I haven't been skating since I was a kid."

"We should go then. I played hockey in high school."

"Let's do it."

On the way back from Kent Gardens, she pulled into a pet supply store. She bought two dog beds and a dog dish. "For the pepperoni," she explained. "We've got to break Rita of the habit of just eating off the top of the pizza anytime she wants."

Ruari shook his head but helped her load them into the trunk of the little Ford Escort. He continued to be quiet as they drove up the road to Maple Hill.

"What's bothering you?" She asked.

He shrugged a little.

Her stomach swooped lower. Geoffrey had been a master at passive-aggressive behavior, leaving her to wonder and struggle when he didn't like something. "Please just tell me. It'll make me crazy trying to guess."

He exhaled noisily. "Invisible ghost dogs, hitchhikers, my

sister. I love your compassion for other people, but you take in waifs and strays at every turn."

"I do not!"

"You do. I'm worried for your safety. Someone's going to take advantage of you one of these days, and you're going to get really hurt."

"Rita would never hurt me or the people I love. Jason is a little annoying, but he wouldn't hurt anyone either. And Erin's your sister. I figured she'd be okay."

"That's my point. You can always think of a reason to let someone into your house. Even when you don't know them very well. Will you be able to kick them out if they take advantage of you?"

"I don't know." He was silent, and she felt there was more to it. "What else is going on?"

He glanced out the window and then back at her. "I don't want to get pushed to the back by your compassion for others."

The tightness in her chest gave a quiver, and she guessed this was the real reason.

She knew she had a tender heart and hated to see others suffer if she could do something about it. Geoffrey had been so controlling that he'd said no to all her waifs and strays unless they were his idea. Maybe she'd gone a little overboard in taking people in now that she could. Ruari was right. People would take advantage of her if she didn't set some limits. Maybe that's what Sarah had been trying to tell her.

"I think you're right that my impulse to help people might lead to trouble." She turned onto Main Street. "I'm not sure how to set boundaries. I'll have to think about that. I'm sorry I invited Rita without asking you. I should have talked to you before I promised her she could stay."

"It's your house, not mine," he said, resigned.

"I know, but you spend a lot of time there, and we're trying to be partners."

He sat up straighter as they pulled onto Violet Lane and gave her a genuine smile. "Okay. Let's hope the new dog beds make Rita feel at home."

Marianne pulled into the driveway, turned off the car, and hugged him across the front seat. "I don't want you to ever feel like you're not important to me.'"

"I love you, Mahri. I just don't want you to get hurt."

Ruari helped her wrestle the two stuffed dog beds out of the little trunk. Marianne put one in the living room opposite the fireplace. It was up against a side door she never used, but she supposed Rita was the one person in the house who wouldn't mind the cold draft. The other plush mat went into the bedroom.

Oscar strolled in waving his crooked tipped tail and sniffed the new mat in the bedroom before stepping on it tentatively. It was very soft, and his feet sank into the plush fibers up to his ankles. He began to knead them and purr.

Uh oh. She hadn't thought about Oscar when she bought them. She didn't blame him in the least. They were awfully soft. "Hey Mister, these are supposed to be for Rita, not you. Should I have gotten you one, too? You have the sofa and the bed. She's not allowed up there."

His rumble grew louder as he began turning around to make himself comfortable. "Let's give Rita first shot at them okay?" She picked up the orange and white tabby and held him close as she walked into the kitchen.

Ruari was putting together some lunch before he went off to the theater. He was close to finishing the sets and thought he needed one more weekend. Scotty had promised to help him.

"Well, the beds meet Oscar's approval. We'll have to see how Rita likes them. Where did you put the dog dish?" She asked.

"I rinsed it out and put it in the pantry on the opposite side from where Oscar's dishes are."

"Good plan."

They ate a couple of sandwiches and some canned soup. Ruari kissed her goodbye and said he'd be back for dinner unless he got going on something.

"See you then. Fried chicken and biscuits, I think."

"I'll definitely be home for that!"

He sounded much happier and Marianne relaxed.

A couple of hours later Marianne got a call from Ruari. She'd been reviewing her notes and trying to think of other avenues of research for Tayloe. She'd intercepted Oscar twice as he tried to sleep on the new dog beds. She wasn't going to be able to keep him off forever, but she wanted Rita to know that they were for her not the cat. Maybe if the two of them accepted each other, it wouldn't be a problem. Until then, she encouraged Oscar to sleep in the office with her as he usually did.

"Mahri," Ruari said, "I wanted to let you know that Fran, who does props, approached me and asked if I could make something for a silent auction they want to hold opening night. She went to visit Teddy Miller in the hospital, and he's recovering, but his bills are going to be astronomical. She wants to raise some money to help him and his wife Mary out."

"Oh, what a great idea! I'm glad to hear he's recovering. I'm sure lots of people would be happy to pitch in for that."

"So, I was thinking, I made a second lazy Susan like the one I made for my mom. I could make another."

"That sounds perfect. People love handmade crafts."

"I'm going to have to spend some time in my studio till I get it done. So, instead of coming home from the theater when I'm done for today, I'll be there."

"Thanks for letting me know. You want me to save some dinner for you?"

"That would be great."

"It'll be ready by six or six-thirty. It can hold in the oven if you're later."

"Have I told you how awesome you are?"

She felt a warmth in her belly. She and Ruari were okay again. "You just like my cooking."

"That too. What are you doing today?"

"I need to call Tayloe and let her know I'm working on her situation. Have you seen her?"

"Only from a distance. She and Katie run the concession stand for the morning cartoons and kid movie. She looked okay to me."

They said good bye, and Marianne dialed Tayloe's number. When she answered, Marianne said, "Hi, it's Marianne."

"Hi. I can't talk for long. I'm at work."

"I just wanted to call and see how you were doing."

"I feel better when I'm not at rehearsal. So, I'm okay for now."

"I think it's a good thing that it's location specific. I wanted to let you know that I've been doing research on the history of the theater, trying to figure out what's going on."

"What have you learned?"

"Nothing specific. I'm still trying to put the pieces together. I just wanted to check on you."

"Thanks, I really appreciate it. By the way, I took your advice and talked to Randall. He was really sweet, and we had coffee together!"

"That's great!"

"I think we're going to try for another date—oops, I have to go. Thanks for calling. Bye!"

"Bye!" *Good for her.*

She stared at her notes. Maybe the source of Tayloe's problem wasn't to be found just in the history of the theater. Maybe there was a ghost element as well. After all, Marianne had relived being trapped in a fire under the influence of a ghost's memory. Actor Loren Demarko and Dane Verplanck both died in the 1909 theater fire. One of them could certainly be a ghostly prankster or the spirit she'd felt on her visits to the theater. Maybe they were influencing Tayloe somehow.

She turned on her computer and searched for information on

the actors. Unfortunately, there was next to nothing. They had not achieved enough fame to warrant Wikipedia entries or fan sites. After an hour she quit in frustration.

Oscar stood, arching his back in a stretch, before leaping off the desk and sauntering down the hall.

"Stay off Rita's bed, Mister," she called after him.

She tapped her pen against her notebook for a moment, deliberating. Finally, shrugging, she picked up her cell and dialed Sarah. She needed more insight than the library or internet could give her, and her mentor was the only person she could think of.

The phone rang several times before going to voicemail.

"Hey, Sarah, it's Marianne. I had some ghost questions about Tayloe's situation and would appreciate a call back. Hope you and Kelly are doing okay."

So annoying. Sarah had made a big deal about being her mentor in all things ghostly and magical before the battle in the cemetery, and then she'd gone off the grid. Kelly had assured her Sarah had recovered and was fine. If she was so fine, why the hell couldn't she call her back?

Somewhat at a loss, she went back to the internet to ask the Big Brain about ghosts, possession, anything that might give her a clue. There were a lot of sites that talked about mystical this and that. A few things felt similar to her own experiences, but some things were just ridiculous or out to sell paraphernalia. There were a few stories about hauntings in old rectories in England that suggested some spirits were unaware of changes to the building they haunted over time. In fact, they seemed stuck in a time loop of their own, endlessly reliving some crucial moment in their life. Attempts to contact them had been unsuccessful. The ghosts were little more than bad silent videos of their own memories, and their spirits had finally faded away.

That was depressing and sad. She'd always thought of death as a release from earthly cares, leading to a happy afterlife in some beautiful place. Had they finally gone "beyond the veil" or "into the light" or wherever it was that people went after death? Or had they been permanently snuffed out like the ghosts that had been consumed by the *draugers* at the cemetery?

After more thought, Marianne felt like she was not much farther than before, though the time loop thing felt important. Now, if she could just figure out how it applied in this situation. She'd have to keep going to rehearsals and explore the theater more if she had the chance. Maybe she could make contact with the Avery's ghosts and ask them what they needed.

❀

Later in the day, Ruari was alone in the scene shop. Tommy, Fran, and The Bink had been in and out several times on one pretext or another. It felt like they were checking up on him after the collapsed flat incident. They were on stage at the moment, their voices floating indistinctly through the legs or side curtains of the stage.

Ruari marked a cut on a board with a pencil and tucked it behind his ear. Pulling his goggles down, he positioned the two by four in the band saw, turned it on, and made the cut. Sawdust flew, and the scent of freshly cut wood grew stronger. He turned the saw off and made sure the blade spun to a stop before retrieving the two pieces. They fitted into place, enlarging the feast table. He tested it for solidness and was reassured. The table was now an eight-foot-long framework with a lighter piece of plywood on top, ready to be painted dark brown with designs swirled along the sides and legs. It was heavy, but someone could dance on top of it if Tommy took it into his head to do that.

Ruari had been both fascinated and horrified to find that the theater was not only the art of illusion but demanded that he make things that were not sturdy and would not last beyond the play. Case in point, the table was destined to be taken apart for something else later. In addition, Scotty's lessons showed him that painting in the theater was meant to give the impression from a distance but up close looked pretty shoddy to his eye.

Granda would have hated it. Vivienne might be amused but ulti-mately dismissive of the whole notion of temporary illusions being the goal.

He paused for a moment and reached for her with his mind the way he used to. There was nothing. She was either profoundly asleep, in a sylvan coma as it were, or she had died and gone to her afterlife.

"Hey mister."

Ruari came out of his reverie. A boy, maybe eight or nine years old, stood in front of him, wearing a flat newsie-style cap. Unruly brown hair stuck out from under it.

"Hi." He looked over the boy's head in the direction of the stage. "Where are your parents?"

The boy shrugged. "My dad's around." A faint cloud of smoke drifted out of his mouth.

Hmm. The boy looked like someone from the cast. Jeremy, was it? Ruari hadn't really tracked the kids. Maybe his dad was still in the changing room?

The boy walked around the shop looking with great curiosity at the equipment and the newly finished table.

"Hey, uh, don't touch anything okay? It's dangerous, and you could get hurt." Ruari didn't want to be blamed if the kid cut himself.

The boy put his hands behind his back. "I'll be careful."

"Do you like to build things?" Ruari remembered being drawn to the things in his Granda's shop.

"Yeah!" He sounded enthusiastic.

"This is the table we're going to use in the feast scene. We have to paint it and make it look more like a table first."

The boy nodded. He looked at Ruari and said solemnly, "I saw them fighting. I think they're going to do something bad. You gotta stop them, okay?" More smoke billowed from his mouth.

"Who? Mr. Verplank and Mr. Binkler?"

"Nah. The actors."

"Casey and Randall? What are they going to do?"

The boy nodded. He turned sharply as if he'd heard his name called and dashed off in the direction of the stage.

"Hey, wait! What are they going to do?"

Ruari walked quickly after him, through the black curtains shielding the wings of the stage from the audience, onto the stage. Binkler and Tommy were standing there staring up at the loft where the lights were.

"Which way did the kid go? Jeremy, I think." Ruari asked.

Both men looked at him in surprise.

"What kid?" Binkler asked.

"He just came into my shop. We talked about building props, and then he ran off like someone had called him. I thought he ran this way."

The two men looked at each other. Binkler said, "No kid ran through here. You must be mistaken."

Jeremy clearly knew the backstage area better than he did. He'd be back for rehearsal, and Ruari could ask him again. "Huh. Okay. I'm almost done with the feast table. I've double checked it for sturdiness. I'll work on the hutch for the dishes next. Is Scotty here yet?"

"Yes, but he's helping us get the lights changed."

"Okay. Send him my way when you're done."

"Will do."

Ruari returned to the scene shop and continued working on props. Jeremy's unexpected visit was clearly a case of a bored child finding things to entertain himself with. Why he would make up malicious stories about his cast mates was beyond Ruari.

Luckily, he had some time to build the dish cabinet that went behind the feast table. At least building a fake one went much faster than building a real one.

CHAPTER 15

id-afternoon on Monday, Marianne drove The
Flea to Mrs. Thomas' house. Her landlady lived in
one of the Victorian "grand ladies" on the uphill side of town.
The stately home was three stories tall with a small, ornately
pillared front porch that stepped down to the street. Golden
yellow siding was framed with a rich chocolate trim around the
windows, eaves, and porch pillars, and a whimsical turquoise
accented the porch ceiling, gingerbread trim under the eaves, and
around the windows.

Hitching her backpack onto her shoulder, she walked up the
front steps, and pressed the doorbell. A distant chime rang inside.
The inner door opened onto a woman in her thirties with short
blonde hair, wearing a dark green turtleneck under casual purple
scrubs. This must be Mrs. Thomas' latest helper, Miss Gina. Her
landlady seemed to change aides frequently.

"Yes, may I help you?" The woman asked.

"I'm Marianne Singleton. Mrs. Thomas invited me for tea
today."

The aide smiled. "Of course! Please come in. She's been
talking about your visit all day."

Marianne stepped inside out of the cold. "Should I take my shoes off?"

"That would be appreciated. You can leave your coat on that chair. I'll let Mrs. Thomas know you're here." Miss Gina stepped into a side room.

The spotless foyer was painted in a tasteful pale gray with darker gray trim. She appreciated the nod to the Victorian era sensibility. A large bouquet of dried flowers adorned an antique side table. She took off her coat and laid it across the arms of an antique chair then slipped off her shoes and tucked them beneath it.

The aide stepped back into the foyer. "Mrs. Thomas will see you now."

Marianne followed her into a front drawing room with a view onto the street. The view was framed by lacy white curtains and blocked by a large number of china figures, photos, and knickknacks on the table in front of the windows. A petite gentleman nodded to her politely from his seat in the corner of the room. She nodded back, wondering who else was here for tea.

Mrs. Thomas was seated in a wheelchair with many cushions. White hair framed her wizened features. Her spine was hunched from osteoporosis, but her eyes were lively, and her cheeks were pink. She tilted her head as Marianne entered.

"Marianne, I'm so glad you came. Please have a seat. Miss Gina will make us tea and bring some refreshments."

Marianne sat in one of the side chairs, facing the man in the corner and her landlady. Mrs. Thomas, who had excellent manners in spite of being forgetful, blithely ignored him. The aide didn't acknowledge his presence either. Miss Gina unlocked the wheelchair and angled it closer to Marianne before locking the brakes again and departing.

Marianne gave the little man in the corner a curious glance. He smiled mysteriously and shook his head slightly. *Oh, they don't know he's here. Maybe that's her husband?*

She cleared her throat and inquired politely, "How was your bingo tournament this weekend?"

Mrs. Thomas' benign features drew down into a scowl. "Marge DeVries beat the pants off me and took first place." She leaned forward conspiratorially. "I think she cheats and has her aide watch all the cards. I tried to get Miss Gina to help me out, but she wouldn't do it. If she didn't make such good tea, I'd replace her. Never mind. I'll win next year for sure! Marge has dementia and won't remember who she is by then."

"Oh, I see," Marianne replied, taken aback. She had no idea that Mrs. Thomas was such a cutthroat bingo player. *Note to self, don't get on her bad side. She might be rather vindictive.* She glanced at the gentleman in the corner, wondering how he would react.

He only had eyes for Mrs. Thomas and was unperturbed by her words. *Yup, he must be her husband.*

"Mrs. Thomas," she cleared her throat, "I came to ask you about the theater."

Her expression turned wistful. "Oh yes. Selwyn and I did a great deal of community theater over the years. It was great fun."

"I've been doing a little research on the Avery Theater and wondered if you could share some of your experiences with me." She got out her notebook. "Do you mind if I make some notes?"

"Please do. We mostly did musicals, you know, but we did a few straight plays as well. *A Doll's House* for one. So serious. I liked the fun, lighthearted ones better. *The King and I, Guys and Dolls.* Did you know, Selwyn and I met during *Peter Pan*? I was Pan to his Hook. He was very menacing with his hook." She giggled like a school girl.

"Did you ever experience any unusual things at the theater? Things that couldn't be explained easily, for instance."

"Oh my, yes. It didn't happen every time, but sometimes there were little jokes that no one admitted to doing." She chuckled. "When we did *Peter Pan,* we came to rehearsal one night and found a mannikin in the middle of the stage. It was wearing Wendy's night dress with Hook's huge feathered pirate hat on top, and the hook and sword lay on the floor as if they'd been dueling. It was quite a laugh! The costumer was very cross that someone had been handling her sewing form, and the props were not put away properly. It was just a bit of lighthearted fun, anyway, and no one was hurt."

Marianne stole a quick glance at Selwyn. He was grinning broadly, brandishing one hand as if it were a hook. Could he be the prankster at the Avery? Probably not. He seemed more keyed to Lily than the theater.

"Was there any speculation on who might have done it? Someone in the cast or crew?"

"Yes, but no one ever confessed to doing it."

"Did you know that similar things are happening during this production?"

"No, do tell!" She leaned forward eagerly.

Just then, Miss Gina returned with an old fashioned tea cart with a full tea service on the top shelf and a couple of plates with different kinds of cookies on the second shelf. Mrs. Thomas appeared to have pulled out the stops and gotten danishes from the Co-op bakery as well. Marianne took her time making a cup of tea and used silver tongs to place a cherry danish onto a white and gold china dessert plate while the aide made tea for Mrs. Thomas and served her an apple strudel. There was a snowy linen napkin for each of them. Miss Gina left the room once her charge was settled.

"Mrs. Thomas, this is lovely. Thank you for making this such a special occasion. My grandmother Selene and I often have tea together."

"She's a lovely person, your grandmother. I like her very much."

"Me too."

Mrs. Thomas leaned forward again. "You were going to tell me all about the *Sleepy Hollow* production! Give me all the gossip!"

"Well, they've had some strange happenings a little like the one you described. Someone took all the shoes and wigs and put them on the backs of chairs in the auditorium."

Mrs. Thomas laughed, clattering her teacup in its saucer. "Oh yes! That was a favorite trick. Another time, all the women's shoes ended up in the men's dressing room and vicey-versy."

"When did this happen? Was it connected with anything in particular?"

"It happened four or five times in all the years we did plays. It never bothered me, though it did make Selwyn cross at times. Other people got quite exercised about it." She grew thoughtful. "I don't think it ever happened during the performances, now that I think of it. Only during rehearsals."

Interesting. Hopefully, there would be some limits on the pranks for this production.

Marianne continued. "I found out that the Avery was built in 1910 after a previous theater, the Averill, burned down. When were you and Selwyn in plays?"

"I was in plays from a very early age. But I'm certainly not old enough to have been at the Averill! That was before my time. I have a couple of memory albums somewhere." She grabbed a silver bell with a wooden handle on the side table and shook it. It made a silvery jingle. "Miss Gina!"

The aide appeared in the doorway shortly after.

Maybe that's why she goes through aides. Running for the bell and being asked to cheat at bingo would get old fast. It doesn't sound like Mrs. Thomas has any first hand knowledge of the Averill. Too bad.

"Yes, Mrs. Thomas?"

"Would you go into my reading room and get my theater albums? The ones with the black and green covers. Be careful, dear, they're fragile." The aide turned to leave, and Mrs. Thomas said conspiratorially, "She's a little careless sometimes if I don't remind her."

Marianne glanced at Gina. Her stiff shoulders indicated she'd heard every word. Marianne wondered if there would be a new aide soon. "You have photo albums of your theater days! I'd love to see them."

"Photographs, old playbills, ticket stubs, news articles. It's all there. Selwyn's and my life in pictures. My parents were in vaudeville and theater too, you know."

"Were they at the Averill?" Marianne perked up

"No, they were in the opening show for the new Avery theater. Before that, they'd been in shows at the Bardavon in Poughkeepsie, in the Catskills, and all over New York in the early 1900s. They came to Maple Hill in 1910, and I was born in 1925. In this very house."

"You've lived here all your life?"

"Yes, I have. I'm a real native. Your grandmother was my first real friend, though. She's true blue, through and through."

"That she is."

Miss Gina returned bearing two large scrapbooks. Mrs. Thomas fussed until they were laid out on the coffee table in front of her. The aide stepped back, and Mrs. Thomas said, "Stay and turn the pages for me, won't you?"

"I could do it, if you're okay with that?" Marianne said. Miss Gina looked carefully neutral.

"Very well. You may go." The aide departed.

Mrs. Thomas had her open the larger of the two, and Marianne was treated to photos of an adorable four-year old girl dressed as a waif, Lily in a frock and wearing Shirley Temple curls, followed by all manner of costumes to the 1970s. Selwyn had joined her in the 1950s, during a fateful production of *Peter Pan*. He'd been a charming character actor, singing tenor roles while she'd sung lyric soprano.

"Mrs. Thomas, I'm writing a short piece about the history of the Avery for the Playbill of the current production. Would you mind if I include some of your thoughts and experiences?"

"Not at all."

As the pages turned, Mrs. Thomas grew more wistful.

"I miss him."

Marianne glanced up from the pages and did a double take. Selwyn sat on the sofa next to his wife, gazing fondly at the scrapbook with them. He caught her eye, winked, and shook his head slightly.

He didn't want to be outed. "I think our loved ones are always near by," she murmured.

Lily Thomas patted her hand. "Of course, you're right, dear. There are days when I feel like he's right here in this room. But it isn't really the same."

A few minutes passed as they turned the pages to the end of the album.

"Is this your parents' album? May I see it?" Marianne asked.

"Of course." The old woman waved her hand at the smaller black-bound book.

She took it carefully into her lap. The covers were heavy cardboard, and the word "Album" was spelled out in graceful, cursive gold foil. Inside, there were only a dozen or so pages compared to the full album of memorabilia that was Lily's life. Sepia toned photos depicted a gorgeous woman with tightly waved dark hair and a handsome man with strong features. Lily's mother had been a babe, and her father would have given Valentino a run for his money. Marianne could see the echoes of their faces in Lily's lips and cheekbones. They had made the cover of *Hudson Valley Theater Magazine* in 1913. Marianne made a note of the title as a potential lead to track down and finished looking at the rest of the album.

She became aware of the silence in the room. Mrs. Thomas dozed in her chair, and Selwyn was gone. Marianne carefully closed the old album and laid it on the coffee table.

"Mrs. Thomas?" She said quietly. "Mrs. Thomas?" Gently she patted the old woman's knee.

"Mmm, yes?" She roused a little.

"Thank you for tea. I loved hearing about your life in the theater. Thank you for sharing that with me. I need to go, and I'll see myself out. Do you want me to get Miss Gina for you?"

"Thank you for coming, dear. I'll be fine."

Marianne put her notebook away and left the parlor as quietly as she could. She went down the hall and peeked in the kitchen. Gina was sitting at the table doing a word search puzzle.

"Thanks for the tea and food. I appreciate it. Mrs. Thomas fell asleep, so I'm going to go. You don't need to see me out."

The aide nodded and got up to check on her charge. Marianne followed her out to the foyer, donned her shoes and coat and slung her pack over her shoulder.

She'd learned more about her landlady than she'd really wanted to know. Although she hadn't had any direct experiences with the Averill, she'd given Marianne a new lead with the *Hudson Valley Theater Magazine*. Maybe Mrs. Caldwell could find old issues. With any luck there would be hot gossip about the *Sleepy Hollow* production of 1909.

On her way home, Marianne parked in the lot next to the Avery and walked to the library. She crossed her fingers it wasn't too late to catch Mrs. Caldwell. She hurried down the stairs to the Historical Society room.

"We're closing for the evening," the librarian said primly.

"I just had a quick question, Mrs. C. Does the library have copies or microfiche of *Hudson Valley Theater Magazine?*"

"Hmm. It doesn't sound familiar." She turned to her computer and tapped a few keys. "No, we don't."

"I came across a reference to the magazine in an old scrapbook and was hoping it might hold some articles about the Averill fire."

Mrs. Caldwell's fingers tapped more keys. After a moment she said, "It doesn't look like anyone has it. There were many little regional magazines for this and that. Most of them don't have surviving copies."

"Rats. How is the request going for *Theater Talk* magazine?"

Mrs. Caldwell checked the records. "That one seems to be scheduled for arrival next week."

Disappointed, Marianne sighed. "That may be too late for me to include in my research for the Playbill. Let me know when it gets here."

"Will do." She looked at the clock over the door. "I'm terribly sorry. It's closing time."

Marianne went home and found Oscar comfortably ensconced on the dog bed in the living room, his head pillowed on his back feet. She shook her head. "What are you going to do if Rita shows up and wants her bed back?"

Oscar flicked his ears and stayed asleep.

She ducked into her office, typed up the notes from her visit, printed them out, and slipped them into the file folder for the theater. She checked her email and found a form reply from the Canopus County Parks and Recreation Department saying they had received her application for a historic plaque for Turner's Pond, and it would take up to six weeks for them to review it. Marianne printed out that email and tucked it into the Turner's Hope/O'Meara folder. At least if Peter O'Meara got restive about his "payment," she could say it was under advisement. If he wasn't happy with their progress, he could go haunt their office, not hers.

This late in November it was already dark by five o'clock. Ruari didn't come home for dinner. He'd texted earlier to confirm he would be working in his shop on the new lazy Susan after rehearsal was over. Erin had spent the day at the dentist's office and texted to say she'd be out for dinner with a friend. The quiet house made her feel lonely.

The last of the fried chicken warmed up in the microwave, and she wondered how she could sneak into the rehearsal tonight. If she could just prowl around the theater again, she might get a better sense of who was haunting the place. But she was going to have to come up with a plausible story if she ran into Dave Binkler again. She was just putting her plate in the dishwasher when she heard a commotion in the living room.

Oscar stood on the new dog bed looking fierce, his back arched and fur bristled out. His fangs were bared and ears were flat against his skull. He hissed furiously at the empty living room. Quickly Marianne closed her eyes and swung her head looking for his attacker.

Rita stood two feet away from the bed, her head cocked to one side, looking more bemused than menacing. Her tail waved back and forth once. Now that she knew where to look, Marianne opened her eyes and saw the faint outline of the big Newfie. Oscar raised his paw and swatted at Rita's nose in a rapid double tap. His claws didn't land, but Rita jerked her head back and growled. She let out an affronted bark, and Oscar leaped from the bed and streaked past Marianne down the hall in a ginger and white blur.

Having won the field, Rita stepped onto the new bed, turned around three times, and lay down with a satisfied grunt.

"What am I going to do with you, Rita? You guys are going to have to get along or you'll have to go live in the garage."

Rita thumped her tail and lay her head on her front paws. Slowly she faded away.

Oscar was in the office on her desk, licking his paws and washing his face. He glared at her balefully as if to say, *Get rid of that dog!*

She sat in her chair and gathered the tabby into her arms. "I know you're unhappy, Oscar. I was hoping you two would figure out how to get along. I got the beds for Rita. If you need a special bed, I'll find something for you."

She tried cuddling the cat. "We've been through a lot together, Oscar. Rita will never take your place with me." He braced his forepaw against her chest and looked away. Reluctantly, she let him jump out of her arms and stalk toward the front door.

"Fine, be mad." It was dark and cold out, but he meowed insistently at the door. Reluctantly she let him out. "This seems like a bad idea, but here you go, Mister." She'd only be gone for a couple of hours, and he'd survived being on the streets of New York before she found him in the shelter. Likely he'd be sitting on the front step waiting for her when she came home.

He exited without a backward glance. He'd always come home before. She had to trust he would do so again. She left for the Avery shortly after.

❀

Of all the obnoxious things in my life, that stupid dog has to be the worst. I can't believe Marianne invited her to stay! I could be curled up on the sofa enjoying the comforts of my own home, but instead I'm standing outside in the cold while that dog gets a new bed. If I stay out tonight, Marianne will kick that mutt to the curb.

Oscar lashed his tail furiously and bounded down the steps as the door opened behind him.

Nighttime muted the outdoors into grays and blues, but the outlines of things were as sharp as ever. *Humans and their weak eyes.* Oscar strolled into the undergrowth at the end of the cul-de-sac and prowled, ears alert for interesting noises. He followed the scent of mice and fainter traces of squirrels.

Who needs a dog anyway? We were doing just fine on our own. First Erin, now a dog. That horrid female with all her awful smells in their bottles, it's enough to obliterate any sensitive nose. Then that big lunk starts hanging around. It's bad enough that she's a dog, but she's a ghost too. It'll make anyone's fur stand on end.

A slight noise made Oscar freeze. His ears rotated trying to find the sound again, but it was gone. After a moment, he continued down the side of a house. The countryside had a lot fewer hazards than the city did with its many humans, cars, and feral dogs. He'd learned to avoid most of those things and felt like the king of his neighborhood most of the time. He knew of a little place where he could shelter out of the cold for a while. There was a house that had an abandoned dog house in the back-

175

yard that was pretty safe. He could stay there until first light and enjoy listening to Marianne calling for him. *Not coming back while that dog is in my house.*

Or I get hungry. Hopefully she'll get the hint by morning, and I can enjoy my breakfast in peace with lots of cuddles and apologies.

Another noise, this one louder and sharper, made him freeze again. Up ahead there was the clank of metal followed by the sounds of tearing bags. Oscar crept closer to the source of the disturbance.

A lean dog had knocked over a trash can and was rooting through the debris, looking for scraps. *Hah, who left Fido out overnight? Bet you're gonna regret that one. Lots of barfs on your carpet and complaints from your neighbors.*

He was about to saunter on, when a slight breeze wafted in Oscar's direction, passing over the scavenger. Instantly, all his fur stood on end. The smell of trash was mingled with the much wilder, sharper scent of danger. That was no dog. Oscar had only smelled coyote in the city once, and it left an indelible impression. This one was lean and hungry, and Oscar was on her menu. He froze as the breeze wandered around aimlessly, banking along the side of the house and doubling back on itself.

Please don't smell me. Please don't see me.

The coyote raised her head, sniffing the air. Then she looked straight at Oscar.

Oh shit.

Bravado vaporized and Oscar ran for it. The coyote decided fresh meat would taste better than garbage scraps. Oscar raced ahead looking for a safe spot, the coyote on his tail. He raced across a backyard and darted through a hole in a fence.

There was a brief scramble while the coyote pushed herself through the boards. Oscar gained a few precious feet. He would have climbed a tree, but they were all stupidly small. He dashed across another yard and under a parked car. The coyote caught up and prowled around the vehicle. She crouched down and tried to push her way under, her stinky breath wafting to his nose.

Heart thudding in his chest, he hissed a warning. "I'll take your face off if you come near me!"

She made no reply but continued searching for another way under the car. Her silent persistence was unnerving. She would get him if it took all night. He wrapped his tail around his feet and watched her warily. At the rear of the car, she began squirming under with more success. Her eyes gleamed with predatory intensity.

Oscar broke and ran, hoping she would get stuck. He fled toward the next yard and recognized where he was. No fence separating this yard from the copse of trees at the end of the cul-de-sac. He was nearly home! He could hide in the garage. There was at least one shelf high enough that he'd be safe. Probably.

The coyote was right behind him, though, paws scrabbling through the dead grass. Oscar could hear her panting. She was gaining on him. He wasn't going to make it.

Oscar passed through a cold patch of air and suddenly there was a thunderous barking right behind him. Another dog had joined the coyote!

I can't outrun two of them.

Oscar sped blindly into the garage and leapt as high as he could onto the nearest available surface. He turned to face his attackers and flexed his claws.

I'm not going down without a fight.

A huge spectral dog stood in the driveway barking furiously at Oscar's pursuer. The coyote stopped and dodged left and right, looking confused, and trying to get around Rita. Rita matched her move for move, teeth bared. The coyote decided a hot meal to go was no longer worth the effort and vanished back into the copse of trees in search of a more docile meal.

Rita let off one more bark, *And don't come back! This is my house!* Then she trotted into the garage and stood wagging her tail at Oscar.

Oscar hissed.

Aw, c'mon. I chased the mean dog away.

Oscar sat down. "Sorry. Reflex."

Can't we be friends?

Oscar regarded her silently as his heart slowed, and his fur calmed down. It felt uncomfortable, out of place. He would need to spend some serious time putting it all in order. He probably would have been safe up here until Marianne got home. But that coyote had a crazy look in her eye. She might just have figured out how to reach him. Oscar might have been able to do some damage on the way, but all that would've been left was a few tufts of fur and a mess. Without Rita he might have been coyote food.

"I guess," he said reluctantly.

Rita panted happily and bounced a few times in place. *Yay! That's great! We'll be the best of friends!*

"Don't get cocky, dog. You still can't open doors or cans of food. Let's get one thing straight: it's my house not yours. I was here first."

Sorry, reflex. Rita grinned and sat down.

Oscar settled down to groom while he waited for someone to come home and let him inside.

Marianne arrived a few minutes before six, parked in the side lot by Ruari's truck, and slipped into the scene shop again. Ruari had felt confident enough in his position to keep letting her in, but she'd promised to be on her own as long as she was there. She shut the door behind her, their signal that she was in. This time her plan was to sneak up to the balcony and watch from there. As long as no one was up there to adjust the huge spot lights, she'd be able to observe without being seen. She tiptoed up the curving stairs to the balcony and slipped into a seat in the far corner.

The house lights were already dimmed, and the stage lights were on. Tommy and his stage manager were seated in their favorite spot four rows from the front. She didn't see Ruari. After a brief talk, Tommy sent people back to the wings to start rehearsal with the scene change.

"Okay everybody, I want you to set up the feast as quickly and quietly as you can. Go!" Tommy shouted. "Make it look beautiful."

Four men in their costumes brought out two long, plank tables. Two women threw a long white table cloth over it and smoothed it out. A whole bunch of people carrying plates, food, baskets, candlesticks, and a host of other props came out. For the most part, they set the table with a minimum of getting in each other's way, and Marianne was impressed. As soon as their prop was placed, each person left the stage.

Tommy pressed the stopwatch in his hand. "That was sixty-five seconds. Pretty good. We'll keep working on it. Remember, the audience is out here waiting for you. They want to see the play, not you setting the scene. Okay, let's go from the end of Maud's scene and take it to the end of Act II."

The cast came out onto the stage and arranged themselves in groups of people enjoying a party. Katrina stood in front with her hands on her head looking down. Ichabod stood at the table of food, pretending to eat and talk with some of the older men. Brom and his friend were surrounded by young women on the other side of the stage. Marianne had just read the original story recently and couldn't remember anyone named Maud. *Ah, this must be the scene the director added. A sort of 'ghosts of Van Tassels past.'*

Tommy said, "Okay, go!"

Katrina straightened and looked around her wildly. Ichabod approached her and said, "Are you well, Mistress Katrina?"

"Yes, I'm fine." She smiled bravely. Marianne wondered what had happened in the previous scene. Jumping around like this during rehearsal was confusing. She looked forward to seeing the whole play from start to finish.

Ichabod took Katrina's hand and made a little bow. He gazed into her eyes and said, "Would you care to dance with me?"

Marianne wondered if Randall was talking to Tayloe in that moment.

Katrina smiled. "I'd love to." Together the two of them danced a little hesitantly, clearly waiting for something. Marianne noticed that there was a painted trio of musicians in the background.

"Stop! Scotty!" Tommy yelled. "Where's the sound cue?"

A distant voice came from somewhere below Marianne. "Sorry, I'm on it."

A burst of folk music resolved itself into a toe-tapping rhythm. Ichabod and Katrina picked up the pace, and four other couples joined them. Brom and his friend danced a little more vigorously than the others and boxed Ichabod and Katrina in. Brom's friend bumped Ichabod, and Katrina careened into Brom.

"Katrina," Brom exclaimed, "come, dance with me!" He deftly swung his partner into Ichabod who let go of Katrina in order to catch the other woman. Brom swept Katrina away, leaving Ichabod and the other woman staring after them unhappily. They stepped out of the way of the other couples. Katrina laughed as Brom twirled her around.

When the music stopped, everyone settled down. A huge spinning wheel came out on stage, and the matron of the house sat next to it while the other women positioned themselves near her. The men brought out long-necked Meerschaum pipes and got flagons, presumably of ale, and sat down nearby. Brom tried to get Katrina to sit on his lap, but she laughed and pulled away. She sat next to her friend instead. The lights dimmed and became more like shadowy firelight.

"Who remembers the tale of poor Major André?" The matron asked as the wheel began to spin.

Marianne appreciated the symbolism of the spinning wheel and spinning tales by firelight.

Together, the cast told two spooky tales of ghosts and enjoyed scaring each other. Finally, someone piped up, "And what about the Headless Horseman?"

Marianne had done a little research on the subject and learned that the Headless Horseman was a figure who appeared in many stories across the British Isles, Holland, and Germany. Washington Irving had travelled in all of those places in the late 1700s to early 1800s and probably drew inspiration from some of them. He'd made the story uniquely American by writing *The Legend of Sleepy Hollow*.

Brom stood up and said, "I myself have faced the Headless Horseman just this summer past." People shifted and leaned closer to hear. He put one foot up on a chair and spread his arms, gathering in his listeners. "I was riding down the old road toward the church near midnight when I came across another rider standing on the side of the road. His horse was huge and black with eyes like embers. The man himself had no head at all above his cloak. He stood as silent as the grave. I approached him and called out, 'Who are you, sir? Are you lost?' "

Brom really got into his story, his voice rising and falling with his words. His stage audience was rapt. Marianne watched Ichabod staring fixedly at Brom with an expression of growing unease while Katrina sat huddled with her friend Katie.

Brom said, "And he answered me not. I thought it quite rude, so I asked again. 'Who are you, sir? I expect an answer!' Finally, I heard a voice saying, 'I am the Horseman of Doom. Ride against me at your peril.' "

Casey lowered his voice to an intense whisper. "His voice did not come from the air above his shoulders. No. It came from the saddle in front of him. His severed head was wedged firmly between his legs and his saddle bow. His dead eyes glared at me."

Everyone gasped and watched in fearful suspense. Even the matron had stopped her spinning.

"I will race you to the churchyard for a bowl of punch! His horse stamped, throwing sparks, and he said in sepulchral tones, 'If you lose, I will cast you into the fires of Hell.' I accept, sir! We race! And I spurred my horse, Daredevil, without further ado.

"We raced at a breakneck pace down the hill and through the close woods. The night was pitch-black, and tree limbs nearly swept me from my saddle. All the while the black horseman raced with me neck and neck, stride for stride. He seemed to pass through the very trees that I had to dodge and jump over. I saw the white bridge over the stream ahead of me, and the silent rider drew ahead. Not wanting to spend the rest of eternity in Hell and wanting my bowl of punch, I spurred Daredevil with my heels and my whip. He surged forward and drew even just as we reached the bridge. I kicked Daredevil again, and he pulled ahead just as our hooves landed on the other side."

There was a collective "oh!" Ichabod looked like he was ready to faint with fear.

"I looked back and saw the Headless Horseman rear up, screaming in rage before he vanished in a flash of thunder and fire." Brom winked at Katrina. "And I never saw my bowl of punch!"

Everyone laughed, and the men pounded Brom on his back and drank from their flagons.

A clock struck three in the background.

Mr. Van Tassel stood up and said, " 'Tis the witching hour and time for us all to be in our beds. This has truly been a wonderful night."

The party broke up with women pulling shawls around themselves and men putting their hats on. There were muted voices of well wishes and farewells and see-you-on-the-morrow. Ichabod drew Katrina aside and took her hand. She looked at him with shining eyes. Brom scowled and departed with his friend. As the crowd thinned, Ichabod and Katrina appeared to be deep in conversation. He knelt on one knee holding her hand. She replied and shook her head. She pulled her hand away, drew her shawl around her, and exited the stage. Ichabod stood looking like his world had fallen apart. He put on his hat and walked dejectedly off stage in the other direction. The lights went down, and there were the sounds of the feast being dismantled.

Marianne was truly impressed. All of Ruari's tales of the feckless Casey had been exploded. He had managed to hold everyone spellbound. She could see why Tommy wanted so badly to bring this play to the public. It had some real moments of magic.

"Come on, people," Tommy shouted and snapped his fingers. "We need to speed up this set change."

Hurried footsteps and whispers sounded from behind the curtain.

The curtain went up again on a darkened road.

Ichabod walked slowly along. He was wearing a prop horse around his waist. Its head drooped, and its tail looked scraggly.

"Come on, Gunpowder, giddyup!" Ichabod danced a little sideways before returning to a plod. The sound of wind and the hoots of an owl added a sense of spookiness. Gunpowder shied away from things before Ichabod tried whistling. It was no more than a thready sounding breath, so he tried singing,"All Hail the Power of Jesus' Name," but his voice came out thin and reedy, and he soon stopped.

"Come now, Gunpowder, we must get home. There will be hot mash for you. Be a good boy. Oh, who am I kidding? I don't have hot mash for me much less for you." He stopped with a jerk. "What was that?"

Another horse and rider had appeared on the opposite side of the stage. This horse was much larger and completely black. Its eyes glowed reddish. A figure sat astride it, but the shadows made it hard to see.

Ichabod halted and said to himself, "What shadow is this? Surely it is no more than a twisted tree trunk." He advanced a few steps and stopped again. "No, 'tis the apparition of a huge horse. The rider is obscured. I say, who are you, good sir?"

The rider said nothing.

"Oh, why won't he speak?" He said to himself. Then he spoke up, " 'Tis a fine night to be out and about, good sir. Speak your name and let me pass."

The rider said nothing. The light on stage improved as if the moon had emerged from a cloud.

"Oh! The rider, he has no head! Are you the Headless Horseman, sir? I have no wish to race you, only to get home to my bed with my skin intact."

Ichabod moved to pass by the silent rider, but the huge horse stepped in his path. Marianne held her breath.

"I pray you, I beg you let me pass!" Ichabod said in quavering tones.

The horseman said in a raspy voice, "I am the Horseman of Doom. Ride against me to the churchyard." A head appeared on the saddle bow.

Ichabod shrieked, "No, just let me pass!" He dodged around the other horse and plunged away. The huge black horse reared up and started to give chase.

"Stop!" Tommy yelled. "You both need to be further over to stage right before you do this. You have to have someplace to run to. Make it look more like you're on a horse, not wearing a skirt. Start again from the top of the scene."

They reran the scene twice more before Tommy was satisfied and let them proceed. When they came to the churchyard and the little bridge, Ichabod had trouble with his horse before finally tearing off the prop and flinging it away. He stumbled onto the bridge with the Headless Horseman right behind him. The Horseman reared up, and the rider flung a round pumpkin at Ichabod. It hit him squarely on the back of the head with an audible thunk. Ichabod reached the other side of the bridge, cried out, and fell. Marianne winced. The stage went dark.

"Bring the lights back up. Okay, let's go back to the middle of the chase. We need to fix some things. Get your props back and let's reset."

Ichabod got up, rubbing the back of his head, a look of fury on his face. Brom sauntered back to his spot clearly ignoring him. Marianne blinked. For a moment, it looked like there were two figures where Ichabod stood, one larger than the other. The same with Brom. But she couldn't be sure because the stage lights came from different directions and cast odd shadows anyway. She blinked again, and they were gone.

Dave Binkler was up on stage. He took the prop pumpkin from Randall and walked it over to Casey. He said a few words and Casey nodded. Randall retrieved his prop horse and secured it around his waist again. Tommy began walking them through the scene step by step again.

Marianne slipped out of the balcony and headed for the

entrance to the side hallway from the lobby. The corridor was empty, but she heard the echoes of voices at the far end. She needed to check in with Tayloe.

Knowing Binkler was on stage, she went down to the door marked Green Room and peeked inside. People in costume sat or stood, filling the room. She recognized Tristan in a tricorn hat, purple jacket, and hose sitting with several children around him. He was folding brightly colored paper. Two of the older children were watching him closely and folding paper as well. He glanced up and caught her eye. Marianne gave a small, polite smile and a quick nod before looking away. Tayloe was sitting at the makeup table looking at her reflection and adding some mascara and lipstick. Marianne tried to catch her eye, but Tayloe steadfastly ignored her.

"Are you looking for someone, dear?" The woman dressed as Mrs. Van Tassel asked.

"Actually, I was hoping for a word with Tayloe."

"I'll get her for you." She stepped away and bent over Tayloe's shoulder. Tayloe looked at Marianne through the reflection in the mirror. Goosebumps prickled Marianne's arms. That wasn't the same Tayloe she'd met the other day. Her rounded cheekbones, full lips, and small nose were the same, but the brown eyes that looked out from under the soft brows were hard.

Tayloe came to the door. She coolly looked Marianne up and down without recognition. "Yes?"

Marianne was taken aback and said quietly, "Tayloe, it's me. You asked me to keep an eye on you during rehearsal."

"No, I didn't." Then she narrowed her eyes and looked at Marianne again. "Wait. You're the one she met with." She shook her head dismissively. "You can go away. She doesn't need you. We don't need you."

"But, you asked me—" Marianne began in confusion.

"Excuse me, what are you doing here again?" Mr. Binkler had approached down the hall without her noticing. "I told you to stay in the public areas." He addressed Tayloe. "Is this woman bothering you?"

Tayloe's expression crumpled instantly and her eyes watered. "Yes, she is. Please make her go away." Tayloe turned away and returned to her seat at the makeup table where she leaned her head in her hands as her shoulders shook.

Marianne was both shocked and impressed by Tayloe's theatrics. She hadn't thought the young woman was capable of it. Clearly, her drama convinced the stage manager.

"That's it," Binkler said with a frown. "I'll call the police if you don't leave right now. I can't have you harassing my actors." He pulled his shoulders back and glared at her, completely failing to look intimidating. But the threat of having the police arrive was a problem.

Marianne put her hands up in surrender. "You don't have to do that. I'm leaving." As she turned, she caught Tristan's cool gaze, watching her thoughtfully until a child in an old fashioned dress tugged on his arm to show him a paper crane she'd made, and Tristan looked away.

"You totally rocked that, man! You were on fire!" Jake slapped him on the back in the crowded dressing room.

Casey grinned. He *had* rocked that whole scene. They'd been eating out of the palm of his hand. Plus he'd brained that idiot good. He flexed his football arm as he pulled on his tee shirt.

How had he ever thought acting in plays was stupid? Well, it had been when he was in high school. He'd spent a lot of time making fun of all the nerds in the Theater Club with his jock friends and never set foot on the stage himself.

But now it was different. Casey figured that was because he was older, and this was a professional theater. When Mom and Dad had suggested he try out for the play, he'd resisted. They'd told him it would "round out his application to college," and they made it sound like he'd better do it. He hadn't made a football scholarship, and his grades had been average at best, lower than average more often. The gap year had been the high school counselor's suggestion along with the idea that maybe he should consider trade school. The apprenticeship at Mom's rental business was supposed to provide "real world experience." But he'd gotten the feeling that his parents were not that excited about his entering the trades. After a month and a half of being with that loser Ruari, he could see their point. Too much work. He was cut out for better things.

He'd auditioned for the play figuring he wouldn't get in. He would have shown his parents he'd done what they asked and then got to spend a fun winter skiing instead. At least his buddy Jake had agreed to try out with him. But then they'd both gotten in. Not only that, Casey had gotten the juicy part of Brom Bones. He was all ready to goof off and do the least he could, but then it had become something he'd never expected: fun.

In fact, the part of Brom came to him so naturally that he'd actually looked forward to rehearsals. When he thought about it at home, he got a little nervous about standing on stage, in front of lots of people, pretending to be someone else. But when he got here, all that went away. It was easier than he'd expected to memorize lines. Even when the stupid director kept changing the script. He'd had to swallow his annoyance that Verplank and The Bink kept insisting he stand in certain places when it felt much more natural to stand somewhere else and recite his lines.

He hung up his Brom clothes more neatly than he did his own. It was important to look cool on stage. Sitting on the bench, he pulled his fancy high tops on. Jake was nearly done, too.

The people had been a surprising bonus. Tayloe Walker was so hot, he had to think about cold showers for the first couple of rehearsals or he'd embarrass himself. Tayloe didn't make it easy, though. She flirted so hard with Brom he was sure she was trying to tell Casey she thought he was a total stud. He'd even asked her out a couple of times, but she'd always found a way to say no. So far. She was so confusing.

When Randall had shown he had it bad for Tayloe, too, that just made Casey simmer. What right did that low-life son of a mechanic have to horn in on his girl? Just because she hadn't said yes *yet*, didn't mean she wouldn't say yes if Casey just asked her the right way.

Then there was the ugly surprise when Ruari Allen had shown up. Ruari had always made him feel like a dumb little kid who couldn't learn anything. And he'd never been satisfied with the job Casey had done, always asking him to do more things. When Mom had told him that Ruari had been fired, Casey had been savagely glad. Then he'd shown up at the theater. Damn these stupid small towns. After the first meeting, Ruari had left him alone, but Casey always had the feeling that the handyman was watching him out of the corner of his eye, waiting for him to screw up.

It might have been a little petty to tweak the set the other night, but at least it meant that Ruari was too busy fixing things to bug him. The others pranks weren't Casey's fault at all, and it made him mad to be accused of things he hadn't done.

"Hey, Earth to Casey," Jake said again.

"What?"

Jake lifted his chin to indicate Randall had come in to change into his street clothes. The locker room—dressing room— was less crowded than it had been. Casey stood up, put on his jacket and grabbed his wallet off the top shelf of the clothing rack and slid it into his back pocket. Jake caught his eye, and they both headed for the door at the same time. Casey took the bump from Jake as if they'd planned it just as he walked past Randall and staggered into the other guy. Randall was knocked off balance, one leg in and one leg out of his costume pants. He would have fallen on his ass if the bench hadn't been there.

"Oh, sorry, man!" Casey said, fake sincere. "You okay? No hard feelings about tonight, right?"

Randall just gave him a furious glare and would have said something, but one of the dads was still in the room, and he clamped his mouth shut instead.

Casey and Jake walked out of the room, holding in their laughter just long enough to get to the hallway. They roared all the way to the exit.

Tayloe pulled off her fancy Katrina ball gown and hung it up with shaking fingers. She tugged the wig off, heedless of the bobby pins pulling strands of her own hair and plopped the hair piece onto the foam head.

Katie touched her arm. "Tay, slow down. What's going on? Are you okay?"

She pulled on her pants and turtleneck. "I don't want to do this anymore, Katie. I'm gonna go to Mr. Verplank and quit."

"But Tay, the show opens in a week! Who's going to be Katrina?"

"I don't know. Golden Years just added twenty hours to my shift. I can't do my job and the play at the same time."

"I'm sure if you told your boss you're in the play and can't do those hours, he'd find someone else."

Tayloe shook her head. She stepped into her sensible shoes and grabbed her purse and coat. "Sorry, Katie." And she flung herself out of the dressing room before her friend could make her change her mind. After tonight, she had to quit. Out on stage, she'd felt powerful, feminine, and supremely frustrated with how Casey and Randall had behaved. Those men, those boys, were childish and infuriating! She'd wanted to slap both of them silly.

And that's what scared her. She'd never hit anyone in her life. Marianne had come to the Green Room at some point in the rehearsal, and Tayloe had acted like they'd never met. Something was wrong with her. She needed to get away from this place, this play. She'd never imagined that her job would feel safer than the theater.

Her feet carried her to the director's office. He was at his desk, putting his notes together after rehearsal. "Tayloe, or should I say Katrina! That was a magnificent performance you gave this evening. The chemistry between you and Brom and Ichabod is fantastic."

She clutched the strap of her purse where it hung over her shoulder. "Um, that's what I wanted to talk to you about, Mr. Verplank. My job is adding twenty hours to my schedule next week, and I don't think I can do the play anymore."

Mr. Verplank's face fell, leaving his mouth comically open in surprise. "But, Tayloe, it's opening week. You can't quit. There's no time to bring an understudy up to speed. Please don't say that!"

"I—I just think I can't do the play justice and keep my job, sir."

"You work at Golden Years Retirement Home, right?"

She nodded.

"I'll give them a call first thing in the morning and make sure they change your schedule. I know someone who works there. I'm sure they'll give you the time off."

Miserably, Tayloe let her shoulders fall. There was no way she could get out. "There's no need for that, sir. I'll stay. I'll make it work."

"That's my girl! Maybe after this play, you'll have more theater opportunities. You have a lot of talent. Maybe you can quit nursing for a life on stage!"

She nodded mechanically and left. She'd invented the added shifts in hopes that would provide a solid excuse to quit. What could she do?

She still had Marianne's number.

"Hello?" Marianne sounded a little sleepy. Tayloe felt guilty waking her up, but the woman had said she could call night or day.

"Hi, this is Tayloe. I'm sorry to wake you up. Do you have a minute?"

"Of course. What's wrong?"

"I'm really freaking out after tonight's rehearsal. I just tried to quit the play, but Mr. Verplank won't let me. I don't know what to do. I'm scared!"

"Okay…"

"I'm sorry I was so rude to you. I don't know what came over me. I apologize."

"There's nothing to apologize for. Tell me what happened."

Tayloe told her.

"That would scare me, too. I once had something similar happen to me. I was not myself." She remembered a certain camping trip all too vividly.

"What did you do?"

"I kept going forward one step at a time. Eventually, I got past the scary part."

"I don't know. This is really freaking me out."

"You haven't hurt anyone or yourself so far, right?"

"No."

"Then there's a good chance you won't. I'm afraid Mr. Binkler asked me not to come back." She thought for a moment. "I can ask Ruari to keep an eye on you. If you're okay with that."

"Does he know what's going on?"

"More or less."

"I guess so." It wasn't great, but she knew she was the reason why Marianne couldn't come back.

"The play opens in a week, right?" Marianne asked.

"Yes. Opening night is next Thursday."

"There are six shows?"

"Eight."

"I'll think of something. In the meantime, I'll make an herbal charm like the ones your aunts Sarah and Kelly make, and you can carry that for protection against negative energies."

"Okay. Promise?"

"I promise. I'll do everything I can to keep you safe."

Tayloe let out a breath. "Thanks. I'm sorry I woke you up. And I'm sorry I got you kicked out."

"No, no. It's okay. I'll see you tomorrow. You'll feel better if you get some rest."

"Okay. Good night."

CHAPTER 17

Tuesday morning, after breakfast had been cleaned up and Erin had left for the dentist's office, Marianne watched Ruari get his things together for the day. There was an endless number of things to do at the theater, and he planned to be there all day.

"I'm going to Hair Magic and Sarah's law firm today and consult with them," she said. "If they act like they're too busy, I'll stick around until they notice me."

"Sounds like a plan," he replied. "I'm sorry they're being so difficult."

"It's like they couldn't wait to get rid of the Protector job. As soon as I said I *might* do it, they dumped both it and me."

"Maybe you're reading too much into it?" He suggested.

She shook her head. "I feel like they're avoiding me. Now they're expecting me to take care of Kelly's niece." She grimaced. "Sorry, I'm just complaining."

He put his hands gently on either side of her face and looked her in the eyes. "They've definitely dumped responsibility on you and that's not fair. It's not your job to take care of someone you barely know. Don't let your compassion paint you into a corner."

She sighed. "You're right. More waifs and strays. But Tayloe is scared, and I might be able to help her. I feel like I need to try."

He thought for a moment. "When I was younger, you know I got into several bar fights, right?"

She nodded. It was an uncomfortable part of Ruari's past. Physical violence always felt scary to her.

"Only the first couple were because I felt like fighting. And Seamus was there," he added with a chuckle. "The other three were because someone else was being picked on who I thought couldn't take care of themselves. I knew I might get hurt and chose to go into the fight anyway. Just figure out what you can handle and know you might get hurt. If you still want to get into the fight, particularly to protect someone more vulnerable than you, then do it. I'll back you up."

A suspicious heat welled up in her eyes and the back of her throat felt tight. No one had ever promised her that before. She hugged him. "Thanks."

"Just looking out for you."

She cleared her throat and stepped back. "Will you be in the studio after the theater?"

"Yup, I need to finish the lazy Susan."

"Okay. Text me if you plan to stay there overnight."

"I'd really rather stay here, but if I'm too late I will. I don't want to wake you."

Marianne got her research materials together and headed into town in The Flea. She could have walked, but it was cold, and she didn't want to. Maybe afterwards she could go to the Trading Company for tea. It was her new favorite place.

She went to Smith, Walgust, and Brown first and parked on a side street. The law firm was in a modest brick building off Main Street, and Marianne put her purse over her shoulder and went inside. She left her backpack security blanket behind.

"Hello, may I help you?" The dark haired receptionist asked. She was in her forties and wore a nice business suit.

"Yes, I'm here to see Sarah Landsman, please."

"Do you have an appointment?"

"No, I don't."

"She is in a meeting all morning but might be free after twelve-thirty. If you give me your name, I'll have her call you."

Marianne gave her name and phone number.

"What is this in regards to?"

Marianne thought about several options: your niece Tayloe is in supernatural trouble, Canopus County business, ghost consultation, but none of them worked. She had no idea how much Sarah's workplace knew about her extracurricular activities. "Just give her my name. She'll know."

"Very well."

Without an appointment, she shouldn't have expected anything else in a busy law firm. Briefly she debated sitting in the reception area until twelve-thirty, but it would be a couple of hours. She had stuff to do, and her time would be better spent elsewhere. At least she'd left a message with a third party. Sarah couldn't ignore that.

She left, determined to stake out Hair Magic until Kelly had a break in her schedule. The salon had a much nicer waiting area anyway. She was two streets away from the law firm when she noticed the blue Honda Civic two cars back. It followed her all the way to the hair studio and then drove past her parking space.

Marianne went into the apple-blossom-scented business and stood near the reception desk. Kelly was cutting hair, and two women sat under heated dryers getting perms or color. No one else was on the floor today. Kelly caught her eye in the mirror and said, "Be with you in a moment, hon."

"I'll wait." Marianne took a seat on the faux leather couch and unzipped her jacket. The coffee table had an assortment of magazines and a photo album. Kelly's sideline was photography, and Marianne leafed through it. The landscapes and solitary objects were beautiful. Kelly had a real eye for composition.

A couple of minutes later, Kelly laid her scissors down and handed the client her glasses. "I'll be right back to blow dry it."

She came to the reception desk with a smile. "Hey, Marianne, do you need a haircut?" She flipped through her appointment book. "I've got some time free next week."

"Sure." That might be the only way to get Kelly's undivided attention. They worked out a date the following Wednesday. "I'm really here because I need to consult with you about Tayloe."

Kelly's smile faded. "Is she okay?"

"So far, but I'm worried. I've never dealt with anything like this before. I think she's—"

Kelly glanced meaningfully over her shoulder toward the clients and lowered her voice. "This is not a great place to talk about this."

"I know, but Sarah won't call me back."

"Opening night is next week right?"

"Yes."

"Okay, we'll be there to back you up. I promise."

"But I could really use some help now!"

Kelly looked uncomfortable. "I'll tell Sarah to give you a call. But we have faith in you. You'll do fine." She raised her voice and said cheerfully, "And I'll see you next Wednesday for a haircut, okay?"

Frustrated, but not wanting to cause a scene, Marianne said, "Fine."

The shop door closed behind her. She stood on the top step, feeling dismissed and annoyed. They *were* avoiding her. What else could be so important that Sarah wouldn't return her calls? She started down the steps and automatically scanned the street for traffic. A blue Honda Civic sat parked near the corner. A person sat in the driver's seat. They seemed to be staring in her direction. Feeling het up and mulish, she hitched her purse higher on her shoulder and walked that way. She drew level with the passenger side door and peered inside.

Tristan Kitteby sat in the driver's seat. Her slow burn ignited.

She knocked briskly on the window. Tristan lowered the glass. She bent down and looked inside. Several origami cranes and flowers decorated the rearview mirror and the dashboard. A faint herbal smell wafted out with the buzz of charm magic. Tristan warded his car, too. Interesting.

"Hi, are you waiting for a hair appointment?" Marianne asked.

Tristan looked uncomfortable. "Not exactly."

"Then why did you follow me from the law firm to here? That can't be total chance."

He grimaced. "How do you know Sarah Landsman and Kelly Walker?"

She lifted her chin. "They're my friends. Are you spying on them?"

He pursed his lips. "Keeping an eye on them."

"Why? You're the Protector of Dutchess County aren't you?"

"I am." He sat a little straighter, his face losing all trace of uncertainty. "Why are you sneaking around the Avery?" He countered.

The low buzz of magic increased. He looked imposing all of a sudden. She reflexively reached for her bag of protective stones in her pocket. After meeting the person inhabiting Tayloe last night, she'd decided to keep it on her. The stones were only body temperature. No Shadow People around. It had also reacted to the evil ghost of Damian Brody when she'd first met him. So no evil ghosts here either. Would it react to spells with ill intent? She backed up a step, hoping that he couldn't cast any spells on her. Sarah had never been clear on what kind of magic was out there, much less how to detect or defend herself from it.

His expression changed again to a conciliatory one. "Look, this is really awkward," he said. "Would you like to go to a café or something and talk there?"

It should be okay to be in a public place with him. "Okay. Where?"

"Do you know the diner on Elm Street?"

"I've heard of it but haven't been there." At least he hadn't suggested the Trading Company. She wanted to keep that to herself and not mess up its good vibes.

"Meet you there in ten?" He asked.

"Fine by me."

He closed the window and started the car. She walked across the street to The Flea. If Sarah and Kelly wouldn't talk to her, maybe she could get some answers out of Tristan. At the very least, maybe she could find out why he was watching their businesses and maybe even why they didn't seem to like each other. If she was going to be part of the Protector business, she needed to know about the politics. Rather like navigating the social dynamics of the history department in grad school. She didn't have to participate, but it sure helped to know what was going on.

She drove to the diner and found another parking space. The eatery looked like a nice place. Before she got out, she texted Ruari, *I'm meeting Tristan at the diner on Elm. I caught him following me and spying on Sarah and Kelly.* At least if Tristan magicked her into a coffee mug or something, Ruari would know where she'd been. The blue Honda Civic was parked up the street. She squared her shoulders and walked in.

Out of his Dutch Colonial costume, Tristan Kitteby looked much more ordinary in corduroy pants, button-up shirt, and sweater under a beige jacket. He was sitting at a booth. The place was reasonably busy for the late morning, and she felt pretty safe. She slid into the red vinyl seat across from him.

"Do you want to order anything?" He asked.

It was after eleven, and she was a little hungry, but that could wait. "Not yet. I'd like some answers first. What is going on?"

He pressed his lips together. "I am the Protector of Dutchess County, like you said. It's my duty to keep it safe. That includes keeping tabs on what's going on in the neighboring counties."

"And?"

"Were you with Sarah and Kelly on All Hallow's Eve?"

"Why are you asking?" She remembered Sarah's theory that the Shadow People were being magically pushed away from Dutchess, Fairfield, and Putnam into Canopus. She'd been wrong. Byron had been focusing his efforts on opening the doors to the Shadowlands and letting the *draugers*, baby Shadow People, out. But Marianne still felt suspicious of Tristan.

"Were you with them on All Hallow's?" He asked again.

"Yes."

His expression shuttered even more. "Then I have no choice but to believe you're working with them."

"Of course I am. What are you saying?"

He regarded her critically. "If you understand what the Protectors do, then you are aware of what happened on that night."

"Yes, I was in the cemetery." She decided to be brutally honest. "It was a mess. We barely survived. If we hadn't called for help, we would have been killed or possessed by Shadow People."

Instead of being sympathetic, he said coolly, "If you summoned them and failed to contain them, then you'd have gotten what you deserved."

She was outraged. "No one deserves to be possessed by Shadow People! It's absolutely horrible. And we didn't summon them, Byron Mandell did."

"That's not surprising. We've been keeping an eye on him for a while now."

"Who is we?"

He named the other Protectors. "Paloma, Marette, and myself."

They hadn't been there. They had no right to accuse her or Sarah and Kelly of anything. "Let's get one thing clear: we did everything we could to stop him. When *draugers* got out, we did our best to kill them or send them back to the Shadowlands."

He was unmoved. "But you didn't succeed did you?"

"What is that supposed to mean?" He had no idea of the chaos, the fire, the insidious evil of the Shadows, and the violent specter Byron was in league with.

"You didn't get all of the *draugers* did you?" He insisted.

"I'm not sure, but I don't think so."

"Because Sarah is working with Byron."

"*What?!*" Marianne reeled back. She remembered the look of betrayal on her mentor's face when Byron revealed who he really was, and how drained she was as she tried to close the spell. No way. Marianne shook her head vehemently. Sarah might be an iron bitch sometimes and had been less than forthcoming both during the trip and in the weeks since, but Marianne was sure of one thing.

"No. You are absolutely wrong. Byron was her mentor, but he betrayed her completely that night. She would never support him again."

He looked triumphant. "Then would it surprise you to know that she's been to his house multiple times since then?"

She frowned. "That doesn't make sense. He's gone as far as we know. He ran into the Shadowlands just before the portal closed rather than face justice here."

Tristan looked grim. "Then I believe she's carrying on his work. I think she's trying to contact him or rescue him from that realm."

Marianne felt ice cold. *She's out of town. She's working on something personal. It's my problem. Above your pay grade.* If Sarah was spending time at Byron's house, then surely she was looking for clues on how to prevent him from doing any more evil. Marianne clenched her jaw. "You're wrong. She would never do that."

"Are you two ready to order?" A chirpy voice interrupted. A high school aged girl with two little pony tails had stopped at their table. They both glared at her. Her smile faltered. "Sorry. I can come back later." She slunk away from the table and back behind the counter.

Marianne resumed. "Even though she was his student, Sarah would never help Byron. He betrayed her completely."

"Maybe you don't know her as well as you think." He looked grim.

Tired of feeling defensive, she gave him a sharp look. "Speaking of which, I don't know you at all. Sarah was pretty clear she didn't like you very much. Would it surprise you to know that we found the initials 'TK' on the wedging charms in several of the stone chambers? It sure looks like you had your own agenda. Maybe pushing *draugers* and Shadows out of your territory into ours?"

It was his turn to look shocked. "Wedging charms?! I would never do that! That goes against everything I hold sacred as a Protector."

He looked genuinely horrified, but Marianne persisted. "And we found red yarn in other chambers that looked like it came from Marette. And there was a little wire poppet near one of the collapsed chambers."

His eyes narrowed. "Are you sure they weren't put there to make you think we were involved?"

"To be fair," she relented, "Byron all but said he'd set the wedging charms with your initials and Marette's yarn to do just that."

He shook his head. "Sarah has never liked me, Marette, or Paloma."

"Probably because Byron never liked you."

He was silent for a moment. "Hmm. When he first came into Canopus County and made it known that he was the new Protector, we tried to welcome him and offered cooperation. He turned us down. But I—we— had no idea he had so thoroughly thrown doubt on us."

"As far as I can tell, Byron only relied on himself even while teaching his protege, Sarah. She was completely loyal to him until he revealed himself. Sarah isn't trying to rescue him, whatever else she's doing. If anything, she's trying to make sure he never comes back."

He sat back and folded his arms. "All right. I'll take it as a working hypothesis for now," he said, looking less grim. "Until something else comes along."

"Good. Changing the subject," Marianne said, "have you noticed anything weird going on during rehearsals?"

He snorted. "Besides the bizarre additions to the classic story by a delusional director and the pranks being pulled by the ghosts of the theater? Not really. But you've been spying on rehearsals haven't you?"

She shook her head impatiently. "I think something else is going on. Something more powerful, but I'm not sure what it is."

"Can you give me a hint?"

"I think it has to do with the three lead actors. Do you see spirits, Tristan?"

"Sometimes, but they have to be very strong. I'm not as sensitive as some people are."

"Well, keep an eye on the three leads. I have a hunch, but I need more information." She wasn't willing to share anything more until she knew more about him and about her suspicions.

He nodded. "I'll be here until the run closes. If I discover anything, how can I contact you?"

She pulled out her cell phone. They exchanged numbers and sent hello texts.

"Done," she said. She stuck out her hand. "Thanks for taking the time to talk to me."

He smiled and shook her hand as if they were properly meeting for the first time. "Likewise. Do you need a coffee now?"

"I'm more of a tea person."

His smile warmed. "I prefer tea too. Can I buy you tea then? As a truce?"

"Sure."

They waved the young waitress over, and she cautiously took their order. Tristan added a piece of baklava. They talked about the play and chuckled over Tommy Verplank's imaginative additions to the original Irving story.

When she left, she was reasonably sure she'd done the right thing by telling him as much as she had and hoped she hadn't misjudged his character. Or Sarah's.

❀

When she got home, Marianne made a sandwich and retreated to her office. Oscar was asleep on her bed and she didn't disturb him. As she ate, she opened her email and felt a pang of dread. Her mother had written a plaintive note asking once again about Thanksgiving. Almost a month ago Mom had asked her to come for Thanksgiving dinner and invited Ruari to come along. Marianne had put off answering her.

After her father had died when she was five, Marianne and her mother had become close. Mom had never found the right man to marry after Dad died, so she'd raised her daughter alone. Even though she'd worked hard to support them, she'd found time to go to all of Marianne's activities and performances. She'd even taken her into the city on occasion to go to a museum or a performance. Marianne had had no problem sharing her life with her mom.

When Marianne had met Geoffrey in college, her mom had been supportive and absolutely thrilled when he popped the question. In hindsight, Marianne thought her mom must have been relieved that her daughter would be well cared for and not want for money ever. Mom had always been understanding when Marianne became more and more wrapped up in Geoffrey's family and his business. Neither one noticed that he was driving a wedge between them. Dazzled by the wealth of Geoffrey's family, she'd raved about their efforts to include her at family gatherings. As her relationship with Geoffrey had disintegrated, Marianne had realized how empty his family's gestures had been. They'd never liked either her or her mom.

Last year at this time, she'd been newly separated from Geoffrey and had eaten Thanksgiving dinner with Mom for the first time in more than ten years. It had been a quiet affair with just the two of them. At the time, Marianne had felt battered by her ex, and the quiet was welcome. In retrospect, it had also been lonely. They hadn't talked much, and Mom hadn't offered much support. It had taken her mom a long time to get over Marianne's decision to get divorced. Mom had since flipped her opinion and called Geoffrey "an awful man," but Marianne was sure she still wished things had been different. That made it hard to share her thoughts with her.

Since Marianne had moved to Maple Hill, so much had happened. She'd hinted at the ghosts in her house, and Mom had quietly wigged out. How on earth would she take Marianne's research into the lives of long dead people in the effort to solve their problems? Or her desire to open a business that was at least in part, a ghost advising business?

She still had to call and say something. It wasn't fair to leave her hanging. She blotted her damp cheeks with her sleeve, sniffed, and tried to relax her face and let the tension go.

The phone rang a couple of times before Christine Singleton answered.

She put on a cheerful voice. "Hi Mom, it's me."

"Hi honey! I was getting worried you weren't going to call me in time. I know you're busy, but it's getting close to Thanksgiving, and I wanted to know if Ruari was coming with you or if it's just the two of us. I need to plan the food. You know how I am."

"Yeah, about that. Things have been really busy down here. Ruari's theater job is taking a lot of time. His sister Erin is living with me temporarily, and she just got a job. I don't know if I can make it this year."

"Surely no one is working on Thanksgiving day! If it'll help, Erin can come too. It's no trouble to add one more person. And if they can't make it, then it can be just you and me. Like old times."

Her heart sank. "I guess I can ask."

"Please do. The more the merrier!"

"Okay. I'll get back to you as soon as I can. Thanks, Mom."

"Of course, honey."

She hung up, feeling miserable. She texted Ruari. *Mom invited both you and Erin to join us for Thanksgiving.*

It took him a few minutes, but he texted back. *That's really sweet but Thanksgiving is a big deal at our house. My parents invited you to join us. Maybe your mom would like to come be with us instead? It would mean more people to buffer between me and Dad :)*

That's a great idea! I'll call her back and see if I can talk her into it.

She dialed her mom's number again.

"Hi Mom, me again."

"Hi honey, did you have a chance to ask them already?"

"Well, apparently Thanksgiving is a big deal in Ruari's family. They've invited both of us to join them. What do you think?"

There was a brief silence. "Oh. I don't know. I was hoping to have you here."

"It means you don't have to worry about food, though. And there'd be lots of people. Ruari's family is much nicer than the Chubbs, trust me. His mom and dad are really great, and Erin's a character. I think you'd like them. Please consider it?"

"Well, I guess I could. Should I bring something?"

"I'm sure they'd appreciate anything you brought."

"I could make potatoes *au gratin*. Or wine. Do they drink? I could bring a bottle of wine. Maybe a nice table decoration?"

Marianne laughed in relief. "Yes, they drink wine. Whatever you choose to bring, I know they'll appreciate it."

"Alright, I'll give it some thought. You'll have to come get me, since you have my car now."

"Of course, Mom. I'll find out when we're expected and let you know."

She hung up and texted Ruari. *She said yes! I'll have to go get her, so you'll have to give me the details as soon as you know them.*

That's great! We usually eat around 3 but I'll confirm. Do we need to ask your grandmother to join us?

She always has her own plans as far as I know. Thank you so much, Ruari!! Love you.

Love you too, Mahri.

While she was still in communication mode, she dialed the number for the Historical Society.

The dry, hard voice answered, "Maple Hill Historical Society, Mrs. Caldwell. How may I help you?"

"Mrs. C, it's Marianne. Could you check on the status of my loan request?"

"One moment." There was a distant sound of a keyboard. "It looks like it hasn't been fulfilled yet." More keys clicked. "Hmm. They may be slower because of the holiday."

"That's what I was afraid of." Disappointment squashed her momentary elation at solving her Thanksgiving plans. She wished she'd found the lead sooner.

"Is this part of your theater research?"

"Yes, I was really hoping to have the information before the play opened," *and maybe find out what the heck is going on at the theater before all hell breaks loose.*

"Hmm. Perhaps I could make a phone call or two."

"That would be amazing!"

"But don't count on it. That library is very by-the-book."

"Whatever you can do, I'd really appreciate it."

"I'll get back to you."

That night at the theater, Ruari caught the end of the storytelling scene. He'd been in the wings, trying to fix a stuck door in the school house flat. Somehow the door wouldn't open or close easily anymore. Luckily, they were rehearsing Act II and didn't need the set piece, so he'd spent the time needed to fix the problem. It turned out that the screws had come part of the way out of the frame. At first he'd thought they'd worked themselves loose by moving the piece back and forth, but they were too far out to really blame movement. The screw heads were also slightly stripped as if someone not too adept had used a cordless screwdriver to move them. Mostly just he and Scotty had been assembling flats and set pieces. But what if someone else had come in over the weekend or tonight and done the mischief? Someone like his former assistant. Who had already cost him his job once.

Annoyance and anger boiled up. Having a loose door wouldn't have hurt anyone, but it would make Ruari look bad. It was reminiscent of the other time when the flat had fallen over during rehearsal because it had come free of its base.

Casey was his top culprit, but he had no proof. Ruari put a lid on his temper and channeled it into checking all the other flats and pieces of stage furniture. It was only a little over a week to opening night. The last thing he needed was to have to rebuild things or for someone to get hurt. So, he methodically checked everything for Act I. The actors were moving things on and off stage for Act II, so he had to wait to check those. Once he finished, he went to sit in the darkened auditorium.

Ruari watched the Van Tassel party break up and Katrina's rejection of Ichabod. Casey and Jake exited stage left the way they were supposed to without looking any more guilty than they usually did. The curtain closed and stage lights dimmed covering the sound of people making the scene change.

There was an abrupt cry of "Ouch, dammit!" Followed by "Ruari! Where are you?"

"Oh God, now what?" Tommy muttered, putting a hand over his eyes and massaging his forehead.

Ruari leapt out of his seat and hastened to the side steps up to the stage. "Coming!"

He pushed past the main curtain and found the two men who were moving the tables still on stage, a painted trestle table between them. One of them was sucking his fingers.

"What happened?" Ruari asked.

"The table top pulled free on one side when we lifted it," Zack explained. "Dennis got a huge splinter. I thought you fixed this?"

"What's going on back there?" Tommy yelled.

The main curtain pulled back showing the three men still on stage.

Binkler hustled up, clutching his clipboard and script. "What's going on?" He asked.

Ruari ignored him and examined the table. Sure enough the

plywood had come free of the frame on one side. "How did you get the table out here?"

"Same way as always," Zack said.

"I thought it seemed loose, but we were in a hurry," Dennis added, peering at his hand.

"Dennis, go take care of the splinter," Binkler ordered. "Zack, you and Ruari move the table off stage and deal with it later. We have to keep the rehearsal going." He gave Ruari a pointed look. "Fix the table later."

Ruari frowned, feeling a strong sense of *déjà vu*. He nodded curtly and helped Zack move the table into the wings. Casey and Jake stood off to the side staring at Ruari. Was there a gleam of satisfaction in the little shit's eyes? Ruari's temper reignited, and he was tempted to haul Casey into the hallway and find out once and for all if he was sabotaging the sets.

Instead, he clenched his jaw and suppressed the urge. He didn't have to be that guy anymore. It might not even be Casey, and he'd be punishing the wrong person.

Yeah, it would still feel good to put the wee bawbag in his place.

CHAPTER 18

Wednesday morning, Marianne was putting the finishing touches on the history piece she was writing for the Playbill. With only a few sources, she had a lingering sense of incompleteness and had to remind herself that this was a fluff piece not a dissertation or a journal article. Still, it would have been nice to have a little more. Oscar stretched and yawned from his customary place on her papers. She sent the document to the printer and the orange tabby jumped down as the machine whirred to life.

Her cell phone rang. "Hello?" She answered cautiously. The exchange was local, but she didn't recognize it.

A dry voice at the other end said, "Is this Marianne Singleton?"

"Speaking. Mrs. Caldwell?"

"Regarding your loan request, I was able to call in a favor with a friend at the lending library. He sent three months' worth of magazines before the fire and three months after the fire in 1909 and 1910. Will that suffice?"

Her heart leaped. "Yes! That's better than I'd hoped. Wait, did you say they're already here?"

"Yes. He had another delivery in the area and was kind enough to send them right away."

"That's fantastic! I'll be there very soon. You are a gem, Mrs. Caldwell!"

"They're very fragile due to age," she cautioned, "so you may only peruse them here at the library. You cannot remove them."

"That's okay. I'm more than happy to read them there. Tell your friend not to worry. I'll be really careful."

"I'm sure he'll appreciate your care," she said wryly, sounding suspiciously amused.

In a whirl, Marianne threw all of her research gear together, let Oscar out, and locked the door behind her. She walked with wings on her feet all the way to the library and arrived in the Historical Society room slightly out of breath. She claimed a table and shed her coat and hat.

The magazines, all twelve of them, sat on the counter. Marianne sighed happily.

"You don't even know if they have what you want." Mrs. Caldwell looked bemused.

"True, but they might. Thank you again. I owe you tea or coffee!"

The severe lines around the old dragon's mouth softened. "I took the liberty of getting these for you." She drew out a pair of white cotton gloves.

"Thank you." Hint taken. No more red gloves.

Marianne carried the precious stack to her place at the table. She loved the musty scent of old paper, ink, and mildew wafting up from the pages. It was the smell of research and history. The magazines of this era had photographs, but they were more like colorized drawings rather than photos. The women's silhouettes had Gibson Girl, hourglass figures with impossibly narrow waists, and big wavy hairdos under huge hats with ostrich feathers. Their expressions were languid and dreamy, while the men were handsome and clean shaven.

The fire at the Averill had happened in early December of

1909, a worryingly coincidental date for the current production, and Marianne made a note of it. She lost herself in the pictures and articles of mildly famous people of the day, enjoying all the advertisements as well. In six issues leading up to the fateful night, she located one that mentioned *The Legend of Sleepy Hollow* production at the Averill and gave profiles of each actor. She read it very carefully, scribbling many notes.

Loren Demarko had played Brom Bones. His photo showed a confident, rakishly handsome man with a chiseled, clean cut jaw and slicked back hair. He'd been in numerous stage plays of the day, playing the lead in romances and dramas. He'd been compared to Douglas Fairbanks once. Interestingly, he'd been a fireman before he'd gotten into theater. He was quoted as saying, "On stage you can die a thousand times. On the street, only once." He'd been proven wrong, though, hadn't he? Poor man.

Once he got into acting, he went whole hog and was in as many plays as he could cram in. He had talent and managed to make each play a step up from the previous one. The final quote was, "After this, the next time you see me will be on the big screen. I guarantee it!"

Wilhemina Trent's photo showed a very pretty woman with masses of curly brown hair. Born to farmers in upstate New York, she'd left home at sixteen and started modeling. She'd been in a number of plays as the plucky, young heroine or ingenue. When asked where she saw herself in a few years, she replied, "I saw my first silent film and fell in love. I'm destined for the big screen, that's where I want to be! Drinking champagne all night and going to parties." With Wilhemina's fresh-faced looks and copious brown locks, Marianne could easily see her by Clara Bow's or Lillian Gish's side. But there had been no mention of her on the internet. She must have faded from the public eye as she grew older. Perhaps she'd lost her youthful looks?

Clifford LaSalle had been in theater for less time than the other two had. His face was more average looking than Loren's heroic features. He was a talented character actor, who had garnered praise for the voices and gestures he'd lent to several villains and side kicks, but he hadn't been a romantic lead yet. Marianne classified the role of Ichabod as a foolish hero rather than a romantic lead. When asked about his upbringing, he said he was an only child and had worked as a clerk in a department store for several years before being discovered. He'd been making his fellow clerks laugh by imitating other people, and a local theater scout had invited him to audition for a play. But, like Wilhemina and Loren, there was no mention of him on the internet. He too had faded into obscurity.

All this young, ambitious talent rolled onto the Averill stage with Tommy Verplank's ancestor's version of *The Legend of Sleepy Hollow.* It would have been a heady mix, and the production might have been wildly successful. The actors might have made it into the silent movies or even transitioned to talkies in the late 1920s. Instead, the Averill Theater caught fire, Loren Demarko had died, and the others had vanished from the public eye. She was beginning to have a very bad feeling about the 2009 edition of the play.

She set the issues leading up to the fire to the side and pulled the next six issues forward. The first issue after the tragedy had nothing about the fire. It must have been committed to the printer when it happened. Two weeks later, however, the mid-December issue had a big article about the fire: "Tragedy at the Averill Theater, Maple Hill, New York."

Much of the basic information was the same as she'd read in the *Maple Hill Register* earlier. However, there was an eyewitness account by a survivor. According to Mr. Brian Hardy, he'd been sitting in the second row when he smelled smoke. The Headless Horseman had just made an appearance on his black stallion.

"The Horseman galloped out onto stage with his prop horse, reared up, and bellowed an evil laugh. Then someone in the audience said out loud, 'Is that smoke? Do you smell that?'

"Well, I tell you, I sat up. Too many people have gotten trapped in theater fires. I got up and started to make my way to the aisle, but then everyone else did, too. The stage manager ran out on stage and said everyone was to make for the exit in a calm and orderly fashion. Well, that didn't last long, I tell you. People were pushing and shoving to get to the exit. No one wanted to get burned alive.

"I looked back over my shoulder at the stage, hoping everyone had gotten off, and I saw the Horseman on his knees. He pulled the pumpkin head off and was choking and gasping. By then the smoke was pretty thick. I wanted to go help him, you see, but the crowd was pushing me to the door, and I couldn't go back no matter how hard I tried.

"Last thing I saw was him lying on the stage looking like he was half dead already. We were all coughing and choking and didn't stop till we got out into the fresh air. The firetrucks came and started pouring water all over the building. We were lucky to get out alive. Last thing I saw that night was firemen dragging poor Mr. Demarko out of the burning building, but they couldn't save him. He was already dead."

So, Loren Demarko had collapsed on stage while wearing the Headless Horseman costume. Mr. Hardy said he'd only just smelled smoke at that time. If Loren had been overcome by smoke, the fire must have traveled really fast. That was certainly possible. But Loren had been a firefighter before his acting career. Presumably he, of all people, would have known how to react in a fire. But he didn't. Something else must've happened.

Marianne reread the account, but nothing new jumped out at her. There was a missing piece of the puzzle. She skimmed the following four issues of the magazine and found no new information about the actors or the fire. There was a short piece about family-owned theaters and children of theaters where Dane Verplanck was mentioned in passing. He was twelve at the time and had been a messenger boy and an honorary member of the crew at the Averill. He'd known the theater inside and out. His death had been tragic, but Marianne couldn't believe that he'd died because of some mistake on his part. He'd worked in the theater for over a year on a daily basis and would have known all the building's secrets. And yet, his body had been discovered inside the remains of the building the next morning. Somehow he'd been trapped, unable to escape. Again, she needed more pieces to the puzzle.

Marianne rose and carefully photocopied the relevant articles and returned them to Mrs. Caldwell. Hours had passed, and her stomach growled.

"Did you find what you were looking for?" Mrs. Caldwell asked.

"I did. But now I have more questions."

She nodded sagely. "That's often the case with history. More questions than answers."

"Are you planning on going to the opening night of *The Legend of Sleepy Hollow?*"

"Most certainly."

"I'll be there. Do you read mysteries?"

"I read history, some of which has mystery in it."

Marianne nodded. "Well, why would an experienced firefighter collapse on stage instead of making for the exit?"

Mrs. C narrowed her eyes in thought. "Yes, that would be problematic. Clearly something prevented him from moving freely. Did his costume constrict him? Was he overly sensitive to smoke having been exposed more often than the average person?"

Marianne tapped her cheek thoughtfully. "Both are good questions. The second mystery is why would a boy who knows the theater like the back of his hand get trapped and die in the fire?"

"Hmm. Maybe he panicked. Or there was structural damage that blocked his escape."

"That seems entirely possible." She shook her head. She felt like she was missing something. She glanced at the clock over the door. "Oh, geez. I've got to go. Thank you for getting these magazines for me so quickly. I really appreciate it."

"You're welcome. Let me know if you need anything else."

Marianne smiled. "I will."

As she walked home, Marianne thought about the descriptions of ghosts being caught in a loop of their own trauma. Loren's and Dane's deaths would absolutely have been traumatic, but she hadn't seen any traces of hauntings that were like that at the theater. Anne Eddy Rutherford had communicated with Marianne through dreams and feelings in the basement at twenty-five Violet Lane. The closer they'd come to the anniversary of the fire that had killed Anne's little brother, the more intense the dreams and experiences Marianne had had.

As opening night approached, Tayloe's experiences were getting more intense. Marianne guessed she was somehow synchronizing with Willa's ghost on the basis of gender, temperament, and role in the play. But Willa had survived the fire. Why would she be needing to relive it? On the other hand, if Willa was compelled to relive the fire, Clifford, and Loren might also be trapped into reliving events. Finally, even though they hadn't seen Dane's ghost haunting the theater or a particular cast member, he might be caught in the loop as well. Four people condemned to live through what was arguably the worst night of their lives. If they were aware of their situation, it must be hellish.

Could she help break the cycle? Would that release them and allow them to move on to an afterlife that was better? Maybe she could find a way to ask the spirits what they needed. But how? She hadn't had much luck during rehearsals. What if she snuck into the theater overnight? She could possibly connect with them through dreams. However, the idea of spending the night at the Avery in order to catch the dreams of the ghosts who'd died horribly was unappealing on so many levels, not the least of which was getting into trouble if she was caught. Being terrified out of her mind if she was successful was worse.

How dangerous was the ghost loop? Was it powerful enough to bend modern events to fit the past? If so, would three or four people's memories of a fire somehow cause a new fire to happen? Anne's memories had made Marianne believe that her own house was on fire so strongly that she broke through a glass window to get away. Four memories might easily be enough to cause a real fire.

Between the faulty electrical system and the potential for ghostly intervention on opening night, she had to talk to Tommy Verplank. Maybe she and Ruari could convince him to stop the play. Maybe if it was put off even by a couple of days that might be enough to disrupt the ghostly reenactment.

They'd have to wait, though. Thanksgiving Day was tomorrow, and the director had reluctantly given the cast the night off. They could approach him on Friday. If they didn't succeed, Tayloe, Randall, and Casey were likely in for a rough ride, and the theater risked being burned to the ground.

Late Thursday afternoon, Marianne and Ruari strolled around the green in the middle of Maple Hill, their stomachs comfortably full from the huge dinner at the Allen house. It was chilly, and they were dressed warmly.

"Well, that worked out well," Ruari said.

"Yup, that went way better than I thought. Though your mom looked a little nonplussed when my mom showed up with a bottle of wine, the potatoes, *and* a turkey-themed table decoration."

He chuckled. "I think she was, but she rolled with it."

"Sorry about that. My mom gets really nervous with new people, but your family folded her right in. Thank you for that."

He squeezed her hand. "I'm glad you didn't have to spend an awkward Thanksgiving alone with her."

"No, and I didn't have to answer questions about whether I'm over the 'ghost thing' or not."

"I'm sorry she doesn't get that part of you."

She shrugged. "It's too bad. At least you understand."

"I love who you are, ghosts and dreams and all."

"Thanks." She leaned her head on his shoulder. "Your dad didn't corner you at least."

"No, he thinks the theater job is marginally better than Gloria's. He's still hoping I get a permanent job with the City of Maple Hill, though."

"You get to do what you want to do. I like the idea of Sylvan Woodworks. I hope you get back to that when the play is over."

"I intend to."

"Good. Erin kept disappearing from the table. Does she always do that?"

It was his turn to shrug. "She's always been a bit hyper. I think it's hard for her to sit still for long. She said she kept getting texts from a friend and didn't want to be rude at the table."

"I suppose. It bugged my mom, but your parents seemed okay with it. At least it seemed to be good news. She was smiling whenever she came back."

He shrugged. "She's a grown up."

They'd completed a circuit around the park. "We'd better get back to the house," he said.

"Yeah, Mom needs a ride home."

"You want me to come with you?"

"Would you? That would be great."

CHAPTER 19

After a long discussion in the car on the way back from dropping Marianne's mom at home, Ruari and Marianne agreed to talk to Tommy as soon as the theater opened on Friday. The dangers facing the play and the theater were too real to ignore. They entered the Avery through the scene shop and made their way to the front of the building in hopes of catching Tommy in his office. With any luck, Binkler would be somewhere else. Given his antipathy to Marianne, it would be easier to talk to the director alone first.

Voices floated through the partially open door. They paused.

"...have your tickets at will call and saved you and Susie prime seats...thank you for the mention in your Playbill for *Guys and Dolls* last week...very kind... Wonderful, wonderful. I'll keep an eye out for you...you too...'bye." The phone went back in its cradle.

They looked at each other, and Marianne felt her stomach sink.

Ruari squared his shoulders, and she nodded. He knocked.

"Come on in." Tommy sounded happy.

Marianne hated to be the bearer of bad news, but they had to make their case.

Tommy looked up from his desk. "Ah, Ruari and Marianne, you'll be the first to hear the good news. Charlie Newsome and his wife are going to be here opening night. He's an old friend of mine and just opened a very successful production of *Guys and Dolls* at the Shubert in New York."

"That's wonderful," Marianne murmured, her heart sinking lower.

Ruari cleared his throat. "Tommy, we wanted to bring some-things to your attention."

Tommy leaned back in his chair, the picture of receptive benevolence. "Of course, what's on your mind?"

"Well, I'm concerned about the electrical panel. The box is old, and the power draw for the lights is a lot more than it can take. We've had blowouts a couple of times since I got here, and the panel gets really hot during rehearsal. I'm worried there's a risk of fire."

When faced with the news that his theater was in trouble, Marianne marveled at how unfazed Tommy was. He smiled knowingly. "The panel is an older model, but it's powered the Old Girl for more than fifty years. It'll last us another couple of weeks."

"But we used the last BUSS fuse last time it overloaded."

"Don't worry, Dave ordered more. A whole box of fuses will be here before opening night."

Marianne spoke up. "But, the power could blow during a performance. It'll interrupt the audience's experience. What if we delayed the opening by a couple of weeks and upgraded the panel at least enough to take the stage lights safely?"

Tommy frowned. "Upgrading the panel would take weeks and, to be honest, it'll cost more than the Old Girl can afford right now. That's why we need a successful run of *Sleepy Hollow* to generate the interest and the revenue, so my backers will upgrade the whole theater."

"But what if the panel blows in the middle of a performance?" She repeated.

His frown eased. "Ruari, you'll just have to station yourself next to the panel and be ready to replace it if that happens."

Ruari looked dismayed. "I was going to be backstage in case there were problems with the sets."

Tommy shrugged. "The panel needs you more. I want you to stay there for the duration of the performance."

Marianne tried again. "You know I'm a historian. I did some research into the history of the Avery."

"I saw your piece. It's a great addition to our Playbill. Thank you for doing that."

"You're welcome. I read about the Averill Theater and that it burned down due to a faulty arc light during the opening night of *Legend of Sleepy Hollow*."

He raised his eyebrows. "And your point is?"

"I'm worried that history might repeat itself, sir."

Tommy looked startled for a moment. "That seems very far fetched."

Not if the same players are involved. "Maybe, but it concerns me."

Tommy raised his eyebrows. "Dave told me that you've been hassling the actors. Is that what this is about? You're worried that they will burn the theater down in some kind of historic reen-actment?"

"First of all, I wasn't bothering Tayloe. She asked me to come see her during rehearsal. She must have changed her mind, and I didn't get the memo. Second, I don't think the actors would intentionally cause problems."

"Then what's your concern?" He looked skeptical.

"All I can say is," she swallowed, "a lot of factors similar to 1909 seem to be lining up with this production. I would hate for all the rest to happen, too." It wasn't a strong finish.

Tommy gave an amused half smile. "Your concerns are duly noted. Although the panel is outdated, it is still a long way from the dangerous arc-lighting used in the old days." He leaned forward and shuffled some of the papers on his desk. "Thank you for coming to me with your concerns. I like to think of myself as an open-minded person, willing to hear everyone out. I believe we have everything under control."

Marianne knew further discussion would be useless. "Thank you for your time, sir."

"Of course. We'll see you on opening night and no sooner, right? Don't give poor Dave anything more to worry about." He gave her a fatherly smile.

"Of course," she said.

They left and closed the door behind them.

She blew out at breath. "Well, that wasn't great."

Ruari held out his hands palm up. "At least we tried. Let's hope that there won't be any dire pranks on opening night and that the panel doesn't melt down."

On Sunday, Marianne and Ruari woke up late. Ruari had spent most of the day before finalizing the sets with Scotty and Tristan, making sure everything was secure, fully painted, and a go for opening night the next week. He'd fallen into bed and curled around Marianne, asleep almost before he'd hit the pillow. It reminded her of the days he'd worked almost around the clock in Scotland. For her part, she was more than happy to stay in bed. They lazed around and spent time with each other under the covers. It felt so good to forget about all her troubles for a little while.

Marianne made French toast out of bread from the Co-op and fried up some sausages on the side. After their Scotland trip, she rather liked them for breakfast. Erin whirled downstairs in the late morning dressed in black skinny jeans and a red turtle-neck under her old leather jacket. Somehow she'd scraped together enough to get her beloved jacket repaired after the tussle at Halloween. Her face was elegantly pale with dark eye make up and dark green lipstick, her hair in a confident red cockatoo crest.

"Where are you going?" Marianne asked.

Erin snagged a couple of pieces of French toast with black-nailed finger tips. "I'm going to see a friend. Can I borrow The Flea?"

"Sure, just be sure to fill it with gas when you bring it back. How long will you have it?"

"Probably most of the day. If that's okay?"

Marianne looked at Ruari who shrugged. "I'll be here," he told her, "if you need to run an errand or something."

She nodded. "Okay. The keys are in the bowl on the mantlepiece."

Erin gave her a big smile, her white teeth flashing behind the dark lipstick. "You're the best! Thanks."

The door banged shut behind her, leaving the house in silence.

"Any idea who this friend is?" Marianne asked.

Ruari shook his head. "I thought she'd broken up with Pat Whelan from the Chamber of Commerce." He referred to a high school friend she'd reconnected with when she moved back to Maple Hill.

"I had that impression too. She must've met someone she's really excited about. I don't think she ever dressed that nicely for Pat." She remembered her girl's day out with Erin and the sad wistfulness Ruari's sister had shown, however briefly. "It must be a little bit of an up and down relationship. She implied she was interested in someone who might be a little out of reach."

"Erin goes all in when she likes someone. She had a couple of crushes in high school and was really down when they broke up."

"Did she have someone in Arizona?"

"No idea, but I don't think so."

"She honestly didn't seem to be that into Pat."

He agreed. "Maybe that was more for the sake of having

someone to hang out with. I think she tried to reconnect with friends when she moved back."

"She said they'd moved on without her. Maybe she met this new person through work? Maybe he, or she, is older, or married?"

Ruari made a face. "God I hope not. I thought she was more sensible than that."

Marianne shrugged. She was just glad Erin had found someone to keep her out of video games and grounded in the real world. "At least she's happy. I suppose she'll share when she's ready."

"Or not. I never know. It's better not to have any expectations."

Together they cleaned up the dishes and sat in their pajamas on the couch to read books. They shared her plush tropical print blanket between them. Oscar strolled into the living room and hopped on the couch. After trying to find a comfortable place on their legs and not being satisfied, he jumped down again. The tabby approached the new dog bed, sniffed the soft cover delicately, and stepped into it. He began kneading his front paws up and down, purring happily. He lay down and tucked his paws under his chest with a sigh.

Marianne shook her head. "I forgot to get Oscar his own bed this week. He really fell in love with the ones we got for Rita."

Ruari came out of his book, *Celtic Designs for Everyone*. "Does she even use them?"

"I think so. They've argued over them a couple of times, and Rita has always chased Oscar away."

Ruari shrugged and went back to his reading. Marianne went back to her haunted hotel in Florida mystery. She was just getting to a good part when Oscar's warning growl started. She looked up in time to see Oscar staring fixedly at something across the room, his tail twitching. Marianne nudged Ruari with her foot. He looked up.

"What?"

"I think Rita's here." She tipped her head toward the tabby's watchful stare.

Ruari tensed and froze. "Where?"

She shook her head. Closing her eyes, she scanned the room. Rita's pale form stood a couple of feet away from her bed, looking perplexed. She gave Marianne a look that said, *That cat is in my bed. Can't you do something about this?*

Marianne opened her eyes. She could still see Rita's smoky shape. She looked at Ruari. "You want to try something?"

"Like what?"

"You can't see Rita, right?"

He shook his head.

"You want to try feeling her?"

He looked dubious but said, "Okay."

"Rita, come here, girl." She tapped the side of the couch with her hand. The big dog gave Oscar a last look and came over. She passed through the side chair and stood next to the couch, oblivious of the coffee table bisecting her body.

Ruari looked down and around, searching for a much smaller dog.

"She's a Newfoundland, so her head is up here." She touched Rita's head about level with her chest. It felt like cold mist.

Ruari drew back. "Jeez!"

"Give me your hand."

Reluctantly he scooted closer to her on the couch and let her guide his hand to the big dog.

"Rita, this is Ruari. He's part of our family. Ruari, meet Rita."

Marianne moved his hand as if he was stroking her head. Rita closed her eyes and panted happily.

"Do you feel that? You're patting her on the head."

"I'm not sure. Maybe? It just looks like I'm moving my hand through the air."

"Stop looking for her with your eyes. She feels cold to the touch. Maybe close your eyes and pretend she's there?"

He closed his eyes. She continued to move his hand along the dog's head and neck.

"It does feel like there's a patch of cold air here. Like a cold layer when you swim in a pond."

"Yeah! That's it."

"But, when I open my eyes, it goes away."

"But you felt her! I bet if you practiced a little, you could feel her more strongly."

He sat back. "This is so wild."

When it was clear no more petting was in the offing, Rita moved back to stand in front of her bed. Oscar lashed his tail but stopped his low growl. One paw at a time, Rita stepped onto the bed, watching the big tabby closely, and moved around the cat and lay down gingerly. Oscar watched her warily but didn't move or hiss.

Marianne murmured, "Not as wild as watching the two of them share the same bed. I guess they called a truce. I wonder when that happened? Well, at least we don't have to worry about them destroying the house when we're not here."

CHAPTER 20

Randall Merritt arrived late to rehearsal on Monday. The play opened on Thursday, and he was both super nervous and excited at the same time. Dad had known he was in the play for weeks now, and after an initial period of ribbing and annoyed looks, his father had left him alone. Randall wasn't sure if he'd bought tickets to see the play or not. He was proud of his work and part of him hoped Dad would show up. The nervous part of him just wanted it to be over.

He'd auditioned out of desperation to do something different besides work on cars all day. He'd learned to diagnose and fix engines since he was very little, but it was his father's dream for him to succeed him at Merritt Motors not his. He just wanted out of the constricting ties of Maple Hill and his father's expectations. That was one of the many reasons he liked Tayloe so much. She was going to nursing school to get away from her father, too. When he was working at the automotive shop, he fantasized they would go together into a happier, if presently fuzzy, future. But things had gotten weird during the play.

The script had come surprisingly easily to him. Maybe knowing how to rebuild an engine contributed to his memory. He also had spent all his free time reading and memorizing the

227

script. Even though Mr. Verplank kept changing things, somehow he was able to keep up. As the weeks went by, he'd even come up with a different voice for the character. A little higher, more nasal. Plus, he got to spend time with Tayloe even if it was just in rehearsal. He'd wanted to ask her out, but his shyness had kept him from speaking up at first. When he was Ichabod and she was Katrina, all the uncertainty went away, and he felt confident enough to respond to her flirtation. They'd gone out several times now, and he felt hopeful they could keep up after the play was over.

The not-fun part was how obnoxious Casey Hopper was. He and Jake had had it in for him almost from day one. They'd never crossed paths in high school or anywhere else as far as he knew. Maybe it was just one of those things: hyenas spot the weak and go for the kill. He'd had practice ignoring such hyenas, but those two grated on him like no others. Their barbs and pranks were like metal filings under his nails or fiberglass in his skin. The stunt with the mice in his pockets made him boil over, but he'd contained himself. Dad had taught him to fight but coached him to choose his battles carefully to ensure a win. He'd find the right time to get even. Casey and Jake would get theirs.

Randall braced himself and entered the men's dressing room. Jeremy dashed past wearing his Dutch Colonial pants and shirt.

"Jeremy, say excuse me!" His father called in exasperation. Jeremy made no answer being halfway down the hall already. "Sorry about that," he apologized.

"That's okay. He's a kid." Randall glanced around quickly and was relieved that Casey wasn't there.

"You'd better hurry," Jeremy's father said, "it's almost time." He hastened out the door after his son.

Randall shed his jacket, tee shirt, and jeans and struggled into Ichabod's shirt, pants, and jacket. The stage manager's voice floated down the hallway, urging everyone to assemble on the stage.

"Shit," he mumbled, shoving the old fashioned footwear over

his dark socks. At least they were slip ons. He plunked the Ichabod wig over his own hair and jogged down the hall to the backstage entrance.

He slipped into the back row of the cast as the director began addressing them.

"As you know we open on Thursday. From here on out, I want to run the show from top to bottom with as few interruptions as possible. You should all know your lines and blocking by now. Tonight, we're going to run the light and sound cues. Be confident, people. You've all worked really hard, and this is going to be a fantastic show. If you—Randall, what's the matter?"

Randall was distracted by a burning, itching sensation on his neck that spread across his shoulders, down his arms, across his back and torso. It rapidly became unbearable, and he began scratching and rubbing his skin trying to alleviate the sensation. He pulled his jacket off and hauled the shirt over his head heedless of the stares as people turned to look.

The people in front of him parted like the Red Sea, and Tommy Verplank stared at him.

"Randall what's going on?"

"I don't know. My shirt…" He looked down at his torso. It was covered in red welts. A fine dust fell from the cloth.

"Itching powder," he said in disbelief.

A cousin had spiked his swimsuit one summer with the stuff, and he'd practically scratched his skin off before his mom had figured it out and doused him with a hose. He'd never forgotten.

Uncontrollable snickers came from somewhere amid the gasps of surprise and sympathy.

"For the love of Dane!" Tommy slammed his fist down on the back of the chair in front of him. "Who is doing this? Casey, Jake, this is not funny! You are sabotaging the play. Get off the stage and sit in the front row. Now!"

"I didn't do it!" Casey said indignantly. "But it's a fair trade off for the thumbtacks I found in my shoes." He glared at Randall.

"I just got here. I don't care about your fucking shoes!"

Randall replied angrily. His skin was on fire, but he would have gladly wrapped the poisoned shirt around Casey's fat head.

"Enough!" Tommy yelled. His usually florid face was bright red with fury. "I don't know what you two have against each other, but for the duration of the play it has to stop. There is no time to find people to take your places, but if there were, I'd throw both of you out on your rears. I want to know who did this! Speak up!"

Casey and Randall said nothing. The cast was silent.

One of the young boys said timidly, "I saw the Headless Horseman go into the men's dressing room earlier."

Tommy glared at Casey and Jake.

"That wasn't me!" Casey exclaimed. He still hadn't moved from the stage.

"I didn't do it," Jake said sullenly.

Tommy turned to Randall.

"I only got here about ten minutes ago."

Jeremy's father spoke up. "I can vouch for that."

"We are not going to continue rehearsal until I find out who did this," Tommy said obstinately.

The cast stood there uncomfortably as the minutes stretched.

"Oh, for heaven's sake!" Tayloe burst out. "What a waste of time. We need to rehearse, and I can't afford to be here until midnight. Casey and Jake, just admit it and let's move on."

Casey looked mutinous and started to open his mouth in a retort.

Katie shuffled forward looking like she wanted to be anywhere else but here. "Um, I was coming back from the bathroom earlier, and I saw the Headless Horseman coming out of the men's dressing room, too." Her face had gone scarlet. "I saw you, Tay, taking the pumpkin head off as you ducked into the costume shop. I'm sorry," she finished in a whisper.

The shock was palpable.

Everyone turned to Tayloe.

Several emotions flitted across her face. Finally, she put her hands on her hips and stamped her foot. "And what if I did? I'm sick of the two of you fighting over me like a couple of dogs over a bone. Well, I'm not a bone, and this dog has teeth! I'll make it in this business without either one of you! So you can just take a powder."

Tommy opened and closed his mouth a couple of times before he said finally, "I am so disappointed." He stared at Tayloe who glared defiantly.

"There will be no more pranks of any kind. From anybody. The show opens in two days. Places, everybody, from the top." He sat heavily in his seat and put his head in his hands.

Binkler, hovering on the edge of the stage, said, "Brendan, would you help Randall take care of his costume and—and get him cleaned up? Randall, will you be able to run through everything tonight? Good. Casey, are your shoes wearable? Okay, good. Places, everyone." He clapped briskly as if nothing had happened.

Brendan accompanied Randall to the bathroom. Gingerly he took the entire costume, leaving Randall in his underwear.

"I think I have another shirt and dark suit in your size," Brendan said. "Be right back."

The door to the bathroom swung shut, leaving Randall alone. He was in shock. Tayloe had salted his clothes with itching powder in a fit of pique? But they'd had such a nice time. Had he offended her in some way? He would not have pegged her as the vengeful type. If Mr. Verplank was disappointed, Randall felt like he'd been punched in the gut.

He'd thought she liked him. He was wrong. Maybe she'd been responsible for all the other pranks, too.

His reflection in the mirror was pallid and damp. The angry red welts stood out on his pale skin, but their sting was dissipating. He splashed handfuls of cold water over his skin and stuck his head in the sink and rinsed just in case. He blotted himself dry with paper towels. When he was a kid, it had taken him a day to stop feeling like his skin had been rubbed raw. At least he was recovering faster.

The door opened again, and Brendan returned with an armful of clothes. "Okay, These will do, even if they're not quite period. Luckily men's fashion doesn't change much."

Numbly Randall pulled on the new clothes, careful to not let the new shirt rub too much. "Thanks, man," he mumbled. "I'm sorry about the Ichabod clothes."

"Not your fault. I'll have them dry cleaned. You're not allergic to dry cleaning are you?"

Randall shook his head.

"Perfect. They'll be ready by Thursday night. You going to be okay? You look pale."

He nodded again and gave limp smile. "The show must go on. Isn't that what the director always says?"

Brendan nodded. "True. Up to a point anyway." He patted Randall's arm. "Don't let this bother you too much. From what I can tell, you've got your lines down pat. It'll be a good performance."

"Thanks." Brendan really was a good guy.

Randall headed out the door, determined to get through rehearsal with his head held high. But it was hard when his heart was in his shoes.

Now that she was banned from the theater during rehearsal, Marianne couldn't keep an eye on Tayloe easily. But her client's panic made her want to do something. So, she slipped into the scene shop through the door Ruari had left open for her and sat in an out of the way corner of the shop. She wouldn't be easy to spot and could hide if anyone came too close. She felt stupid having to be so sneaky and tensed every time someone other than Ruari entered the shop to get something. She overheard the commotion when Randall's costume was sabotaged but didn't know what had happened. Ruari filled her in on the details when he had a chance.

"Tayloe would never have done that. It must have been Wilhemina," she whispered.

"I don't think it matters at this point. Tommy is upset, but it's too close to opening night to make any casting changes." He left again to be on call in case the sets needed him.

Marianne's heart went out to Randall. It must have been an awful shock to think Tayloe had been so mean. Marianne used the two hours of rehearsal to think and came up with a tentative plan. It was a terrible idea, very risky, and depended completely on what Tayloe had to say. She texted Ruari the bare bones, and he texted back, *Are you sure?*

No, but it's the only thing I can think of.

I'll back you up.

While she waited for rehearsal to be over, Marianne went up the hallway to the lobby, listening and looking with all of her senses for ghostly manifestations but felt nothing. Finally, she heard many footsteps leaving the stage area and hastened back to her post in the scene shop.

She texted Tayloe. *I need to see you when you're dressed. Come to the scene shop.*

It took a few moments, and Marianne fretted that she'd have to call to get her client's attention. At last she answered. *Okay.*

About ten minutes later, Tayloe and Katie entered the shop. Katie spied her and said, "Tayloe's not feeling well. She needs to go home. Maybe you can talk to her another time."

Tayloe sounded weary. "It's okay, Katie. Marianne's a friend. You go on. I'll be fine. See you tomorrow, okay?" Her lips stretched in a bright, brittle smile.

"Are you sure, Tay?" Katie looked dubiously at her friend.

Tayloe nodded. "I'll call you later, okay?"

Reluctantly, with a couple of backwards glances, Katie took her leave.

"Have a seat. " Marianne motioned for her to sit on one of the folding chairs.

Tayloe looked shellshocked. Her eyes glistened. "I can't believe this is happening. My parents would be so angry with me."

Marianne said gently, "What happened? Tell me from the time you got here tonight."

Tayloe took a deep breath and pulled herself together.

"I got here a little early, like usual. I always need a little time to let go of whatever happened at Golden Years and get myself into this headspace, you know? Katie wasn't here yet. My memory is a little fuzzy, but I remember wanting to go to the costume shop. Brendan had been going on about the Headless Horseman costume being so cool, and I wanted a sneak peek. He wasn't there. The pumpkin head *was* really cool. I tried it on and put the cape on too. It was a little hard to see through the mesh behind the mouth, but I could. I looked amazing in the mirror and thought I'd take a little stroll down the hall."

She stopped speaking and gave Marianne an agonized look. "It's not like me to mess with other people's stuff. Father always says, 'If it isn't yours, don't mess with it,' and he always gave us a smack if we forgot. I don't know where the impulse to put on the costume came from." Silent tears began spilling down her cheeks.

Marianne took her hand and squeezed it gently. "I hear you. I don't think it was you doing that. I've been doing some research. A hundred years ago, the theater did the same play. An actress named Wilhemina Trent played Katrina. There was a fire on opening night, and the theater was destroyed. She survived, but there were two deaths connected to the fire. I think she, and maybe the other actors, are trying to relive the days up to the fire. I think she's using you to relive those days." She held her breath, hoping Tayloe would understand.

Tayloe's eyes widened. "You mean I'm being possessed? By a ghost?"

Marianne nodded slowly.

She closed her eyes and scrunched up her face. "That makes a kind of weird sense." Her eyes flew open. "Please don't tell my parents! They'd kill me! They'd say I need an exorcism." She put her hands on her head. "Maybe I do. This can't be happening."

"You don't need an exorcism." *Being borrowed by a dead actress is way better than being possessed by Shadow People, trust me.* "I promise I won't tell them. Can you remember what happened next?"

Tayloe stared into the middle distance trying to remember. "I'm not totally sure, but I remember going down the hall to the men's dressing room. I found Casey's shoes and put my hand in my pocket. It was full of thumbtacks. I have no idea how they got there." She gave a helpless look. "They weren't there when I left Golden Years. Somehow she put must've put them in there."

"Who?"

"Her. Willa."

"Okay, and then what?"

"I —Willa put all of them in his shoes. I remember putting the shoes back where I'd found them and thinking, 'I hope his feet hurt!'" She stopped. "Marianne, I don't like Casey, but I would never deliberately hurt him."

"I know. You're a nurse. You help people. And then what?"

She thought hard and then shook her head. "I have no idea where the little can of itching powder came from. But Ichabod's suit was easy to pick out. I," she gulped, "Willa sprinkled it all over the inside of Randall's shirt and hung it back up. We heard footsteps coming and hid the can under the cloak. A little kid came into the dressing room as we were leaving. He saw us, but we hurried back to the costume shop, and took the cape off, and hung it up where we found it. I put the can in the trash and left. I had no idea Katie saw me, but she did give me a strange look when I went into the dressing room. We didn't talk about it because it was almost time for rehearsal."

Tayloe took a shuddering breath and more tears leaked down

her cheeks. "Randall is never going to believe me," she whispered, and her breath hitched in a silent sob.

Marianne squeezed her hands again. "Don't give up yet. I think Willa was angry with the men playing Brom and Ichabod and wanted to get back at them. Randall and Casey just got in the way. I don't know exactly what happened all those years ago, but I think Willa and maybe the other two actors need to work out their differences. Do you think Casey and Randall are being possessed as well?"

Tayloe sniffed hard and wiped her face with both hands. "I don't know. Maybe? I've never met either one of them before, so I have no idea. I hate that Randall thinks it was me who put that stuff in his clothes."

"We'll see about that. When Willa is with you, how does it feel?"

She considered and then nodded. "It's really weird, now that I think about it. Willa is all confident. She's the one who remembers all the lines, not me. We get mixed up sometimes when Mr. Verplank changes the blocking, but it's important to follow his directions, so I make us do it. She's the one who is really flirty. I think she was a good actress when she was alive. When I get nervous, she takes over, and I let her because I stop being nervous. I kind of float along." She looked guilty. "It's kind of fun to be so good on stage. Does that make me a bad person?"

Marianne smiled. "Not at all. Here's the thing: do you think you could stop Willa from doing something you didn't want to do now that you know she's sometimes with you?"

"I don't know. I felt very distant when she was sabotaging the costumes. I could sympathize with her frustration. Casey's such a jerk. Maybe the other actors..."

"If all the old actors are tracking the same roles they had in the past, then Loren Demarko would be with Casey, and Clifford LaSalle would be with Randall."

She nodded slowly. "Yeah, that feels right. Loren and Cliff fought over Willa, and I think she thought it was cute and flattering at first, but then she got sick of it and was mad at them. All I could feel tonight was anger at the two of them."

Marianne's mind was racing. This was incredible. Three ghosts reliving their past in parallel with similar circumstances in the present. It tracked with her own experiences with Anne Eddy. But once the fire had been relived, Anne stopped being quite so present. Would that happen with these three? Or was that unique to Anne? Would the three dead actors decide they liked possessing the living and try to continue past the opening show?

"Tayloe, do you feel like Willa is with you outside of the theater? Does she go home with you or to Golden Years?"

She shook her head. "No, I'm just me then. If I didn't have to finish the play, I would leave right now! This is only going to get worse isn't it?" She sounded wretched.

"Do you think you could keep Willa from doing something you didn't want to do?" Marianne tried again.

"Maybe. What do you think is going to happen?"

"I'm not sure. I think that we have a chance to help Willa and the others if we let them play out their problems."

Tayloe's eyes widened. "Wait a minute, you said the theater burned down! What if Willa set the fire?"

"The old newspapers said the fire was started by a faulty arc light not a deliberately set fire. So, I think we're okay there."

"If you think so. What if one of the others set the fire? Are you going to talk to Casey and Randall about this?"

"I'm going to try. You'll have to come to rehearsal for the next couple of nights until the opening. You can practice keeping Willa under control. I'm hoping that the old actors will work out their differences either on stage or back stage before anything gets too wild. Ruari knows about this too. He'll keep an eye on Casey and Randall. Your aunts Sarah and Kelly said they would be at opening night. So you'll have lots of help if something happens. What do you think? Do you want to try this? It's okay to say no." She crossed her fingers behind her back.

Tayloe took a deep breath and let it out. "You think Willa might let me go if she works out her issues?"

"Probably. I think it's worth a try."

She nodded. "I'll try. If I think it's getting out of control, I'll try to tell you somehow."

Marianne hugged her briefly. "Okay, if you're willing to let Willa in, I can't give you a protection charm. You're a brave woman, Tayloe. I won't let you down."

She gave a shaky laugh. "Can't be a nurse if I'm not brave. Though this was never part of my training."

"Do you need a ride home?"

"I'd appreciate that."

Ruari came into the scene shop. "You're still here."

Marianne nodded. "Yeah, we're ready to go home. Would you mind dropping Tayloe off at her parents' place on the way?"

"Sure, no problem."

The ride home was quiet. Tayloe slipped out of the truck looking like a pale ghost. They waited until she'd opened the front door of her house and waved at them before continuing back to number twenty-five Violet Lane.

"How did she take your suggestion?" Ruari asked.

She shrugged. "About as well as you'd expect. But she's game to try, and I promised we'd be there to help her through it. Now I have to figure out how to talk to Casey and Randall."

"Good luck getting through to Casey. He's practically bullet-proof when it comes to his ego."

"You're probably right. What about Randall?"

"I don't know him. He's worked on my truck at his father's auto shop before. You might be able to catch him there on a break."

"I've only got two days left, but I have to try."

CHAPTER 21

The night before the opening Marianne lay awake unable to sleep. The more she thought about her plan of letting the ghosts possess the three leads and work their issues out with her mediating, the worse it sounded. What a dumb idea. What was she thinking? The three leads would be completely vulnerable to whatever whims the ghost actors had. She'd never tried to reason with more than one ghost at a time. What if they completely ignored her and did something that hurt their living hosts? What if they decided to jump into different cast members? What if the old investigation was wrong, and one of the three original actors *had* started the fire? What if there were more ghosts she didn't know about? There were no existing copies of *Hudson Valley Theater Magazine*. What if one of those issues held all the answers?

She pulled herself up sternly. This was like the night before her PhD defense, spinning around in ever shrinking circles, thinking of only the worst outcomes. Except failing her defense would have only impacted her. Failing Tayloe would be potentially devastating. But she wasn't alone this time. Ruari would be behind the scenes, and he could prevent any fire from getting out of hand if that happened. She could protect the rest of the cast by making charms. The next hurdle would be getting the cast to keep them for the duration of the show. She began chasing down all the possible ways she could get charms to the actors. Finally, exhausted she slipped into an uneasy sleep.

She woke up tired, but there was no time to sleep in. Ruari and Erin left for their respective jobs, and she headed for Main Street. The herbal components for protective charms were a little hard to come by in November, but between the florist shop and the fresh produce section at the Co-op, she found enough to protect most of the cast. At home, she fashioned decorative sprigs of lavender, sage, mint, and cedar tied together with a bit of decorative ribbon. She added a safety pin on the back of each one in hopes of fastening them to costumes. They were pretty and fragrant at least.

When she was done she gathered them all together in a bag and headed for the Avery. It was overcast and threatening to snow or rain, and she crossed her fingers that any bad weather would hold off. At this point, she just wanted all the uncertainty to be over.

It wasn't hard to slip into the theater through the scene shop. Ruari was consulting with someone on stage, and she decided it was better for him if he didn't know she was there. She padded down the hall to the changing rooms. Midway through pinning a charm to the main costume of each actor, Brendan walked in.

"Marianne, what are you doing here?" He looked at her in surprise.

She stabbed her finger painfully. "Oh, you scared me! I made these little corsages and thought it would be nice for the cast on opening night," she answered. She'd been working on an explanation.

"Did you clear this with Tommy?"

"Um, no, I didn't."

Brendan hung up the three costume pieces he'd been carrying. "May I see one?"

He looked at the little bouquet. "It's a sweet idea, but Tommy is really picky about his costumes. He's very likely to say no when he sees them."

"Well, can I leave them anyway? I have one for each cast member. They've all worked so hard. I thought they deserved a little thank you." She crossed her fingers.

Brendan shrugged. "You can try. But if he hates it, he'll ask them to take them off."

"That's all I can hope for. Is it okay if I go into the men's room?"

"Sure, no one's using it yet." He looked at his watch. "It's almost three-thirty. You've got some time."

She flashed him a grateful look and went next door. A sprig got pinned to the inside of the children's trouser pockets, and she put one under the lapel of the men's jackets. A sweet herbal smell wafted up from each one. Hopefully, if Tommy made the cast take them off, at least a few would stay in place. She wasn't sure how magic worked. Maybe the remaining charms would benefit those who weren't wearing them, rather like herd immunity for vaccines. She shrugged. It would have to be good enough.

Ruari came home for a shower and a quick early dinner before putting on their fancy clothes. While he changed, she slipped into a mid-calf, wrap dress with gold and black swirls and settled it over her curvy frame before zipping up the side under her arm. She wiggled again to align the seams and inspected herself in the mirror. She'd last worn it to one of Geoffrey's awful office parties. This was a much better occasion. She checked her makeup. She didn't wear it often, but tonight was one of those times. She heard a faint whine, but it sounded like something in the kitchen.

Ruari came up behind her and wrapped his arms around her. "Shimmy like that again, and we'll be late for the opening."

He kissed her temple, and she turned and met his lips with her own. "I may need help getting out of this when we get home," she murmured.

"I'll volunteer for that."

He put on his one good navy blue blazer over a button up white shirt. "How do I look?"

She tugged the lapels straight and made sure his collar was even. "You look wonderful. I don't get to see you dress up very often. Someday, I'll have to see you in a tux."

"I thought about it, but it'll be easier to change out the fuses in this when the lights go out. Did you have any luck talking to Casey or Randall?"

She sighed and checked her evening bag, a black and gold clutch big enough for keys, phone, a comb, a lipstick, and her charm pouch. "You were right about Casey. He was never far from Jake and was completely uninterested in talking to me. I gave up on him. I went down to Merritt Motors yesterday with no luck but managed to catch Randall outside on a break this afternoon. I explained the situation as best I could. He was upset when I explained that Tayloe was being 'borrowed' by Willa Trent who was angry at Clifford. He didn't want to hear it. Someone called him back into the shop before I could explain anything else." She shrugged. "So, I have no idea if I helped or made things worse for Tayloe."

Marianne put her hands on Ruari's chest and looked up at him. "I don't know how this is going to go tonight. Nothing might happen, or it might be a huge disaster. At this point, I can't worry about Tommy Verplank or his show. I just want Tayloe and Randall to be safe. What if I can't communicate with Willa and the other ghosts?"

"You'll be fine. You'll find a way."

She felt a small shot of adrenalin course through her. "Oh, shoot!"

"What?"

"I completely forgot to get more holy water! What if Shadow People show up?"

Ruari folded her into his arms. "Calm down. Have you seen any signs of Shadow People?"

"No."

"Then let's hope they stay far away. We'll do the best we can. I'll keep an eye on the backstage area and try and prevent any fires. By the way, I have something for you." He pulled a box out of his coat pocket.

"What's this?" For a wild moment, she thought he might propose.

"I stopped at DreamTime and got you a little something." He opened the box and pulled out a necklace. "Come stand here," he said, nodding at the mirror.

She stood between him and the mirror and watched as he put a necklace with three onyx medallions set in silver around her neck. Onyx protected the wearer from negative energy and provided emotional and physical strength. She felt an unexpected prickle of tears. Geoffrey's gifts to her had all been for his benefit, to be seen as a generous husband who had money to lavish on his wife. This was the first gift she'd gotten in a very long time that was meant for her.

"Ruari, I love it. It's beautiful."

He gave her a wry smile. "I can't have my lady unprotected because some stupid designer didn't put pockets in her dress."

She hugged him and dabbed at her eyes carefully to keep the mascara from running. "It's perfect." She took a deep breath and checked her reflection. Her makeup was still good. She heard another whine and felt a cold nudge against her hand.

"Rita, no girl. We're going out, and we'll be back later."

Ruari looked around the bedroom. "Is the ghost dog in here?"

"Yes. Maybe she wants food or something." Marianne stroked the invisible head, feeling the cold slip of spectral fur under her hand.

Ruari shook his head, dismissing the impossible for now. "We'd better hurry or we'll be late. Is Erin coming with us?"

"No, she borrowed The Flea, saying she had to pick someone up."

"Maybe we'll get to meet her mystery boyfriend tonight," Ruari mused.

"Maybe. Clearly, he doesn't drive." Marianne collected her black wrap and clutch and then stopped. "Rats. I need to pee before I go."

"I'll get the truck."

"I'll only be a second. Meet you out front." She detoured through the kitchen on the way out and left a couple of slices of pepperoni in the dog dish.

The marquee outside the Avery was brightly lit for the first time since Marianne had moved to town, and there was a nice crowd of people outside. The big black letters proclaiming, "100th Anniversary Show. The Legend of Sleepy Hollow," showed up beautifully against the newly washed white background.

Marianne took Ruari's arm and grinned up at him. "This is so exciting! Having everyone here to see it somehow makes it feel different from rehearsal." Even if the night was a catastrophe, this moment made her happy. Marianne had texted Tayloe an hour ago, assuring her she would be in the audience and watching over her. Tayloe had texted back, *Ok, thank you.*

He grinned back. "It does."

He flexed his shoulder, wincing a little, and she added, "All the work you and Scotty did to clean the marquee looks great."

"Thanks. If I haven't said it enough, you look gorgeous tonight. The necklace looks really good on you."

Marianne squeezed his arm. "I should've asked before we left, do you have the charm I made you, just in case?"

He tapped his pants pocket.

She spotted a distinguished figure with iron gray hair talking to a woman in a wheelchair.

"Oh, look!" Marianne exclaimed. "Grandma's here! And Mrs. Thomas. And, oh my gosh, is that John Irving? I know you need to get backstage, but let's go say hi first." She tugged him through the growing crowd.

Grandma Selene looked up and smiled as her granddaughter approached. She held out her arms. "There you are!" She embraced Marianne. "You look beautiful, lovey."

"I'm so glad you came tonight! Mrs. Thomas, it's nice to see you."

Her landlady peered up sideways around the hunch in her shoulders. "Hello, Marianne. I wouldn't miss an opening night for the world. Young man, I'm looking forward to your sets."

Ruari smiled. "I hear you're a long-time theater person. I hope they pass muster."

"I'm sure they will. I wish Selwyn could be here. He'd love this."

Grandma Selene said, "John agreed to accompany us tonight."

Marianne turned to him "I'm so glad you came!"

He looked better than he had the last time she'd seen him. He was dressed in a nice jacket over a clean dress shirt with a dark blue bow tie.

His mustache twitched with a smile. "Thank you. I haven't been to the theater in years. Your grandmother is very persuasive."

"Do you have your tickets or are they at 'will call'?" Marianne asked.

Mrs. Thomas said, "Miss Gina has them, don't you, dear?"

Miss Gina wore her usual purple scrubs over a turtleneck under her overcoat. Marianne shook the aide's hand. "I'm so glad you're here. I hope you enjoy the show."

"Thank you."

"You'd better find your seat before any more people come."

"Thank you, lovey," Grandma Selene replied. "We'll see you after the show. Perhaps we can go for a light supper afterwards."

"Sounds wonderful." She'd always loved late-night drinks at a café after a show when she lived in New York City.

John offered his arm to Grandma Selene who followed Mrs. Thomas and her aide through the front doors.

Ruari squeezed her hand. "I've got to go check on things. Text me if you see anything amiss."

"Absolutely. Cross fingers everything will go smoothly."

He nodded and kissed her cheek. "Remember, I won't be able to do much. I'm stuck next to the fuse panel. See you at intermission." He threaded his way through the crowd to the side of the theater and headed for the scene shop entrance.

Marianne walked through the main doors into the lobby. Everyone in Maple Hill sure liked the excuse to dress up, she thought with a smile. She'd been worried she had over dressed and now felt justified. Women wore formal dresses with a hint of sequins here and there, and men wore suits and ties and the occasional tuxedo. She took her black wrap coat to the check room.

"May I take your coat, ma'am?" The coat checker asked blithely.

Marianne did a double take. "Erin? How did you end up here?"

"We—I came early and found out that the person who said they were going to do it had bailed. I offered to help out. I figured this would be a good vantage for spotting anything spooky happening." Her usually spiky red hair was gelled back into a sleek auburn cap accented with a little black barrette with a sequined skull on it. Her black eyeliner had swoops at the corners, and her lids were highlighted with beige and a tinge of maroon. Her deep red lipstick complimented the dark red sleeveless dress she'd found at Renata's Closet. A black pendant necklace completed the outfit.

"You look terrific," Marianne said as she handed her coat over the counter. Erin gave her a playing card with a two of hearts in return. Its twin was clothes-pinned to the black coat before being hung up.

"So do you. Love the black and gold. You're so lucky you can wear that. Gold looks terrible on me. Nice necklace. Too bad it isn't a gold setting. Kinda clashes."

Marianne caught a glimpse of movement behind Erin. Someone was hiding behind the coats. Before she could investigate any further an older couple arrived at the counter. Marianne stepped aside, and Erin took their coats.

She tucked the playing card into her tiny evening bag on its black twisted cord over her shoulder. Another brief flash of white caught her eye. The older couple left.

"Is your friend back there?" Marianne asked, peering past Erin again.

"What? No." Erin replied a little too quickly.

Marianne scanned the back of the small coat room. "Hello, is someone else in here?" A pale face with dark, bobbed hair peeked out from behind the last row of jackets. "Toni?"

Erin looked flustered. "Yeah, Toni wanted to see the show, too. I invited her. It's not like she'll take up a seat or anything."

"I'm...I'm just surprised." Was Toni Erin's mystery date? Well. Suddenly all the borrowing of The Flea made more sense. Erin's happiness. The day they'd visited John Irving when she'd gone walking and not gotten Marianne's text. She smiled and waved at the spectral young woman. "Nice to see you, Toni."

Hi, Marianne. Nice to see you too. She leaned awkwardly against the back wall, dressed in her usual blue jeans and white tee shirt. *I figure I'll stay in here. I don't really have dress-up clothes.*

Marianne heard the voice in her head in spite of the noise of the crowded lobby.

"I hope you get to see some of the show at least."

Thanks.

Three more people stepped up to the coat check counter.

"I'll see you later, Erin."

Erin nodded in Marianne's direction, relieved at the interruption.

Wow. Erin certainly had done a complete one-eighty on her feelings about ghosts. Was Toni her new special someone? A dozen questions popped into her head, and she had no time to think about any of them. She had to stay focused on this evening. Maybe she could sit down with Erin tomorrow after all this was over.

A modest banner on the left side of the lobby caught her attention. "Silent Auction Fund Raiser." Marianne made her way over and saw a couple of tables draped in dark red tablecloths holding a variety of items. A card off to the side explained that this was a benefit to help pay for Teddy Miller's hospital bills after he'd been injured during the course of the production. Ruari's two lazy Susans, inlaid with dark Celtic knot work on a light background, made her proud. He really did beautiful work. Even better, there were at least two bids on them for substantially more than the starting price. There were at least a dozen other goods and services including some Headless Horseman and Sleepy Hollow memorabilia.

As she stood there, an older couple approached the table and bid on several things. Marianne put down a modest bid on a gift certificate to the antique store and hoped someone would be inspired to outbid her. Although she'd never met Teddy Miller, she hoped they raised enough to help him and his wife.

Marianne scanned the lobby. It seemed nearly all the people she knew had turned out for this event. She crossed her fingers it would be okay. She caught sight of a thin woman about her height with gray hair in a tight bun. Mrs. Caldwell had decided to come on opening night. A boy of about ten dressed in a stiff navy blazer stood next to her. She wondered if the boy was a grandchild or nephew and realized she had no idea if Mrs. C had a family. As she watched, the boy asked her a question, and Mrs. C tilted her head down to listen with a smile. That smile took a dozen years off her and softened her fierce visage. Marianne was amazed by the transformation of the grumpy old librarian. Her view was abruptly blocked by people walking by, and Mrs. C turned away.

❦

Still smiling, Ruari headed for the scene shop entrance hoping to avoid any further social obligations. He wanted to check all the sets one more time to be sure nothing went wrong.

He was almost to the corner of the building when someone said imperiously, "Excuse me!"

In all the years he worked for Talmadge he'd met Gloria Hopper only a handful of times at company picnics and a couple of rare personal visits to the Maple Hill office. But her voice was an unforgettable hoarse alto. He grimaced.

It was dark. Maybe he could keep walking as if he hadn't heard her.

"Ruari Allen, I want to talk to you." She pursued him relentlessly.

He stopped and faced her, hoping to keep things civil. "Good evening, Mr. and Mrs. Hopper."

Gloria was dressed in a fur coat over something full length that glittered below the fur hem. Her husband Ned was in a dark wool tweed coat, the light glinting off his thick-framed glasses.

Maybe they were just here to wish him all the best for the opening show.

She advanced on him, hissing like an angry goose. "I expected you to teach our son some responsibility and a work ethic. Instead, you nearly got him killed! "

His hackles went up instantly. He clenched his fists. The Hoppers had no hold over him or his job. He could finally say what he wanted to. "You should've taught him that. Instead, you taught him to be entitled. Your child is inattentive, lazy, and reckless, completely unsuited to working as a handyman. It was only a matter of time before he did something really stupid."

"How dare you!" Gloria sputtered. "If SueAnn hadn't fired

249

you, I would have. You're not fit to mentor him or any other young person!"

"Casey is destined for much better things than being a glorified janitor," Ned added.

"SueAnn didn't fire me. I resigned." He stalked away, not trusting himself to say anything else.

Shaking with fury, Ruari let himself into the scene shop. The sooner the show was over, the sooner he could leave the horrible Casey and his miserable parents behind. He took a breath and let it out, then a second breath. The smells of cut wood, paint, and dust filled his nostrils. He had a job to do. Gloria Hopper's accusations were infuriating, but she had no more power to hurt him.

Dave Binkler, his pale pompadour sprayed into place, hailed him with some exasperation. "Ruari, you're here finally! I need you to check the schoolhouse set. It was wobbling a lot last night."

The stage manager was another person Ruari was looking forward to leaving behind. However, he was positively sweet in comparison to the Hoppers. Taking off his jacket, he laid it over the back of a chair. He grabbed a cordless screwdriver and followed The Bink backstage.

In the lobby of the Avery, a statuesque woman in a blue silk sheath dress stood like an elegant column. Her long blonde hair was twisted up in an chignon, held with a black lacquered hair pin. By her side was a familiar, shorter woman with chestnut hair. Marianne made her way over.

Kelly's watchful expression relaxed when she saw Marianne. "Hey, hon, nice to see you here." She enveloped Marianne in a warm hug.

"I'm glad you came," she replied. "I wasn't expecting you."

Sarah tolerated a quick hug from Marianne. "Tayloe is our

niece. We wanted to see her play and be here just in case. I hear things have been weird."

A flash of resentment warred with her relief that Sarah was finally present. She swallowed her waspishness, determined to stay focused on the potential problems.

She lowered her voice and leaned in a little. "I think the spirits of three actors from 1909 are borrowing the leads to work out their differences. Short of closing the play down, there was no way I could stop it. So, I'm just keeping an eye on Tayloe, Randall, and Casey. With any luck the play will go on without too much trouble."

Sarah opened her mouth to say something.

"Check your ten, babes," Kelly interrupted. She'd unconsciously taken up a guard position while Sarah was focusing on Marianne.

Sarah cast her eyes across the lobby and scowled. "What are they doing here?"

Marianne looked past her. "Who are you looking at?"

Kelly tilted her head in the direction and murmured, "See the tall woman in the black dress and the woman in green next to her? That's Paloma Xerxes and Marette."

The other two Protectors.

Marianne picked them out. "They're probably here to see Tristan Kitteby. He's playing the Narrator."

Sarah snapped her head back to Marianne. "You didn't tell me Tristan Kitteby was in this."

Marianne raised her eyebrows and said coolly, "You haven't exactly been available by phone or otherwise."

"You still should've warned me."

Marianne frowned. "I would have loved to, but leaving messages in the void strikes me as stupid after a while."

"I got all your messages."

"I had no way to know that."

"I was busy."

Marianne was nettled. "Yes, apparently you were going

through Byron's house. Multiple times. Care to share what you were doing?"

Sarah looked startled. "How do you know that?"

"Tristan told me. He followed you."

"That nosy bastard. It figures. He—"

Marianne put her hand up and cut her off. "Before you say anything more. All three of the other Protectors were convinced you were in league with Byron and looking for ways to rescue him from the Shadowlands or take over where he left off."

Both Sarah and Kelly were shocked into temporary silence.

"However," Marianne continued, "I told Tristan there was no way you would ever trust Byron again, and you would never betray your duties as a Protector. So, what were you doing?"

Sarah gave her an opaque look. "This isn't the best place to discuss this."

"Probably not, but I don't seem to be able to get your attention otherwise."

Sarah gave a frustrated huff of breath. "I was looking through his papers and effects to figure out what he was doing. If he was up to anything more, I want to be able to stop him before it happens."

Something inside Marianne uncoiled. She hadn't guessed wrong. "Good."

"Babes, they're coming over," Kelly murmured.

Paloma and Marette approached. Paloma was easily six feet tall, matching Kelly eye to eye, while Marette was barely Marianne's height. The four women regarded each other with mutually suspicious stares, sizing each other up like dogs at the park. No one seemed inclined to say anything.

Marianne stepped around Kelly and smiled at the tall, striking woman. Now that she knew it was Paloma Xerxes, she vaguely remembered a photo in the news about the artist and one of her shows in Putnam County. Middle-aged, Paloma bore herself with a regal, easy grace. Her cane seemed more of an accessory than a necessity. The woman next to her looked like she was fifteen. She wore a green knitted dress with complex cables and flowers worked into the fabric. The pattern gave Marianne a slightly giddy feeling if she looked at them for very long.

Tristan was friends with these women and trusted them. Hopefully, he'd relayed to them the conversation they'd had about Sarah and Kelly. Marianne offered her hand and the bright smile she'd used to greet her ex's powerful work colleagues.

"Hi, I'm Marianne Singleton. Tristan has told me a little about you. It's nice to meet you."

Paloma looked at Marianne's offered hand for a moment as if it were a Dollar Store gift she didn't want to accept. Then she took Marianne's hand in her cold fingers briefly. Marianne ignored her disdain and shook her hand firmly.

She turned to the younger woman and offered her hand with a smile. "You must be Marette. It's nice to meet you."

Marette regarded her solemnly with large brown eyes that would have been at home on a deer. She nodded slightly, ignoring the proffered hand. Marianne wondered if she was averse to touching people in general.

Marianne turned her hand palm up and gestured to Sarah and Kelly. "These are my friends, Sarah and Kelly. I believe you know each other?"

The women stared at each other coolly without speaking. Marianne resisted rolling her eyes.

Instead, she plowed on. "I believe there have been some misunderstandings in the past, but I would like to put that aside, at least for tonight. I don't know what Tristan has told you, but I think there are spirits with old grudges who will be present on stage tonight. I would appreciate it if all of you would keep your eyes open and be willing to intervene if things go wrong."

Paloma gave Marianne a hawkish stare. "Yes, we're well aware of the disturbances in the spirit world. Whatever you're doing, you need to stop before it gets out of hand."

Marianne bristled. It was just like grad school history department politics all over again. "Excuse me? I may be relatively new to dealing with ghosts, but I know what I'm doing."

"If you did, there wouldn't be reverberations clear across three counties." She turned to Sarah. "What do you think you're doing by allowing this…person to stir up the spirit world? You know what the consequences can be."

Sarah replied coldly, "Marianne is quite capable."

"We'll see. What are you doing with Byron's notes, I wonder? Stepping into his shoes? Helping him return to this world?"

Sarah bared her teeth. "I wouldn't dream of telling you."

"Then I have no choice but to assume the worst."

Sarah growled. Kelly tensed.

If things went any further, there would be bloodshed. Marianne took a breath and tried to dial it back. "Forget that for now. If things get out of hand tonight, can we count on you to help us?"

Paloma stared down at her. "This is your territory. We're here for damage control and to make sure things don't spill over into our counties."

The lights in the lobby dimmed and came up twice in succession.

Paloma gave a wintry smile. "Enjoy the show."

The two Protectors turned and headed for the auditorium.

"And that's why we never work with them," Kelly muttered in disgust.

Sarah said, "Never mind. Marianne, we've got your back."

That was something at least. "Thanks. Check in with you at the intermission."

They left for the nearest entrance to the auditorium. Still boiling, Marianne got a program and went to her own seat near the back of the house. What was wrong with those two? She'd offered an olive branch, and they'd thrown it away. Clearly there was more to this longstanding feud than she was aware of. It was curious that Marette hadn't said anything, letting Paloma set the tone. Maybe Marette was fearful of her? Or shy? Or perhaps she agreed wholeheartedly and was content to let the other woman speak for her? Maybe if Marianne could speak to Marette alone, she'd have a chance to build some bridges. That would have to happen later, it was too late now.

She pushed the worn velvet seat down and sat. The seat was near an exit in case she needed to duck out and go through the side hall to the Green Room, or, perish the thought, run for the stage.

CHAPTER 22

$\mathcal{M}$arianne felt her clutch purse vibrate. She pulled out her cell phone and saw she'd missed three messages from Ruari.

Fifteen minutes ago he'd written: *Just saw Casey/Randall/Tayloe talking together. It didn't look happy. Auras dark.*

Twelve minutes ago: *T stormed off. C and R still at it. I asked if there were problems. They said no but they were lying hard/smoky. They didn't seem to know me. I'll keep an eye on them.*

Five minutes ago: *Lost them for a couple of minutes over a set question. Randall came out of the costume shop?*

Just now: *Headed for fuse box. I'll keep the door open.*

Marianne texted back: *Sarah & Kelly here. Met the other Protectors. Did not go well.*

I ran into Casey's mother. Also did not go well.

Sorry to hear that! Never mind. Screw them. We just do the best we can.

She got up for several people as they made their way in from the aisle. Luckily, no one she knew was sitting near her. She'd caught a glimpse of Paloma'a tall figure across the auditorium near the front. The lights dimmed, and David Binkler came out on stage looking dapper in a dark blue suit and freshly styled hair in his trademark swirl pompadour.

"Welcome, ladies and gentlemen. Thank you so much for coming to our production of *The Legend of Sleepy Hollow* this evening. We have a few announcements. We'd like to draw your attention to the fundraiser in the lobby. Any money raised goes to pay the medical bills of our long-time friend and colleague Teddy Miller who was injured during the making of this show. Please be generous and open your hearts to help him out.

"During the show there will be some special effects including flashing lights. Patrons that may suffer from epilepsy and other visual light stimulation are advised to close their eyes or look away. In addition, we warn you that we will be using a synthetic smoke machine in a few scenes. For now, please silence your phones and refrain from taking photos during the show as it may distract the actors and other members of the audience. And now, without further ado, *The Legend of Sleepy Hollow.*"

There was a scatter of polite clapping, and Marianne was aware that the auditorium was nearly full. She was both glad for Tommy Verplank and all the more anxious for the bystanders should anything go wrong during the play. She touched the charm in her clutch bag and touched the necklace at her throat and thought, *By Earth and Sky and Fire and Water, bless this production, and keep all the people here safe!*

The red velvet curtain drew silently upward on a bucolic scene of woods and meadows with the Hudson River in the background. Tristan Kitteby in his beautiful deep blue coat with shiny gold buttons strode out on the stage. He had shaved his beard off in the style of the period, and his makeup had somehow given his rounded face a decade of years. He swept off his tricorn and bowed gracefully before placing it back on his head.

"In the bosom of one of those spacious coves which indent the eastern shore of the Hudson, at that broad expansion of the river denominated by the ancient Dutch navigators the Tappan Zee," he began, his voice a rich and vibrant tenor, "lies the drowsy hamlet of Sleepy Hollow. It is an old Dutch settlement of complacent, prosperous farmers and gardeners. These peculiar inhabitants live comfortably far away from the hurry of modern life. They love nothing so much as bounteous harvests, good food, and a place by the fire under a tight roof. They are given to trances and visions and prone to seeing strange sights. Sometimes they hear music or voices among the sleepy bird calls. Anyone who tarries here also begins to see spirits and apparitions. Come with us now and visit the be-spelled settlement of Sleepy Hollow."

The scene changed to a country lane. A white painted bridge had been placed mid stage. Ichabod Crane came strolling purposefully along singing a refrain from a hymn as he went. He walked as if his arms and legs didn't quite work as well as a regular person's, and it made him look slightly insect-like. Over his shoulder was a stick with a tied-up bag swinging at the end. He crossed the bridge, and the projected scene melted into that of a prosperous village with buildings made of fieldstone and clapboard. A white steepled church rose above them. People in colonial dress entered going about their daily lives. Several children chased a hoop with a stick. Marianne was relieved to see at least a couple of sprigs still attached to the bodices of the women's clothing.

An older man approached Ichabod. "Good morrow, sir! Are you here to stay or passing through?"

"I am Ichabod Crane, your new school master, here to teach your children reading, writing, and arithmetic."

"Welcome to Sleepy Hollow, Master Crane! Let me introduce you to our families and show you your school house."

"Much obliged, good sir. And, may I inquire, what is your name?"

"I am Baltus Van Tassel."

"Pleased to make your acquaintance."

The audience was drawn into Sleepy Hollow and all the goings-on there. Marianne had to remind herself to keep an eye out for anything odd. All eyes were on Brom when he entered the scene. He was clearly the local darling, dressed well and greeted by everyone he passed. He slapped Ichabod on the back when he welcomed him. For a moment it looked as though the two men might become friends. But when the beautiful Katrina arrived, she favored Ichabod with smiles and giggles, and Brom's expression changed. From then on, there was an edge to his lines, and the pranks began.

The first break in the flow was during the singing lesson when the smoke from the plugged up chimney belched from the stove. The lights went out. Marianne didn't remember that from rehearsal. As the darkness stretched beyond a few seconds, the audience began shifting in their seats. Suddenly the lights went back on, and the scene continued. Marianne got out her phone and texted Ruari.

Everything okay?

Yup. First fuse. Are the lights back on?

Yes.

A discreetly cleared throat from the person next to her made her put her phone face down in her lap and cover it with her purse.

Act I continued, and Marianne watched the covert looks and underlying sharpness of the three leads. It was like watching a real-life soap opera. They certainly had the rapt attention of the audience. The lights went out a second time during Ichabod's crossing through the cemetery after a visit to the family of one of his school children. In the pitch dark, Ichabod continued whistling for almost a minute. The audience grew restive again, but the lights came back on, and the scene continued.

Marianne knew Ruari must be frantically trying to keep the power board from overloading and hoped he was okay.

When the invitation to the party at the Van Tassel's house arrived, Ichabod ended school early. The children left amid whoops of delight, and Ichabod began getting ready for the party.

Brom lingered in the doorway to the schoolhouse giving Ichabod ill-favored scowls.

"Is there something else, Master Van Brunt?" Ichabod asked as he tugged his shirt straight and smoothed his worn black coat down.

"Only take care on your way to the Van Tassel's house. The roads can be treacherous."

"I will keep a watchful eye out for vagabonds and highwaymen."

The two men glared at each other before the lights went out and the curtain closed. The house lights came up, signaling intermission. Marianne got up, folded the seat, and laid her Playbill over the front edge to indicate it was taken and went out to the lobby.

The concession stand was open and serving cocktails to people over twenty-one, as well as selling sodas, and small packets of nuts, candy, and cookies. It was staffed by a couple of volunteers. The coat room was open, and Erin was back at her post in case anyone needed their outerwear.

Her phone buzzed, and she checked her messages.

One act down, one to go! I have three fuses left so cross fingers we won't need more than that, Ruari wrote. *How's the play? Any signs?*

You could cut the tension between the leads with a knife. There is definitely some departure from the script since the last rehearsal I saw. Bet Tommy is worried, she replied.

Gotta go check on the set.

Good luck.

She went to the concession stand to get herself a small bottle of water. She stood behind the director and a well-dressed man and his wife.

"Well, Tommy this is quite a production." He sounded impressed in spite of himself. "You've managed to update the legend and focus on the rivalry between the two men over the girl. I'll be interested to see where you take it in the second Act."

"Charlie, I think you'll both be surprised and entertained," Tommy laughed.

Marianne thought Tommy's reply sounded a little strained. She bet Tommy was sweating bullets, hoping that the play didn't go off the rails any more.

"Susie and I were sorry to hear about Teddy Miller. It's nice you've got a little fund raiser for him. We bid on a few things, didn't we, Sugarcake?"

Susie's elegantly styled hair was sprayed into place to show off her diamond earrings. "Yes, the carved trays are so rustic. They'd look sweet in our Hamptons home. I do hope we get them."

Marianne down-checked her assessment of the power couple from New York by several notches. Rustic indeed! She'd met more than a few people like Charlie and Susie during her years in New York and was so glad to have left all of that behind. She didn't miss it or them at all. She reminded herself that it didn't matter as long as they plunked down a lot of cash and helped Mr. Miller.

The three notables were served small plastic flutes of champagne before moving off. She purchased a small bottle of water for a dollar and left a donation in the jar. From the side of the lobby she watched the crowd. Paloma and Marette stood on the other side of the room talking to each other. Marianne wondered what they were saying and shook her head, determined to ignore them.

Mrs. C threaded her way firmly through the crowd to Marianne's side, little boy still in tow. She was dressed in a dark gray skirt with a dark green velvet blouse. She looked stern.

"Mrs. Caldwell, nice to see you tonight!"

"Marianne, this is my nephew, Paul."

"Nice to meet you, Paul. How do you like the show so far?"

Paul said, "I like it. Those two sure hate each other don't they!"

"I guess they do." Marianne looked at Mrs. C. "What do you think?"

"Well, it's taking some liberties with the original, but I can see that it's following the spirit of the story very well. I'm looking forward to seeing how the director handles the climactic ride through the woods. I've seen all the adaptations both on stage and screen. The entire show is made or broken with that scene."

Paul tapped his aunt on the arm. "Aunt Milly, can I have a snack?"

"May I. And yes, here's some money. Be sure to leave them a tip." She pulled a five out of her purse. Paul hurried to stand at the end of the line. Mrs. C kept a watchful eye over her charge.

"Paul is very polite," Marianne observed.

"We're working on it. My brother is a good father but busy."

Brother? *She must have a much younger brother or she's much younger than she looks.* Either way, she's a good aunt, taking her nephew out for an evening of theater. Marianne's estimation of the formidable librarian rose. She changed the subject. "I didn't realize you were such a fan of *The Legend of Sleepy Hollow.*"

"Oh, yes. Ever since I was a little girl. The first time I read it, it scared me to death. I was determined to understand it inside and out from that time on."

"I see. Well, I hope you won't be disappointed."

"We shall see. I do hope we won't have any more outages."

"Oh, you noticed that did you? Ruari's in back keeping everything going."

She snorted. "This old building ought to be condemned. It's in terrible shape, and Verplank has never really taken care of it. He'd rather chase another dream than take care of the one he has."

"You sound like you care about the Avery."

"Of course I do! It's a national landmark. Or it would be if it wasn't about to fall down." She shook her head. "Well, maybe someday it will get a much needed renovation."

"I'm sure Mr. Verplank is very hopeful of that, too."

"Humph."

Paul returned with a bag of mint candies and gave his aunt the change. He opened the box and offered Mrs. C a few before having a handful. She took them graciously.

The lights dimmed and came up again in quick succession. Marianne threw her empty bottle in the trash. "Time to go back to our seats. Paul, I hope you like the second half of the show."

He nodded, trying to wolf down the last of his snack.

Mrs. Caldwell replied with a glint in her eye, "Yes. Time to see if the ride is worth the wait."

I hope it is, too, she thought.

CHAPTER 23

The play resumed with Ichabod riding a borrowed horse, Gunpowder, through the woods to the Van Tassel's party. The prop horse was worn around Ichabod's waist and looked like the broken-down nag it was supposed to be. Its head drooped, and the mane and tail were scraggly. The front and back legs swung foolishly, while the actor moved forward. Marianne was impressed that it didn't look nearly as ridiculous as it had in rehearsal. Ruari told her that Fran had spent hours building it and the more impressive Daredevil horse prop for Brom. Casey and Randall must have practiced for hours getting the movement to look right. Her hopes for an exciting chase scene rose.

As Ichabod made his way through the forest, tree branches dropped and bushes shook, making Gunpowder shy and causing Ichabod no end of trouble. It was hard to tell if Brom and Jake were behind the mischief or whether it was part of the spooky atmosphere of Sleepy Hollow. Ichabod looked out of place in his worn black suit among the villagers in their finery.

The scene changed, and the actors brought out the long table and set it. They talked and laughed, welcoming each new addition as they set the huge feast. In spite of Tommy's concerns, they managed to include the audience in their excitement.

After the first half of the Van Tassel party, the ghostly Maud Van Tassel exited through the back of the fireplace. Katrina held her head, moaning with great feeling. For a second, Marianne had the impression Tayloe was fighting Willa. When Ichabod took her hand to dance, she looked a little wild-eyed.

Uh oh, Marianne thought.

But Ichabod smoothly led her into the steps of an English country dance. The lively folk-music brought the other couples onto the dance floor, including Brom and his buddy Jake with a brightly dressed dance partner each.

After a few turns, Brom forcefully careened into Ichabod and Katrina. Brom flung his dance partner at Ichabod, startling both actors and then snatched Katrina into his arms. He gave his line, "Katrina, come dance with me!"

Katrina got her balance after one turn and planted herself, pulling away from Brom. "Stop it! Let me go! I am sick of you yanking me around, Loren!"

Marianne sat up abruptly. Tayloe's face had subtly changed, becoming rounder, her lips more full and bow-shaped. It was Willa. And she was furious. Marianne tensed, wondering if Tayloe would be able to regain control. Marianne was maybe twenty rows from the stage. A short dash, up three stairs, and she'd be there.

"Then stop making eyes at him!" Brom said. His face had become older, more square-jawed as Loren took over. Marianne wondered if anyone else could see the surreptitious change in the actors' faces. She spared a glance at the person sitting next to her. They appeared to be watching the stage with interest but not alarm or confusion.

"And so what if I do? I can like whoever I please!" Katrina replied.

"You told me I was the one for you. You said when this was

over, we would leave this hick town and make it big together." Brom grabbed Katrina by the wrist.

Ichabod strode over and seized Brom's shoulder. Ichabod no longer looked like the hometown mechanic Marianne had met a day ago. In his place, an older, plainer-faced man stood. He was no longer awkward but confident and menacing. "Let go of her. She doesn't love you. She thinks you're nothing but a bully and a cheat."

Brom released Katrina and turned, his fists bunched. "Back off you two-bit little clerk. I got here first. You weren't even their first choice. It was only after the first two were sacked for being drunks that they even considered you. When you arrived, she called you a pathetic, no name amateur." His laugh was ugly.

Ichabod looked stunned and hurt. He turned to Katrina.

She looked anguished. "Cliff, that was before I knew you. I would never say that now!"

Ichabod stared at her. "Willa, you said I was talented. You said you loved me." His expression hardened as he looked between Brom and Katrina. "It wasn't just him. It was both of you together all this time. Every prank, every slight."

Katrina said, "Cliff, no! I wasn't part of that! Don't go!" She grabbed Ichabod's sleeve.

Transfixed by the spectacle, the audience seemed unsure where this was going. It was like watching your neighbors fighting through an open window: embarrassing, but you couldn't look away.

Ichabod pulled free of her scornfully. "I'm done with you." He looked at Brom his face contorted in a sneer. "You deserved everything you got."

Brom looked confused and then realization dawned. "You? You poisoned the pumpkin head?"

Ichabod's lip curled. "After that day when you got so sick over a little hot pepper sauce at lunch, I knew I had you. I just had to bide my time. I dabbed little hot sauce on the inside of the mask. Some firefighter you are, afraid of a little heat."

Brom's face darkened with fury. "*You* killed me! It wasn't the fire or the smoke. I couldn't breathe." His fists curled, and he looked ready to attack Ichabod.

Belatedly Marianne vaulted out of her seat and ran for the stage as fast as she could go, her purse bouncing along her hip on its cord. She had to stop this before it got totally out of hand and help Tayloe.

Ichabod tensed, more than ready to respond with his own violence. "The fire wasn't my fault, but it sure was convenient."

The huge red curtain descended in a rush, blocking the audience's view. Tristan in his Narrator's outfit emerged hurriedly from the wing. Marianne narrowly avoided colliding with him and darted behind the curtain.

After a startled look he regained his composure and spoke in the voice of the Narrator. "Katrina Van Tassel became completely disillusioned by both of her suitors during the party. The appearance of her great-grandmother Maud had a powerful effect on her, and she refused to marry either one of them. Her beaus were distraught and angry by her rejection and left the party soon after that."

On stage behind the curtain the lights had come up. Katrina, Brom, and Ichabod were arguing heatedly with each other. The cast stood staring in shock at the unfolding confrontation, completely flummoxed as to what to do next. Dave Binkler stepped in between the three combatants.

"What are you doing?" He hissed. "This is highly unprofessional! Go back to the top of the scene and let's do this again."

"Get out of the way, little man!" Brom said, pushing him aside.

"I beg your pardon!" Binkler said huffily.

"Mr. Binkler," Marianne said, "May I have a word with you please?"

He turned to her, his brows lowered. "Get off the stage! You don't belong here!"

"I need to speak with you, now!"

"No, we may be able to salvage this if we hurry."

"Listen to me. Can you call another intermission? Something to delay the audience? I just need five minutes."

A look of outrage crossed his face. "Do you have something to do with this madness?"

"No, but I think I can fix it. Just give me five minutes."

Fuming, Binkler stepped away from the three leads. His white pompadour trembled in agitation. "The longer this goes on, the more we lose them."

"I know. Tristan is out there trying to patch it together. Let me work with Tayloe and them. Just give me five minutes. Maybe skip to the chase scene instead?"

Binkler wavered and then nodded. "Five minutes." He stepped away clapping his hands and ordering the rest of the cast to change the scene. Relieved that someone had taken charge, the cast moved to take the feast scene away.

Marianne stepped over to the three who were still arguing. Up close the faces of the dead actors completely overwrote the living ones. For once, it wasn't hard to focus on the spirits at all.

"Hey, Willa, Cliff, Loren!" The three actors turned to her. There was no time to lead them gently into the situation. She just dove right in. "The three of you are ghosts of the actors you were in 1909. You've been stuck at the theater since you died. You need to accept it and move on. I'm here to help you."

Glad someone was listening, Loren jabbed a finger at Cliff. "He knew I was allergic to hot peppers and deliberately caused a reaction."

Cliff replied heatedly, "I didn't mean to kill him. A fatal humiliation only."

"I died from your idiotic prank! I've been trying to get back at you ever since."

Willa stared in shock. "Wait, Cliff, you *murdered* Loren? How could you?" She looked disgusted. "I felt sorry for you for years! But you *killed* him!"

Cliff reached for her. "Willa, I loved you with all my heart, but you wouldn't see past him and look at me."

She recoiled from his hand as if he were a toad. Then she added suspiciously, "Did you do something to Dane? Did you kill him, too?"

Cliff was taken aback. "No! He was just a little kid. I just needed him out of the way long enough for Loren to put the mask on. He was going to tell!"

Willa shrieked, "You slimy little horse turd! You killed him too! He was like my little brother! I felt guilty for years!"

Cliff said in anguish, "I didn't mean to! The fire happened and everything was chaos. I just wanted to get out of there. I was sure he'd get out on his own."

Willa's face contorted. "You murderer!" She launched herself at Ichabod, raking with her fingernails and shrieking like a banshee.

Cliff put his arms up to block the blow, and Loren wrapped his arms around her and pulled her away. Willa struggled for a minute then slumped in Loren's arms and sobbed.

A whiff of something acrid curled into Marianne's nostrils. At first she thought it was the smoke machine, but that smelled more like ozone and dust, not like burning refuse. A zing of alarm shot through her.

There was a murmur from the other side of the curtain, and someone said, "Do you smell that? Is that smoke?" They sounded unsure. "Is this part of the play? What's going on?"

As the voices became more strident, Mrs. Caldwell spoke up in a clear, commanding tone, "The play is over. Would everyone please make your way to the exits now. Go outside through the lobby and gather on the sidewalk. Take your coats and belongings with you and move quickly please. Now!" She clapped her hands sharply for emphasis.

Seats thudded as people stood up and voices became more purposeful.

Binkler said in despair, "Oh this is a catastrophe! We'll never get them back now. We might even have to refund everyone. We'll go broke!"

Marianne shook him. "There's no time for that!" She looked at the rest of the cast. "Everyone, go outside! Hopefully, you can pick up your things later, but you have to go outside now just in case!"

Parents took charge of the children and hustled them off stage. The others left, looking confused and alarmed. Marianne pulled her phone out and texted Ruari. *Play's over. There's smoke out here. Is there a fire back there? Get out!*

The main curtain rippled as someone walked along trying to find a way through. Kelly and Sarah emerged from the wing. Thank goodness. They would be able to handle Willa and Tayloe.

They hurried over and extracted their weeping niece from Brom's grip and said, "We've got her. We'll get her outside." Sarah looked at Marianne. "The fire department is on the way."

Katrina looked dazed, her makeup streaked and smeared by tears. She meekly went with her aunts.

Marianne turned to Cliff and Loren. Somehow she had to separate Loren and Cliff from Casey and Randall. But how? Unfinished business. That's what kept people here. How could they get closure? Maybe without Willa here, they could focus better.

She shook Ichabod's arm to get his attention. "Cliff, why did you sabotage Loren's costume?"

Cliff looked sullen again. "I was sick of the practical jokes, stolen costume parts, and broken makeup."

Loren sneered, "You had no interest in pursuing a career in theater. Whereas it was my life's dream."

"Loren, you were a firefighter up until you got into acting. You'd only been an actor for a couple of years," Marianne pointed out.

"There was no future in that." His face twisted. "How bitterly ironic that I should die on stage of asphyxiation during a fire."

No contesting that. "It sounds more like you died from an allergic reaction."

Loren flashed an angry look at Cliff. "One that he created on purpose!"

"It was the only way to stop you from tormenting me!"

"Cliff, you could have left the play," Marianne said. "You ended up killing your cast mate and a little kid."

"I didn't mean to." He sounded sulky and unrepentant.

Time was passing. She had to hurry this along.

"Cliff, why are you here?"

"I thought Willa loved me and—and I thought I'd killed that little boy. I couldn't live with myself."

He'd died in obscurity about ten years after the fateful fire, Marianne remembered.

Loren snorted derisively. "She didn't love you! She wanted Hollywood as badly as I did."

They moved toward each other again, looking to finish their fight. Marianne put a hand on each man's chest, keeping them apart. She gave them each a sharp look. "Willa thought it was flattering to have the attention of two men. She played you off each other. To be fair, I don't think she loved either one of you. You need to let that go."

"The little minx told me we would go to Hollywood together," Loren said resentfully.

"She probably would have gone with you, but I doubt she would have stayed. Cliff, did you lock Dane in a closet or something?"

He nodded. "He saw me doctoring the pumpkin prop and said he would tell his father. I couldn't let him." He looked anguished. "I was going to let him out after the play was over! He would have been fine!"

No, he would have been traumatized, but never mind. It was her job to save Randall, not get Cliff therapy. She made a choice. "Cliff, Dane's death was an accident. It's not your fault." It was better to lie as long as he left Randall and moved on.

Cliff looked hopeful. "Not my fault?"

She gave him an earnest look. "No. You can leave. You don't

have to stick around anymore. Randall, I know you're in there. You have to help Cliff leave."

"Not my fault?" Cliff repeated.

Marianne took the actor's arms and shook him a little. "Randall! I need you out here. Now!"

"Not my fault." Randall/Cliff shuddered and blinked. Randall looked at her. "I'm here."

She sagged a little in relief. "Good, you have to get out of here! There may be a fire." She pushed him toward the wing exit. "Go! Tayloe's safe outside already."

He nodded and stumbled away.

She turned back to Loren. But he'd wandered away to center stage. He stood panting and swallowing reflexively like he might be sick. His face was flushed and sweating. He was trying to loosen his collar and shirt.

"Loren?" She started toward him.

"Mahri!" Ruari ran onto the stage. "Thank God you're alright!"

"I'm fine. Is Casey allergic to hot peppers?"

"What?" He looked at his former assistant for the first time.

Casey had dropped to his knees and was gasping for breath. "Of all the times to be overly dramatic," Ruari snorted.

"He's possessed by a man who died of anaphylactic shock." She dropped to the young man's side. "Casey!" She shook his shoulder, but he ignored her. She looked at Ruari. "Is Casey allergic to hot sauce, peppers, capsaicin?"

Taken aback, Ruari replied, "Um, no? I don't think so. He always ate pepperoni pizza slices and added pepper flakes."

"Great." She shook the young man's shoulder. "Casey! I need you to listen to me! Loren is allergic to hot sauce, but you're not. You can breathe fine. Fight Loren!"

The stocky young man kept gasping, his face turning from red to purple. Ruari shouldered her to the side, pulled Casey up off his hands and knees, ready to slap him silly for all of his offenses.

All of Casey's strutting, shirking, smirking, slacking, and the occasional flash of pride at doing something right flashed across Ruari's mind. The look of pure fear in the boy's eyes now as he gasped for breath made Ruari's anger drain away. Casey was just a kid.

"Hey, snap out of it." He shook him roughly. "You're not allergic, you stupid twit!"

Casey blinked, saw Ruari's face up close, and shuddered. He took a deep gulping breath of air only to cough as an acrid wave of smoke billowed across the stage.

Ruari shoved his former assistant toward the wing exit and said, "Casey, you have to get out of here, now! There's a fire! Go out the front doors in the lobby."

Casey lurched away.

"We have to get out of here, too," Ruari said.

They turned to follow Casey, but stopped at the sound of heavy footsteps running across the stage behind them.

Erin dashed across the stage. Her snug red dress was complimented not by spiky heels but by her black Doc Martins polished to a mirror finish. Only Erin could pull off that look. The only thing amiss was an odd bulge ruining the line of the dress at her hip. Toni's translucent form trailed after her.

Erin said, "We smelled smoke, and everyone rushed out the door, but I didn't see you guys. Someone said the fire department is coming. What happened? Where's the fire?"

"Who is that?" Ruari said looking at the pale form next to his sister.

"You can see her? That's Toni. I forgot to tell you." Marianne said.

Toni raised one hand at Ruari. *Hi, we met at the cemetery.*

Ruari looked confused. "I don't remember…never mind. We were just leaving."

Marianne shook her head. "We can't leave yet. I have to find Dane."

"Who the hell is Dane?" Erin said.

"A boy who was locked in a closet. He was caught in the fire of 1909 when the theater burned down and he died."

"Isn't it a little late to find him, then?" Erin said in a voice richly laced with sarcasm and fear.

"We don't have time for this. We have to go," Ruari said.

Marianne replied, "But he's the fourth ghost. If we don't find him, this whole scenario might play out again in the future."

"But this is a completely different theater than the Averill!" Erin protested.

"Yes, but it was built on the same footprint."

Erin put her hand up. "Let me get this straight. We're looking for a ghost kid stuck in a ghost closet?"

"Yes, but I'm looking for him. You are getting out of here."

"Oh for fuck's sake!" Erin threw up both hands.

"I'll be as quick as I can," Marianne stated.

Ruari looked at both of them. "Are you crazy? This is a terrible idea!"

I can help, Toni said. *If you go down the corridors, I can go into rooms even if they're locked.*

Erin looked at Marianne's high heels. "Toni's right, we can check the hallways faster than you can."

"No, I've got this," Marianne insisted, leaning over to slip her shoes off.

Ruari took Marianne's elbow firmly. "Absolutely not! We are all leaving. Let the firefighters deal with it."

Marianne looked at them in anguish. "If he's a ghost, they'll never find him! We'll be doing this whole thing again tomorrow night. We have to break the cycle."

"He's a fucking ghost, he'll be fine!" Ruari snapped, pulling Marianne toward the exit.

"Please!" Marianne said.

Erin had a determined look. "Don't worry, Marianne, Toni

and me got this!" She ran off before either one of them could stop her.

I'll keep her safe. I promise! Toni called as she followed Erin.

"Erin!" Ruari shouted. "Dammit."

Another wave of acrid smoke rolled across the stage, making them both cough. He pulled Marianne toward the exit, crouching, trying to get under the smoke layer. The smell scalded the back of her nose and throat.

They made it to the lobby, and he pushed her through the front door.

"Wait, where—" she said.

"I'll be right back. I'm going to get Erin," he said and disappeared before she could say anything more.

Marianne breathed in the cold night air and coughed. Her lungs felt raw from the smoke. Red lights strobed across the front of the building and swept the sidewalk. A large group of people were gathered waiting to see what would happen or perhaps to be given the all clear to go back into the building. Cast members still wore their costumes and huddled in groups, shivering. Firefighters in full gear were donning masks and gloves, getting ready to enter the building. She shivered. Ruari should have found Erin by now and be bringing her out. But the smoke was thickening inside. She hesitated on the top step, still coughing.

The lead firefighter approached her. A woman's voice asked briskly, "Is anyone else still inside?"

"Yes, my boyfriend is looking for his sister. They were right behind me."

"We'll find them, ma'am. Please move down to the sidewalk for your safety and let us do our job."

She nodded and moved down to the sidewalk. At least the the weather had cleared, and it wasn't snowing or raining. She scanned the crowd looking for Grandma, Mrs. Thomas, and Mrs. Caldwell. She identified Casey flanked by a man and woman in evening dress who Marianne assumed were his parents. Randall looked a little lost, and she almost went to check on him, but Mr. Merritt descended on him and began talking. Randall shook his head, and the two walked off together.

She continued scanning the crowd looking for a silver-haired woman. There was no sign of her or a wheelchair. Her muscles trembled with cold and tension, adding to her fear. Where was Grandma Selene?

Someone called her name. "Marianne! Marianne!"

She jerked her head to the left and saw Grandma Selene waving at her, a familiar white haired man with a large white mustache next to her. They both looked hale and healthy, and part of her unwound a fraction. She hurried over.

"You got out okay!" She said a little breathlessly.

"Yes. It was a little tricky getting Lily's wheelchair out with people behind us getting pushy, but we all kept our civility."

John Irving said, "We're alright. Don't worry about us."

Marianne didn't see Mrs. Thomas or her aide. "Where's—?"

Grandma Selene answered her unfinished question. "Gina thought it best to take her home rather than have her sit out in the cold."

"Of course. Maybe you should go too, Grandma."

"Not yet. Where are Ruari and Erin?"

Marianne cast an anxious look back at the front steps. The firefighters were getting equipment off the truck, preparing to enter the building. She felt a stab of guilt. She was the one who'd suggested they look for Dane instead of exiting a burning building. She should have done it herself or not suggested it in the first place. She'd just been so focused on breaking the cycle of haunting. She said miserably, "I don't know. He went back inside to look for her."

Grandma said, "They'll be alright. The firefighters will find them, I'm sure."

Marianne fervently hoped they wouldn't succumb to smoke. She asked, "Did you see Sarah and Kelly come out? They had Tayloe with them."

"I think they're over there." Grandma indicated with a nod of her head.

Sarah, Kelly, and Tayloe were standing in a close knot. They seemed to be deep in discussion. She wondered where Tayloe's family was.

"Excuse me, Grandma, John, I should make sure they're okay."

"I'll keep an eye out for Ruari and Erin," Grandma Selene said.

"I'll keep an eye on your grandmother," John said.

She gave them a grateful look and hurried over to her friends. On the way she noticed two figures, one tall with a cane, the other small, standing side by side watching the unfolding drama.

CHAPTER 24

Tayloe was still in her Katrina ballgown, though her wig of blonde curls was askew.

"I'm fine," Tayloe was saying as she pushed Sarah's hands away.

"I'm trying to make sure you're okay," Sarah said sharply.

"Stop pestering me!"

"Tayloe, honey, we're just trying to help," Kelly interjected.

"Is everything okay?" Marianne said as she arrived.

"We're fine," Sarah said. Her tone indicated Marianne didn't need to be there. Marianne ignored her.

"I just want to go home," Tayloe said.

Marianne gave Tayloe an assessing look. The cold street light, punctuated by strobing red flashes made it hard to see her features clearly. She tried to catch the younger woman's eye. "Tayloe, where are your parents?"

"They'll be here soon enough, I'm sure," Sarah said caustically.

"They didn't come to this," Tayloe replied. She refused to look at Marianne.

"Of course they did. I saw them in the audience," Kelly answered, looking confused.

"Willa, is that you?" Marianne asked.

"Sarah, Kelly, you said you'd take me home," Tayloe insisted, pulling away and looking toward the street. "Tell this woman to go away."

"What do you mean 'Willa'?" Sarah said sharply.

Marianne put her hand up, forestalling any further comments. To her relief, Sarah clamped her lips shut on what she'd been about to say. Kelly looked alarmed but stepped in front of their little group, blocking them from the crowd.

Marianne took Tayloe's forearms in her hands and caught her gaze. Her eyes were a little disoriented and spacey. "Willa, you can't stay here," she said firmly, "You have to go on."

Willa looked at her and straightened, looking defiant. "Why can't I stay? I haven't left the theater in years. I just want a look around for a little bit."

"No, Tayloe lives here, not you. My friends are getting Dane out of the theater as we speak. You said he was like a little brother to you, remember? He's not trapped anymore. He's free to go. You have to move on and let Tayloe live her life."

Willa's gaze grew steadier and harder. She lifted her chin. "I like it out here. You can't imagine how awful it was to be stuck in nothing but memories of that old play over and over again. It's worse now that I know what Cliff did!"

Marianne shook her head. "That's done. We broke the loop you all were trapped in. You don't have to go back. You're free to move on."

"I just want a chance to live my life the way I meant to."

Marianne shook her head. "No, Willa, you had your chance. You don't get a second one. Not like this. If you move on, for all I know, you'll have another chance, another life. But you can't have this one."

Willa said wildly, "You don't know that! This little girl just wants to be a nurse. How boring! We could be stars of stage and screen! I was really good at that. It's not my fault that Loren and Cliff ruined my life."

Marianne changed tactics. "Tayloe, I know you're in there."

She shook the young woman a little. "Tayloe, we talked about this. You have to be brave and fight! You can push Willa out if you try hard."

"I see what you're doing! I won't let you!" Willa tried to pull free of Marianne's grip, but Sarah had stepped behind her, blocking her escape.

"Tayloe, keep trying. Remember Randall, remember your friend Katie, remember your job at Golden Years. You want to be a nurse and help people."

"I'm…trying…" she gasped.

"Guys, hurry up," Kelly said. She stood blocking them from the crowd on the sidewalk. "Tayloe's family is coming over, and I won't be able to stall them for long."

If she couldn't get Willa out now, Marianne thought, who knew what would happen? Tayloe had said something about her parents demanding an exorcism and thought at the time she'd been exaggerating. Maybe not.

Starting to feel desperate she said, "Tayloe, your family is coming. You don't want them to see you like this. Push hard!" Marianne took hold of the girl's forearms again and shook her again.

"I'll try to buy you some time," Kelly said.

Just then Ruari and Erin hurried up.

Marianne barely had time to register them.

"What's going on?" Ruari asked.

"Willa is still here and she won't leave," Marianne replied.

"I got this," Erin said, fumbling in her pocket. She pulled out a bottle, uncorked it and flung the contents in Tayloe's face. "Begone you stupid bitch! Get out and leave her alone!"

Tayloe gasped from the cold and the shock and possibly from the aroma of patchouli, dust, and smoke. She shuddered in Marianne's grasp and shook her head.

"Get out!" Tayloe said firmly. Her muscles tensed into cords for a couple of seconds as she fought the intruder. Then she sagged in Marianne's grip.

"Tayloe?" Marianne said.

She nodded, panting. "It's me. She's gone."

Erin looked around wildly. "Where did she go?"

"I don't know, but she's not in me anymore."

"Get out of my way, Kelly, I want to see my daughter!" A man's strident voice shouted. Kyle Walker was as tall as Kelly and had the same handsome features. But his ash blond hair was center parted and feathered in a bad '80s cut and anger twisted his features.

"Let go of my child!" He grabbed Tayloe's arm and pulled her away from Marianne. "Tayloe, are you alright?"

Tayloe straightened and pushed her shoulders back, pulling herself together. Gently but firmly, she pulled her arm out of her parent's grasp.

"I'm fine, Father," she said lightly. "Aunt Sarah and Aunt Kelly made sure to get me out of the theater. They were just making sure I was safe."

"Oh." He seemed taken aback by his daughter's words. He rallied and said, "It's time to go home. You can return these… clothes to the theater tomorrow."

"Yes, Father. Is Mother alright?"

"She's worried sick about you. I told you this whole theater thing was a mistake from the beginning. The car is over there."

Tayloe nodded and gave Marianne a grateful look. "Thank you. I'll call you tomorrow." She gave Sarah and Kelly a quick hug. "Thank you for getting me out of there. I'll call you later."

Tayloe's father dismissed Marianne and the others with the selective blindness of the righteous. He put a possessive hand under her elbow and said, "Why are you wet?"

She pulled her elbow free again and walked towards the curb. "Let's not keep Mother waiting."

After they'd left, Kelly said dryly, "Brother Kyle's still a dickhead."

"I'm impressed she had the presence of mind to tell him we'd helped her," Sarah said.

"Yeah, she's getting more independent. I think she'll be just fine," Kelly agreed.

"Erin, what was in that bottle?" Marianne asked.

Erin looked pleased. "I brought holy water. Just in case."

"Hah! But why did it smell so odd?"

Erin grinned and held up the little faceted bottle. "Grave Dust perfume."

Marianne laughed. "It seemed to be what Tayloe needed to help her push Willa out." A wave of relief left her feeling weak. She was so glad to see both Ruari and Erin that she tried to hug both of them at once. "Omigosh, I'm sorry I said we needed to look for that little boy. I should never have said that."

Ruari hugged her hard. "The firefighter found us in the hallway before we'd gone too far. She yelled at us for being stupid, but she got us out the rest of the way."

Marianne suddenly started shaking in earnest as cold and reaction set in. Ruari took off his jacket and wrapped it around her shoulders, holding her close. "Thank heavens you're okay," she said.

He wrapped his arms around her. "We're fine."

Erin stepped back, looking tense again as she scanned the crowd. "I don't see Toni. Does anyone see her?"

Sarah said, "You mean that girl from the cemetery on All Hallow's? How did she get here?"

Marianne said, "Long story."

Kelly put her arm around Sarah. "I don't think they're going to let us back in to get our coats anytime soon. We should go home, babes."

Sarah nodded.

"I'll get the car and meet you here." Kelly left in the direction of the street.

Sarah looked at her appraisingly. "Marianne, that was well done." She looked reluctantly impressed for someone who'd called her too empathetic not so long ago.

"Thanks." She'd be happy about Sarah's praise later. Right

now, there was a more pressing question. "Do we have to worry about Willa coming back and doing this all again?"

Sarah was thoughtful. "If the other members of the loop have successfully moved on, probably not? There's a chance she might haunt the theater for awhile, but it's like being an addict without the crowd who keeps you addicted. It's not nearly as compelling. We can come back in a few days and check."

"I'd like to know how to help someone move on. Is there some kind of spell or charm to help them?"

"There are a couple of things you can do. I'll show you."

"Good. Not now. Too tired. What happened to Paloma and Marette?"

Sarah's expression was stony. "They left as soon as they got a chance. I told you they were useless."

Marianne shook her head.

"Go home and get some rest," Sarah advised. Looking over Marianne's shoulder toward the street she said, "Ah, I see Kelly." She took off without another word.

"Is it my imagination or is she just rude?" Ruari asked. All this time he hadn't left her side, holding her close while she shivered.

She sighed. "That's just Sarah. Erin, where are you going?"

Erin craned her neck back toward the front of the theater. "Toni isn't out yet. They're never going to see her! I have to go back!" Erin started toward the front doors again.

"Hey, hey, Sis. None of that." Ruari let go of Marianne and grabbed Erin around the waist. "If Toni is a ghost girl, she'll be fine even if the building is on fire. She'll come back."

Erin looked anguished. "You don't know that!" After a brief struggle she allowed Ruari to hold her. They watched as fire fighters dragged hoses into the building through the front doors. The strobe lights continued to knife through the darkness, and the crowd watched in morbid fascination. Ruari tucked an arm around both of them. Finally, Marianne caught sight of a familiar figure.

"Erin, look!"

Toni's pale form emerged from the building, supporting another smaller figure whose arm was flung over her shoulder. Together they came down the front steps. No one moved to help them. Marianne was sure they were coming their way, but Toni veered off.

Marianne followed their progress to a little knot of people on the sidewalk. The crowd had thinned, but this tightknit group stood staring at the theater intently, watching the disaster unfold. Toni approached them. A man and a woman stepped up and gently took Dane from Toni's care. They hugged him, and three smaller figures piled on, hugging their brother. The woman spoke a few words to Toni who nodded.

Toni stuck her hands in her jeans pockets unaffected by the cold night air. She half-glided, half-sauntered over to Marianne, Ruari, and Erin.

Erin tore herself out of Ruari's grasp, closed the distance, and threw her arms around her. Toni embraced her.

"I thought I'd lost you!" Erin said thickly, sniffing back tears. "I was gonna go back for you."

I'm glad you didn't. I'd never want you to die to be with me. Toni draped her arms around Erin's shoulders. She was slightly taller than the redhead.

"You know I'm not scared to do it."

Yeah, I know, she said sadly. *And that's the problem, sweetheart.* Toni stepped back. She gazed into Erin's tear-stained face. *I wish I'd known you when I was alive. Being dead sucked until you came along. Maybe that's what I was waiting for? I had to give up being mad at my father and stepmother. Meeting you, being with you has been the best part of my life both before and after death.*

"For me too," Erin replied.

But you have to live your life here first.

"What are you saying?" Erin asked. "We have plans. You're coming with me to Boston. Or I'll stay here and get a job if you can't leave. It'll be great."

She shook her head. *I'm sorry. I can't.*

Erin frowned. "You're not leaving me?"

I have to, for a while. But I'll be here waiting for you when you're old and gray.

Erin's face crumpled. "No. You can't leave. I need you!"

You'll be fine.

"But I love you!" Her voice broke.

I love you too, Erin. You're the coolest, most brilliant, most dangerous, badass babe I ever met. I'll wait for you. On the other side. You can count on it. She smiled, touched her fingertips to her lips, and touched them to Erin's lips. Then she faded out of Erin's embrace.

"You're supposed to stay with me!" Erin shrieked. "How can I live without you?" Tears ran in black streaks down her face. Ruari put his arms around her, and she sobbed into his shoulder for a few moments. Marianne put her arms around her from the back, sandwiching Erin between them.

After a few minutes, Erin took a shuddering breath, sniffed hard, and said in a more normal voice, "Okay guys, I can't breathe."

They broke apart, and Erin wiped her eyes and nose with the back of her hand. "Well, shit."

"Let's go home," Ruari suggested.

Marianne put her arm around Erin. "She found Dane and got him back to his family," Marianne said.

"Damn right she did." Erin sniffed again.

"Let's go home."

Marianne, Ruari, and Erin threaded their way through the remaining bystanders. Grandma Selene and John Irving were still there, looking cold and tired. Marianne hugged her grandmother and said, "We're all safe. Thank you for staying, but please go home and rest."

Grandma Selene kissed her forehead and said, "I couldn't hear what you were saying, but it looked like you handled everything admirably. Well done. Go home yourself. Ruari, take care of both of these ladies."

"Will do."

"Drive safe, Grandma."

"You too, lovey."

They continued making their way to the side parking lot where most of the cars had gone. The white truck was at the far end, and the little Ford Escort was a couple of spots away. A light mist curled through the air along with a skirl of leaves. Marianne was exhausted after all the excitement. All she wanted was a cup of cocoa, possibly a hot shower, and to go to bed, preferably sandwiched between Ruari and Oscar.

"Erin, I don't think you should drive yourself," Ruari said. He sounded as tired as Marianne felt.

"I'll be fine," she said listlessly, fishing for her keys.

Marianne could picture the woman driving out to the cemetery to look for Toni at this hour. "Nope, I'll drive."

Ruari interjected, "We're all tired. Let's just leave The Flea here. We can get it tomorrow, no problem."

"Okay," Marianne agreed.

He deftly removed the keys from Erin's hand before she could protest and steered her towards the white truck.

It was a tight squeeze in the cab, but they managed. Erin slumped against the window on the passenger side. They pulled out of the lot and turned left toward home.

Beyond the theater, Maple Hill looked deserted at this hour. Only a few people were out, bundled against the damp cold. As they passed the Co-op an odd thudding sound started up.

"What's that?" Marianne asked.

"I don't know. Maybe something got caught in a tire," Ruari answered. "I'll look when we get home."

They drove another half block as the thudding noise got steadily louder.

"Um, guys?" Erin said. "Why is there a horse on the road?"

Marianne turned and saw a huge black horse and a cloaked rider keeping pace with the truck. Her heart leapt into her throat. The horse pulled ahead and veered into the roadway.

"Ruari, look out!"

The headlights flashed off the glossy, muscular hindquarters. Ruari swore as he jerked the steering wheel to the side. They careened around the huge black beast, mashing them into each other in the front seat. He jammed on the brakes, throwing them all forward.

The road ahead of them was empty.

"Holy shit!" Erin said. "You saw that, right?"

"Where did it go?" Ruari said, looking for the horse.

The hairs on the back of Marianne's neck stood at attention. "We need to get home as fast as possible. I warded your truck but not that strongly. The house is the safest place we can be."

The engine growled as Ruari accelerated. They passed another block and heard hoofbeats again, this time on the driver's side. One moment there was nothing; the next, a huge black beast cantered next to them. Ruari cursed and jerked the wheel again, veering away from the horse and narrowly missing a parked car. He gunned the motor and drove the last couple of blocks before turning onto Primrose Lane. Marianne and Erin braced themselves as they careered around the corner. The horse and rider kept pace.

They flew down the three blocks to the turn for Violet Lane and took the corner at speed. Ruari gunned the engine again and raced for the cul-de-sac at the end of the street. Marianne prayed there were no dog walkers and no cats out this late. The horse pulled ahead of them and beat them to the end of the block. Ruari slammed the brakes barely in time to keep from hitting the animal.

The horse reared up, flailing its hooves over the hood of the truck. The street lights on either side exploded in a shower of glass, and the hooves struck the hood with loud clangs, shaking the cab and leaving sizable dents in the metal.

Ruari threw the truck into reverse and backed up, heading for the sidewalk next to Marianne's house. The horse and rider soared over the white picket fence and landed in the front yard, where they turned and blocked their way to the front door. The rider's cloak obscured his form, but now that they could see it, a jack o'lantern with jagged teeth and glowing eyes rested on the shoulders where a head should have been.

"Are you fucking kidding me?" Erin exclaimed.

Ruari braked and stared at the rider, the truck engine idling loudly. "What the hell is the Headless Horseman doing here?"

"Somehow we have to get into the house," Marianne said. "We can deal with it from there."

"I don't think its's just going to let us go," he said.

"If it's that stupid Casey kid, I'll kill him!" Erin declared.

"He was in no shape to find a horse and chase us all the way down here," Marianne said. "Same for Randall and Tayloe."

"It can't be real. Just ram it, Ruari!" Erin shouted.

"The dents in the hood say otherwise." He watched the silent rider on the lawn. "We could sit here until dawn. Wasn't the Headless Horseman dispelled by daylight?"

"I feel stupid sitting in your truck, big brother, being held hostage by a fairy tale monster," Erin said. "Marianne, what should we do? You're the ghost expert."

"I'm thinking." Marianne glanced out the back window. "Ah shoot," she muttered. "Go home Mrs. Branson. Don't walk your little dog down here." *Go home, go home, go home,* she thought as hard as she could.

Her nosy neighbor from several doors up the street was airing her little fluffy, yappy dog and heading purposefully down the sidewalk toward them. No doubt to complain about the noise at this hour.

She approached the truck where it idled in the street and knocked on the driver's window. Ruari rolled it down.

"You do realize how late it is, Miss Singleton? You woke me and Prince up from a sound sleep. That muffler is a menace. There's a noise ordinance, you know." She clearly couldn't see the huge black horse in the front yard.

Marianne looked around Ruari and said, "Hi Mrs. Branson. Sorry for the noise. We'll get it fixed. Please don't worry." Ruari killed the engine.

"I should report you to the police anyway."

"Please don't. See, no more noise. We're going inside now. Good night, Mrs. Branson."

The old woman harrumphed and headed back up the street.

Just go home, Mrs. Branson.

Prince caught sight of the huge animal in the front yard and began yapping loudly, his whole little body convulsing with the effort. He was not so selectively blind as his owner.

"Guys, look out!" Erin warned.

The horse moved through the gate and neighed loudly at the dog.

Mrs. Branson looked up in time to see the enormous black beast rear up again. She shrieked and fell onto the sidewalk.

Erin opened the truck door and nearly fell out of the seat. Raising her arms, she yelled, "Hey, you! Over here!"

The rider pivoted, crashing down to the cement and lunged toward Erin.

Ruari opened his door and sprinted toward Mrs. Branson.

Marianne slid across the seat and out the driver's side, keeping the truck between her and the horse.

The rider barely controlled the lunging mount as Erin dodged the hooves and the heaving body.

"Your little girlfriend isn't here to save you, Missy!" The rider said.

Understanding electrified Marianne. "Willa, stop!"

"Took you long enough!" Willa took the pumpkin head off and shook out her hair.

"What are you doing here?"

"Isn't it obvious? My greatest role ever."

Erin scrambled out of the way and dodged behind the safety of the truck.

"Why? I thought you moved on."

She let out a derisive laugh. "You threw me out of Tayloe's body. There is no 'moving on.' "

"You don't have to stay here, Willa."

"Where would I go? Dane went back to his family. Loren and Cliff are gone. The theater would be totally empty and boring. Now that I've figured out how to do this Headless Horseman gig, I think I'll stay. It'll be much more fun to harass you and little missy here. And when I get tired of that, I'll go visit Tayloe. Maybe she'll even let me in again. And if she doesn't, I'll come back here and haunt your neighborhood. I'll make sure everyone knows it's your fault. And when you move, I'll follow you."

Marianne could totally picture it. And she couldn't let that happen to Erin or Tayloe or any of her neighbors. She caught a movement out of the corner of her eye and saw Ruari ushering Mrs. Branson across the road. She had to figure out how to derail Willa. Ghostly Jason managed to touch her jacket using sheer concentration, and George Rutherford had been able to manifest by drawing energy out of the lights and air around him. But for how long?

"You won't be able to hold that shape forever, Willa. Then you'll go back to being invisible to everyone but me, and I have ways of keeping you away. It'll be a pretty sad afterlife." She was making things up and hoping something worked.

"Maybe, but it's better than being at the theater anymore. No one likes a sad ghost. Besides, you can't save everyone, Marianne." With that she hurled the pumpkin head at Marianne and spurred her mount up the street past the next lamppost. It promptly shattered, dimming the roadway further.

Marianne ducked her head as the squash flew over and shouted, "Ruari, look out!"

Willa rode after Ruari who grabbed Mrs. Branson and pulled

her behind one of the huge old trees that lined the street. Willa laughed and turned to race back down the road toward Marianne and Erin, hooves pounding on the asphalt.

All the noise was going to draw more people out of their homes to see what was going on and provide more targets. Marianne needed to end this. Willa wanted her, fine. She pulled the charm bag of herbs and polished stones out of her purse and got ready to hurl it as hard as she could. Maybe she could startle the horse and make it throw Willa off. She was counting on the protection of the onyx necklace to keep her from serious harm, but she had to wait until the beast was close enough that she couldn't miss. Her heart pounded, and she drew her arm back. The thud of the hooves shook the pavement as they passed the bed of the truck.

Three things happened at once.

Marianne launched her bag of stones at the horse's face and threw herself to one side.

Two heavy projectiles flew out of the darkness and struck the hindquarters of the horse accompanied by a shriek of fury.

And a huge spectral dog ran out of the yard barking.

The horse shied away, eyes rolling wildly. It snorted, and half reared. Willa struggled to regain her seat. The dog stood stiff-legged, hackles raised between Marianne and the horse belting out huge barks.

Erin picked up her shoes and flung them again, screaming, "Leave her alone, you fucking bitch!"

The horse screamed in panic, threw its rider, and galloped off up the street away from the things it was sure would kill it. The hoof beats faded quickly into nothing.

Willa landed on the pavement in a crumpled heap and lay still. Rita barked once more decisively and went to nose the fallen cloak. Marianne got to her feet, feeling a dress seam split, and approached Willa. Erin retrieved her shoes and stood panting, ready to hurl them again at a moment's notice.

Marianne crouched on one knee, feeling the seam of her snug dress tear further. Footsteps approached as Ruari ran up.

"Are you alright? I saw the horse run you down!"

"I'm fine. Erin and Rita spooked it, and it tossed Willa."

Marianne touched the cloak and pulled it back from the still form. The actor snatched the fabric away and hugged it to herself as she sat up. Rita barked again.

Willa's face twisted as she cried furiously, pale tears streaking down her face.

"I hate you! You ruined everything!"

"You brought it on yourself, bitch!" Erin retorted.

"Erin, please, that's not helping," Marianne said.

"Fine, I just want her to know that I'm ready to kick her sorry ass if she tries anything else."

"When I get my horse back, I'm coming to get you first," Willa hissed.

"Till then, you got nothing." Erin flipped her off. "I'm going in, 'cause Rita's got your back, and I'm cold."

Marianne wanted nothing more than to follow her inside with Ruari, but she couldn't leave Willa in this state. She might very well be able to get another horse and carry out her threat of haunting Tayloe and following Marianne wherever she went. She reached up and took Ruari's hand.

"Willa, that was the best Headless Horseman ride I've ever seen. It was a thousand times better than the ones I saw in rehearsal. You really nailed it."

The actor glared at her and wiped her face with the cloak. "I've wanted to do that scene ever since the beginning of the play. Loren in that rinky-dink costume horse looked so stupid."

"Casey was totally lame. You were magnificent." She didn't even have to pretend to sound sincere.

"I could go back to the theater and be the Headless Horseman again," Willa stated.

Marianne shook her head sadly. "It's time to move on. I can help you cross over."

"To heaven?" She scoffed. "They'd never let me into a place like that."

"Maybe. From what I've read, it doesn't have to be Heaven or Hell anymore. Besides you cared about what happened to Dane and now you know he's safe. I think you'd be welcome."

Willa considered. She gave her a suspicious look. "How? I've been stuck here so long. Didn't I miss the boat?"

"I think you can go if you want to go. It doesn't matter how long you've been here."

She sniffed again. "Do I get another chance to live?"

"I don't know. Maybe. But you have to go through the door first and find out."

"What door?"

"The door between here and the Other Side."

"What's over there?"

"I'm not sure, but I think it's good. Your family is there if you want to see them again." She felt Ruari's solid presence behind her, and his hand squeezed her shoulder.

Willa said bitterly, "I doubt they want to see me. I ran away from the farm to be an actress."

"You might be surprised."

"I don't know how." This time she sounded tired.

"Let me show you." She swallowed. Sarah never had shown her what to do. She'd looked it up on the internet this afternoon and hoped she could pull it off.

"There is a door," she began. "Behind it is a white light. It's the most intense, most beautiful thing you've ever seen." She imagined the door opening, brilliant beams spilling out. "Can you see it, Willa?"

The ghost looked away over the empty street. "Oh. I can." She sounded surprised and a little awed.

"You're allowed to go through. It's there for you. Don't be afraid."

"I'm not." She stood and turned toward the imaginary door.

For a brief moment Marianne saw the door and felt the

warmth and light spilling out of it like the most welcoming glow of coming home. A part of her longed to see what was on the other side. Then it closed. She felt like crying.

"Is that it?" Ruari asked quietly.

She swallowed hard. "Yeah, she's gone."

"What happened?" He asked as he helped Marianne stand. "When the horse disappeared, Willa did. I only heard your side of things."

Marianne felt stiff and cold and a little sad. "She went through the door."

"That's good, right?"

"Yeah, she won't haunt the theater or anyone else." She heaved a sigh, feeling immensely tired. "Can we go to bed now?"

In the distance they heard cars approaching.

"On the off chance that Mrs. Branson called animal control and or the cops," Ruari said, "we should get inside. Hopefully, no one will be the wiser since we can't explain any of this." He slipped inside the cab and parked the truck more carefully against the curb.

Together they moved to the front stoop and up the steps. Erin had left the door unlocked, and they went inside and turned the lights off.

Two vehicles with lights on but no sirens drove through the cul-de-sac, one a cop car, the other a small van. They peered through the curtains and held their breath until the vehicles moved up the street and stopped at Mrs. Branson's house. The officers spent several minutes there before they returned to their cars and drove away.

"I feel a little bad for Mrs. Branson," Marianne said, "but I plan to deny everything."

"She was a little shaken up but otherwise unhurt. Prince seemed fine too," Ruari commented.

They got ready for bed as fast as they could and crawled under the covers together.

"You scared the crap out of me," Ruari said. "I thought you were going to get killed."

"I'm sorry I scared you."

"Please don't do that again."

"I'll try not to."

He was quiet for a moment then said, "Was that Rita out there barking at the horse?"

"Yup."

"Huh." He climbed out of bed and disappeared down the hall. Marianne did her best to warm her freezing hands and feet. A few moments later, he got back under the covers wafting a faint smell of pepperoni on his hands.

"Rita did a good job."

"You're all clear to go back in," the chief firefighter said, her mask tipped up so she could be heard clearly.

"How much damage is there?" Tommy asked. It was almost eleven, and the crowd was dispersing, now that the excitement was over.

"There doesn't seem to be any." She shook her head. "We found a lot of smoke, but couldn't find any fire. It's the damndest thing. But I'm confident there is no fire. The smoke seems to be dissipating rapidly."

"That's good news!"

"However," she said sternly, "that fuse box is dangerously out of date, and you should have it replaced immediately. It's not safe to operate."

"Thank you. I'll do that."

"Call us, if you smell smoke again."

"Absolutely. Thank you for coming. I'd be happy to give you and your team complimentary tickets to tomorrow night's show."

"Thanks for the offer." The fire chief strode off to finish getting everything back on the truck.

Tommy wasted no time in reentering his beloved building, Dave Binkler on his heels. He walked through the whole building making sure everything was really okay. The till was still safely stashed in his office. Costumes and street clothes were haphazardly scattered in the dressing rooms. The stage was half-transitioned between the feast and the chase scene. Random coats, dropped hats and gloves, and Playbills were scattered throughout the auditorium. But the Old Brick Bitch was still intact. She was not burned down. Tommy thought he might faint from relief.

"Are we going to offer refunds?" Dave asked, tentatively.

"Why? We just gave people the show of their lives." He thought quickly. "What's the seat count for tomorrow night? If we still have open seats, we can offer people who were here tonight a chance to see the play tomorrow night for half price. That might fill the house."

"I suppose. We could just deal with people if they call. On a case, by case basis."

He nodded. "Yes. Let's not get too crazy. Dave, what happened at the end of the party scene?"

"I don't know. It was almost like there was a whole other set of people there. But that woman, Marianne, got them sorted out. We might have been able to continue if it hadn't been for the fire scare."

"We'll have to talk to the cast about that tomorrow night before the show. I don't want a repeat of that *mishegoss*."

"We're going on tomorrow night?" Dave asked.

"Of course! Did you see the chemistry between the three leads? It was absolute gold! Before they went off the rails, of course. If they can pull that off again, that would put this show on the map! We could extend the run, advertise more widely, bring more people in. We could really save the Old Girl."

"You know I believe in you, but I have a feeling that the cast was a little rattled after tonight's performance. They might need a day or two to recover."

"Nonsense! When you fall off the horse, you get back up and

ride. I want you to send an email to the cast and crew. Something like, 'we apologize for the regrettable interruption in the performance tonight but expect to see them on time tomorrow at 5:30.' " He waved his hand vaguely. "Tell them how good they were and that the audience loved the show. This time we'll finish out in style. We might even get an ovation!"

Dave scribbled a hasty note in his binder on the margin of the top sheet. "Got it."

"In the meantime, we'll have to put everything back. I don't suppose anyone is still here to help out? Scotty? Ruari? Fran?"

"I don't think so. It's after eleven."

Tommy shook his head. "Really? Okay, we'll tackle this first thing tomorrow morning. I'll lock up. You might as well go home and get some rest."

Dave looked relieved. "See you tomorrow."

Tommy let the silence stretch after the front door swung shut.

Yes, indeed. That had been the best performance he'd ever seen on this stage. The three leads had been on the verge of actual jealousy and fisticuffs during rehearsal, but he'd never supposed they would take it that far. He'd have to head *that* behavior off at the pass tomorrow. Tell them to channel all that creative emotional energy into their characters.

He locked the front doors and went to his office. He cocked his head to listen for the customary rattle, but there was nothing. Odd. He shrugged. He reached out and straightened the picture of his grandfather and family automatically.

As he pulled on his coat and his old navy blue fedora, he wondered, *who the hell are Willa, Cliff and Loren?*

CHAPTER 25

"How is she doing?" Marianne asked.

She and Ruari were standing in the kitchen in their pajamas two days after the last ride of the Headless Horseman. Marianne wore her fluffy bathrobe and warm slippers. It had taken ages to warm up, and she finally felt comfortable again. Ruari had on an old pair of sweats and his "Edinburgh" sweatshirt.

"I knocked on her door and left her a mug of coffee on the desk," he replied.

"Is she up?"

"She's asleep as far as I can tell. Oscar was outside the door just waiting."

"Was Rita there? She and Oscar have been camped out there since yesterday."

He started to shake his head, then stopped. "Now that you mention it, there was a cold draft around my feet when I left the coffee."

Marianne nodded.

"I'm kind of surprised she's taking this so hard," Ruari said.

Marianne turned the bacon and made omelettes. "She really loved Toni."

"But Toni is dead. God that sounds weird."

"Yes, but they really clicked. It's a shame they didn't meet when Toni was alive, but Erin wasn't even born then."

He shook his head.

"You said she'd had crushes in high school and maybe college but nothing serious. So maybe this is the first time she's been in love?"

"We should get her out to do something fun if she doesn't come down by the end of today."

"Good idea. I'm not sure I want to go to a club though."

"I'll give it some thought."

Marianne finished cooking the last of the bacon and ham and cheese omelettes. Maybe the smells would bring Erin downstairs for breakfast.

"Do you have to go back to the theater today?" She asked.

"We're striking the sets."

"I wondered what Tommy would do."

"I think it killed him to close, but even he couldn't pretend the show was any good."

She winced. "How is Tommy holding up?"

"Not very well. He poured everything he had into this show, and I don't think his finances are in very good shape."

"Do you think he'll try to stage another one?"

"Maybe. But the word is that the theater will be closed until further notice. Even the movie nights and cartoon weekends."

"Yikes. I feel bad for him."

"Me too. At least the silent auction raised money for Teddy Miller. Fran rescued the items and tracked down everyone who bid. She made sure they paid up." He laughed. "I wouldn't want to get on her bad side. She just wears you down until you do what she wants."

"How much did they make?"

"A little over $2,500."

"How did your pieces do?"

He smiled. "One went for $350 and the other for $425."

"See, your work is amazing! Did they go to Tommy's awful friends?

"No idea."

"I guess you can't ensure every piece goes to someone you like. I hope you go back to opening your own studio."

"I definitely will. I'm pretty sure I'll never see a paycheck from Tommy, so that's a write off. But it was a good experience."

There was a noise in the hallway. Oscar came sauntering in, crooked tipped tail waving high in the air. Erin shuffled after him, wearing her baggy black sweats, MCR concert tee, and carrying a mug of coffee. Her hair stuck out at all angles like a chaotic red hedgehog that had been run over by a minivan.

Marianne cracked two more eggs. "You want an omelette and bacon?"

"Sure." She sounded listless but got herself another mug of coffee. She added enough vanilla creamer and sugar to make Marianne's teeth ache, but at least she was out of her room. She slid into a seat and slouched, elbows on the tabletop. Marianne finished cooking, turned off the stove, and Ruari brought all the plates to the table.

"I was thinking," Ruari said after several bites, "the ice skating rink is open today. Marianne hasn't been skating since she was little, so we were going to go. Want to come?"

Erin gave a one shouldered shrug and continued eating.

"Erin and I learned to skate on a local pond when we were little," he explained. "One time she got too close to an open patch, and the ice cracked under her. I had to rescue her with a broom handle."

Erin didn't look up. "Not my fault," she said dully. "Terry dared me to see how close I could get."

"And you never met a dare you didn't take."

She continued to eat slowly. "Not true. You dared me to eat a frog one summer and I didn't."

Ruari gave Marianne a wink and continued. "Only because you wanted to put horseradish on it, and I told you you couldn't."

"I felt bad for the frog."

"When I took up hockey, Erin followed me around. She insisted on joining the pickup games."

"Damn skippy. You could skate fast, but your stick handling was really lame." She drained her coffee and looked marginally better.

He laughed. "Between us we were a whole player!"

"I only stopped because they wouldn't let me play after I turned eleven."

"Only because they knew you would beat their pants off."

"And you would have spent your whole time beating up the players who checked me into the boards instead of playing hockey."

"Fighting *is* playing hockey."

"I never got into hockey," Marianne said, "but I watched the ice dancing and figure skating at the Olympics every time they came around."

"Ice dancing always seemed a little prissy to me," Erin said.

"You have no idea how hard it is, the hours of practice that go into being able to jump, turn, balance. At speed. On ice." Marianne sighed. "My mom paid for lessons, but I didn't get very far."

"I bet you could still do some of that stuff," Ruari said. "It's like riding a bicycle: you never forget."

"We should go find out," Marianne said decisively. She looked at her phone. "Let's get out of here in half an hour and go to the rink."

Erin slumped again. "Have fun."

"Uh uh, nope. You're coming with us," Ruari said.

"I don't feel like it."

"Then sit on the side. You're not sitting in your room for the rest of the day. I bet I can still out skate you, Goth Girl."

A spark flickered in her eye. "You wish."

"Then show me. I dare you."

She made a big show of getting up and dragging herself to the kitchen with her dishes. She started to leave them in the sink, but Marianne said mercilessly, "All the way into the dishwasher."

She sighed loudly and obliged, clattering them loudly then slouched upstairs.

Marianne and Ruari finished cleaning up in the kitchen. "Good going, big brother. Do we need to ask her about how she's feeling?"

He shook his head. "I sat with her the morning after the fire scare. She's hurting, but she'll be okay."

"Okay, you know her better than I do."

They piled into The Flea and drove down to the ice rink in Fishkill, rented skates, and spent a couple of hours remembering old skills and finding out that falling still hurt. Hot chocolate in foam cups capped the fun.

Wednesday after the disastrous opening and closing of *The Legend of Sleepy Hollow*, the weekly edition of the *Maple Hill Register* came out. Marianne didn't subscribe but bought a copy from the Co-op and brought it home. It was snowing lightly outside, and the radio said more was coming in the forecast.

There were two articles on the theater and a review of the play. She sat under her plush tropical blanket on the sofa and read them aloud to Ruari and Erin. He sat with an old towel in his lap, whittling on a piece of wood. The dentist's office had hired a full time replacement, and Erin was once again out of a job. She sat in the armchair with her legs draped over the side, reading a slightly water-stained copy of *My Grandmother Asked Me to Tell You She's Sorry*.

When Marianne raised an inquisitive eyebrow, Erin shrugged. "I don't read books much, but Toni recommended it." Wisely, Marianne did not say she'd given that very copy to Toni herself.

Oscar was nestled on top of the blanket between her and Ruari, and she thought she detected a faint dog-shaped depression on the bed on the floor. Her heart was full. It was really nice to have all these people in her life. She shook open the paper.

"Uh oh, there's a review of the play," she said.

"Let's hear it," Ruari said.

She cleared her throat and read.

" '*The Legend of Sleepy Hollow* opened and closed last week at the Avery Theater. A creative adaptation of the original short story by Tommy Verplank, the play was a curious and not always smooth blend of spooky hijinks, *A Christmas Carol*, and heavy-handed moralizing about the evils of small town social dynamics.' Ouch. It didn't seem all that heavy to me. Anyway, 'the play would have been nothing but a rather run-of-the mill adaptation without the humor of the Arnault version or the true horror of the Bloedel and Bloedel version, but the unexpected chemistry between the three lead actors, local talent Tayloe Walker (Katrina Van Tassel), Randall Merritt (Ichabod Crane), and Casey Hopper (Brom Bones), kept the scenes lively if a little chaotic. They managed to infuse the play with real drama in spite of the plebeian lines. In fact, Tommy Verplank was clearly unable to control his actors because they veered off script during the second act after a bizarre appearance of a ghostly Van Tassel played by Sally Whiting.

" 'Reeling from this peculiar interjection that deviated from the original by many miles, the audience then struggled to catch up with the sudden argument that broke out between the three leads. At first it seemed to be the outcome of the tension between the characters, but then careened into nonsense. The curtain closed shortly thereafter. The Narrator (Tristan Kitteby) did his best to cover for the madness happening behind the curtain but was unable to rescue the play. Smoke drifted into the auditorium, an apt ending for a play that was a total dumpster fire.' Ouch.

" 'The second night only proved the point that the actors were not in command of their lines at all. It was exquisite torture to watch them lurch from line to line with muttered prompting from various ensemble members. The chase scene everyone missed due to the fire the night before was ludicrous in spite of the prop horses made by Fran Turk. The horses should have been turned out to pasture rather than ridden by complete idiots. We can thank the theater muses that we have been spared further renditions of this production.'

"Wow. Guess she didn't like it," Marianne finished.

"Who wrote that?" Ruari asked.

Marianne scanned the page. "Rachel Vingen. That sounds familiar, but I can't place the name."

"DreamTime," Erin said without looking up. "She's a bitch. I interviewed for a job, but she turned me down."

"Oh, that's right. She must do reviews as a side gig. Damning with faint praise at best."Marianne rustled the pages. "Here's the news article about the fire. 'Firefighters were called to the Avery Theater last Thursday night after a report of smoke during a performance of *The Legend of Sleepy Hollow*. Everyone was evacuated safely from the building, and no cases of smoke inhalation were reported. Fire Chief Jana Wilson and her crew investigated the building for more than thirty-minutes. They found smoke but no evidence of fire anywhere. The smoke dissipated, leaving no damage. No cause could be found, although the electrical panel was declared unsound, and the building was closed to the public until the wiring could be brought up to code.' Wilson is quoted as saying, 'What the f***? With that much smoke, half the building should've burned down.' "

Marianne smiled. "When smoke from a ghost fire gets in your eyes."

Oscar stood up arching his back and yawned before settling down again. Marianne stroked his fur.

"I, for one, am glad the play is over even if it bombed," she said. "Christmas is coming up, and I want to celebrate in peace."

Ruari stopped carving and took her hand. "It'll be our first Christmas together. Maybe we'll get some more snow."

"Brrr! I hope not. It's cold enough without it."

"We need to get a tree," Erin said without looking up.

"And lights, we need lights," Ruari added.

"I don't have any ornaments," Marianne said.

"That's okay." He held up the little carving of an ice skate he'd been working on. "I'll make a few of these."

"DreamTime is selling blown glass ornaments," Marianne added.

"Renata's Closet was selling vintage Christmas things," Erin said. "We should totally go see what she has."

It would be a grand Christmas whatever happened.

ACKNOWLEDGMENTS

My father, Thaddeus J. Gesek, was a set designer and professor at Vassar College for forty years, so I grew up in and out of the Avery theater on campus. I was always aware of when he was working on a new play because we'd have new music on the record player, and torn out pieces of magazines and books with paper-clipped pages littered his desk. All of that source material would turn into sketches for the set designs. He'd stay late and go in on weekends while the show was going up. The close collaborative relationship he had with the other members of the department meant so much to him. He never mentioned whether the Avery at Vassar was haunted or not. It was not something he would have noticed or subscribed to. In spite of that, I think he'd appreciate this Avery Theater in Maple Hill.

Washington Irving's short story, "The Legend of Sleepy Hollow," first appeared in 1820 in Irving's collection of 34 essays entitled *The Sketch Book of Geoffrey Crayon, Gent* (Wikipedia 2025). It became an American icon, firmly embedded in the literary history of the Hudson Valley of New York. I quote the opening lines in my book and refer to and embellish the details of Irving's story during the course of *Legends and Dreams*.

I tied most of the story to things available in 2009, but I took a few liberties. The Haunted Home Renovation books by Juliet Blackwell, the Haunted Haven books by Carol J. Perry, and Fredrik Backman's book *My Grandmother Asked Me To Tell You She's Sorry* were all published after 2009, but they fit with the story, and I recommend them.

I had lots of good help in writing this book. My writing group, Sanan, Angela, and Miles, read a very early version of this storyline when it was part of the road trip story in book three. They wisely told me the two stories needed to be told separately. My writing sisters Cara and Helen are my cheering squad. Cara also jazzed up my book blurbs and reminded me to be visceral in my descriptions.

Austin is always my first and last reader. He provided feedback and ideas both at the beginning and the end. Kelton and Orion gifted me with a thorough read-through and detailed analysis of characters and scenes providing concrete ideas on how to make individual storylines stronger and more satisfying. Penny and DeeDee gave me suggestions on how to improve the theater parts, as well as making sure Ruari didn't sell himself short. Jamie was my sensitivity reader and reminded me that colloquialisms and expressions that are familiar to me aren't necessarily common everywhere. Andy Slaughter of Pilcher Illustrate created the wonderful frontispiece art. We hope to collaborate again and create a fully illustrated version of this book in the future.

Thank you, everyone! You've made this a much better story, and I couldn't do it without you and your support.

My dear readers, I hope you enjoy the ride.

ABOUT THE AUTHOR

 Elizabeth R. Alix has always been fascinated by ghosts and ghost stories. She has a degree in anthropology and done archaeology in the remote Aleutian Islands. She currently lives in a formerly haunted house and works as a professional archaeologist in Eastern Washington. She writes cozy ghost stories and is the author of the Maple Hill Chronicles. She can be found at PalouseDigitalPress.com.

Dreams of Fire by Elizabeth R. Alix

Book 1 of the Maple Hill Chronicles

Stalked by her unrelenting ex-husband, Marianne and her cat Oscar move to Maple Hill, a place she's known since childhood. Shaken but determined, she begins to make a new life for herself. An electric encounter with Ruari, a handsome handyman, offers a second chance at love. But her charming new home is the safe haven she thought it was. When her clairvoyant dreams take a terrifying turn, she faces the possibility that her house is haunted. To make matters worse, her ex is determined to find her, and Ruari doesn't believe in ghosts.

Marianne will need courage and help from new friends to face her fears or the past will consume her.

Available at Amazon.com in paperback and digital formats as well as on Kobo, Barnes and Noble, and Apple Books in digital format.

Sylvan Dreams by Elizabeth R. Alix

Book 2 of the Maple Hill Chronicles

Marianne has defeated both her horrible ex and the ghosts in her house. Her prospects for a job are promising, and her love life is back on track. Life is good. But she's still seeing ghosts. When she picks up a hitchhiking ghost who won't leave her alone, she has her hands full. Ruari starts missing dates with her, and that may be more than her bruised heart can stand.

Ruari Allen is at a crossroad in life. His job is thankless, and he longs to start his own woodworking business. Marianne makes his heart sing, but, having broken someone's heart before, he's afraid of hurting her. When he starts seeing colored haloes and smoke around people, he worries about his sanity. Especially since he's also started dreaming of a mysterious red-headed woman who claims to have known his dead grandfather.

Relationships are hard enough without supernatural forces getting in the way. If Marianne and Ruari's relationship is going to have a chance, they'll need to take drastic steps. Will a desperate journey to Scotland bring them together, or forever cast them apart?

Available at Amazon.com in paperback and digital formats as well as on Kobo, Barnes and Noble, and Apple Books in digital format.

Hallowed Dreams by Elizabeth R. Alix Book 3 of the Maple Hill Chronicles

Illustrated by Andrew P. Slaughter of Pilcher Illustrate

All Hallows' Eve looms, and Marianne embarks on a road trip with Sarah, her mentor in all things ghostly, to protect Canopus County from supernatural danger. As Marianne struggles to learn magic, the trip takes a perilous turn. Needing to prove to herself that she can stand on her own two feet, Marianne refuses to bail out and go home.

Meanwhile, Ruari cools his heels at home in Maple Hill. When his fiercely independent sister, Erin, asks for his help out of the blue, something is really wrong. A trauma from Erin's childhood might just hold the key to Marianne's dangerous journey.

As the clock ticks toward a showdown in the Maple Hill Cemetery on Halloween night, Marianne will have to learn magic and convince some rowdy ghosts to help her or doom Canopus County to suffer from an ancient, malevolent hunger.

Available at Amazon.com in paperback and digital formats as well as on Kobo, Barnes and Noble, and Apple Books in digital format.

Legends and Dreams by Elizabeth R. Alix Book 4 of the Maple Hill Chronicles

What's going on at the Avery Theater in Maple Hill?

After an exhausting battle in the cemetery on Halloween, Marianne, Ruari and his sister Erin, need some serious down time. A community production of *The Legend of Sleepy Hollow* seems like just the harmless diversion they need to regain a sense of normalcy. Ruari finds a lifeline building sets for the play, but it has just as many pitfalls, even as his sister interferes with his domestic life.

But someone with a sick sense of humor is playing dangerous pranks on the cast. To protect the actors Marianne has to expose the culprit whether they're living--or dead. Marianne's mentor, Sarah was only a phone call away before Halloween, but now she's ghosting her just when Marianne needs her help protecting the production.

Marianne's knack for history and Ruari's handyman skills may be the only thing standing between the theater and disaster.

Available at Amazon.com in paperback and digital formats as well as on Kobo, Barnes and Noble, and Apple Books in digital format.

9 780999 852439